RELIGION, POLITICS,

and a

PARTICULAR WOMAN

A Tale of Political Persuasion in our Time

BY
JOHN F. LYNCH, JR.

Jakobean Publishing Co.
Morristown, NJ

This is a work of fiction, an imagining of a thread of happenings and intentions behind observable facts of our time. Where historical people are identified I have tried to be accurate about their biographical facts, but their interactions have been invented. For example, General Griffith and Professor Zeman did exist and did publish their books through Oxford University Press. Whether they ever met is a possibility but here it is an invention, considerably less than a surmise. As for the main characters, they are inventions and any similarity to actual persons living or dead is an unintended coincidence arising from the thought experiment described in the Preface.

Publisher's Cataloging-In-Publication Data
(Prepared by The Donohue Group, Inc.)

Names: Lynch, John F., Jr., 1939-
Title: Religion, politics, and a particular woman : a tale of political persuasion
    in our time / by John F. Lynch, Jr.
Description: Morristown, NJ : Jakobean Publishing Co., [2016] | Includes
    bibliographical references.
Identifiers: LCCN 2016909582 | ISBN 978-0-9976998-0-7 |
    ISBN 978-0-9976998-1-4 (ebook)
Subjects: LCSH: United States Military Academy--Officials and employees-
    -Fiction. | Fathers and daughters--Fiction. | Propaganda--United States--
    Fiction. | Religion and politics--United States--Fiction. | United States--
    Politics and government--21st century--Fiction. | LCGFT: Political fiction.
Classification: LCC PS3612.Y63 R45 2016 (print) | LCC PS3612.Y63 (ebook)
    | DDC 813/.6--dc23

PREFACE

FIFTY YEARS AGO AND EARLIER the government formed to serve We the People of the United States did so through officials from internally diverse political parties who engaged in respectful disagreement of how best to serve those people. Often they reached helpful, if not all-pleasing, compromises. Today the same government seems blocked from serving by my-way-or-the-highway factionalism.

Has that change been intentional? After study—and being favored by friends with more than 2,500 stoke-the-base emails—I worry that intentional change is not only possible but likely.

That led to a thought experiment asking three questions. If, in 1963, a couple of young men had wanted to change American politics from what it was then to what it is now:

Who would they have been at the outset?
Why would they have done it?
How would they have done it?

This book is based on that experiment. It is an explanation of the political history of American in our times as told by those men to the idealistic daughter of one of them, as her father invites her to carry on his life's work. It is neither history nor journalism but simply a story re-verse-engineered from effects observed to causes surmised.

Respectfully,

Jack Lynch
Morristown, New Jersey

I Need Your Advice
Late Spring 2014

R EADER? WELCOME. THANK YOU FOR coming. I'm Kate Wilson, "Colonel Wilson" to the cadets swarming out of these classrooms. I'm the one who called and asked you to come.

First, let me apologize for that delay at the security stop at the entrance to the Post. I'm sure you understand, but since 9/11 getting on the grounds here at West Point isn't as easy as it used to be. But now that you're here, let me tell you more about why I called.

As I explained on the phone, I have a troubling problem and need some serious, thoughtful advice. Several of my friends knew you well, spoke of you as having wisdom, and suggested I seek you out. Some, I sense, also thought you have more of a real world view of things than I do and that I could use that sort of help.

Truth be told, I need more than advice; I need counsel. So an appropriate place to start would be for you to understand some things about me, at least those that seem to bear on why I'm having a hard time with this. I had hoped you could attend my 11 o'clock class and get a sense of what I do and what is important to me. But time, tide, and class hours wait for no man—not even Post Security.

1

Let's go to lunch. We can catch the cadets' noon meal formation on our way.

My next class is at 2:00; I hope you can stay for that. In the meantime we have time to go over the problem. At lunch I thought I'd give you a short, and I hope relevant, version of my biography. I'll tell you about this morning's class insofar as it bears. Then I have a couple of notebooks of material for you to consider that lay out the problem. I'd be grateful if you would take them home and go over them at your own pace. After you read them I'd like to meet again, at a time and place of your choosing. Or maybe, since we both travel a lot, it may be best if we carry this forward by phone or e-mail. My email address is at the end of the written material. OK?

Fine.

My problem sounds like a common one. Obviously, I'm in the military. Like most before me I've reached a point where I have to decide whether to get out or stay in. Unlike most who face that decision I've already been in for a little over 20 years. Others of my seniority who face that decision usually just have to balance their outside opportunities and compare leaving with a 50% pension or staying for a full career and getting a 75% pension after 30 years' service.

But my problem is more complicated than that. I love what I'm doing. There wouldn't even be a decision to make except for a meeting I recently had with my father. My Dad has been a very important part of my life; we've been very close, especially since my mother left when I was 12. That makes this all the more difficult because he has offered me an opportunity to join him in carrying on his life's work. And I'm uncomfortable about it.

After we talk and if you're still willing to help, I'll give you the two ring notebooks to take with you. One is something my father prepared to explain the roots of his enterprise and the other contains my notes of a recent discussion with him about how it has progressed since its beginnings. Together they give the details of my problem. Of course, they also show more about me and my family than I'd care to be public. So, if you agree to give me your counsel, I'd ask you to promise confidentiality. OK?

Great; let's go out that door and up the stone stairs back up to the level where you parked.

Bit of a climb, wouldn't you say? Over there, in the shadow of the old stone barracks those cadets are forming up to be marched to the mess hall. You know, we talk a lot about this place educating these young people to be leaders—and we do, and I think we do it very well. But when I look at formations like that, or the full dress parades on Saturdays, I often think that we spend more effort training them to be followers. Some say you have to know how to follow to know how to lead. The tough part is giving them a sense of when they shouldn't follow. In a way, this afternoon's class tries to get them to think about that problem. But we'll get to that.

This building we're entering now, Grant Hall, is where we faculty members usually eat lunch. It's a newer building; brick, not granite. But this school has been here since 1802 and everything is built to convey tradition; here they do it with a design to evoke a medieval knight's hall—high ceilings, gothic windows, and those painted state "shields" on the roof beams.

Oh, milk, sodas, and the like are in the coolers on your left; prepared sandwiches are further down along the far wall; and, as you go around there's also hot food on the cafeteria line. I'll meet you at the cash register, my treat. Don't fuss; you're helping me out. Then we'll take a booth over there.

Did you find everything you wanted? Good.

Let me start with some background. I'm 43 years old, widowed, and the single parent of a daughter, Joy, who's a math whiz studying meteorology at Georgia Tech. It's her passion. She's doing very well in school and one of her professors has hooked her up with a summer internship at The Weather Channel. I'm sure she's found a career in which she can succeed. The net of that is that my family situation is stable, so I don't see it as a major part of my current problem. It's mostly only my sense of what matters in my own life that makes this decision the problem that it is.

The simplest way to say it is that I had a privileged childhood. My family was and is, frankly, very well off. My father still lives in the village where I grew up. It's called New Vernon but, formally, it's Harding Township, New Jersey.

In my lifetime my dad, Bill... er, well, let me leave his last name out of it… has always worked in New York in the investment business his grandfather founded. When I was little I didn't follow it all but, as far as I understood, he was busy building the significant wealth on both sides of the family into more—largely through banking and insurance. When Dad started out he bought banks. Banks were smaller then and had geographical limits. Importantly, individuals were allowed to own multiple banks while corporations could not. As those rules changed he was able to sell his banks into ever larger conglomerates, remain on their boards, and use them as springboards to board membership in all manner of companies. With the proceeds of some of his sales he made more diverse investments, largely in property and in extractive industries like oil and gas. All of those investments, and now many others, are in privately held companies. Most of the companies are off-shore, at least nominally.

During my childhood my mother kept very busy as a club woman and super organizer of her regional charitable events and Dad's very extensive local, state, and national political network. My mother is elegant, intellectual, and a bit reserved. Dad has charm but he can be blunt, gruff, combative, and inclined to use the "sailors' vocabulary" he picked up in the Navy. Both are still as fit as their lifetimes of tennis could make them. They have been active in their church and consistently charitable, particularly to the arts, their colleges, and the private schools that they, my brother, and I attended. Also, a lot of their charitable funding goes to "think tanks" and such.

My older brother, Tom, and I were raised on my Dad's "farm" which was remarkably large considering we were only 30 miles from Wall Street—so close Dad commuted by train. We went to a private grammar school. Then, my brother went to an all-boys prep school. By the time I was ready it had merged with a girls' school and was co-ed.

My brother was groomed from childhood to go into the family business. By the family business I mean the investments I've mentioned. And there was something my Dad and his friend (and Tom's godfather) Doug VanArsdale called "Our Enterprise;" it's the enterprise whose roots he has written about in his notebook I'm going to give you. For most of my life I assumed it involved common investment projects going on since Dad and Doug met in the Navy. When I'd ask what "Our Enterprise" meant, they'd joke with a wink that it was English for "Cosa Nostra," and then they'd change the subject.

My brother Tom and I always understood that only one of us could go into the family business and Tom, being older and—I supposed, given the times—being male, was the one. Still, Dad supported and helped me every bit as passionately as he did Tom. I remember that when I became interested in horses at the riding stable in the county park system he jumped on it with his usual enthusiasm. He bought a horse perfectly sized for me and paid for lessons from a top-of-the-line instructor moonlighting from the U.S. Equestrian Team Training Facility a few miles down the road. From that point on Dad and I took long rides together at least every other week. I think he dreamed of me as some sort of dressage champion—Olympics, maybe.

Every summer my mother and I would spend a month with her parents on their farm about 50 miles west of D. C., just north of Middleburg, Virginia. Down there I could ride over vast farms—old plantations, really—for uninterrupted miles. I did so alone, pretending I was riding point for "Jeb" Stuart or Phil Sheridan reconnoitering behind enemy lines on the old Civil War battlefields I would read about in the local library. No surprise, I suppose, that I came here. Maybe it even had something to do with my going into military intelligence. Anyhow...

But back to Dad. As I grew older he encouraged me to do whatever I wanted. He made it clear I could pursue any career, or none, as I might choose, and he and the family would support me. In fact, through trust funds and such, I have shared in the businesses' success. He has said that when he passes on I can expect to inherit half of his share of the wealth that he and Tom have been managing. Whether that now depends on how I resolve this problem—that is, whether I let him down—I don't know.

I'm getting ahead of myself. For you to best understand my point of view I think it's important to say that while I was in grammar school my parents worked hard on Reagan's 1980 campaign. Dad was busy jetting about dealing with fundraisers, campaign strategists, speechwriters, and the like—the mechanical side of politics. Mom basically added class and intellect to the social tea and formal dinner network in D.C.—the people side. When Reagan won they were so happy I thought they'd burst. Tom and I shared the joy. I was about ten years old but I had already been listening to Reagan's speeches and short radio spots. With his election I did so even more. The soaring phrases struck a chord: "America, the last great hope of mankind;" and, "America, the city on the hill."

Eventually, I graduated from here in the early '90s and, as you know, I teach history now.

My husband, Dave, was also in the Army, a graduate of MIT. We met at my first duty station after graduation when I was a Second Lieutenant in Military Intelligence and he was a Captain in the Corps of Engineers. He was a country music fan and he used to say we got married in a fever, hotter than a pepper sprout. True enough; and it just kept getting better. We had a couple of great years in grad school together. Young marrieds, young parents, and an academic freedom I hadn't known here at The Point—I didn't think it could have gotten any better but, surely, it was going to. But it didn't. His next assignment was in Middle America and mine was in a joint military command in Italy, just outside Naples. I had Joy with me when we learned he had died in a construction accident while working on the Ohio River Locks Project. One of his men was tangled in some rigging and was being pulled under; Dave tried to save him.

It was very tough emotionally at first and it got tougher, practically, after that. It's been many years. I dated a bit, still do but never re-married. I guess I have felt that having an unrelated male in the house with a beautiful daughter is looking for trouble. Anyhow, Joy and I made it through and, as Dave would have said, she and I are closer than white on rice.

I'm now a Lieutenant Colonel with a bit more than 21 years in, so I've qualified for a 50% of base pay pension. I'm no longer doing much in Military Intelligence though I've put in a couple of summers in Afghanistan. Instead, I'm a career academic with, essentially, the equivalent of tenure here at the Point. I had more than enough field deployments and leadership responsibilities early in my career to have earned my spurs and stand before these kids as "real Army." I was just selected BZ (below the zone; that is, a year early) for full, "bird," Colonel, so I probably can stay in and do what I'm doing at least until I reach 30 years of service. That would mean a 75% pension in excess of $100,000 a year for life, even more if they don't do away with cost-of-living adjustments. (It looks like the new budget will cut something off those adjustments). Mind you, it's not about the money. I don't need it. But it would be welcome as a symbol of the worth of my life's work.

It's possible I might even be selected to be the head of the History Department. If so, I'd retire as a Brigadier General. In the meantime I'm living in Colonel's Quarters on the post and they're something special.

I guess that's about all you need to know about my personal circumstances to give me the help I need. But you're going to have to know a good deal more about what I have come to believe is important.

THE CLASSROOM
TEACHER IN ME

A S I SAID, THE HOUSING is something special but the job is even more so. I suppose any professor standing in front of a morning class of gangly 17- to 19-year-olds with a deer-in-the-headlights look of their first week in college could well ask herself, "What am I doing here?" I remember thinking that one day during the first week of the academic year last fall. I carried that thought with me to lunch here in Grant Hall. Then, on the way out and while simply choosing between the right and the left exit doors over there, I was caught by that portrait set eye-level between the doors—Eisenhower. One of my awkward students may someday have to face the kinds of responsibilities… Well, that's my answer. Like I say, the job is something special. This morning's class was a good example.

As I was studying history in high school I watched for things that would help me understand mankind's need for the hope that Reagan said America provided. In a way, this morning's class—the one I hoped you could attend—was designed to get my cadets to think about the same things.

The course is first year survey of military history. In it the cadets

8

have reviewed many of the history's better known wars. At the end of each classroom session I gave one cadet the assignment to research why the common soldier fought in that war and give me a short written report a week later. I asked them to explain why the human beings in the mass of their war's infantry agreed to leave their families to go where they were at significant risk of losing their lives. I did not want the cause of the war; I wanted the cause of the common man's service.

Did the infantryman in the Trojan War really feel it would be all right if he died because some guy's wife ran off with another guy? I mean, once on a battlefield a soldier may be willing to put his life at risk to save his buddy next to him. That buddy would have done the same for him and their chances of survival were better for it. But why did the common man in the Trojan War agree to go on the battlefield? If his own wife ran off, would a single one of his countrymen have risked death to regain her? Would so many of his countrymen join his pursuit that they'd fill a thousand ships? Would even one choose to leave his home for ten years in the effort?

Another cadet had to report on why the common man went to the battlefields of the Wars of the Roses, a dispute between two wealthy families about which should rule over the common man and his family. Another was asked to explain why the common man carried his spears and arrows onto the fields of the religious wars of the 1500s in which princes fought to determine which one would get to choose the common man's religion and thus get to say which common men they could call "heretics" and execute.

After weeks in which each cadet received such an assignment, in this morning's class we had a free-for-all discussion looking for the common threads. The main one was, of course, that they went to war because their social order required it. And that order was such that there were other human beings—who for reasons of history, usually violent battles past— had acquired the power to put their own personal interest above the interest the commoner had in his own life. Most often the power was based on the powerful person's ownership of all the land on which the common man and his family lived or could live. Refusal to serve was not an option.

It was also a common thread that, except in revolutionary times, the powerful person who ordered the war had inherited the power. Rarely did the first person to gain power peacefully show disrespect for the interests of the common folk of his generation who had ceded it to him.

Then I drew them into discussing how wars fought by soldiers sworn to 'support and defend' the American Constitution differed from those earlier wars. Do the soldiers my students will lead have a different reason to serve? I wanted the cadets to know that I believe those soldiers do—and, when these cadets graduate they ought to remember that as they lead.

Back in school, when Reagan's speeches first caused me to ask myself questions, I could see that people in all times and places have an instinct to patriotism. A leader could announce boundaries to the land the people live on, raise a flag to symbolize it, announce a real or imagined threat, and march them off to his war. But, I believed, America was different; it was more than real estate and symbolic cloth. I became, unabashedly, an American Exceptionalist.

For me that exceptionalism was a basis for humility, not arrogance. I came to see the Constitution as a declaration of the need to respect the humanity of the individual citizens, the common men. It was based on realistic understandings of the possibilities for human good and ill that James Madison and others had derived from the history of distant lands and of colonial America. I came to believe that the "last great hope" that the Constitution gave the common man was the hope of living a life in which he was not simply a tool to be used to serve the interests of a synergy of princes, popes, and people with the power of wealth. It is, after all, the essence of a democracy that the rules that govern the lives of its citizens are made by those citizens in proportion to their numbers, not in proportion to their wealth.

Other nations, of course, have since adopted their own written constitutions and become more democratic, so the hope has spread. But I believe our nation's leadership of the movement for written rights-giving constitutions has remained important to the rest of humanity.

In short, Reagan's images inspired me. It's not too much to say it was because of them—more, even, than daydreams on horseback in Virginia—that I decided to serve, to go to West Point. Standing on Trophy

Point on R Day, oh, sorry, Reception Day, as a teenager and taking an oath to "protect and defend the Constitution of the United States from all enemies foreign and domestic" was a thrill. And taking the same oath in Michie Stadium at graduation, as one of the top graduates in my class, was no less so. I felt to my core that this was a career worth a life. I still do.

These are the things I try to inspire in the students who sit in my classroom.

By the way, of course I never became a dressage champion. But my Dad was there for the highlight of my riding career, being one of the first females to gallop an Army mule onto the field at an Army-Navy game. I don't think dressage could have made him as proud.

I've given you a bit about my teaching. But being a professor is more than that and you should know something about my life and views as an academic.

THE ACADEMIC IN ME

A FTER I GRADUATED I DID a couple of field tours. Then at that point in an officer's career the Army sends those with promise to get post-graduate degrees. The Army sent Dave and me to Brown for those great grad school years I mentioned. He got his Masters in Civil Engineering while I earned a Masters in American History.

Then, after Dave's death, I pointed my career toward teaching at the Point as the way to best serve the Army and still be the mom Joy needed. If I stayed in Military Intelligence I'd have been sent on assignments to sand-filled tents in God only knows where. At the Point I would serve in one place. I hoped to teach the aspects of World History that led to the U. S. Constitution and U.S. History with an emphasis on Constitutional evolution, if I could. My academic record at the Point and Brown had been good so the Army was willing to make me a career academic. It sent me for more graduate study to prepare me further.

Broadly speaking, my core interest in American History rested on the Constitution. As a person born to the "Party of Lincoln" I was brought up admiring him and sensing something profound in his concept of a new nation being brought forth on a politically virgin continent. I wanted

12

to study the Constitution as a social compact formed to avoid those aspects of European history that it could avoid because it was adopted on an isolated continent. And I wanted to understand how that social compact has evolved, especially as a result of the events of Lincoln's time.

I decided to pick a university located in a state with a Revolutionary War history. I figured most good Ph.D. programs encouraged some elective work in other schools within the university, so a university with a top-flight law school would allow me to take some constitutional law courses to bridge from the Constitution's historical aspirations to its as-applied reality.

In the end I chose Columbia probably for no better reason than I could commute from New Vernon where my daughter could have something of the childhood I had enjoyed so much. And, I figured, when intense study brought long hours, I would be only a subway ride from my father's in-town apartment across from Central Park. Another reason for choosing Columbia was that it would be easy for me to return to the University's library to complete my dissertation, if I needed to, after I was posted back to the Point for duty.

One of the great things about the study of the Constitution is the availability of The Federalist Papers. As you probably know, the main authors of the Constitution wrote them to answer opponents during the ratification process. Generally, the opponents wanted a smaller government. When I was looking for a dissertation topic uniting my interest in the Constitution and Lincoln (who led the fight "to save the Union") I decided to focus on a single Federalist Paper, specifically, Number 10. It was written by James Madison, the principal architect of the Constitution, and was entitled "The Union as a Safeguard Against Domestic Faction…" My dissertation reviewed the historical events and prior written political analyses that inspired Madison's views expressed in Federalist #10.

As Madison saw it, governments are formed to serve the public good and the main enemy of public good is private interest. For him, the fact that people have different interests is so fundamental that the "principal task of modern legislation" was the regulation of those competing interests. He had a dread of small groups, "factions," succeeding in their pursuit of private interests. History had shown him that factions seek to advance or maintain the "unequal distribution of property" or to pursue "their zeal over different opinions about religion." Those factions were "the source of mortal diseases under which popular governments have everywhere perished."

He worried that in the America of his dreams, as in the democracies of history, men "of sinister design"—by success with "the vicious arts by which elections are too often carried"—may first obtain the vote of the common man and then overcome the common man's interests. For him a large "Union" of people of diverse interests was the best available defense against those risks.

So that's what the Constitution strove to do. And ultimately, in Lincoln's time, it was the pursuit of private interests by slaveholders that almost brought the Union to its end. Heady stuff; 1780s theory morphing 70+ years later into reality with a murderous war resulting.

After completing my doctorate I left most of that behind as a teacher. But even here at the Point we have a version of the classic "publish or perish" system that haunts most academics. So I've been publishing articles based on the evolving history of the constitution. Writing those articles is like putting money in the bank by qualifying me for an academic appointment elsewhere if I want one after I retire from the Army. (And my Dad has read all my articles as soon as they were published. His plainly evident pride in me and them has been compensation enough for extra effort.)

Most of my professorial articles have dealt with the history of the evolution of specific Constitutional concepts. The articles have taken a change—say, the changing view of "separate but equal" or the changing view of the need to exclude unconstitutionally obtained evidence from criminal trials—and analyzed the demographic, economic, and sociological factors behind that change and, equally interesting, behind the forces opposing each change.

A focus of my interest and my writings has been on the ways the Constitution, as applied or ignored in reality, hasn't always given people the liberty its words and theory promised. Federal religion was forbidden but state religions existed until the 1840s. It took nearly 100 years for society to implement the 14th amendment's command that states had to respect that their citizens of African ancestry had national rights transcending their state's power to deny them.

Even the one of only three personal rights granted in the original body of the Constitution (as distinguished from granted in the Amendments) that "...no religious Test shall ever be required as Qualification to any Office or public Trust under the United States" didn't stop the people running West Point and Annapolis from limiting the minor office of First Captain of the Corps or Brigade Commander to Protestants until the 1950's. They simply said, "That's the way we've always done it" or justified themselves by saying that Protestant Sunday services were so central to the institutions' purposes that the student leaders had to participate—therefore, they had to be Protestant.

That example is trivial, but it's not an aberration. "That's the way we've always done it"—or some hollow pretext—is often the way the aspirations of common men, even the ostensibly protected aspirations, are brushed aside by those who see their advantage in opposing change. The Constitutional right of the people "peaceably to assemble, and petition their government for redress of grievances" didn't stop the use of fire hoses, attack dogs, and mass arrests against non-violent, but non-white, people to preserve the way part of the country had "always done it"—denied them the vote.

Yet changes such as the exclusion of evidence from beaten confessions, provision of counsel for indigents, and *Miranda* warnings illustrate how new generations have taken the ideas of the Constitution, applied them to the facts and understandings of their time, and worked toward perfecting a justly functioning society. Americans who sense a wrong have a ready-made answer to the "that's the way we've always done it" crowd. They can say, "Maybe so, but that's not right; it's not even constitutional."

The more I studied, the more I came to believe that America *was* the last great hope of mankind. The evolution of the American Constitutional system remains an important part of the advance of mankind. We were the shining city on the hill and, stumbles aside, we remain so. Reagan was right.

Over the last few years I've been troubled by some trends of our times including: a growing respect for wealth and disrespect for the worth of the common man; the grasping for social control by those who "know" they speak for God; and, the jingoistic programs of those who see the nation's military as something more than a way to "provide for the common defense." All that seems to me to be a violation of the trust we have been blessed to receive.

Earlier this year I persuaded the National Endowment for Democracy at Johns Hopkins to invite me to write an article for an upcoming issue of its Journal. It's due in September for publication in January. It's my first attempt at an article that doesn't just crunch numbers to explain changes in the past—my first attempt at history applied in the present. In my drafts I've come back to Madison's concepts. I've been exploring whether the factors of mass national electronic communication and the concentration of wealth have become so powerful—and national intellectual diversity so diminished—that private interest now has the potential to overwhelm public good, despite Madison's Constitutional design.

I'm sorry. I'm running on about all this. My friends are forever telling me I'm too passionate about this stuff. Sometimes I think they're right. But, that's who I am. It's idealistic, I know. But that's a big part of why I'm having a hard time with my decision. It's the main reason I'm asking your help.

I've said all this because it is important to me and my decision.

It's a nice spring day and we still have an hour until my next class. Let's dump our trays, take a walk, and continue this discussion in fresh air.

I know. You're probably saying, "Fine. Let's take a walk. And I get that this is important to you. But what's the problem?"

Well, about three months ago my brother Tom, who seemed to be in perfect health, died of a sudden heart attack while training for a triathlon. After the deeply emotional times had passed my Dad started a campaign to persuade me to leave the Army. He wanted me to take Tom's place in their businesses and that thing he and his service buddy Doug call "Our Enterprise."

At first I told him that I was not at all sure I wanted to leave the life I had fashioned for myself. He said he understood that, but, he suggested, I couldn't make a rational final judgment about that until I understood the alternative. Once I did understand, he said, I would see that this was a unique opportunity. It was also one that, given the nature of it, would probably not be available almost a decade from now when my Army career had run its full course.

Then about a month ago he sent me a history he had written explaining the concept on which the Enterprise was founded and how, during its earliest years, he and Doug learned about the tools they would need to implement that concept. He asked that I read it as soon as I could. And I did. Two weeks ago he invited me (I might even say "summoned me") down to his farm for a weekend centered on an all-day Saturday session with Doug at which they explained how the Enterprise has evolved and succeeded since those early days.

If you're willing to counsel me on all this, before you leave I'll give you a copy of Dad's history of those early days, "The Roots of Our Enterprise." And I'll give you a set of the notes I've prepared about my discussion with Dad and Doug on that Saturday. Those are the two ring notebooks I mentioned earlier.

But first, since you've agreed to go to this afternoon's class, let me tell you about it. Like most classes here it's small—about 15 cadets are seated around the perimeter while I walk about in the open center of the room. Today's format will use the Socratic questioning process to get the students to think, speak, and learn from each other about the day's topic.

The course is American History and today's topic is Watergate. In the first part of the session I hope to bring them to an understanding why the people around Nixon obeyed rather than opposed the nuttier ideas in that fiasco.

I'm going to try to bring the cadets to a realistic understanding of the pressures on someone who is not independently wealthy, someone with a family to support and a career to pursue, who is told to do something he doubts should be done. You know, the "You do it or I'll get someone who will" problem.

At about halfway through the hour, I throw the curve. I'll remind them of our earlier class session on the Depression and ask them to imagine they were Douglas MacArthur when, in July of 1932, President Hoover told him to use the troops to break up the encampment of the

World War I veterans, the "Bonus Army," on the Mall by the Washington Monument. Was MacArthur's obedience to Hoover consistent with his oath to support and defend the Constitution? Remember the vets were, in terms of the First Amendment, people 'peaceably assembled to petition the government for redress of a grievance.' Should MacArthur have obeyed? In MacArthur's place, would they? If they didn't, would they be subject to a Court Martial under the Uniform Code of Military Justice for disobeying an order? Would the Code's Article 92's limitation to "lawful" orders provide them a realistic defense? Do any of those legalisms matter to one's career? If MacArthur had refused to obey the order, would they have even heard of MacArthur? Should the consideration of preserving a career, the ability to continue to serve, be part of the decision whether to obey an unlawful order?

What are the right answers? I don't know. But even teaching students that not every problem has a clear right answer, that there are things about which reasonable people can differ, has value, especially here at the Point.

Then I'll ask whether MacArthur's position was materially different from John Mitchell's in Watergate? I'll come back to these questions in a later class when we consider the actions of the service academy types around President Reagan at the time of Iran-Contra, and whether lying to Congress out of loyalty to a president is consistent with supporting and defending the Constitution of the United States. These are very bright young people. It should be fun.

After the class I'll give you a tote bag with the ring note books. Hopefully, they will give you an understanding of why I'm deeply troubled about the choice I have to make. I do need your insights into all of this. The way I see it now, my problem presents many aspects. But it all boils down to this: should I accept his invitation to join Dad's Enterprise?

Thank you very much for taking this on.

THE WARDROOM OF
THE OLDENDORF

Reader,

What follows over the next several chapters is what Dad wrote to explain the beginnings of his Enterprise, the origins of its concept, and the things he and Doug learned to equip themselves to pursue it.

Respectfully,
Kate

K ATE, WHAT WE NOW CALL Our Enterprise started when I was serving in the Navy on the Oldendorf. That tour ran from after I graduated from Boston College in 1961, until August '63. The Oldendorf was a destroyer with a wardroom of intelligent, well-educated, and thoroughly enjoyable young men.

I suppose that throughout the fleet there were many similar groups; such were the times. On my ship, the group included top graduates of Ivy League schools (Harvard, Columbia), major State universities (Michigan,

Minnesota, and Washington), and smaller excellent schools (Tufts, Lehigh, and Georgetown). We also had 3 or 4 top-10%-of-the-class Academy grads. There was no reason for these high-achievers to be together except for the call of service and the Destroyer force's promise of significant responsibility at an early age. Corny or not, that's the truth of it.

With my modest academic record at B. C., I was at the bottom of the barrel. But, hey, it was a high quality barrel.

Three of this group of early 20-somethings already held advanced degrees. One of them was Tom's godfather, your "Uncle Doug," who had been on a Navy scholarship studying civil engineering as an undergraduate at Rennselaer Polytechnic Institute, up by Albany. Then, with the Navy's blessing, he stayed at school to earn an MBA before reporting for active duty.

Doug was about 40 pounds lighter then. But he was just as striking when his hair was a darkening blond, not so grey. He already had the gravitas that projected wisdom as well as intellect.

Doug and I held comparable positions, Division Officers in larger Departments. He was in the Weapons Department managing Gunner's Mates and Fire Control Technicians, the men who maintained and operated the guns and the equipment which aimed them. I was in the Operations Department in charge of the men who operated and maintained the radios and did the short-range visual communications using lights and flags.

We were both fully qualified as "Officers of the Deck, Underway," the senior watch standers who drove the ship while others worked or slept. Talk about early responsibility! We were each trusted by the Navy to drive our destroyer, maybe steaming through a hurricane at night in formation with a dozen or so other ships, responsible for the lives of a couple of hundred men asleep below. Hell, when I qualified I was 3 years younger than I had to be before Hertz would trust me to drive one of its Ford Falcons.

I've described the group of officers as being "in the wardroom" of the Oldendorf. But I need to say something about the idea of a wardroom itself.

The term "wardroom" refers, of course, to the ship's officers' dining room/lounge. In the room itself, the officers share meals and, in off-hours, often gather to pass the time playing cards, reading, and such—all the while building a community, a brotherhood.

The conversation in a wardroom has definite limits though.

At meals with the Captain, your boss, sitting at the head of the table and in earshot, you were not going to ask the guy next to you when his sailors are going to fix your pump, winch, or whatever. A Captain like one of those we had—a self-satisfied, all bright-work and no substance, passive-aggressive priss—would jump all over both of you, and thereby turn a low-priority job into a cause. That'd just make the job of getting the right things done in the right order harder. So, wardroom discussions, particularly as led by the first Captain we served under, were superficial and as good a reason as any to finish the meal quickly, ask to be excused, and leave the room.

But even in happier commands such as the one we had under the next Captain, there were some universal conversational prohibitions that applied even during games of hearts, cribbage, or acey-deucy. The best known was that "in the wardroom you never discuss religion, politics, or particular women."

Some joker would always mutter "women who ain't so particular, that's different." But it wasn't different. The rule was wise. One man's not-so-particular woman might be another's Venus. Men have beliefs about their religions, their politics, and their women that they hold more deeply, more emotionally, than they can rationally defend. Any actual two-way discussion of religion, politics, or a particular woman could quickly escalate into frustration, anger, and a loss of the officers' mutual respect and camaraderie upon which the ship depended.

Still, beyond the hearing of the Captain and away from the wardroom and while still honoring its rules, we had some very interesting and substantive conversations. In fact, the ship's number two, the Executive Officer, the XO, "Woody" Hartzel, made a point of arranging those discussions.

After dinner, when the pace of operations and the weather permitted, the XO would invite those of us not going on the 8-to-12 watch that evening to join him up near the bow, on the "foc's'l" (that's the "forecastle" to you ground pounders, the open part of the main deck up by the bow—basically the ship's front porch), to watch for the "green flash." The green flash was supposed to be a moment exactly at the instant of sundown when the sky flashed green. Most of us figured it was just another legend of the sea. We had never seen it and we argued there wasn't any scientific reason why it should happen.

Nevertheless, we developed a ritual to gather and watch for the flash. Actually, the reason we gathered was the XO, not the flash. He was strong, quiet, wise, and respectful of every one of us and our thoughts, no matter how less wise than his they might be. He brought out those thoughts by having a topic and getting us talking.

The range of the conversations was unlimited; the tone was civil, rooted in our mutual respect. This was not a locker room.

Sure, we all had our nicknames—the head of the Weapons Department was "Weeps." It was a term obviously derived from his job title. The self-appointed purveyor of official nicknames sought to avoid appearing unimaginative by suggesting it meant Weeps wasn't lucky at cards—you know, "Read 'm and weep." The Engineering Officer was GORCE for "Good Old Reliable Chief Engineer." He, as you can guess, was the purveyor of the names. My name and its source are things I'm not going to volunteer to my daughter, even if she is a field-seasoned Army Colonel. I'm sure there were other names now lost to memory.

But I do remember that Doug became "Reggie." It was a reference to a TV skit character, "Reginald Van Gleason III," a tuxedo and top hat wearing super sleuth serving the super-rich. The skits played on the common man's stereotypes of the too-rich, too-inbred, and too-stupid for their own good crust of society. Doug did nothing to earn the nickname other than have a last name that started with a "Van." Yet "Reggie" it was and it stuck.

What the rest didn't know, and I learned thumbing through a family copy of New York's Social Register on a weekend home, was that Doug's family was, in fact, well into the super-rich category. I later learned that their wealth derived from real estate, shipping, and other aspects of international trading dating back to the days of Nieuw Amsterdam.

Normally, talk among a group of young adult males would be

banter, ribbing, bonding at best, but in truth would actually be a series of mini-battles of attack and defense directed toward arranging a social pecking order.

Yet, except for our use of status-neutral nicknames, our green flash meetings were different. We knew our social order. The Navy gave it to us. There was the XO, a 'gray beard' 34 year-old career officer, and the rest of us, first hitch junior officers. The struc-ture gave our conver-sations comfort. We were equals, a team, people whose lives were often in each other's hands. There was not a hint of any of us undermining anyone else in the group.

Then there was the sheer beauty of it all. The skies were clear at the horizon or we wouldn't be looking for the flash. Sometimes there were a few of those small, but tall-ish, translucent tropical clouds that evaporate as the day's heat fades. But, if there was to be a flash at the moment of sunset, those few clouds had to float well above the horizon as they often do in the tropics. The ship's 12-15 knot movement through calm-weather swells added a peaceful rhythm to it all.

As much as I've told you over the years about how bad the rough days were, most days were clear and peaceful. And, though I've probably told of long days with interminable hours of standing watches, drilling at battle stations, and doing the routines of managing dozens of men at work, these green flash sessions were a time to take in the beauty, think deeper thoughts, and share them.

Usually the green flash session broke up when the sun set or when the XO and the Department Heads went aft for a short review-the-day session called "8 o'clock reports." Sometimes, as in the picture I've in-cluded, the XO made 8 o'clock reports a part of the green flash session. But sometimes when the green flash session broke up and most of its participants went to watch the wardroom movie, some of us stayed on the foc's'l a while longer.

Rarely, at first, and then more often, Doug and I stayed. We built a deeper friendship as we swapped stories of our privileged youth, of growing up affluent, stories that would have been out of place among the others. Hell, one buddy, a Japanese-American with a Master's degree from Columbia, had spent a good chunk of his childhood in a "War Relocation Camp."

Doug and I swapped tales of our prep school years—mine in an urban religious school, his suburban in a school with barely a hint of its distant denominational roots. Like most, we had stories of bullying—his more subtle, but both borne in silence due to the futility of any other action. We had stories of dates and proms in an era of sexual repression which your post-pill generation would not believe. His repression was imposed as the requirement of gentility; mine came in the form of a threat of eternal damnation.

The early discussions were ordinary enough, only the recurring theme of affluence set our stories apart from what we might have shared with others. Between the two of us we were able to speak unapologetically about the satisfaction of privilege. It was as we peeled back that onion Doug opened a subject that had been troubling him that he couldn't discuss with the others.

Doug's Concern

S O IT WAS THAT ONE evening Doug started to talk about some wondering he had been doing. Would privilege survive? Would wealth last, at least through our days? He asked me to hear him out as he described his outlook at length. He drew mainly on his brief undergraduate studies of history, economics, and sociology.

On the economics side, his classwork had first aroused a mixed bag of questions about the enduring status of "elites" controlling capital. Then later, he came to wonder about the effect of wealth concentration on those who did not participate in it, the common lives lived in the average household, typical lives among those living a capital-constrained paycheck-to-paycheck existence.

Most people would call the head of such a household the Average Joe. I called him what your grandfather had called him, a "wage earning schmuck." Ever the gentleman, Doug was offended by that name and worried that others would be too. So he made my name for Average Joe into an acronym, "WES." He tried other acronyms for that class of people, a way to refer to them in the plural. But they never stuck and over the years he'd simply come to use "WESs" for the plural.

Doug went on about his worries about the long term effect of Marx's call for radical social change—taking capital away from the wealthy and giving it to the government, then putting those who had held that capital back on the bus with everyone else.

From the political side of his education, though, Doug didn't think a Marxist "dictatorship of the proletariat" was a likely real threat to the American "elites."

But he did see a threat in the American Constitution's mechanisms for change. He went on about how the trend of American history was to lessen the power of the vote of the privileged. Doug reviewed the changes in voting rights since pre-Revolutionary Americans raised a rabble seeking their "voting rights as Englishmen." Kate, as a history professor you probably know this stuff better than he did. But as he told it, in Colonial times even in England only about 5% could vote; the English WESs (peasants and tradesmen, not wage earners) were told they had "virtual representation" either because their landlord's vote voiced the needs of their region or because all of Parliament represented all of England. The American Constitution let State Legislatures decide who could vote for members of the U.S. House. The Constitution also limited votes for the U.S. Senate to those State Legislatures, and it limited the vote for President to electors.

The course of history from those times to ours had seen the vote for those offices become more directly popular in form while, at the same time, the list of those who could cast a popular vote was expanded to "otherwise qualified" Negroes in 1870, to women gradually but finally totally in 1920, and to the last American Indians in 1947. At the time we were speaking, blacks in the South were attacking interpretations of "otherwise qualified"—interpretations purporting to be based on principle, like poll taxes and subjective literacy tests—that had the effect of denying them the vote.

In short, Doug's pessimism about the future of privilege in America was threatened by the ability of common men to vote away the privileges of wealth.

And, according to Doug, that was exactly what was happening. In 1913, the WESs amended the Constitution to give themselves the right to impose a graduated income tax. While the original top rate (the rate paid by the highest income payer on the last dollar earned) was 6%, here we were only 50 years later and the top rate was 91% and had been so for as long as he could remember. I said, "Yeah, but that's just the rate our folks pay on the next dollar they earn, the 'marginal' rate. On all the dollars they earn they actually pay a much lower percentage. That rate, their 'effective rate,' even for the richest, is about half that 91%." (Actually, Kate, I looked it up recently on the IRS website for SOI, Statistics on Income. It's amazing what you can find out with a few key strokes these days. In 1963 I'm sure Doug's parents and mine were among the top tax filers who reported income over $1 million. That group's effective rate averaged just over 46%.)

But Doug kept going about his worry about privilege in our lifetimes. He said that, led by FDR (a "traitor to his class," our parents said), the WESs had voted themselves the right to promote union-favoring limits on capital's prerogatives through the National Labor Relations Act. They put the government in the insurance business through Social Security and in competition with private utilities through the Tennessee Valley Authority.

Doug summed up by saying that now, in different cultures—Eastern Europe and America—history was developing along two strongly similar lines. Marxists were seeking the ascendency of the working class by the elimination of the wealthy through violent revolution. In America the working class was seeking its own ascendency through the ballot box. In both cases, those with wealth were at risk of losing the privileges they enjoyed.

Meanwhile, he said, those of us with wealth are being fed the line that "to whom much is given much is expected," the noble were obliged—like we're supposed to give it away. Doug wasn't buying it. He said that he thought having more money than the next guy was a good thing. He said we've got it and all those forces have declared an intention to separate us from it. He thought we'd be wise to grab the rope and heave the other way.

But, he wondered, how? Abolish the ballot box? No way. We all know that slogan, "taxation without representation is tyranny." Most people in this country, at some level, believe that. That meant that in order for us to stop the trend we'd have to get the far more numerous WESs to vote against their economic interests and for ours. I said "That'd be "pissin' up a rope.". (That's Navy-speak for "lots 'o luck.")I wanted to respond right then and there. Instead, I told Doug I had some of my own college-based opinions on that subject. If he gave me a couple of days to sort them out I'd like to try them out on him.

PERSUASION AS A COUNTER TO DOUG'S CONCERN

A FEW DAYS LATER WE HAD another "discussion into dusk" as we were calling our sessions. It was my turn to ramble and explain my optimism about the future of privilege. I also drew on observations made in college, both in course work as a history major and as an intercollegiate debater.

I said that my optimism was based on the fact that people have been acting against their obvious interests across history. They did so because somebody *persuaded* them there was some higher principle. To put it another way, my message was, 'Don't ever underestimate the power of persuasion.'

I explained why I felt that way, starting with an experience I had in intercollegiate debate.

One year the national topic was Right to Work Laws, the state laws that voided any provision in a union contract that required an employer to make a deduction, payable to the union, from the pay of each worker the union represented, even if the worker didn't join the union. Remember, once a majority of a category of a plant's workers vote to certify a union to represent them, federal law requires it to represent every worker in that category, union member or not.

Well, anyhow, when you started to research the debate topic, the Chamber of Commerce and the National Association of Manufacturers would send you reams of stuff, quotes from this famous guy or that, decrying the unfairness of making a poor worker pay dues to a union he didn't volunteer to join. It interfered with the worker's right to work! Get it? And, besides, the Chamber's material crowed, it was demonstrable that employment in the states with such laws was growing faster than employment in other states.

Most of us bought those arguments and crafted our "pro" speeches with quotes from guys like Barry Goldwater about the injustice to that imagined oppressed worker. *It was a matter of principle, damn it!*

When you went to research and build a case for the other side, the AFL-CIO would send you fewer reams of stuff, quotes from this less-reputable guy or that, decrying the unfairness of having the federal law require unions to represent a worker and then having state law force the union to do it for free. That was the "free-rider" argument. And besides, Big Labor's stuff noted, in a society ruled by majority vote, involuntary consequences to the minority were an accepted fact of life. Some guys bought into that. In any event, all of us crafted our "anti" speeches around that. *It was a matter of principle, damn it!*

Then we memorized our speeches and went out on road to weekend tournaments with finely-tuned, quote-laden speeches believing, with some justification, that debate was a matter of presentation, of stage presence and subtle theatrics.

But one tournament—Dartmouth, I think—ended with something more than the usual simple tabulation of points from the five or so rounds. We all attended a final round. At that final, the team opposing the Right to Work Laws—the debaters from Kansas State at Emporia if I recall—went outside of the box. At least out of the box I had been in.

In essence they said all this emphasis on *principle* was hogwash. The true test of whether a policy should be adopted was one of *effect*. What was at issue with Right to Work Laws was strength at the bargaining table. That table was the place where capital and labor met to negotiate an appropriate balance of their interests—their interests in the share of the wealth that resulted from their productive combination. At that bargaining table they hashed out a balance between the workers' interests in pay and working conditions vs. the capital contributors' interest in the lessening effect of those wages and conditions on profitability.

Against that background what mattered about these laws was their *effect* in decreasing the economic strength, the bargaining power, of those on the workers' side of the table. The size of the strike fund, the salaries of those representing the workers, the amount available for public relations to shape local public opinion, for hiring lawyers, etc., were all lessened where payment into the union's coffers was made a matter of individual choice. After all, free choice to pay union dues was going to be made by low wage folks who had other demands on those wages.

No law subjected the capital side of the bargaining table to division of its economic power. Given the nature of the modern corporation, even if an individual investor would choose better things to do with his share of the company's capital than absorbing the cost of a strike, or paying for negotiators, lawyers, and local PR, he didn't get a choice. The united power of the capital at the bargaining table was employed as management saw fit. At their most basic, a Right to Work Law was about pitting capital unity against labor division—pure and simple.

And of course, the argument went on, it was natural that states without dues check-offs were gaining jobs. Capital was moving to where it didn't have to pay union scale or pay as much attention to workers' conditions.

Those debaters were right. In that hour I realized I had been persuaded by high sounding appeals to a principle by people who had no interest whatsoever in that principle. What the hell were the management entities, the National Association of Manufacturers and the Chamber, doing by putting so much effort into speaking for the "poor workers" oppressed into paying for the services they received from the union? Why the reams of stuff purporting to urge workers' rights?

In fact what was with this title, "Right to Work Laws?" Ostensibly it was the little guy's right to work without paying dues. But would the NAM or the Chamber urge, for one second, that the little guy who had been loyally doing a good job for 19 years had a right to keep that job, a "right to his work," if the company wanted to fire him because his plant manager had it in for him, or the company wanted to save money by closing his plant before his pension rights vested at 20 years, or any other reason at all? No, the title of the laws was as much plain hypocrisy as the arguments invoked to sell them.

In that hour I realized I had been bamboozled by high-sounding principles which were really just self-serving crap. At the same time that debate went a long way to teach me the power of persuasion, because on the surface that self-serving crap did persuade. It also taught me that the correct way to judge any argument was not on the abstract principle it advanced but rather by its *effect* on people in the real world. It is to achieve effects that men shape their speech. Most often, when they want to achieve an effect the audience might want to avoid, they call upon their audience to honor some high-sounding principle they assert should control.

Then I gave Doug another illustration of the power of persuasion that came to me from my college history courses.

Throughout history people were persuaded to act against their true interests all the time. Just think of all the millions who have marched to some avoidable war, put their lives on the line, and then died for no good reason at all.

That idea had really hit me in college during my year abroad at the University in Bordeaux. I was taking a long weekend across the Spanish border in the great little city of San Sebastian. Climbing a hill in some parkland, I came across a small, mostly overgrown English cemetery for soldiers killed in some war in 1835. Why did they die so young?

The Crusades, the Thirty-Years War, and who knows how many other wars were all about my God is better than your God, even though they're the same God. Those wars were fought by people who had been persuaded that they should put their lives on the line to make the other guy see God "our" way. I had long understood how men could be persuaded to fight in wars like that.

And I understood wars of national pride (Napoleon and Hitler) or national greed (the wars of colonization and the American wars against the Indians). But why was there an English cemetery in Spain for soldiers who died in the 1830s? It was less than one hundred and thirty years earlier and I had been a serious student of world history, yet I had not even heard of their war. Turns out it was something called the First Carlist War. I still don't know what it was about.

Somebody conned those poor bastards into dying—for what? I don't know. But that alone said something to me about the power of persuasion.

And look at our Civil War—600,000 died, but it sure as hell wasn't the people whose interests were at stake. Who knows what that was all about? If, in the agrarian South, it was to defend slavery—it sure wasn't the slave owners doing the defending. The grunts got drafted but the slave owners were exempt. On the other hand, if (as the Southern revisionist economic determinists say) it was about high tariffs to protect Northern industries, it wasn't the industrialists doing the protecting. The grunts got drafted but the owners of industries, if they could spare 400 bucks, were exempt. The Southern grunts had been *persuaded* to "defend our way of life" and probably to spare their women-folk the imagined sexual depravity of slaves. The Northern grunts had been *persuaded* about the nobility of freeing the slaves and the necessity of forcing the Southerners to remain in a Union that no longer served their interests.

Doug interrupted to say we did know what the Civil War was about; it was about freedom for slaves. "The songs said it," he said, "you know: 'Let us die to make men free;' and 'Singing the battle cry of freedom.' That sort of thing." I told him he was forgetting that the Southern grunt didn't think he was fighting to oppress people; he thought he was fighting for freedom—freedom of Southern whites from the moral judgment of Northern whites. For the Southern soldier the war was about freedom of a nation's minority to reject the will of the nation's majority. Lincoln knew that. That's why, for him, it was about whether the four-score-and-seven-year-old Union could endure without resolution of the split between the moral judgment of Northerners about slavery and the determination of Southern slaveholders to spread their system, the source of their wealth, over the new lands in the west.

But that's just one war. I told Doug men have been persuaded to put their lives at risk in every war. Often they marched off believing they were doing the right thing, the thing that needed doing. And in almost every war, on at least one side and often both, they were marching and dying for an interest that wasn't worth their lives or the effect on their families.

Look at us, I said, we're in uniform ready to do or die to defeat communism. OK, formally, we're sworn to "protect and defend the U.S. Constitution of the United States against all enemies..." Fine. But communism? It's an economic system—one that the people of the United States could, under the Constitution, vote to adopt if they wanted to. They would have to amend the no-takings-without-just-compensation clause of the 5th Amendment, but they could do it.

But someone has made "communism" a hated word. It looked to me like several someones had made it a code word to persuade people about their pet issues. Only a very, very few saw communism as a threat to their individual wealth; for the average wage earning schmuck the sled dog rule applies, "If you're not the lead dog the view never changes." But a greater number saw "communism" as a code word for totalitarian dictatorship. Many others used it as a code word for Russian imperialism. The churches saw it as atheism-militant and urged their followers to "oppose Godless communism."

After a rational political debate, the American people could probably craft a form of communism as a structure for their economic activity which honored individual freedom in all matters except private investment. It wouldn't work very well because we'd lose the healthy tension between markets and government power, but they could do it. And they could craft a communism that protected our national borders. They could fashion a communism which allowed religion. The one thing they couldn't do is make a communism with wealth still in the hands of the wealthy.

Just suppose it was the few very wealthy who leveraged their money to persuade the nationalists, the individual freedom people, and the churches, to fight the wealthy's battle? I was saying, suppose these groups, the nationalists, the individual freedom types, and the make-the-world-safe-for-religion types had each been whipped up to vent against communism by the people who were most at risk, the ones Marx was at war with, the wealthy. If our nation went to war against communism the average grunt would be hearing a constant chorus of reasons based on threats to his patriotic instincts and his longing for religious and personal freedom. He'd be persuaded to be willing to fight and even die—perhaps unwittingly to protect somebody else's wealth.

I was saying it can be done. People can be persuaded to act for your interest while believing they are fighting for theirs. As you know, Kate, history is the story of how often they are.

And, I said to Doug, it's not just some other grunt I'm talking about. It could be you and me. If we die fighting communism, which interest will the winner say we put above our interest in living? An economic system? A social system? National independence? Power for the Vatican? Or maybe even some interest we haven't figured out yet. "Shit, if we'd gotten our asses fried in that Cuban Missile flap last year, some historian might say we died to get the Mob back in Havana."

By the time I finished, Doug admitted I had given him some hope that protecting privilege was possible. That night we had gone on so long I barely had time to hit the head, stop by the wardroom to grab a mug of coffee, and head up to the bridge to take the mid-watch—that is to drive the ship from midnight to 4 a.m.

A few weeks after that discussion, all the officers were gathered again on the foc's'l. By then, it was mid-May. I was really into trying to see the green flash before I was rotated off the ship, or at least be so sure I had given it such fair effort that I could firmly conclude it was just a baseless legend.

The main topics discussed that evening were the space program, the loss of some of our friends on the submarine Thresher, and the happier discussion of things to do on the ship's 7-month Mediterranean deployment scheduled to leave in early September.

The movie in the wardroom that night was so bad that the receipt that came with the film cans from the last ship bore a bold and very unofficial grease-penciled legend: "NFG!"

That evening, after the others drifted off the foc's'l, Doug and I stayed to move our private conversations to some conclusion.

The net of it all, we concluded, was that Marx was right—there was class warfare in progress—it was the wealthy versus the not wealthy; the haves versus the have-nots, the affluent against the paycheck-to-paycheck workers and their families, our types against the Wage Earning Schmucks.

Beyond that we agreed: we were among the wealthy and we liked it; we should commit to become class war warriors so that privilege would endure for ourselves and our descendants. We even decided we should do more than participate—we should set our sights on winning that war.

We committed to a friendship dedicated to doing so. We also confirmed a tentative assessment that our principal weapon in that war would be persuasion.

(Later that year, after Joe Valachi's Senate testimony about the "Cosa Nostra," we began to call that purposeful friendship "Our Thing" but eventually, somehow, we came to call it "Our Enterprise.")

By the way, Kate, about the green flash? I'm not sure I ever saw it. I certainly didn't see the sky inexplicably flash green. But there was one very clear evening when I did see something. As the sun first touched the very sharp horizon, it was its usual darkening yellow. As it sank to become a progressively smaller arch on the horizon, it grew orange and darker. By the time it had shrunk to a dot, the size of a pencil lead, it was bright pure red. And then it was gone. In that instant that spot went Kelly green. Something I learned from a high school science teacher about complementary colors even made that plausible. But…like I said, I'm still not sure.

In any event, Doug and I were due for transfers.

Reader,

I think this is where my discomfort started. I never thought "class warfare" was real, just a way to describe a byproduct of competition in the marketplace. But treating it as a fact and entering it to win? Really?

Kate

7

SHORE DUTY IN NEWPORT

BY THE SUMMER OF 1963, both Doug and I had been Division Officers on the Oldendorf for a full tour and were due for a reassignment.

With some planning and effort, we both wangled shore duty in Newport. Doug was to become the Admiral's aide at the Naval War College; he had the bearing and the charm such aides usually had. I was to be posted to the staff of the newly enlarged "type command" on Pier 2. A "type command" administers to the needs of a type of ship. Our command, DESLANT, had provided for all east coast destroyers but it had just been merged with the cruiser command to become what we irreverently called CRUDLANT.

Of course, Doug and I had to move off the Oldendorf and find digs in town. Fortunately, we had learned of a great place that was routinely rented out to naval officers rotating through on two year tours, 222 Nottingham Lane. We had been there for several "wetting down" parties toasting friends' promotions.

222 was at the end of a peninsula. The Lane approached the property from the rear, touched just enough of it to allow entrance to the

sea-shell driveway and detached garage behind the house, then looped away and back toward the main road. The house itself was a good-sized, frame Victorian. But its best feature was that it was right on the ocean. Its large front lawn sloped away from the wide porch as it descended about 25 feet in a distance of about 100 yards before making a last 10-foot rocky drop to the sea. The nearest land to the south was 650 miles away in Bermuda. The nearest toward the west—across a cove—was a set of low cliffs which bore the enormous mansions that had been the summer cottages of the ultra-rich of the Gilded Age. We had the better view; we looked at their grandeur and they looked at us.

Our old Victorian had been divided into 3 apartments: one to the right of the entrance hall; one to the left; and one upstairs. Our timing had been good; we were able to lease the large upstairs apartment. It had just been vacated by a young officer being shipped off to Arco, Idaho, in Admiral Rickover's involuntary draft of several hundred officers into the nuclear power program that was roiling the Navy at that time. Our lease began on the first of August.

The remaining apartments were leased to a couple of Navy officers based on the other side of Narragansett Bay, at Quonset Point. One was a pilot whose squadron and its carrier were going on the 7-month Mediterranean deployment with the Oldendorf. The other was a civil engineer Doug had known at RPI. (He was the one who told us of the upstairs opening.) He was in the Civil Engineering Corps, the Seabees, about to spend the summer, our winter, in Antarctica. We arranged to pick up most of the rent for both of those guys with a promise to hold their digs for their return. As a result of that, by the end of September Doug and I would become the sole occupants of 222 until spring.

Our orders to our new jobs said "when relieved in August 1963 proceed…" and so forth. With our fresh-out-of-school Ensign replacements already on board, we had some flexibility about picking the day we'd be relieved. And the orders' use of the term "proceed" meant we would have four days of paid unofficial leave, time intended for people who had to move their household effects further than we had to move our meager possessions.

The Oldendorf was leaving for the Med on the Tuesday after Labor

Day. For most of August it was in a nest of ships alongside the repair ship Yosemite, being fitted for the deployment. So, aside from having in-port watch one night out of every four, we had the August evenings to settle in at 222.

We scheduled our relief and departure from the Oldendorf so that we had the last week of August off. We planned to check into our new jobs and get right down to work on the day after Labor Day.

I should mention that the world beyond the Navy was dealing with other events at that time. The Thursday of that week was the day of Dr. King's "I Have a Dream" speech, and the following Monday was the day of President Kennedy's Labor Day message, a message that holds some weak, but haunting, parallels to Lincoln's Second Inaugural. Both Dr. King and the President addressed the society's larger picture and, in a way, reminded us that the momentous was possible.

Doug and I knew our new jobs could be either mind-numbingly dull or an opportunity to start Our Enterprise. Throughout that August, we continued our discussions-into-dusk above the sea—now on a seaside bluff instead of a foc's'l. We talked ourselves into a progressively deeper resolve to arm ourselves to join class warfare and to be winners in that war.

We knew we had to learn a lot before we could engage. We had little doubt there was such a war and only slightly more doubt that persuasion was the principle weapon. We convinced each other that our new jobs, particularly Doug's, presented extraordinary opportunities to study something we needed, the discipline of warfare.

No, Kate, seriously. We figured that some serious academic understanding of war, a thoroughly studied form of achieving goals, could serve us well.

As it turned out, that study has helped us more than we could have hoped. But that was all in the future during those evenings above the surf. At that point we were strengthening our resolve to learn anything relevant at every opportunity.

In those discussions we formed the view that more opportunities would present themselves if we only looked.

One of the things we had discovered about each other in the long discussions-into-dusk on the Oldendorf was that we both liked the bits of wisdom buried in the songs of Broadway musicals. Here in late August that regard brought us to talking about The Music Man. You may know it was the story of a salesman who came to a sleepy Iowa town alert for something that would present a sales opportunity. He learned the only thing new in that town was a pool table at the old billiard parlor. He took that fact, persuaded the local folks that pool was a threat to their children's souls, and sold the town a whole band's worth of instruments and uniforms.

By that Labor Day weekend we were prepared to tackle our new assignments giving the Navy full value. But we were also primed for learning warfare (and mass persuasion if we could) for our own purposes while keeping an eye out for what we came to call some "Music Man Moments."

Learning Warfare, Clausewitz

A S YOU WOULD IMAGINE, DOUG'S job as aide to the President of the War College made him only a little bit more than the Admiral's go-fer. Yet, it opened doors for him that his own lowly rank would not. He soon found that the courses that most closely matched what we were looking for were the courses in Basic Warfare Theory I and II taught by Marine Colonel Vincent Hardeman and Navy Captain David Knorr.

As the semester began, Doug approached them with the idea that we'd like to use our off-duty time in Newport to learn warfare. We didn't completely tell them our goals, but we were truthful with them. We said that when we got out of the Navy we expected we'd be in competitive businesses and we sensed that studying warfare theory would help.

We also worked on building a good, respectful, relationship with them and their families.

There were several circumstances that helped build that relationship. For one thing, the lawn at 222 was a great spot to have their families over—the kids played badminton or had Frisbee catches while the adults prepared the barbeque. For another, Doug had a modest but impressive sloop he moored at Ida Lewis Yacht Club. A third was that we were all avid, if not accomplished, golfers.

One of the greatest things about Newport in those days was that for an incredibly cheap price, and subject to modest tee time restrictions, Navy officers could play at the otherwise private Newport Country Club. Newport Country Club, for God's sake! A founding member of the U. S. Golf Association, site of the first U. S. Open, and better yet, the course with the finest turf I'd ever played. To be specific, a weekend round with a tee time before 10 a.m. cost about the same as a sleeve of 3 golf balls. (The local members played later and the mansion dwellers even later than that. Kate, there were a couple of times earlier that year I came off the 18th green while President Kennedy was on the 1st tee just across the driveway. His father-in-law's farm, which had become the summer White House, was just up the road from the entrance to the Club.)

On the personal level and away from the base, we earned a first-name-basis friendship with our instructors. We came to know the Colonel as "Vince," and the Captain as "Tug." As for becoming our personal informal warfare instructors, they were glad to help.

Teaching us warfare theory put little added burden on them. For our purposes they figured they didn't have to teach us all the details of their courses. We needn't bother with tactical concepts, such as "capping the T" a la Nelson at Trafalgar or Jesse Oldendorf at Surigao Straight—except to know that it's better if you can shoot at your opponent with more guns than he can at shoot you. And they thought we wouldn't have much need of Alfred Thayer Mahan's ideas about geopolitically import-ant choke points on the world's trading routes—except to know that even in a battlefield as broad as the sea one can find some positions that are more important than others.

Instead they commended us to start with *On War* by Carl von Clausewitz. They agreed to meet with us for about an hour once every week or so—usually on Doug's sailboat or after eighteen holes. There they'd take on the role of teachers leading seminar-like discussions on chapter assignments they would give us. So it was that over cold Narra-gansetts and bowls of pretzels and salted nuts we absorbed the subjects they taught in their courses.

It turns out that *On War* was the profoundly thoughtful and influential product of its author's life's work. As an Army officer, Kate, you've probably read it. But if you haven't, I strongly recommend it. Unfortunately, his ideas were still evolving, particularly with regard to limited wars, when he died from a flu epidemic or some such in 1831. So the book was published in a somewhat disjointed, but still worthy, form.

Colonel Vince was right when he said, "this book leaves you saying this guy was a genius." He also said that too many of his students tried to treat it, as they had most other texts in their careers, by looking for a few central take-away tools they could use. Two weeks later, at our second session, he chided us saying that we were trying to do just that.

Doug and I read the chapters when and where we could. Then we turned our evening discussions at 222 into study-group conversations. Eventually we figured you could divide Clausewitz into two parts: bedrock immutable structural concepts about the enterprise of war; and, diverse elusive considerations for use by commanders called upon to engage in that enterprise.

About the structure Clausewitz was clear and repetitive. "War is nothing but the continuation of policy with other means." "War is an act of force to compel our enemy to do our will."

It was key to his work that Clausewitz saw the conduct of war as the interplay of three things: the political aims of the government; the primal violence of the soldiery; and, chance. It is chance that presents the commander with the circumstances to which he must, in an agile intelligent way, apply soldierly violence in service of the political aims.

To be a bit more specific, Clausewitz taught that if the political leadership has a *policy*—today you'd call that *policy* a '*mission*'—and if the political leadership decides to serve that *mission* by war—it becomes the task of the War Department to gather men and material and adopt a *strategy* appropriate to a war in furtherance of that *mission*. Then it must select the *engagements* in which the available men and materiel are likely to advance the *strategy*. Again it must do so consistent with the controlling *mission*. Within those *engagements* the on-scene commanders must seek to succeed by sound *tactics* using the available men and materiel—always being alert to chance and ready to change *tactics* accordingly, even by withdrawal from an *engagement* when appropriate—again, always in a way consistent with the stated *mission*.

This sounded a bit abstract, so Vince and Tug suggested we apply those ideas to what we knew of Germany's actions in WWII.

They asked us to consider that Hitler's *mission* was to obtain his personal domination of, at least, Europe. He, aided by his inner circle, chose a *strategy* of successive individual conquests. Then they and the General Staff had to choose the *engagements*. Different commanders then had to choose different *tactics* in those *engagements*. The first *engagement* was to convince the German people he was seeking power for them in a "Thousand Year Reich." Follow on *engagements* included: pacifying Austria; subjugating Poland; co-opting Italy; conquering France; and, so on.

We concluded that such an outline and the Hitler example give a good summary of Clausewitz's ideas about the structure of war.

But looking for take-aways from Clausewitz's ideas about the conduct of war was a maddening task. I suspect that if you put most any question about war to Clausewitz, other than about its structure, he'd probably answer, "It depends." You might want to dismiss him as useless. But he'd be right. In his book, time and time again, he enumerated factors and then railed against trying to prioritize them without consideration of the unique facts and policies in play.

I guess you would look at his view of the conduct of war as one part the Kantian distinctions of means and ends and one part the engineering methodology of "form follows function."

Concentrate your forces or divide them? It depends.

Choose to attack or wait? It depends.

Pursue a battle until it is done or disengage? It depends.

What did it depend on? He'd probably say, "How best to use the men and materiel in the existing circumstances to serve the national *mission*." That is, what form best fits the function? What means best fit the ends?

All of that can be maddening, mostly so for a student who dreams of someday being a commander and then, win or lose, finding comfort in the fact that he did his job by the book. But for the commander with confidence in his own creative ability, in his own genius, the Clausewitz approach is liberating. Yet, at the same time, it compels that commander to undertake the hard discipline of learning, as exhaustively as he can, all the factors involved in the choices actually before him.

By the third seminar session we were about getting the hang of it. Then, at that point and out of the blue, we saw our first "Music Man Moment."

LEARNING WARFARE, SUN TZU

WE HAD ALREADY SENSED THAT part of any such "Moment" would be the outlook of Doug's boss, Admiral James McKinney, the new President of the War College. He was a dynamic fireplug of a man who had been a two sport All-American in his Academy days. He came to the War College determined his tour would be extraordinary. Maybe it would be his last on active duty and would leave him with a sense of life-justifying accomplishment. Or maybe it would be so noteworthy that it would lead to an even higher command. Either way, it was clear he was there to change things for what he saw as the better.

But the second part of the "Moment," the part that turned the Admiral's ambition into a very helpful force, came in the form of the 1963 publication of the first English translation of Sun Tzu's *The Art of War*.

The translation was by a remarkable man—a linguist, combat hero, and Oxford scholar—a retired Marine, Samuel Griffith. When he retired, he put his Marine tunic in the closet with a general's star on the shoulder and the Navy Cross he earned for "extreme heroism and courageous devotion to duty" at Guadalcanal on its chest. Then he took his linguistic skill and his insights into Chinese military tradition, both earned during his long tours in China before and after the War, to Oxford. In England he studied among Oxford's great Chinese scholars. He even consulted on ancient armaments with Cambridge's Joseph Needham, the subject of that Manchester book you recently mentioned, Kate, *The Man Who Loved China*. General Griffith translated Sun Tzu for his thesis and emerged with his Ph.D. Then, working for the Council on Foreign Relations, he published his translation of *The Art of War*.

Incidentally, it was clear that both General Griffith and those who reviewed his book believed that it held lessons applicable beyond the military. Many pointed to the wider use of the original text in Asia, particularly in the Japanese business community. That view of the work suggested that it was particularly relevant to the goals Doug and I were pursuing.

What was immediately clear to everyone at the War College was that this 2400-year-old "new" book deserved an honored place in the curriculum. And at the War College the most logical place for its study was somewhere in the Hardeman/Knorr Warfare Theory courses.

When we heard of the book we saw the obvious "Music Man Moment." Doug started a frenetic round of shuttle diplomacy among Vince, Tug, and Admiral McKinney. Doug's message was that the College needed to revise the lectures and teaching materials for the Warfare Theory courses to accommodate *The Art of War*. Then he argued that, given their already considerable teaching responsibilities, Vince and Tug needed a qualified assistant to change the course materials promptly and well. With help, Sun Tzu could be a major part of the courses as soon as the January-May semester.

Doug bolstered his contention that he was the man to provide the help for a couple of reasons. First, because of our widely known scholarly sessions with our friends about Clausewitz, he was already fairly familiar with the existing curriculum. Second, he was able to play up his experience in grad school. There he had been a research assistant to the Dean, D. W. Karger. As an assistant he had worked with Dean Karger on the articles that had become part of the Dean's just-published and very favorably reviewed text, *Managing Engineering and Research,* a primer on how to lead scientists and other inherently creative types. (Of course it was easy for Doug to get a glowing recommendation from Dean Karger because by then Doug was engaged to Karen, one of the Dean's daughters.)

Vince, Tug, and Doug persuaded Admiral McKinney that Doug could take on that job without lessening his service to the Admiral as his aide. In fact, they convinced the Admiral it would help Doug's service to him because, if the Sun Tzu additions to the curriculum were made quickly and well, the War College would be changed for the better. The Admiral might even be called on to promote the changes to the other war and staff colleges throughout the Armed Forces of the United States and possibly even to the similar schools throughout the English-speaking world.

It worked. Doug was tasked to provide scholarly assistance to the Colonel and the Captain as they set to the task of curriculum revision. And, if I may say, he did it astoundingly well. I helped as much as I could and made no secret of my help either within the War College or back at my job at the other end of the Base. The career Navy people involved appreciated the energy we gave to their project. They all knew that our personal goals were a bit different from theirs. But they also knew that, as far as the effort required, our motivation was totally aligned with theirs.

As the task gained momentum, urgency, and credibility, and with the help of Admiral McKinney, the Profs and Doug were able to persuade my boss, the Admiral's classmate, Admiral Bob Gamba, to let me join them for one day a week. Of course, Doug and I piled up many more hours than called for by our day jobs on long nights in the War College library. The net was that both Doug and I were being paid to immerse ourselves in the study of warfare. The Navy had its reasons; we had ours. I honestly think we served both well.

At its most basic, our task was to harmonize the 130-year-old Clausewitz text with the 2400-year-old wisdom of Sun Tzu.

To start, of course, we had to study Sun Tzu to the depth we were studying Clausewitz. Thankfully, and no doubt because we were official-ly pursuing the matter for the War College where General Griffith had, about 15 years before, been a faculty member and tinkered with the same problem, we were able to meet with him a few times. And we were able to routinely call on him, by note or phone, to keep us headed in the right direction.

I have already told you about many of the key things we learned from the study of Clausewitz. Let me do something similar about what we learned from Sun Tzu.

First of all, as far as style goes, it struck me that their styles were the exact opposite of what one might expect from ethnic stereotypes. In my view (which differs somewhat from the historian who wrote the intro to Griffith's translation), the German's style had been quite an enigmatic open-ended recitation of considerations for a commander. The Asian's work was much more declarative, more Germanic if you will. It consisted of statements of rules (often presented with illustrative anecdotes and commentary).

To put it in terms you might identify with, you could say that the style of Sun Tzu's work has more in common with Machiavelli's *The Prince* than Clausewitz's *On War*. I suppose that shouldn't surprise. Clausewitz was a practitioner simply writing to tell other practitioners of his craft what his experience and studies had led him to believe about it. Machiavelli and Sun Tzu were practitioners writing to display their competence by giving guidance to those who would employ practitioners.

That said, there was undeniable wisdom in the ancient work.

Some of Sun Tzu teachings can be put forth as quoted maxims: "All warfare is based on deception;" "To subdue the enemy without fighting is the acme of skill;" "To capture an enemy's army is better than to kill it;" "What is of supreme importance is to attack the enemy's strategy. Next best is to disrupt his alliances;" "A victorious army wins its victories before taking battle;" and, "Management of many is the same as management of few. It is a matter of organization."

Other core teachings are not so easy to quote:

> Anger and confuse the opposing commander;
> Keep him under strain and wear him down;
> When his forces are united, divide them;
> Political leaders should pick able generals and not interfere with them; and,
> A general in the field conducting operations consistent with his mission need not obey orders from higher authority about the details of operations.

One of the more interesting and valuable of Sun Tzu's teachings is his view that to conduct war without spies is virtually immoral. He said that a general who approaches a decisive battle yet, because he begrudges "… a few hundred pieces of gold remains ignorant of his enemy's situation, is completely devoid of humanity."

Sun Tzu expressed the other side of the coin with an interesting corollary: in order to make it impossible for the opposition to learn the commander's program through its spies, he should set troops to their task without disclosing its full design. Very few needed to know that much.

Another tidbit we have found most valuable is the advice to, "Bestow rewards without respect to customary practice … Thus you may employ the entire army as you would one man." We had heard rumors about generals deciding before Normandy how many Congressional Medals of Honor would be awarded—both in total and to each of the service branches. (The book and later movie, *The Americanization of Emily*, were based on that rumor.) Sun Tzu's idea was that if rewards are earned by action, not granted or denied by such a customary formula, everyone in the army would get the message that reward would be attainable by action, and not denied by whim. And, incidentally, the award itself would not be cheapened.

These two geniuses wrote in different ways, constructed different outlines, and didn't always come to the same conclusions.

For example, Sun Tzu most famously said all war is based on deception while Clausewitz thought "cunning" was overrated, largely because execution of it wasn't worth the effort required. Sun Tzu taught the ultimate skill was in winning without violence while Clausewitz taught that anyone who thought he could win a war without violence was kidding himself.

Some apparently different conclusions turned out to be not so different on further study. They could both be asked the question, "attack or wait?" Clausewitz would say, "It depends." At least at first, it appeared that Sun Tzu, considering the realities of a home-front economy, would urge quick action by saying "No nation ever benefitted by a protracted war." But deeper down he did suggest not only that "it depends" but he set down rules for what it depended on—for example, he listed which course to take when your forces are half the enemy's, or equal, or twice, or ten times. So it was that the more we studied their writings the more we found many things about which they agreed. Despite his more declarative assertions of relevant considerations, we found places where Sun Tzu, as Clausewitz more than two millennia later, decried attempts to prioritize those considerations in the abstract, without consideration of the context in which they presented themselves.

Both took time to note the importance of debasing the authority of the opposing commander. Clausewitz spoke of personal attacks on him, *ad hominem* attacks, for this purpose. Sun Tzu, as I've mentioned Kate, urged efforts to anger and confuse him.

On their bedrock teachings they were very similar. Clausewitz saw total victory in the enemy's loss of military strength, his loss of morale, and his open admission of those factors by giving up his intentions. Sun Tzu opened his work by listing five fundamental factors in war. The first of these was "moral influence" which he defined as "that which causes the people to be in harmony with their leaders." When you worked it through, his definition of "moral influence" is virtually identical to Clausewitz's definition of "morale."

That was the hook we had been looking for. When you searched for the central bit of wisdom about warfare true across the ages and cultures that separated Clausewitz and Sun Tzu it netted to realizing that the core object of warfare was the moral commitment of the competing populations. Wars were won by sustaining commitment among your troops and countrymen and weakening it among the enemy. In that light, the study of mass persuasion was a legitimate, even essential, subject of study for future combat commanders.

That was our next Music Man Moment. We had found a military justification for learning about, as the military would say, "the capabilities and limitations" of what we had concluded would be Our Enterprise's principal weapon—persuasion. Persuasion was the most direct means by which the commitment of a population could be sustained or attacked.

Reader,

For most of us in the American military the idea of wars being decided by the comparative commitment of populations of the warring nations is painfully clear after Viet Nam. Still, I'd studied both Clausewitz and Sun Tzu and I never came to the conclusion that persuasion linked them. But coming at those texts from Dad's perspective I'd have to say his idea makes sense.

Kate

ORGANIZING A LECTURE SERIES ON PERSUASION

W HEN DOUG AND I DISCUSSED ways to learn persuasion, we agreed that we learned better from good teachers than we did from good textbooks. Looking for a tutor to give us private lessons at 222 wasn't likely to produce a top-notch teacher. And if it did, we'd have to pay top money with after-tax dollars.

To solve that problem, we worked on a plan to get the War College to conduct a series of Spring Semester seminars on 'persuasion in the career of senior naval officers.' Sun Tzu's *The Art of War* and its core harmony with Clausewitz' *On War* on the object of war—the populations' support of the war—had given us an opening.

We mentioned our thoughts to General Griffith. He thought we were on the right track but he reminded us that others had gone down that track before, particularly in then-recent wars with radio's ability to evade print censorship in the enemy's homeland. But they didn't call those efforts persuasion; they called them propaganda. He thought that, between wars, the military forgot about those less-than-manly efforts and would be the better for a reminder.

He also pointed us to a fellow he met at Oxford, Professor Zybnek Zeman, a scholar in the field of 20th century European history. Dr. Zeman was about to publish a book about the use of propaganda in Germany, 1919 to 1945. That's how General Griffith had come to know him; they had worked with the same set of editors at Oxford University Press. The General thought the Professor would be an ideal addition to our seminar series.

With General Griffith's introduction and a couple of pay-by-the-minute transatlantic phone calls, we got Professor Zeman's tentative thoughts on our plan. He was willing to get on board.

Then we approached Admiral McKinney. We explained our belief in the importance of mass persuasion in war and General Griffith's agreement with us. (We also mentioned the importance of persuasion for officers who must go to their seniors or Congress for funds for their programs.) We told the Admiral that we could find funds for a series of about five half-day lectures, probably on successive Fridays toward the end of the spring semester, taught by some of the top minds in the field. We proposed establishing a foundation and inviting contributions from civilian corporations while offering attendance to people in their marketing departments. With 3 Ivies (Brown, Harvard and Yale) within 100 miles we couldn't have a better location to find teachers. The 75 miles to Boston also gave access to the scientific tradition at MIT and the Jesuit tradition at Boston College.

We would be able to gather a group of excellent professors for a weekend session to design a course outline. Then we'd have pairs of them prepare and conduct the chosen sessions. We figured the whole thing would cost about $50,000. (Even if Doug and I had to pay it all, we could deduct the $50,000 from our other income. Effectively those 50,000 dollars were at the top margin of our income so, at a marginal tax rate of 91%, about $45,000 of it would otherwise have gone to the government.) As it turned out the invited companies covered most of the nut.

We proposed to the Admiral that we finish with a War College-only session specifically addressing wartime persuasion—*i. e.*, propaganda—and more specifically that we invite Professor Zeman to lay out the use of propaganda by the German leadership. The Admiral agreed to the seminars but suggested we open that session to the contributors as well. They may not come, he said, but the invitation would justify the use of some of the collected funds to defray the cost of Professor Zeman's participation. And, he said, he would invite the CIA to send a couple of reps and chip in some of their budget toward the cause. Admiral Jim was no dummy.

By phone and judicious use of the Admiral's letterhead we reached out to specific professors from each of the schools I mentioned. A gratifying number accepted our invitation.

At the first weekend session we and they hashed out a course outline shaped serve both our purposes and the Navy's. We still had to make arrangements—meeting rooms, publicity, meals and base passes for the guests, that sort of thing. But mostly we were glad to be on our way to getting started learning the inner workings of persuasion, our war's principal weapon.

LOGIC VERSUS
CHARACTER AND PASSION

I N THE FIRST SESSION OUR Professors started with the ancients, primarily Aristotle and his idea that there are three ways speech can persuade: the Character of the speaker *(ethos)*; the Passion he instills in his audience *(pathos)*; and, the Logic of the argument *(logos)*.

Aristotle was convinced that persuasion was not the same as demonstrating the truth of the issue. If truth were all, then Logic would control. But Aristotle believed that the Character of the speaker was the most persuasive factor.

As Doug and I discussed that idea on the porch one evening, we took that thought further. It was certainly clear that Character, Passion, and Logic were not a set of 3 equal forces. It was highly likely that Character and Passion, if combined, could whip Logic damn near every time.

That was heartening. After all, we were looking to persuade a mass of people to act on beliefs that were, in Logic, contrary to their interests. We wanted them to vote less wealth for themselves and more for us.

Next our professors addressed the two classic forms of reasoning: formal (or syllogistic) and informal reasoning.

In Catholic schools I had several teachers explain formal reasoning, the syllogism. You remember, it's the form of argument that starts with an indisputable **major premise** followed by a **minor premise** leading to a **conclusion**. The hackneyed example is, "All men are mortal; John is a man; Therefore, he is mortal."

That form of argument is neat as a pin. But its elegance and authority make it useful in persuading an audience in part because they hide its flaws. When true, it rarely teaches you anything you didn't already know (or were conditioned to believe). Also, it puts control of the discussion in the hands of the speaker who proclaims the major premise. A major premise about how one should act is often a principle. Formal reasoning assumes only one major premise, one principle. In the real world there are often several principles that must be weighed and harmonized before the wisest course can be selected. But by using formal reasoning a speaker can declare a single true (but insufficient) principle, mate it with carefully selected facts, and make an argument more compelling than it ought to be.

The other major form of argument, informal reasoning, was never mentioned by my teachers. Still, we all use it to come up with new ideas or support ones intuitively formed.

Where formal reasoning's syllogism has three parts, informal reasoning's structure has four. There are three main-line parts: **evidence** which creates an **inference** that the **proposition** is true. The fourth element is one or more **warrants**; they support the **inference** of the truth of the **proposition**.

Diagrammatically, Kate, informal logic looks like this:

$$\text{Evidence} \rightarrow \text{Inference} \rightarrow \text{Proposition}$$
$$\uparrow$$
$$\text{Warrant(s)}$$

For example, suppose that during an Oklahoma spring there is evidence that a strongly colder dry air mass is moving toward an area of sun-heated ground covered by a hot humid air mass, and that is happening right beneath the jet stream. From that evidence I can infer the proposition that there may well be a tornado outbreak. In a backyard conversation I could use a simple warrant for the inference, "That's what happened under those circumstances last spring." For a different audience I could use a different warrant—perhaps getting into all manner of meteorological principles, even the complex mathematics of spirals.

Informal reasoning doesn't yield certainty; it leaves room for doubt and produces conclusions reckoned in terms of probabilities. That allows people who disagree to air different ideas. They can do so secure in the uncertainty of the opposing position, and correspondingly humble about the uncertainty of theirs. Such logic doesn't control its listener, it engages him.

Long before Aristotle, recorded court trials had reached actionable, if less than certain, conclusions based on evidence and inference. And thousands of years before that, peoples all over the world used evidence from the heavens to infer propositions—predictions—about good times to hunt, fish, plant, and harvest. Nowadays such reasoning is the core of the scientific method.

The different forms of reasoning fit different forms of political persuasion. Informal reasoning held sway in Greece's Age of Pericles and was honed in debate in the Roman forum. When the Roman Republic was replaced (through force) by an emperor, governance justified by formal syllogisms took over. Formal reasoning is the logic of absolutes, of certainty; it is a weapon of power. An Emperor's pronouncements were not invitations to discussion. Neither were a pope's. It wasn't until the printing press made dissent possible again that informal logic re-emerged. Galileo's 1633 trial (for challenging the orthodox concept of the cosmos) was a classic battle in the war between formal and informal reasoning. In it, prelates (with an interest in preserving their power by limiting knowledge to major premises they could proclaim) fought against a common man (representing those who had an interest in seeking to know the unknown). In our time fundamentalist preachers were reenacting that battle—this time in response to Darwin, not Galileo.

After that session we suggested to our profs that this business of formal and informal reasoning seemed to be getting a little bit away from what the Navy and we were interested in. We weren't looking to persuade an individual. We wanted to be able to persuade a society and understand how the other guy persuades his society. And, besides, these concepts related to *logos*. Hadn't Aristotle suggested that Logic was possibly the least important means of persuasion?

They promised that, in the next session, they'd get to that—surprisingly by again invoking Aristotle. We were beginning to understand that the things we needed to learn were timeless.

PERSUASION OF GROUPS

I T SEEMS ARISTOTLE HAD INTRODUCED a concept called an "enthymeme." That word apparently meant "in the mind." He taught that some audiences could be persuaded by a speaker who called upon premises or warrants already 'in the mind.' For those audiences some parts of the persuasive argument need not be stated.

For an example in formal logic, if Greeks were conditioned to believe—if they had it 'in the mind'—that the Oracle at Delphi only spoke truth (major premise), then one need only say that the Oracle predicted easy victory (minor premise) to persuade the Greeks that a planned attack was worth the effort (conclusion).

Argument based on ideas already in-the-mind works just as well in informal logic. There the thing 'in the mind' is the validity of a warrant. Consider, Kate, "Jesus loves me, this I know, for the Bible tells me so." If the proposition is that Jesus loves me, and if the evidence is a biblical passage, the inference will only work in a society conditioned to believe the Bible is worthy of being, at least, a reasonable warrant for that inference.

In both examples an independent observer, unaware of the

unspoken beliefs 'in the mind' of the audience, would conclude that these arguments were not logical and should not persuade.

Persuading people to mass action is not a matter of persuading enough individuals. Persuasion leading to mass action is different—and using what is 'in the mind' of that mass is a major part of that difference. Members of a society that has a set of beliefs different from the rest of mankind can be persuaded to act as the rest of mankind might not.

The profs said that 'in the mind' arguments particularly abound within religious denominations and political parties.

With that I sensed the profs were getting to that wardroom rule again—religion, politics, and particular women, the power of emotion to override fact.

The profs used different terms, but what came across was that the things shared 'in the mind' of people within a religious or political group often created a "nation" as Robert Ardrey would later use that term in *The Territorial Imperative*. Such an entity, a "nation," has one fundamental characteristic. It has boundaries. Inside the boundaries you are one of the "us." Outside you are not. Within the boundaries a disagreement is an individual dispute to be resolved with civility (up to shunning or expulsion). Across boundaries a disagreement triggers collective animosity and it permits conduct, such as violence, otherwise unethical.

We were getting to an idea central to mass persuasion: we are social beings; we need societies. We need membership in something that defines the "us' as distinct from "them." Without societies there would theoretical liberty but profound individual vulnerability. In such a world a 10-man cohort could rule. The 10 could define an "us" that others would want to—no, have to—join.

The profs emphasized that joining necessarily involves submitting to, or adopting, things that are 'in the mind' of the group. For example, did we think a multitude of people would independently just come to believe all the things recited in the average denomination's creed? Yet people born to (or joining) a society which has chosen a multi-faceted creed, have gone to war, shed blood, and sacrificed their lives, apparently over differences about such things as the nature of a wafer in a religious ritual, or name of the same "one true God," or which cleric had the right to succeed a religion's founder a thousand years earlier.

Persuading people to act on a belief can be very different from persuading them to actually believe. And that's not just by putting a gun to their head or threatening to burn them at the stake if they don't—though threats of some negative consequences can certainly help. If a person is a member of the group he is expected to act, or to assert a belief, as the group's leaders intend.

Among half a million *Sieg Heil*-ing Germans at a Nuremberg rally (many compelled to attend), or among a million Chinese rhythmically pumping Mao's Little Red Book to the sky there had to be some people with doubts. But, by participating in chorus behavior proclaiming that they had no doubts, they were convincing the people near them to assert the same belief as a condition of fellowship in society, of membership in a tribe.

In short, there's more to mass persuasion than valid logic spoken by a noble character attempting to gain intellectual acceptance of an idea. There is also a social phenomenon. By it an exalted character, the leader of a disciplined group, can use social pressure and emotion to induce action by its members quite independent of their individual thoughts. It's even possible that, eventually, a member of such a group will not even allow himself such independent thoughts because they would trigger an internal sense of disloyalty.

That week's session ended there.

During a less hectic part of the academic year Doug and I probably would have spent a good part of our weekend on the golf course, or on the boat, kicking our new ideas around. But the year was winding down. Doug was off to Rennselaer to see Karen for a planning session for their upcoming August wedding. I put in a weekend with Colonel Hardeman and Captain Knorr assessing how the Sun Tzu-enriched Principles of Warfare courses could be improved.

13

COMMERCIAL PROPOGANDA AND FALLACIES

A CCORDING TO OUR CURRICULUM, THE next session was to cover fallacies. But our corporate guests had asked us to let them talk about how they used things 'in the mind' to persuade in marketing.

Doug and I expected them to give examples of the sort described and criticized in Vance Packard's popular 1957 exposé of advertising trickery, *The Hidden Persuaders*. And such examples came up, to be sure. But these practitioners focused on more fundamental ideas from Edward Bernays' 1928 book titled, simply, *Propaganda*.

For an hour they led a lively interactive discussion. Ideas of many informed and experienced practitioners rattled around the room with an energy I had never experienced in a classroom setting.

I borrowed a copy of Bernays' book and read it in a week. Bernays defined modern propaganda as "a consistent, enduring effort to create or shape events to influence the relations of the public to an enterprise, idea or group." Then, two paragraphs later, he convinced me that we were on the right track:

So vast are the numbers of minds which can be regimented, and so tenacious are they when regimented, that a group at times offers an irresistible pressure before which legislators, editors and teachers are helpless. The group will cling to its stereotypes…making of those supposedly powerful beings, the leaders of public opinion, mere bits of driftwood in the surf. When an Imperial Wizard, sensing what is perhaps hunger for an ideal, offers a picture of a nation all Nordic and nationalistic, the common man of the older American stock, feeling himself elbowed out of his rightful position and prosperity by the newer immigrant stocks, grasps the picture which fits so neatly with his prejudices, and makes it his own. He buys the sheet and pillowcase costume, and bands with his fellows by the thousand into a huge group powerful enough to swing state elections and to throw a monkey wrench into a national convention.

To be sure, Bernays' book, like those of Sun-Tzu and Machiavelli before him, was largely a commercial for his services. But that passage and what Bernays said in his chapters on "Psychology" and "Propaganda and Political Leadership," have served us well over the years.

After an hour of almost rowdy discussion, the profs decided we had to return to the planned curriculum if we were to cover all the points they thought fit the purpose of the course. So they brought us back on track and addressed fallacies. They said that, normally, fallacies are taught as offenses to correct reasoning. But, for propagandists, fallacies are tools. They went on to describe particularly useful ones.

Some fallacies in formal reasoning are pretty obvious. The average person can see that kind of falsehood the moment he senses it's there. Yet there were other fallacies which often can lead a listener to a wrong conclusion. But what makes them pernicious to truth, yet usefully persuasive, is they are not always wrong. They could support a correct conclusion; so their falsehood is less obvious.

Consider the personal attack on people speaking for the other side—an "*ad hominem*" attack. This is an application of the negative side of Aristotle's idea of the persuasive importance of the Character of the speaker. The Character of a speaker has no sure connection to whether his side of the issue is right. True, a flawed speaker is often on the false side of the argument. But the mere fact that he is saying something doesn't make it false.

A similar form of could-be-true-fallacy is ridicule—reducing the opposing proposition to the absurd—a "*reductio*" argument. This form of fallacy can be particularly helpful in opposing new ideas, in resisting change even when that change is needed. "Give women the vote? Nonsense!" "Interracial marriage? Preposterous!" If you want an example touching your life, Kate, look up the press coverage when, in the fall of 1956, a Congressman gave a service academy appointment to a Mary Ann Bonalski. She was serious and worthy and her quest was an idea less than 20 years before its time, yet it was treated in the national press, and by the Navy, as a joke.

Personal attacks and ridiculing arguments have been well known fallacies since the time of the ancients. Even more importantly for our purposes, they have power both within a receptive group **and in creating such a group**. They help identify the "us" in the sociologically eternal battle against the "them," particularly when they are served up in some humorous form.

There's science behind that use of humor. Every after-dinner speaker senses it. Freud explained it. In his book about jokes, commonly called "*Der Witz...*," he argued that jokes release common, natural, but socially repressed, thoughts. That release lies behind the chuckle elicited by bathroom, sexual, and targeted aggression jokes. That audience release, shared with speaker who inspired it, tends to build a bond among them.

Then the profs ran through a second group of fallacies, arguments which were capable of misleading. I took furious notes. Some were verbal trickery. Some were structural flaws. The "straw man"—misstating the opponent's argument and then disproving it by attacking a weakness inherent in the misstatement—was a venerable and effective one of those. The fallacies of this second type don't do quite so much in creating a cohesive receptive group. But they work far better among people in a group already conditioned to be receptive.

Two fallacies of this type deserved special mention.

One goes by a shortened form of its Latin name, *Post hoc.* The full name translates to something like, "After this, therefore because of this." It presents an inference that, since A happened before B, A must have caused by B. Cross-examining lawyers use it often. "Mary was shot with this gun after you borrowed it from Louie, wasn't she?" (If you can't prove that you returned it before she was shot, you're in trouble.) The fallacy is attractive because time sequence is important to causation; the flaw is that people instinctively give time sequence more weight in considering causation than they should. *Post hoc* is a particular favorite of conspiracy theorists.

Another of these fallacies is guilt (or innocence) by association. "You should believe him because he went to the same school as Dr. Smith, the saint." (Or "…not believe him because Dr. Smith is a lout.") Guilt by association is particularly useful because it works as well for or against ideas as it does for or against people. "The XYZ theory is correct (or bogus) because it was Professor Jones' idea and he was the fellow who came up with the great (or flawed) ABC theory."

All weekend after that session Doug and I batted around the idea of growing a mass of followers that would evaluate each new idea about government with our principles already 'in the mind.' Suppose our followers had 'in their mind' that they and we are patriots, and that there is an unpatriotic opposition they should hate, one we could tag with one word. Then, if we associated an idea we opposed with that word, our followers would be passionate opponents of the new idea even if, had they seriously thought about it, they would see it would be good for them.

As the weekend wore on, we also toyed with an idea from the week before: the power of a cohort of 10 as a disciplined and dissent-proof core of a political group..

After work the following Monday we made our usual stop for a couple of beers at the weekly sing-along at the piano bar in the small Officers' Club annex on the hill above the piers. Normally we'd have sung about some Michael rowing a boat, or about when "husbands and wives, and itty-bitty children lost their lives" on the Titanic. But this time we were in Broadway mode and felt a need to lead a deep-throated chorus of the old Romberg/Hammerstein march:

Give me ten men who are stout-hearted men
Who will fight for the right they adore.
Start me with ten who are stout-hearted men
And I'll soon give you ten thousand mor-ore.

It was coming together. And we still had to hear from General Griffith's friend, Professor Zeman.

THE ZEMAN SEMINAR

W E WERE GETTING TOWARD THE end of May. Memorial Day weekend was next on the calendar. Because we figured the War College students and the corporate types would be itching to get out the door on that Friday afternoon we moved our last session to Thursday.

Professor Zeman flew Pan Am into Boston's Logan on Wednesday afternoon. I picked him up and drove him back to Newport. Conversation with him was a delight. If Doug and I could have, we'd have asked him to stay at 222. But the two of the guys who had left in the fall had returned. So, the Admiral had invited him to stay at the Admiral's quarters, and that was the plan.

That evening Admiral and Betty McKinney hosted a formal dinner for their guest. They had invited Admiral and Joanne Gamba; Captain Knorr and his wife, Beth; and Colonel Hardeman and his wife Doreen. Doug and I came stag. It was quite a formal affair; white mess jackets with gold cummerbunds, wives in formal dress. It had to have been on the War College's budget, not the McKinney's.

On Thursday morning we held a prep session. We had gone over what he should cover on the phone a couple of weeks earlier. In turn, he had sent us a complete version of his book. It was simply titled, *Nazi Propaganda*. The CIA's two representatives joined for that session as we had asked them to add an inside view of the contemporary propaganda.

Professor Zeman's session described how the propaganda machine of what we later came to call "The Movement" shaped Germany's national purpose. He knew his material well. In addition to living through and studying those times generally, he had studied Hitler's book, Goebbels' diaries, and the speeches of both of them.

His most valuable lesson for me had to do with Hitler's *Mein Kampf*. He said that, as impenetrable as most of the book was, when it came to propaganda, Hitler was lucid. He recommended, if we really wanted to understand mass persuasion, two specific chapters: Chapter 6 of Book One; and, Chapter 11 of Book Two.

Dr. Z. saw the mission of Hitler's Movement as the pursuit of power. Its leader craved power for himself. He gathered a relatively small inner circle of people to whom he offered power they would not otherwise have. And together they promised the ordinary people, the Wage Earning Schmucks whom he called "the masses," a share of world dominating power if they came along. More immediately his Movement provided those "masses" a feeling of the power in belonging to a strong and resolute community.

I quickly sensed that if we substituted the concept of wealth for the concept of power, The Movement had a lot to teach us. To be sure, Doug and I were not going to use violence to herd the schmucks, the masses, but we could see that there were probably enough kinds of economic inducements of inclusion and exclusion that herding was possible.

Professor Z. noted that The Movement was, nominally, the "National Socialist Democratic Workers' Party (NSDAP)." But all that really mattered in NSDAP was raw "N," Nationalism—that is, "patriotism"— the 'last refuge of scoundrels.'

To understand the effectiveness of The Movement's propaganda, in Dr. Z's view, one had to understand The Movement's organizational structure. It was organized into two classes of supporters: members and followers. The small core gathered Members, strongly committed people who supported its objectives and funded its propaganda operations. The followers, gathered by that propaganda, were the committed masses.

In passing, Dr. Z. said a basic rule, mentioned in Goebbels' diaries, was that though the message and its spokesmen were obvious, the machinery behind them was not to be disclosed. The marionettes were there for all to see, but sight of the strings and the string pullers would spoil the illusion.

The propaganda machine was responsible for more than putting out the message. It was responsible for destroying the means of communication of contrary messages. At first it used scornful dismissal of the free, non-Hitler adoring, press. Then, gradually, The Movement centralized, and then eliminated, every alternate source of information to the masses.

As for the actual content of The Movement's propaganda message Dr. Z. said it had a very short list of hard core issues intended to inculcate a nationally-unifying emotion—a sort of self-justifying hatred of anyone who was not a follower. The core issues played the eternal theme of zealots seeking to lead masses, "We are victims (or are threatened). They are the victimizers. Unite behind me and together we will be strong." In Germany the alleged sources of the victimization were three: Jews; Communists; and, the Versailles Treaty that ended World War I.

Those core points aside, The Movement's propaganda had no consistent message. It was an opportunistic set of ideas, ideas calculated as needed to fit the moment in order to gain or appease followers. The Movement felt absolutely no need to appear consistent to its short-memoried followers. For example, early on it scorned working farmers as the hated "them" to its "us," the out-of-work followers. But when the farmer's economic lot sagged they were quickly welcomed to grow the ranks of "us."

Another idea shaping The Movement's propaganda was that before the mass of followers could be led to act they had to be led to a "well-nigh religious conviction" of its dogma.

From his years on the post-WWI political stump, the leader came to learn that the way to motivate concerted action was not by intellectually persuading individuals but by using the emotion of the masses to persuade those individuals. And the way to convince those masses was through emotional rhetoric and the projection of strength of character, not reason.

Yup, viewed one way, the leader sought an unquestioning, 'in the mind'—based acceptance of his declarations. Viewed another way his main technique was to put Aristotle's Character (*ethos*) and Passion (*pathos*) into action.

The Movement used the negative part of Character as well. Character assassination of political opponents was a constant. Opponents, non-included groups, and differing ideas were subjected to a theatrical form of ridicule attack not usually described in texts on logic or rhetoric: scorn. A cynical, sneering dismissal was often persuasion enough for an audience of committed followers. Among the followers a sweep-away arm gesture could win the day against many an argument which might seem unassailable to a neutral party.

One of the most powerful and unique hallmarks of the leader's rhetoric was something classic texts on the subject didn't teach—the cause-serving power of lying. He did not regard truth and objectivity as ideals worth pursuing. He did not meet the opposition's lies with truth. He countered with bigger lies. By his lights demonstrating the falsehood of the opponent's lies was too complicated for the masses to follow.

That was related to his appreciation of "The Big Lie" outlined in *Mein Kampf*. I'll paraphrase, but only for simplification of his Germanic sentence structure. He said that the great masses of people, in view of the primitive simplicity of their minds, more easily fall victim to a big lie than to a little one. Since they lie only in little things and would be ashamed of lies that were too big, awareness of such a falsehood would never enter their heads. Even when enlightened on the subject, they would long doubt and waver, and continue to accept some part of the lie as true.

For its emotional content, the propaganda machine made every effort to convey that The Movement was the embodiment of spirits deep in the common German soul. Many observers have wondered how it could have succeeded in so cultured a nation as the Germany of Beethoven, Bach, and Goethe. But the leader knew how to exploit darker aspects of the German culture. He used the centuries of Germanic calls to violent anti-Semitism (including in Luther's *On the Jews and Their Lies)*; he drew on 400 years of politicians' invocation of the ideal of Germanic "racial purity" harkening to observations in *Germania,* the ancient book by the Roman historian, Tacitus; and, he insinuated his organization into the nation's soul by identifying the party with the state, then calling upon patriotism to advance the party/state. (This patriotism tactic was employed in crescendo fashion—a little at first, then more during Hitler's 1932 election campaign, and finally massively after the Enabling Act made the nation a dictatorship.)

The Movement's leader was very aware that humans are creatures given to respond to symbols. So his propaganda machine made generous use of places and totems purporting to convey spiritual power. Professor Zeman reminded us of movie footage of the leader solemnly taking various Wehrmacht units' colors into his hands and touching them to the party flag carried at the beer hall putsch, as though the touching conveyed some spiritual power from that past event.

Of course, the red, white, and black swastika-emblazoned flag was the central totem of them all. And its transition from party flag to national flag in 1935 was the strongest invocation of patriotism to advance The Movement's interests.

The most important media for The Movement's social persuasion were large, live, performances. As Goebbels had lamented, The Movement's rhetoric did not play well in the written media where it could be met with study, analysis, and telling reply available to the same people who had read the original message. On the other hand, the grand rallies maximized the opportunity for exalting the Character of the speaker and magnifying his emotionally persuasive effect, the Passion aroused in the audience. From the elevated rostrum the leader could arouse the emotions of the assembled masses and watch that mass emotion persuade individuals in the crowd to action.

What the leader actually said at the Nuremburg rallies was not uttered in a forum that permitted rebuttal. For one thing, the crowd-shaping presence of the Brown Shirts insured all response would be exulting; no small group could start a dissenting chant and drown Hitler out with a chorus of the German version of "Bull shit! Bull shit!" and live to tell about it. And the media coverage—both newsreels and Leni Riefenstahl's documentaries—relayed the rallies to the broader audience in a way that focused on the spectacle, not the content, of the event.

When Dr. Z. finished, the Yale-ies from the CIA contributed some stories about the tactics of their Agency's predecessor, the OSS. They described the division of propaganda into white (helpful truths) and black (vexatious falsehoods either in fact or in attribution of authorship). But they said nothing about the then-current propaganda operations either in Eastern Europe or in the powerful radio signals directed at Cuba. It seems they agreed with Goebbels that revealing the strings and the string pullers would spoil the illusion.

The next morning Doug drove the Professor to the Copley Plaza to spend Memorial Day weekend taking in Boston. At Symphony Hall the Boston Pops was in season playing the new Beatles music with classically trained musicians bopping about 'air-guitaring' with their cellos. And at Fenway the Red Sox were hosting the Twins—Harmon Killebrew and the Green Monster—a bit of Americana always worth the price of admission.

Karen and her parents were meeting Doug in Boston for some pre-wedding household-formation shopping at a local predecessor to today's "Black Friday" sales stampede, a one-day out-of-town-warehouse clearance sale for an in-town department store—talk about Americana! They offered to host the Professor through as much of the weekend as he might choose.

After what the Professor, in a 'thank you' note, described as a gloriously beautiful weekend, Doug took him to the airport late Monday and then drove back to 222.

Reader,

I understand Dad wasn't intending to repeat the leader's crimes of mass slaughter and initiating aggressive war. But I was becoming more uncomfortable that he was planning to repeat the Movement's Original Sin—self-serving disrespect for masses of other human beings.

Kate

Applying the Military Lessons of Newport

THEN IT WAS JUNE. DOUG'S service obligation was going to be up at the end of the month. My obligation and our lease ran two months beyond that. It was time to gather our thoughts about what we had learned; decide whether our ideas had any chance of succeeding; and, if so, what we should do next.

The front porch of 222 was no longer ideal for that sort of discussion. The two original tenants who had returned were as welcome as we to sit on the porch. Even if they stayed inside reading or watching TV, they'd likely have their front rooms' windows onto that porch open after a day of sunshine had heated those south-facing rooms. We meant no offense, and I think we gave none, when we moved the old cross-legged picnic table to the seaward end of the lawn. There we carried on what we described to them as after-the-Navy business partnership planning.

We put in full days for the Navy and when a heavy workload loomed at those jobs we preferred to tackle them by going in early. We tried to get off the base as soon after "knock off ship's work" as we could. Usually, we were at the picnic table by 6.

Bachelor eating habits are seldom ideal and rarely time-consuming.

We set up a rotation with our housemates that, Monday through Thursday, one of us would start a charcoal fire in the grill. Each of us would then use it as suited him that night.

At first, the discussions-into-dusk Doug and I had at the picnic table were not organized; they were more a free form opportunity to air and respond to ideas from three sources: what we had learned so far; what ideas were prompted by the different books we had chosen to study; and, the spontaneous thoughts about what the future held for Our Enterprise.

We quickly agreed that nothing we had learned during our year in Newport showed our basic ideas to be flawed. Neither did anything suggest that implementing our ideas would be easy. We also agreed that we should approach the problem in the structured way of warfare taught by Clausewitz. So that's what we set about to do.

At first we spent a good deal of time seeking a simple, direct statement comparable to Clausewitz's concept of national *policy*. We had to define the interest which our war was going to advance. As you would say, Kate, we were defining the *mission*. Eventually Doug suggested that our *mission* was "to maintain and grow wealth for ourselves and our descendants." That worked for me.

We noted that The Movement's leader had not pursued power for himself by declaring that's what he was doing. Instead, he told his party's members that his efforts would gain them more power than they could get by any other means. Then, together, they told his followers in his party, and later in his nation, that if they united behind him he would lead them to the power inherent in their national destiny. In like manner, we decided we would privately state our strategy to our closest associates, those analogous to his party's members, as "More wealth for the wealthy." And we would have our allied media, office-seekers, and office-holders tell our followers we were seeking "A more prosperous America."

Our *strategy* was obvious; installation of government officials who conformed, rigidly, to our will. There were more than enough people whose ego drove them to seek public office. If we ran Our Enterprise correctly we could identify those who would be compliant, then deliver the campaign facilities, the financial contributions, and the votes of our loyal followers to install and maintain those politicians in office.

We intended to win wealth from the WESs, the "masses" as the leader would say, by getting them to fight our war against their financial interests. In our national democracy that meant we would have to persuade the Wage Earning Schmucks to install the office seekers we had judged to be obediently compliant. The WESs would do that if they were 'in the mind'-sensitized followers of our cause.

We recognized that we'd have to spend money to make money. History (and the leader) taught that the return from a propaganda campaign could be well worth the cost. But we took some time to estimate if that would be so for us. To do that we had to get some sense of what government (that is, obediently compliant office holders) could do for us. A Clausewitzian analysis would have us consider the *engagements* we would undertake in furtherance of our *mission*. It was far too early in the game to actually choose the *engagements*, but at least we had to estimate them to make a preliminary assessment of whether the effort would be worth it

The most obvious way government could provide more wealth for ourselves and our descendants was, of course, tax policy. We made a list of which tax changes could help us (noting at the outset that, unlike the Wage Earning Schmucks, most of our income came from investments). It came out something like this:

Ordinary income tax:
- Reduction of rates on high-salary income
- Reduction of rates on dividends received
- Reduction of rates on interest received
- Reduction of rates on short-term capital gains

Long-term capital gain tax:
- Reduction of rates
- Reduction of holding period to attain long term status

Corporate tax:
- Reduction of rates
- Faster allowable depreciation (or investment tax credits)

Estate tax:
- Reduction of rates
- Elimination

Staying with taxes, government could help our investments by fore-going tariffs. Tariffs limited the profits made by our overseas investments, protected higher domestic wages, and lessened incentives to make goods more profitably where wages were cheaper and regulations fewer.

Social Security was another potential risk in the tax area. We saw it for what it is: a wealth transfer tax from the employed to the retired and disabled. It was the one federal tax that was flat; that is, it was the one tax with only one rate. That tax didn't apply to our primary types of non-wage income and didn't apply at all above a very modest limit, even on wage income. If the WESs wanted to tax themselves to pay their elders, we didn't care. But if they ever tried to change the format we'd have to be ready to meet the challenge.

A key corollary of our 'more wealth for ourselves' objective wasn't complicated. We of wealth do not want the WESs to use their votes to get us to pay any of their expenses.

The world-wide trend to tax-supported health care was then only a distant concern in America. But obviously, anyone with even a rudimentary understanding of market economics knew that its basic idea was that the general welfare is best advanced, resources are most efficiently allocated, when people are able to decide when something has become too expensive and they are able to buy a substitute. You know, Kate, cross-elasticity of demand and all that jazz. But people who had that understanding of markets also understood that logic didn't work for health care; for health there is no substitute.

But gaining a favorable tax policy and defeating efforts to put the cost of the WESs' health needs on us were just a couple of ways obedient office holders could serve our goals. There was the matter of an enormous amount of government land. We could insure it remained available for our use and that we need pay only low prices for that use—lease payments for such things as logging rights and grazing permits, and royalty payments for oil, gas, and mineral extraction. And, if low royalty payments could be enhanced by permissive operating regulations or lax controls on our accounting for units removed, so much the better.

It also seemed to us that the WESs had been waging a 75-year campaign to have government restrict the self-serving choices people of wealth could otherwise make: antitrust laws against price and market division agreements (the Sherman Act) and against the use of price differences to favor our friends (the Robinson-Patman Act); securities laws abolishing the rule of buyer beware in the financial markets (the Securities Act and the Securities and Exchange Act); and, a law against the combination of banking and brokerage operations that had proved so damaging to the WESs in the Hoover years (Glass-Steagall). We could benefit by the repeal, or the conscious neglect, of those laws.

The WESs were also using their votes to convert more of their values into expenses for our corporations. We didn't see how far that would go. Yet we sensed that any government which undertook to protect labor unions, regulate working hours, and define minimum wages would find more ways to dictate that we bear expenses it thought appropriate.

It's not that we saw all of the occupational, product, and transportation safety requirements coming. Or interference with our factories' waste disposal practices. Or a requirement that we actually fund our corporations' pension promises. But we did see the trend toward using government to make our companies serve more values than our prime value of profit-maximization. This trend alone was enough to tell us that the costs of the class war had to be borne.

One evening a thought brought us up short. We knew we intended to persuade the Wage Earning Schmucks to fight our battle for us at the ballot box. We were not fighting against them as people; we were only fighting against such of their interests as could lessen our wealth. So who was the enemy? Who were the people we intended to defeat?

I'll spare you all the back and forth, all the hypothetical answers to those questions advanced and rejected.

In the end we came up with this. The people we had to defeat were those few who valued any interests the WESs had which would cost us money. From among those we need only defeat those who were willing to devote their life's effort to advancing or serving those interests.

At first it might seem that most of the WESs would be against us. But throughout history they had shown that they were not usually willing to devote their life's effort to confronting forces at work beyond their immediate neighborhood. Except in eras of extreme stress and when they had extraordinary leaders, they were docile. The fact was that the demands of making a living had as much call upon their life's effort as they could deal with.

So who was left?

Well, first, there were unions, of course. Then there were two eligible groups of politicians—those who believed in promoting the general welfare and those who believed that promoting the general welfare would get them re-elected.

Next were the people who studied and wrote about government, law, and all manner of other social disciplines from the comfort of academia and who were not indebted to us or committed to advancing our interests. Trial lawyers who represented the WESs in court made our enemies list. So too did people in the media who believed that serving the interests of the WESs was either the right thing to do or would cause WESs to read their papers or tune in their stations. The last people we identified were in that segment of the clergy which preached or acted upon the social message of their religions' historical founders and early leaders.

We quickly realized that our target enemies were few and diverse. Such a group would have difficulties opposing us. Save perhaps the clergy, they embraced open discussion and respectful disagreement. Their opposition to us would be made harder by funding difficulties; those they served were less likely than those we served to advance that service with monetary support—donations are made from the discretionary part of one's wealth—WESs had very little discretionary wealth. Only labor unions had ready funds. That shaped our preliminary assessment that they deserved special attention.

These enemies also had limited lines of communication by which to mobilize WESs to support them. The main entities which could bring them to united action were government itself, the pulpits, and a free press fairly informing WESs of troubling facts of their time.

On those pleasant June evenings we'd sit above the sea's edge, reading as long as light permitted and often talking well beyond that. When in our reading one of us came across a new idea he'd blurt it out and we'd start a discussion on how it fit. It started out all very free form, a good way to fill both of our minds with a common understanding about things we hoped to deal with in the future.

But it proved to be not as free form as it seemed. It was just our way to focus on details. We found that, occasionally, we needed to step back and look at what we were saying to each other from a broader perspective.

Time and again we'd find ourselves using terms of ruling or governing. "In the world of individuals, a cohort of 10 rules." Stuff like that. But slowly at first, and then more frequently, we'd remind ourselves that those were terms of power, of ego. We weren't about ego, we were about wealth. By constant reminder, we conditioned ourselves so that "Wealth, not Ego" jumped out of our mouths with the certainty of a Pavlovian response when we heard ourselves crossing the line. We sought faceless effectiveness, not acclaim. As Truman and Marshall were fond of saying, "There's no limit to what a man can achieve if he doesn't care who gets the credit."

We also had to remind ourselves that we were not starting a war; we were joining one. Others before us had been at it for generations. Many of our elders were experienced and active in the war as we spoke, though they were probably not as focused as we. For example, the on-going "Unions are ruining this country" diatribes and the Right to Work Law efforts were clear instances of our elders using persuasion to attack those who stood between them and more wealth.

The combination of two thoughts, faceless effectiveness and an on-going war, caused us to consider just where we hoped to fit in. We didn't want to just become grunts in someone else's army. Still, we were willing to support others' efforts while we learned what was really going on—what worked and what didn't.

We developed an analogy to where we would fit in if we were in a traditional war. We saw Our Enterprise starting as a small, supportive, but independent ally of people with goals similar to ours. We would support them with a view toward earning their indebtedness and respect. Through that phase we would be scouting for those the leader would have called "members" and whom we came to call "Allies"—people we could induce to align with us. Meanwhile we would build and train our own "persuasion organization." We would put our alliances and persuasion organizations in the service of carefully chosen individual politicians who were most committed to our privately stated cause—more wealth for the wealthy.

As Our Enterprise grew we would continue our participation in this class war through alliances, not an ego-advancing structured hierarchy. Our fellow warriors would be our Allies, not our subordinates. Our Enterprise would be so dynamic and so amorphous that many of our Allies would not even know themselves to be part of our organization.

In those June evenings we had formed a workable outline of our policy, our strategy, our potential engagements, our enemy, and his capability and limitations. We had also come to a better understanding of who we were and where we hoped to fit in all this.

Now, as our own General Staff, and following the teachings of Clausewitz, it was time to address our manpower and weaponry needs.

Reader,

Militarily speaking, "Wealth, not ego" allows them to bring their guns to bear without giving the opponent a hard target. Clever.

Kate

CHOOSING OUR BIBLE

E ARLIER I MENTIONED THAT OUR evening picnic table discussions would often arise from thoughts prompted by the books we had chosen. As between organization and propaganda, Doug undertook to take the lead on organization. He had a sense he could develop a fundamental synergy between Clausewitz's *On War* and Dean Karger's *Managing Engineering and Research*. So, he usually sat there with the Dean's book open and *On War* and *The Art of War* available for a cross-check.

According to Doug, Dean Karger's second and third chapters—planning and organizing to meet objectives—dove-tailed with Clausewitz's guidance on policy implementation through strategy, engagement selection, and responsiveness to change. For example, the Dean wrote that there were all kinds of possible organizations. You could organize engineers by function (electric, mechanical, testing) or by product line (Impala, Corvair, Corvette) for example. Which one? It depends. And Doug saw reinforcing Clausewitzian parallels in one chapter after another.

Persuasion, propaganda, was my turf. So, at first, I had Dr. Zeman's book open and *Mein Kampf*, Aristotle's *On Rhetoric*, and Bernays'

Propaganda at the ready.

But as we thumbed from one book to another and popped up to make a point or listen to one, we came to realize something. We were trying to start a movement. Of all the authors we were looking at, only one had actually successfully started one. And he had set down how he did it. The relevance of *Mein Kampf* became more clear every night.

When that idea first hit us, Doug worried that there was a danger to our plan if WESs found out we were using that book as our foundation text. He had a point. We assured ourselves that distancing ourselves from that hated movement was fair to the facts. We wanted no part of what came to the minds of most when Nazism was mentioned. We were about family wealth not personal power and we were not intending any violence.

Still, Doug's concern triggered a memory of a story my uncle Fred told me when I was barely a teenager. I told it to Doug.

It seems an executive was driving to a very important meeting on the proverbial dark and stormy night—hurricane, actually. Near the top of a steep hill he had a flat tire. He got out, took off the hubcap, removed the lugnuts, and put them in the hubcap. Then he jacked up the car and went to get the spare tire from the trunk. Just then, a strong blast of wind carried the hubcap and the lugnuts whirling and rolling into the darkness, the woods, and who knows where all else. He stood there bewildered, frustrated, angry, and without a clue as to how to get to the meeting.

Then he heard a voice above him. He turned and saw he was outside an insane asylum. One of the inmates was leaning out a window and said, "Take a nut off each of the other wheels and put them on that one and you'll be fine."

He thanked the inmate, did what he suggested, and was ready to go on his way. But he looked up to thank him again and then said, "Would you mind if I ask a question?"

The inmate said, "Do you mean how come I knew what to do and I'm in here?"

"No offense, but yeah."

"I'm crazy, not stupid."

The way I saw it, I told Doug, Hitler was crazy. But, when it came to organizing a movement or persuading people to blindly loyal follower-ship, he wasn't stupid.

So I suggested we keep on using *Mein Kampf* as a guide, but refer to it more abstractly. Ultimately, we decided that, since the German prec-edent had ended less than 20 years before our discussion, we could just refer to *Mein Kampf* as the "Modern Experience." We also determined to refer to "The Movement" and "the leader" when we were speaking of the German Party and its Fuehrer. You've already seen me do that in this story of our enterprise's roots.

Finally, one evening, we decided to stop the random back and forth and to take some time for each of us to extract lists of teachings in *Mein Kampf* (the Modern Experience) that seemed likely to serve as guidance for our respective tasks—Doug's concerning organization, mine concern-ing persuasion.

We've kept and used our lists through the years. In preparing this history of our Enterprise for you I've attached them, updated with cita-tions from the 1999 Mariner Books edition. (And from here on in this story of our roots, when I'm quoting *Mein Kampf*, I'll use italics.)

With our distillation done and the extracts almost committed to memory, Doug went back to thinking about how Our Enterprise would be organized and, more creatively, how it would be funded.

Reader,

I've put those lists, those Mein Kampf extracts, at the end of the notes I've promised you about the Sat-urday conversation. Doug's extract on organization is Appendix A and Dad's on propaganda is Appendix B. In my notes I've continued Dad's use italics when I quote them.

Kate

DOUG'S PLANS FOR ORGANIZATION AND FUNDING

D OUG SENSED THAT FOR OUR purposes Clausewitz's manpower and weaponry ideas paralleled the two areas The Movement excelled at: organization (manpower) and propaganda (our
weaponry). He decided we'd do well to organize Our Enterprise as Dr. Z.
had suggested—we should serve as the core group controlling "members"
and "followers." However, because our organization would be less rigid,
less hierarchical, we would call the members "Allies."

He decided that in order to limit the Allies' input on the direction
of Our Enterprise they would be chosen on a case-by-case basis with an
eye toward their zealous support of our view of that particular issue. That
was in keeping with the leader's idea that The Modern Experience was a
movement, not a debating society; Doug thought Our Enterprise should
be the same.

Given the difference of our times Doug decided that, at least in the
early years, we would not personally stir up the lunatic fringe with any of
what the leader called "radical and inflammatory propaganda." But we
would keep an eye on the fringes that grew of their own accord. Then, as
each fringe movement faltered, we would approach the most radical and

well-funded people in it to offer them a better way to reach their (our) goals.

Doug focused on the shape of the organization and, true to his engineering training, he used a "form follows function" approach.

Our Allies would serve two functions. First, they would provide the resources needed to support our efforts to gain followers. Second, on an issue-by-issue basis they would form the network of mutual support which would give our side in the war a momentum and continuity not previously seen in American politics; they would be our movement's flywheel. As for their motivation, generally these would be people whose wealth would be increased by our success. They'd be people for whom that increase would more than compensate them for their efforts.

We'd also need staff, typists and clerks to be sure. But I also mean professionals. Some would be part-time, often academics who would loyally give us knowledgeable advice when called upon. Some would be full-time, paid practitioners of the rhetorical art devoted to crafting, vetting, and disseminating our party line.

I suppose that if any other pair of guys from the wardroom of the Oldendorf had dreamed about doing what we were, they would see themselves as just 2 guys in a country of 200 million. But we had wealth; we had connections. We were not naked in the face of opposing forces.

Still, our wealth was limited. So managing it required some consideration. Doug applied some serious thought to that aspect of our organization.

He had an instinctive understanding of the power of the leverage available from spending tax-deductible dollars in an era of high marginal tax rates. It was simply a use of the age-old concept of funding your business with OPM, Other People's Money. For starters he would look to our Allies to join their funds with ours. They were one part of the "Other People" in the "OPM" theme.

But Doug had bigger plans. He set about to create instruments that were tax deductible to our Allies and us. By employing tax deductible funds from high-income people, most of the funds we would use to change the government would, in essence, be government money. That is, it would have gone to the government in taxes if our entities hadn't grabbed it first. Using tax deductible funds he would effectively make the tax-paying little guys a major part of the "Other People" who would be funding our class war against them.

To put that another way, Doug decided we would act through 501(c)(3) organizations, that is, entities which qualified under that section of the tax code. The money contributed to them could be deducted from the donor's taxable income. In those days 91¢ cents out of every dollar contributed by the wealthy would have gone to the government for its purposes. Instead, through 501(c)(3)s, the 91¢ would go to our the purposes. (If we acted through a political party instead, 100¢ cents of every dollar would be out of our pockets—stupid, that.) The trick was making the 501(c)(3) look like a charity to the government and look like an organization which would do their political bidding to the rich donors. The John Birch Society had been successfully doing that since the '50s.

Endowing and controlling professorial "chairs" in universities was another way to use 91% government money to gain the allegiance of professors who would advise us when called upon. We'd need them to generate high-sounding academic defenses to our least defensible ideas—defenses that would receive character-of-the-speaker value, *ethos*, by their personal credentials.

Think about it. It was clearly better for us to contribute tax deductible funds to a university or a compliant 501(c)(3) "think tank" than to contribute non-tax-deductible funds to a political party. And, for corporations, contributions to a 501(c)(3) was one of the only ways to fund political power since they weren't allowed to make direct political contributions.

With that Doug realized we could also make use of privately held for-profit corporations. What IRS auditor would have the nerve to deny a corporation's deduction for demographic sales research? How could such an auditor prove that the research was actually in support of political— that is, electoral—ends? And how could such an auditor challenge the deductibility of a salary expense for a highly paid "executive" who was, in reality, just an out-of-office politician being rewarded for service while in office?

Then Doug realized that both 501(c)(3) entities and private

corporations could also address a problem that office holders have to face given the nature of the American political system—the risk of being unemployed when the political winds turn against them. Truth be told, we could provide jobs for such folks at little cost to our members through the public for-profit corporations which we controlled, or at least influenced, through Board of Directors memberships. Within those Boards, our membership on Executive Compensation Committees could enhance that influence even further. Even more, all three of these types of organizations—501(c)(3)s, private corporations, and public corporations—could help politicians' family incomes even while they were in office by hiring their spouses and children as long as the officeholders did our bidding.

With all that, a well-organized and well-funded group focused on a *mission* such as ours could make the lives of obediently compliant career politicians much better than the lives of their more independent counterparts.

Through control of these enterprises we could also influence mass media. Our corporations could use their advertising expenses (deductible, of course) to support the media that advanced our cause. They could also withhold their advertising dollars from media that opposed us.

Doug came out of those June sessions saying simply that the tools to gather and herd political and media sheep were there for us to use; we only needed the determination to use them.

Meanwhile, I was doing a similar analysis.

Taking the Lessons of Newport from Daydream to Reality

B Y THIS POINT WE KNEW we needed followers—millions of them—who believed in our movement, who saw it as safe harbor away from the scary seas of changing ideas and economic fortune all around them. We wanted their support to be so strong that they would follow our lead even on issues where reason would dictate they should do otherwise. Even if they personally felt we were wrong on an issue, their membership in our movement would be so much a part of them that they'd feel somehow disloyal if they didn't follow our lead. They would be the soldiers in our army, our Wehrmacht. We were confident that with their committed support, their votes, we could win our war against their class.

Remember, in the Modern Experience there were only three core, passion-inspiring, messages—hatred for Jews, Communists, and the Versailles Treaty. Every other message was simply an opportunistic reaction to the problems of the day used to advance the cause. As to those consistency was not required. We had to select three core passion-inspiring messages that would serve our cause as well as those three had served to persuade the Germans to do the irrational in the '20s and '30s.

89

Again Doug counseled selecting our core themes on a "form follows function" basis. Clearly, as both Sun Tzu and Clausewitz taught, we should attack the opponents' lines of communication and their alliances. In this context we saw that we had to convince the WESs that **government is bad;** that was Core Message #1. And it meant conditioning the WESs to distrust, even to actively refuse to listen to, any part of the media we did not control; so Core Message #2 was **traditional media (later "main stream media") is bad.** And if we needed three Core Messages, and the rhetorical teachings of Cicero suggested we did, we could use the flip side of the government is bad tenet, and so, Core Message #3 became **the "free market" (that is, a market free of government regulation) is good.**

There were some problems, of course.

For one thing, The Movement used mass meetings, a format that was largely gone from our society.

Except for political conventions, there were few mass meetings left in our society. We'd have to find an alternative. But in June of 1964 that was a problem for a future day.

Another problem was that the work of building The Movement in Germany was led by a charismatic leader who was visibly on the stump. Part of what his book said to us was that movements were driven by agitators who knew the psychology of the WESs' emotions—not by bookish intellectuals, however better reasoned and academically valid their ideas. Neither Doug nor I sought such a role. And, frankly, we knew we didn't have the personalities needed to carry off such a role.

That, too, was a problem for another day.

What was clear was that if we wanted the mass of individual WESs to act with a sense of being reinforced by membership in a great comprehensive body, our best hope lay in creating a society in which each of them had our core messages "in the mind." We had selected those core messages; we had to drum them into the WESs' minds.

But we still needed a forum in which the persuaded WESs would be committed by a deep emotional bond to a comforting community of fellow believers. If they carried in their hearts an "us versus them" feel, they would sense that any thought, based on an individual exercise of rational contrary choice was an act of disloyalty. That sense required a community based on passion, the emotions of hate for the "other" and the comfort of the crowd of the "us."

It seemed unavoidable that the community committed to such a "well-nigh religious belief" would be a political party. After all, a party's capacity for instilling commitment as emotion-laden as a religion had been a foundation of the old wardroom rule.

Any party would do. And we had to remember that we did not want to manage a political party—an inefficient, after-tax burden. We simply wanted to use it to hold a banner that our passionate followers would rally around. We would require politicians elected under that banner to implement the policies we would demand.

In the U.S., third parties have not done well since the Whigs and the Know Nothings collapsed in the 1850s. And a problem with third parties was that they tended to take votes away from the party closest to their point of view. You've seen that in your lifetime, Kate, as Ross Perot took enough votes away from the Republicans to make Clinton the president and Ralph Nader took enough votes away from the Democrats to make "W" the president. So we reasoned that our best course was likely to take an existing party and, as fast as possible, make it our instrument.

Looking at both major parties we could readily see that, traditionally, the Republicans had been more favorable to wealth than the Democrats. But the Democrats held more allegiance among the wage earning schmucks. So our choices seemed to be to enter the party of the schmucks and change its philosophy or enter a party with a compatible philosophy and attract the schmucks to it.

Tentatively, the Republican Party seemed the way to go. It was weak. Its only President in 40 years was a middle-of-the-road war hero who carried it to the White House rather than the other way around. Its weakness suggested it would be presumptively more receptive to new energy. Even if it were not receptive it would be less able to offer resistance.

That spring we had a more pressing problem with our plan about entering the class war and winning: how to take it out of our two-man mental garage and into the real world.

Earlier that spring Doug had mentioned our interest in political involvement to his parents. They suggested that, if we wanted to see politics up close, there was an almost once-in-a-lifetime opportunity coming up: the Republican National Convention scheduled for mid-July. They were going; Doug's politically active mom was a delegate from New York.

The suggestion made a lot of sense. From the comfort of June evenings on the lawn at 222 all our study seemed to have generated some fine theory. But we knew that, if we were on the brink of turning our theorizing into action, our ideas needed a reality check. A trip to the Convention could give us a good feel for whether the stodgy Republican Party could be the tool to gather a passionate army of WESs for class warfare against the WESs' economic interests.

Doug would be out of the Navy by the beginning of July; I had a couple of months more, but I'd start July with 60 days leave on the books. We were thus free, to different degrees, to test the reality of our ideas a continent away from our East coast roots at the convention in San Francisco.

When I think back on the decision to drive west, somehow John Belushi is in the frame shouting, "Road trip!" Did he ever really say that, or was it just "Toga party!?" I guess it really doesn't matter; the spirit was the same. For us, "Road trip!" seemed the parting yelp of our youth. We had gotten our schooling and done our service; we were about to enter the real world of our adult lives.

Reader,

Dad always said there were 2 kinds of people—those who control their environment and those who are controlled by it. This chapter reminded me that I've thought a lot about the fact that my environment is other people. Can a life in control of others, not in service to them, be ethical? I suppose it's a matter of degree, but where's the line?

Kate

THE TRIP WEST

I F YOU'RE A BACHELOR OFFICER on a ship in the Navy, every-thing you own—uniforms, skivvies, civvies, shoes, and sword—can be packed into a sea bag. When you're ashore you don't have much more—some books, a few pots, not much else. So, in late June, Doug was able to pack all of his gear into the back seat and trunk of my white 1958 Plymouth Belvedere convertible. His golf clubs were already there. He left for New York on the first Newport-to-Jamestown ferry on Saturday morning the 27th, transfer to the Stand-by Reserves and orders to "pro-ceed" home in hand.

I had the weekend duty on Pier 2 and stayed in Newport until the start of a 3-week leave the following Wednesday morning, July 1. Then I drove to New York in his too-small-for-golf-clubs Porsche. There we switched cars and headed west in my older but more spacious Plymouth. That's right, contrary to what you've heard him repeatedly bust me about, it was the space, not the push-button vs. stick-shift transmission, which governed the choice.

I don't know what we expected out of the trip. We had decided to drive rather than fly because we wanted to see the country. Between us we had seen much of Europe either in school or, earlier, on trips with our parents. On Oldendorf's last Mediterranean deployment we had seen Southern Europe: Barcelona, Cannes, Genoa, Naples, Brindisi, and Piraeus. Our Navy time in the Western Atlantic had taken us to Bermuda, Norfolk, Jacksonville, Key West, and throughout the Caribbean. But, those trips and ports aside, we had lived our lives on the east coast within 200 miles of New York.

We took Route 22 across New Jersey and survived its stores-on-the-median madness. We were headed for Harrisburg to pick up the Pennsylvania Turnpike hoping to make Pittsburgh by nightfall. We hadn't gone much beyond the Delaware River when we saw our first "Impeach Earl Warren" billboard. "John Birch Society; 91% government money," Doug said. I'm not talking about the Deep South; I'm talking about Pennsylvania within 100 miles of New York. I'm sure we saw the Earl Warren billboard well before we saw our first barn painted black and advertising Mail Pouch Tobacco.

About then the content of the broadcasts we could get on the car radio changed.

You have to remember that, in those days, cars only had radios as an option you paid extra for (so, too, a heater, outside mirrors, and seat belts). And the radios were AM-only with no scan feature. Both Doug and I had done a lot of nighttime driving between Newport and New York so we knew about the big 50,000 watt clear channel stations like WWVA in Wheeling and WOWO Fort Wayne. But you could only get them at night. By the same token those stations knew they were serving a good part of the nation. So, except for a slightly higher Country music content (they called it Country and Western back then) for the truckers they were keeping awake, they could have passed for East coast stations.

But local AM radio west of the Delaware and out of daytime range of the big cities was different. Religion. Religion from one end of the dial to the other. I guess around Boston I had become used to hearing Cardinal Cushing droning out the rosary to people stuck in evening traffic on Route 128. But there, at least, you had choices among your radio's four other buttons. This was different. I'm not just talking about the radio preachers we could already identify like the simple Oliver J. Greene or the scientifically aware Garner Ted Armstrong. Every valley seemed to have its own 250-watt tower selling salvation from sin and the need to prepare for the 'end times.' Often, as in the small valleys between the tunnels on the Pennsy Turnpike, the mountains left your radio dial with only one choice and that was either from the local pulpit or from a tape of a travelling preacher who was scheduled to appear at that pulpit within the month.

Many of the preachers, like the Cardinal in Boston and Brother Greene, were simply calling on their listeners to consider the spiritual needs of their individual souls and live moral lives. Had there been more diversity on the radio dial we'd have listened awhile and then tuned to other stations. But that option was not available. So we listened past the point of welcome. Soon we realized that many of these preachers were not speaking to individuals urging personal belief and conduct—they were invoking religious language and biblical prophecy to define America. Their focus was on the nation instead of the person; they were speaking of the nation's place in history. Yet I should say they were not yet preaching today's Dominionism (the doctrine that there's a biblical imperative for believers to actively work to spread Christian dominion over all the nation's citizens and the rest of the world).

But they were getting close. It didn't take a genius or a long time to identify the most common theme—the scriptures of old were leading up to these times and America was uniquely intended by God to do something great. Only the "something" varied—crush Godless communism, visit retribution on the Jews who "killed our God," defeat the evils of the papists, wipe pornography off the planet, and such like. "The blood-soaked cross and the red, white, and blue—arise and follow! And contribute to support this messenger." The messages boiled down to Christianity, the Declaration of Independence, the Constitution, and clerical compensation. Never mind that the specific illustrations invoked beggared the concept of behaving toward strangers as the Good Samaritan would or respecting that other people also were endowed by their creator with unalienable rights. It was God! It was our nation! It was the principle, damn it! Onward, Christian soldiers! Onward, believing Americans!

Religion and politics, all that was missing was a particular woman. The tone of the pulpit polemics were worth studying. Besides, what else was there to do?

At the end of the first long day on the road we found a tolerable motel near Pittsburgh. The next morning, starting a practice we had planned for breakfasts, lunches, and dinners, we found the nearest off-highway local eatery and started to take the pulse of the nation by respectfully chatting up some locals. "What's new around here?" "What do you think of Gold-water?" "Do you have an opinion about school busing?"

Then we set off, leaving the Turnpike and taking Route 40 to Terre Haute. Partway through Ohio the hills gave way to flatter land. With that the number of accessible radio stations increased. Our choices improved. Of course, there were more country songs. But they were a better selection than the current Top 40 anyhow.

The next day, continuing our diner, luncheonette, and cafeteria meal plan, we headed to St. Louis, picked up Route 66, and (with a short departure from 66 for dinner and to check Arkansas off our States-vis-ited list) we ended the day camped in Grand Lake, Oklahoma. By then the "something" part of the radio preachers' vision of God's purpose for our Republic often included fulfilling the Deity's manifest intention to advance the glories of the white race. (And because they were airing this stuff the stations were earning 'good boy points' with the FCC for broad-casting religious thought. As that comedian with the Russian accent would have said, "Vhot a country!")

The rest of our planned route was Oklahoma to Tucumcari, New Mexico; Tucumcari to Kingman, Arizona; Kingman to Yosemite; and, finally, Yosemite to San Francisco arriving on the 9th. We had a 2-day cushion built into the trip to provide for any unexpected problems like a car breakdown, or unexpected traffic or routing problems. We planned that, in the absence of problems (and we had none), we'd have a two day lay-over at Yosemite. Those days would give us days to relax, absorb what we'd seen, and do some light reading.

We had been in the Navy for 3 years and the Navy, at least in those days and even in "green flash" sessions, was not a place to be on top of current events. Neither a 7-month Med deployment nor a two-week-out/two-week-in Atlantic training rotation allowed newspaper subscriptions or TV news to be a routine part of your life. Even a subscription to a news magazine, by the time it found you through the Fleet Post Office system, couldn't keep you current.

Still, you'd have to have been deaf, dumb, and blind not to know that "the times they were a changin'" at least in the area of civil rights. 1963 had seen Kennedy speak on TV urging civil rights legislation and Medgar Evers murdered later that night. It had seen Dr. King's "I Have a Dream" speech followed by the Birmingham bombing which killed 4 little girls at their Sunday school. In Selma, Alabama, when 30-some black school teachers applied to register to vote, they were fired.

So far 1964 hadn't been any better. What you know as the *Mississippi Burning* incident, the murder of 3 young voting rights activists, had happened in late June. Their bodies had not yet been found as our drive made its closest point of approach. There was important legal change— during our trip President Johnson signed the Civil Rights Act of 1964— but still less than 1% of the eligible black adults in the county around Selma, Alabama were registered to vote. On the day we drove into Yosemite, back in Selma 50 blacks went to the Courthouse register to vote. The Sheriff arrested them.

When we arrived in Yosemite we took the opportunity to try to make sense of the news, the Gospel as interpreted on our car radio, and the passions of the folks we had met in 2000 miles of pancakes, hamburgers, and (starting in Tucumcari) burritos.

But mostly we set out to brush up on our Goldwater. We had each brought a 4-year old copy of his book, *The Conscience of a Conservative*. Four years earlier, in 1960, we had each listened to, and were stirred by, his speech at the 1960 Republican Convention. We were fans.

That wasn't odd. Wardroom rules aside, there was no doubt that all but one of the 25 or so officers who served on the Oldendorf at various times during our years on board were staunch Goldwater supporters. Goldwater's message was strong, simple, and direct. It suited our lives.

I mean, at sea the Navy was the simple life. At least, that's what a shipmate, Mike McCabe, said one day as we steamed out of a foggy harbor. He explained, "At sea you collide or you don't collide. You sink or you don't sink. It's simple. Ashore life's got too many strings tuggin' at you. You can try to weave them into something, but you rarely know if you got it right." Goldwater had no such doubts.

THE CONSCIENCE OF
A CONSERVATIVE

B ACK IN OUR SEPARATE COLLEGES Doug and I had read *The Conscience of a Conservative* and it had moved us. It announced approaches to contemporary problems that felt right to us, maybe because they were a path to protecting our privilege. But we thought it was because of his emphatic assertion of simple righteous principles, damn it.

Now we had just finished some serious study of the mechanisms of logic and persuasion; we came to the book to judge the form of its arguments, not its conclusions. For two days, as we sat in armchairs at the Ahwahnee Lodge or on glacier-smoothed granite above the floor of the spectacular Yosemite Valley, we dissected Goldwater's arguments. Simply put, we were appalled.

By any measure, Goldwater's book was remarkable and revolutionary. Written by a Republican during a Republican administration it tore into that administration more than the opposition. Goldwater held special contempt for the Supreme Court headed by a former Republican governor of California, Earl Warren. On his first page he criticized both the Republican president and the Republican vice-president for statements

98

Goldwater saw as apologies for conservatism. His attack against Nixon was for saying, "Republican candidates should be economic conservatives, but conservatives with a heart." His revulsion toward Eisenhower was based on the president's statement, "I am conservative when it comes to economic problems but liberal when it comes to human problems."

Writing at the end of the decade, the 50's, most Americans think about as happy days, which itself followed the decade in which the greatest generation proved its mettle, he dismissed all that and called for the country to acknowledge his view that, "America made its greatest progress [in some unspecified distant and better era] when conservative principles were honored and preserved." This was a pride-inspiring call for the return to a view of freedom, essentially freedom <u>for</u> the powerful, that best fit an age before mankind decided governments were necessary—or at least before some people decided even the powerless deserved a voice.

He called his movement "conservatism." In the Republican Party of my youth that term meant what it had to Lincoln, a preference for the old and tried over the new and untried. But, as you know, Lincoln's Republican administration had responded to changing facts and opportunities of its time and given the nation the new and untried. It not only freed the slaves and built iron warships; its laws gave land away in the Homestead Act, authorized and worked out funding for a transcontinental railway, and set aside Yosemite Valley as parkland. Goldwater's movement could not be called "conservative" in that mold. "Authoritarian reactionary" fit better. Yet, "conservative" sounded nicer and so fit his purposes (and ours) well.

Goldwater denied his "conservatism" was essentially economic. Rather, and prophetically, he asserted it was moral. He claimed morality and then asserted that morality required government to take positions that were amoral at best. He was on our wavelength.

His recurring method of persuasive argument was to start by asserting something to be a principle, as if it were always and everywhere true—the only principle to be considered. Then he would ignore any consideration of the effect of that principle on the reality of his times. Finally, he concluded with the assertion that the principle required that established wealth be served in some way or another. Universally, this or that governmental response to the facts and understandings of the time was wrong. For Goldwater just about every element of national government, other than the military, was wrong. All forms of persuasion other than force and declaration were for weaker souls.

His arguments had the simplistic form of formal logic—but, worse, it only used two parts of that logic. He left out the fact part, the "John is a man" part. It was as if he felt no need to acknowledge facts, the realities (or even the existence) of the 19th and 20th centuries.

For example, he argued against the nation being a means for its citizens to help bear each other's burdens. Local efforts were best, "Who knows better than New Yorkers how much and what kind of publicly financed slum clearance in New York is needed and can be afforded."

It was as if he never bothered to learn the lessons the 1800s taught about a nation's role in meeting regional problems. Goldwater's view that the nation had no business dealing with the social issues of New York's urban poor echoed the view of Great Britain's elites that its national government had no business dealing with the 1845-50 famine in the Irish part of the then-newly-unified nation. For the Lords in London it was a matter of principle; if the Irish couldn't buy potatoes, they should use the free market and buy something else. (Of course, the Irish weren't buying potatoes; they were growing their own. They had no money; royally-favored people in England owned the land and the Irish paid their rents with labor. Most of the rest of their economy was barter.) Then, when overwhelmingly large numbers of Irish escaped the famine to the nearest port in England, Liverpool, and packed into communal disease-promoting poorhouses, the Lords held fast. Who knew better than the people of Liverpool what and how much aid the poor of Liverpool needed and how much could be afforded. Principle required that the welfare problems of Liverpool were for Liverpool to deal with. One effect of this consistent but fact-ignoring philosophy was that the wealthy in London never had to open their purses to aid their poor countrymen. Another effect, according to a book on the subject I had read the previous year, Woodham-Smith's *The Great Hunger*, was that 3 million of those countrymen died.

Goldwater's call to honor his unsupported and devoid-of-context principles was a call for the American national government to ignore the reasons the Constitution created that government, especially including, as the Preamble stated that purpose, the promotion of the general welfare.

More than that, Goldwater's call was a call to ignore his own ideas of morality. He wrote, "The conscience of a Conservative is pricked by anyone who would debase the dignity of the individual human being." But he also wrote that states' rights trumped that dignity. About civil rights he declared that, "I believe that the problem of race relations, like all social problems, is best handled by the people directly concerned." The reality of the way 'the people directly concerned' were handling the problem, as seen in lynching photos in the tabloids of my childhood and school desegregation riots shown on the nation's TV screens throughout the '50s, was not even mentioned. Establish justice? Insure domestic tranquility? Forget effect; it's about a principle, damn it!

Notwithstanding that he was in Congress, the branch constitutionally given the power to make laws to insure that "no State shall deprive any person the equal protection of the laws," he declared that, though he was for civil rights of course, he was not going to impose his ideas on "the people of Mississippi or South Carolina." "Social and cultural change, however desirable, should not be effected by the engines of national power."

In short, he was willing to ignore specific national powers earned in blood in Lincoln's Civil War and made constitutional law in the 14th Amendment—and, by ignoring them, to leave the rights of black American citizens in Mississippi to the 'druthers of local whites.

If there had been any doubt about that when the book was published in 1960, there was no doubt by the summer of 1964. Goldwater was the presumptive nominee of a major political party, the Party which had long prided itself on being the party of Lincoln, yet he had been one of only six Republicans to oppose the Civil Rights Act Johnson had just signed. He voted against it twice: first against the resolution that ended a 75-day filibuster to block a vote on the bill; then against the bill itself.

His book went on to claim that the moral high ground of protecting the individual dignity of workers required the nation to check the power of those who spoke for them, the unions.

Then, despite the constitutional amendment giving the government the right to levy a graduated income tax (which had then been in effect for over 45 years), he declared that principles, damn it, required a flat tax "I believe the requirements of justice here are perfectly clear:

government has a right to claim an equal percentage of each man's wealth and no more." He went on to declare that a graduated tax was immoral. Here again his approach was to assert control of the major premise, assert a high moral principle and leap to a conclusion with nary a thought about the effect of the conclusion on the average citizen.

His tax argument, like his other arguments, was not three-part formal logic. It did not proceed from the assertion of principle to the consideration of the facts (or effects) before reaching its conclusions. It went like this—equality is fairness, equality requires a flat tax. He simply ignored the reality that the low income wage earners spent their last dollar, their marginal dollar, on food, clothing, and shelter while our coupon-clipping class did not. He also made no mention of the fact that the tax code already recognized equality—both the poor man and a wealthy man paid the same tax on their first $10,000, on their first $20,000, and so forth. What was unequal was the rate imposed on the marginal dollar earned by the wealthy compared to the rate imposed on the marginal dollar of the low-income family. His was an argument for equal treatment of dollars, not equal treatment of We the People. Ignoring reality and resting on his assertion of principle, he simply declared that morality required a change—no matter that the effect of that change would put a greater burden on the ability of the wage earner to feed, clothe, and house his family while it put more wealth in the pockets of the wealthy.

From a broader perspective, the essence of his moral high ground for what he called "conservatism" was his argument that it is not proper for America's government to address the problems the Constitution had formed that government to address.

Most Americans in 1787 and in the 1960s saw the Constitution as a social contract among the citizens to use their combined strength to protect each other's opportunity to live lives free from the excesses of popes, princes, and the power of wealth. Goldwater saw the Constitution as a contract among citizens not to use their combined strength at all, especially against freedom for the powerful to pursue excess.

So it was that in case after case Goldwater announced an unsupported principle, sometimes from an out-of-context Constitutional provision, and went on to reach a not-otherwise-supported conclusion. He specifically said that morality required the elimination of: social welfare, government support of education, public power, agriculture, public housing, urban renewal, federal regulation of nuclear power plants, and on and on.

Goldwater wasn't ignorant. He must have known that state regulation of nuclear power plants would mean a competition among states to adopt the most lenient, least costly regulations in order to get the tax revenue a major nuclear power plant would provide. The real world effect of state-by-state regulation would surely involve a race to the bottom of both the safety and the cost ladders in pursuit of profit. If he wasn't ignorant then he must have been sure of the ignorance of his audience.

Wherever you looked in Goldwater's book through the lens of what effect its conclusions would have on society, it boiled down to a polemic for more power for the wealthy and less cost for them to bear. *Principles*, damn it, demand more wealth for people like us. The likely *effects* of the "principles" on the people generally were insignificant trifles, lamentable perhaps, but righteous. Our kind of guy.

As I mentioned, four years before, as we read this book alone in our college dorms, Doug and I had been enthusiastic, even passionate, believers. Now we were re-reading it in a collaborative way, in a beautiful valley, with a greater understanding of the techniques of persuasion born of study, and with a greater understanding of America born of our Navy service and our 2000-mile drive.

We had been looking for the book's formal logic or its informal reasoning from evidence though warranted inference to conclusion. But late on the second day, as the heights were cooling and the warmed valley floor was starting to send a breeze up its granite walls, Doug put his finger on the problem. Goldwater's assertion of morality was a personal claim to his Character as the speaker. His message was an assertion of what his two audiences, the wealthy and the bigoted, wanted to hear, were pre-disposed to believe. To those people, his was the logic of that touched what was 'in the mind.' It told them what they already believed. He was inflating his Character before the masses by cloaking himself in morality then inflaming their Passions. It was clear to us that he was using the core techniques of Aristotle, Bernays, and the leader.

We knew that Goldwater's message was our message. But his was an angry and disrespectful tone. He preached contempt for the American society of his time. That society, which in the previous 20 years had repaired the economies of Europe and Japan, invented the first solid-state semiconductor, defeated polio, made a commercial success of jet transportation, television, etc., was by his lights shackling itself by offending his principles.

But we also saw his book as a collection of dogmatic statements uttered in what the Modern Experience had taught was the wrong medium for that form of persuasion, the easily studied and rebutted printed word.

There was no mention in the book that the nation formed and selected its government in order to "promote the general welfare and secure the blessings of liberty." Goldwater was asserting that the nation's government should abandon its efforts in pursuit of the common good and serve his ideas. It was a matter of principle, damn it!

We were on our way to the convention at which, at his urging, the party of Lincoln would turn its back on civil rights, moderation, and its patrician concern for the mass of the nation's citizens. Lincoln said he favored policies yielding the greatest good for the greatest number; Goldwater was saying the greatest number should fend for themselves.

On the morning of July 9, after two restful days testing the Goldwater message against our new-found understanding of persuasive techniques, we left the Yosemite. As we drove, a radio station in Modesto told us that, back in Selma, a judge had issued an injunction forbidding three or more people to assemble under the sponsorship of a civil rights group. But that seemed worlds away. Our reality that day was the spectacular near-wilderness through which we drove alongside the rapid Toulumne River toward a revolution about to explode in San Francisco.

Bring it on.

Reader,

I suppose an important part of my growing discomfort was how well Dad saw through the bull and yet remained intent on using it.

Kate

SAN FRANCISCO

W HEN WE HAD OUR FIRST thoughts about making the trip we had asked several people to advise us about how to get the most out of it. Doug's parents had been the most helpful. They were experienced hands at conventions and alerted us to the types of events worth attending and what to observe when we were there. At the same time they told us what activities would likely be all glitz and no substance; the sort of thing that would be, for our purposes, a waste of time.

When Doug had spoken to them in mid-May, they counseled that we make immediate reservations because very few hotel rooms would still be available. They also recommended that we plan to arrive in San Francisco early and stay with the Goldwater forces who would be gathering at The Mark Hopkins Hotel. Mingling with them would give us one view of things by reason of proximity. And we would have access to the other view, the view of the Rockefeller/Scranton forces, without having to stay at their hotel. Doug's parents would be there and that would provide us access enough.

We were able to get one of the last rooms at The Mark Hopkins, with arrival scheduled for the Wednesday before the convention proper, July 9. The hotel was already solidly booked for the next week so we'd have to vacate on Sunday before the convention proper started. For the convention week itself we arranged to stay with friends of my mother at their home overlooking the Bay high up on the first block of Broadway, by the Presidio.

As soon as we checked in, we made ourselves known around the Goldwater organization. Doug presented himself as a true believer just out of the Navy and out from under its Hatch Act restrictions on political activity. He wanted to help in any way he could. I was his buddy. But since I was still in the Navy for a few months I was just there to observe. We told them I was thinking about writing a political novel and was there to get color for it if I could. But, we said, mainly I wanted to absorb convention politics for possible future involvement. We did not push the fact that we were members of the rising generation of wealthy, traditionally Republican families. But we didn't hide it either.

Doug pitched right in by aiding a large group of 30-something organizers in whatever ways they needed.

I drifted, asked some questions, but mainly listened to what people were saying as they bustled. I spent a good deal of time reading all manner of press reports. Some newspaper distribution agency was supplying The Mark Hopkins with newspapers flown in. The convention was the first West Coast convention in the jet era and we generally had same day newspaper service from all across the country.

The work that Doug did often lasted well past midnight. My wander-about-and-observe format had some structure during the days but became much more free-form in the evenings. Each evening was different.

On one of the first nights we had dinner at the Fairmont with Doug's folks. They were true believers from the core of the old Republican Party, the wing that was about to get a thrashing from the Goldwater forces. At dinner I asked Doug's Dad what he thought of Goldwater's rhetoric. He gave a patrician, economics-based, but empathetic perspective, "Goldwater speaks as if the economic lessons of the last 200 years mean nothing. Those lessons teach that markets, like every person, animal, and thing on the planet, have capabilities <u>and</u> limitations. At best, when working well, markets only serve one of society's values, the efficient allocation of resources.

"Even from an economic perspective unregulated markets have limitations; they don't police themselves. Monopolizers can eliminate competitors; colluding companies can charge more than a competitive market would permit. Unregulated markets don't prevent dishonest vendors or adequately punish them; that's true whether the things being sold are goods, services, or financial instruments. That's why Republicans like Sherman sponsored antitrust laws and Republicans like Teddy Roosevelt enforced them.

"Beyond that, markets don't work well economically in a society with great wealth concentration; in that situation they allocate more resources to the frills of the wealthy than the basic needs of the common man. And they don't work at all when the people don't have enough money—think the famines in Ireland, in India during the last war, or in Africa south of Sahara with every drought—even think of what happened here when credit collapsed and unemployment rose after 1929. A song of praise for 'free' markets in such circumstances has a sound of telling people rioting for lack of bread that they should eat cake.

"But worse than all that, it is we Republicans who have stood for the right but unpopular ideal of equal treatment for all America's citizens, especially the Negroes. We have lost election after election holding true to that ideal in face of the power of the Solid South. Under Kennedy and Johnson the Democrats finally came to see things our way and now this bastard is going to rob us of our victory."

But that wasn't the only evening conversation I remember from that week. I made it a point to meet as many people as I could and find out as much about the world view of these political types—much as Doug and I had learned about the average American's world view on our drive out to the convention.

I struck up conversations in a well-known touristy seafood place down by Fisherman's Wharf, in a Chinese restaurant on Grant Avenue, and at a steak house off Union Square. But most evenings after those excursions I'd find myself back at our hotel's famous top floor bar, "The Top of the Mark."

If, when you entered that room, you looked left to the far corner you'd see an ordinary double hung window. But that window held a special place in Navy lore as told by many of the senior officers we had known at the War College. They called it the "Widows' Window." They would tell, with barely restrained emotion, of the days when their WWII colleagues had spent their last night ashore at the Mark Hopkins with their young wives. Then in the morning the wives went with them to the wharf where the guys boarded the ships that would take them to sea. The wives would return to the hotel and, a couple of hours later, gather around that window. They'd watch as their husbands' gray battleships, aircraft carriers, troopships, whatever, silently steamed through an often gray morning toward the mouth of the harbor, under the Golden Gate Bridge, and into the dense fog that waited there. For too many young women that was their last visual memory of a loved one.

The Navy's collective memory of the window was an effective conversational gambit. It helped me break the ice with some very interesting people.

One evening I fell in with a group of Goldwater political strategists who were in serious need of unwinding from their day's efforts. I bought a round and invited them tell me about themselves. After a while I bought another and asked them to step back from the details of the day and tell me where they saw the Goldwater movement in the big picture of American politics. After all, some newspapers saw their efforts as destroying the Republican Party. And, Lord knows, from what I had seen at the committee meetings at the St. Francis Hotel, there was a lot more anger and confrontation than I had expected.

One of them said those were just the labor pains of change. Another said, "This party needs a painful change. It has a great opportunity for power if it can just get out of the middle of the road." The guy next to him, who came with a head start on the drinks, slurred the predictable, "The only things in the middle of the road are dead skunks and horseshit."

I asked something like, "Yeah, but hasn't the opposition built a pretty formidable consensus from the middle of the road?"

The first fellow, the apparent scholar of the group, said, "They act like they have a consensus, but what they have is a coalition, the Roosevelt coalition. It doesn't make sense. Its main components don't fit together. Ask yourself what these groups have in common: the Solid Segregated South (based on hatred of the Party of Lincoln since the Civil War and Reconstruction); the working class urban ethnic Catholics (who built urban political machines to stand up to the patrician Republicans who were in power when the ethnics came to this country); the northern Blacks (who left the Party of Lincoln when President and Mrs. Roosevelt showed them some respect); and, Jewish liberals.

He went on by saying, "Neither the segregation-forever Southerners nor blue collar white Northerners have a natural affinity for Northern Blacks (the Southern Blacks are irrelevant, they don't vote) or educated Jews. In short, the Democratic Party is vulnerable and its power is there for the taking.

"LBJ is throwing away the Segregated South. Truman did that before him. But the old Republican Party was just too patrician, too dignified, and too noble to accept the gift. In 1948 they just hoped that Strom Thurmond's Dixiecrat split would leave them the winners. It carried four states but that wasn't enough. We're not so passive. We aim to accept the gift.

"The urban ethnic working guys have done well but the Democratic Party is vulnerable with them because of its success in helping them. There's nothing that makes a man conservative more surely than giving him something to conserve."

I steered the conversation back to my genuine interest in their biographies, noted the names and home towns of those who impressed me, and let the conversation drift on from there. If I came away from that table with a single thought it was, **"Target: the Roosevelt Coalition."** Sun Tzu came to mind: "What is of supreme importance is to attack the enemy's strategy. Next best is to disrupt his alliances."

I wanted to test their personal motivations so I asked them, if the Democrats had helped the little guy, why were they using their skills in service of the other side? Their answer was a simple question. They asked "What did Willie Sutton say about why he robbed banks?" I said, "Because that's where the money is." "Well," they said, "we're professionals in the persuasion business and persuasion in aid of the wealthy is where the money is." My kind of people, no illusions.

Elsewhere in The Mark Hopkins—in the halls, at breakfast, in conference rooms—something was impressively clear about the style of the Goldwater forces. It was in their faces. They were uniformly very serious, very focused, very determined. Somehow, collectively, they lacked grace. Simply put, they didn't smile. Just passing them in their individual rush to wherever they were hurrying I could see this was not going to be a convention at which differences from the primary season were resolved, at which compromises were reached, and from which a unified party would venture forth toward the general election.

Throughout the hotel the tone was—how shall I put it? Strident? Angry? No, perhaps best, militant. The core supporters of Goldwater, under the direction of campaign manager Richard Kleindeinst, were a high-handed and highly disciplined lot. Consistent with my well-lubricated discussion with the strategists, one of their core beliefs was that the only way to beat President Johnson was with a candidate whose racial views could carry the South. And in the Republican Party of that era that meant Goldwater and virtually nobody else.

Those 'my way or the highway' intentions of the Goldwater forces became actions outside The Mark Hopkins. The Eastern Republican establishment had arrived aware they had been beaten in the primaries. Rockefeller had already withdrawn in favor of Governor Scranton of Pennsylvania. But they came with at least a hope that Goldwater's radical views could be moderated. The futility of their hopes became clearer every day at the committee hearings I was attending at the St. Francis Hotel.

For example, if elected, Goldwater intended to delegate the decision to employ nuclear weapons to military commanders in the field. High military men had been frustrated when Kennedy refused to use the bomb in Cuba or Berlin in 1962. Our local congressman, Peter Frelinghuysen, a respected patrician moderate with four generations of United States Senators in his lineage, saw the danger in Goldwater's proposal and urged the Platform Committee that the platform should make clear that the decision to use nuclear weapons should be the President's alone. His motion was soundly defeated by the Goldwater forces.

Similar defeats occurred at the Credentials Committee and the Rules Committee. Meanwhile, over at The Cow Palace, the Convention site, when the pundits' unofficial vote tallies went way beyond the number needed for nomination, the easterners floated a trial balloon suggesting Governor Scranton for the Vice-Presidential slot. But the Goldwater forces laughed it off. They obviously knew a lesson the leader had taught, *[I]t is the highest task of the organization to make sure that no inner disunities within the membership of the movement lead to a split and hence a weakening of the movement's work.* Compromise, the moderating force of American politics, would not be tolerated.

Every day brought a new story in the newspapers about the rejection of attempts at moderation by the likes of Henry Cabot Lodge, George Romney, and William Scranton. Herbert Hoover was lionized but Eisenhower was barely tolerated.

(Kate, when I was writing this I checked the internet for entries about the convention to see if they reminded me of anything I forgot. I saw some that said that Ronald Reagan gave a sort of political coming out speech at the convention. The story had it that he was trying to get a boost for '68 in much the same way the Goldwater's speech in '60 gave him a boost for '64. Back in January, 2012, I had even downloaded a copy of the speech. I didn't remember it; but, more than that, it just didn't fit my memory of the mood. In that crowd Goldwater was God; it didn't make sense that such a crowd was going to be grooming a god in waiting. Turns out someone found out that the speech never happened and copies of it have now been pulled off all manner of websites.)

So the week went. Goldwater won resoundingly on the first ballot. He rejected any attempts to accommodate the middle of his party when he chose as his running mate an upstate New York Congressman who, as chairman of the Republican National Committee, had done a good deal of the political groundwork for Goldwater's rise.

At the end of the convention Doug was going to stay to offer his services to the Goldwater campaign. But I had to drive back to Newport before my leave expired. So I left San Francisco mid-morning on the 16th, before the convention finale.

Reader,

When I teach this period of American History I focus on the events of 1968. From Dad's perspective they were merely fruits of things planted in '64. Interesting.

And I think I'll use Dad's experience with that website's Reagan speech hoax as a lesson to my students about checking their sources.

Kate

22 RENO

I LEFT SAN FRANCISCO BEFORE THE convention ended intending to reach Reno by evening to watch Goldwater's acceptance speech in some neighborhood bar—the kind of place where a dime could get you either a beer or one of the pickled sausages soaking in God-knows-what in the large jar by the beef jerky sticks.

That evening I found just such a place, introduced myself to a few of the guys, and—mentioning I was active duty Navy—got some of them sharing war stories. The stories were not so much about personal combat heroics but remembrances of friends long gone, shipboard or foxhole living conditions, and where they were when they heard of something important that happened somewhere else—the Pearl Harbor attack, D-day, Roosevelt's death, the bomb, things like that.

I read the twenty or so guys in that bar as the natural constituents of Goldwater's movement and future followers in our war against their interests. They were nice aging white guys, most of whom had served in Korea or WWII. These men were probably as smart as those in any group I knew, but they were under-educated and stuck at the lower end of the economic ladder, barely above the blacks. I doubted if any of them had read Tuchman's *The Guns of August* or shared the caution that it had inspired in Kennedy as the missiles went into Cuba or the wall went up in Berlin. These guys lived simple lives and were given to simple answers.

I brought the conversations around to their views of Goldwater. Most were enthusiastic supporters. One thing about Goldwater did trouble some of the older guys. It was all his preaching about success through self-reliance. It sounded nice in principle but their life experience through the Depression and the great national effort in the World War had taught that success didn't lie in some kind of fantasy about unrestricted individual liberty; it lay in a more subtle reality of a society pulling together, enjoying freedom consistent with functional order, but achieving improvement through mutual reliance.

As one of the older guys put it, "That stuff is easy for him to say. But it sounds to me like he's saying 'be like me, go out and inherit a department store.' For the rest of us it ain't that simple."

But conversations like that faded as the TV broadcast of the convention neared the time of the acceptance speech. I moved to the back of the room to watch the speech and, more tellingly, watch the crowd at the bar.

Finally, the TV showed Goldwater striding toward the podium to the martial strains of "Battle Hymn of the Republic." Until that moment I had never sensed a conflict between the emotions stirred by that song and those inspired by "America the Beautiful." Each song had spoken to a part of my single soul. But now the Battle Hymn pointedly announced the reality of Goldwater's world. He did not seek to crown our nation with brotherhood. Nor was he calling on the nation to work for a day when its cities would be undimmed by human tears. His was a call to join his God's righteous march with a ready blunt-force answer to any problem; he had no inclination to confirm the nation's soul with self-control. He was unencumbered by any peaceful distractions of spacious skies, purple mountains, or waving grain.

His speech was in the classic form of 'you are victims, they (the Democrats) are the villains, unite behind me and ye shall be saved.' It used the same bald-assertion format of his book—principles were not supported, they were proclaimed; consistency was not required; consideration of the consequences was unnecessary.

The speech was built around phrases of strength, total dedication, and freedom. Consistent with his musical choice Goldwater told his Republican Party that it was on the side of God and martial morality. His Party would remember why "the Lord raised this mighty nation", while the Democrats followed false prophets. The Democrats had not given the nation moral leadership. (I'm sure the Democrats thought their civil rights initiatives, taken at political peril, were an exercise of moral leadership, but to Goldwater they were error based on a false notion of equality.)

During this early part of the speech the TV broadcast convention delegates' cheers for just about every sentence. And among the crowd bellied-up in Reno there were spontaneous shouts of "Amen;" "You tell 'em!;" and, "Fuckin' 'A,' man!" The tavern crowd was particularly emphatic when the speech played on fears of racial unrest: "the license of the mob and of the jungle;" "violence in our streets;" and, "keep the streets from bullies and marauders."

But all that was prelude. The speech's main theme was hard core militaristic foreign policy.

During their years the Democrats let a billion people fall under Communist rule. (I thought, the Democrats caused that? I thought that, basically, the size of the Red Army in Eastern Europe and Mao's Army in China were the causes. But, *post hoc*, the Democrats were in power, so they must have "let" it happen.) In contrast, during their years in control the strong Republicans had used power 'courageously' in the Formosa Straights (Kate, have you ever heard of Quemoy and Matsu?) and Lebanon. (Inferentially, the cowardly Democrats deserved no credit for leading the nation's containment efforts in The Berlin Airlift, in Greece, with NATO, or in the Korean and the now escalating Viet Nam wars.) He didn't even mention the Cuban Missile flap where the Democrats put my ass on the line less than 2 years before. I suppose it was just another fact that would interfere with his dogmatic assertion of their weakness.

The enthusiasm among the war vets in the bar moderated somewhat as they sensed the gravity of the rhetoric, but the roar of cheers broadcast from the convention floor grew louder. I could see the difference between the emotions in the mutually reinforcing crowd on the Convention floor and the emotions in the tavern. The roars if the Convention echoed those of a Nuremburg rally—the relative silence in the tavern grew from individual thinking about the reality behind the speech's words. The difference between the two moods grew more obvious as some around me in that dive, those we'd now call Reagan Democrats, chilled when they felt themselves dismissed from their nation's future by the line, "Those who do not care for our cause, we don't expect you to enter our ranks in any case." Goldwater was not out to lead a unified nation; he was out to use national power to serve only his people.

But then came the two sentences that ended Goldwater's hopes.

Having built a crescendo of militancy he said, "I would remind you that extremism in defense of liberty is no vice. And let me remind you also that moderation in the pursuit of justice is no virtue."

To men who had, in 1945, seen the ultimate human cost of strident speeches urging extremism, those sentences were troubling. But the absolutely wild deafening roar of approval from the convention floor stunned them far more than the words themselves. It did more than stun them. It scared them.

The bar went quiet. The speech soon ended. None of the men waited for any commentator's post-speech analysis. This was no longer the gathering of comrades who would have normally stayed together until closing. One by one they left the bar in somber silence.

I stayed only long enough to see them go. Then I followed them out into a night turned to a false day by the flashing wall of neon lights on the commercial marriage mills across the street. I took it all in and then walked back to my motel.

THE SIX MONTHS AFTER SAN FRANCISCO

I ROSE AND SHOWERED VERY EARLY, then drove across town and toward the east. I remembered that at sea, on the bridge of a destroyer, the morning 4 to 8 watch was a glorious time of day, the time when the night's first dim light builds its crescendo to dawn. But on that morning as dawn came to Reno the growing light turned the city's glitz to sleaze. By the time I reached the city limits I felt I needed another shower. But I drove on toward a breakfast in Winnemucca and a hard day's drive to Salt Lake.

As I drove I thought about Goldwater's total failure to capture the hearts of the guys in the bar with what was, essentially, our message. I considered the total absence of formal or informal logic in his bombastic declarations—both in his book and on the podium. My tentative conclusion was that his was an attempt at justifying the prejudices of the persuaded. It failed because not enough time or intelligence had been expended to put our basic doctrines "in the mind" of the nation. Only the already-believing and those subject to the psychology of the convention floor (those who had *succumbed to the magic influence of what we designate as 'mass suggestion'*) were inspired. Or maybe it was just that

Goldwater's stark declarations simply lacked the disarming charm, the quiet humor, of someone like Reagan.

As I drove across the Great Basin's desert, many of my thoughts were about how much I had learned in the past three weeks. But among all the insights I had gained, none was stronger than my deepening belief that there were three areas that I needed to learn a good deal more about. They were: religion and its relationship to politics; psychology and its relationship to prejudice; and, the law and its mechanisms for change.

I had formed ideas about those categories, at a vague level, before I left Newport. But the drive across the country had been one long shout that Doug and I had to have far more learning on those subjects if we would have any hope of gathering the millions of WESs we needed as followers. The ignorant certainty of the radio preachers was touching something in the hearts of the heartland with an intensity that I did not understand but I knew could serve us well. The passions that had led to the events in Mississippi and that flamed in the eyes of the locals we had met at more than two dozen eateries were exactly the kind of logic-resistant passion, *pathos,* we meant to employ. And as for the law, what had focused my attention wasn't so much the fact that a federal law was passed to establish new civil rights, it was that a judge could issue an injunction denying old civil rights.

Back in Newport I faced a month and a half teaching my replacement on Admiral Gamba's staff his duties. My year on the job had taught me that it involved a lot more than I had been told when I came on board. I had developed a list of people throughout the Navy he would have to deal with and I had a bit to say about each person—things that, prudence dictated, should not be put in writing.

Besides, I had more wrap-up work with Vince and Tug over at the War College including working out funding for a biennial repeat of the Persuasion for Naval Officers seminar.

While I was driving east Doug stayed in San Francisco to deepen his connections among the Goldwater campaign forces. Mostly he let them know he was a person of substance, someone who could do a lot more for them than just set up tables, give out straw hats, and do the hustle-about donkey work he had been doing in the hubbub of the convention.

At the end of July we got together again for the festivities surrounding Doug and Karen's August 1st wedding where, as you know, I met your mother.

A few days after the wedding, and for a brief hour, it looked as if life plans for all four of us were going to have to change profoundly. Doug and I had reserve force commitments for the first couple of years after our separation from active duty. On the Tuesday after the wedding President Johnson addressed the nation about what was called the Tonkin Gulf incident. His speech was a clear declaration that the country was going to enter the Viet Nam War with both feet. Only at the very end of the speech did he announce he was <u>not</u> going to call up the reserves.

Doug and Karen have not mentioned the effect of that part of the speech on their honeymoon.

As for me, the Navy asked me to stay in until the end of the year and I agreed. That was no problem beyond the fact that my lease was up, so I moved into the Bachelor Officers' Quarters behind the War College. My work ramped up. We had been scheduling ships through a peacetime routine of local training operations, shipyard overhauls, Guantanamo refresher training, and 7-month Mediterranean deployments. The schedule had been essentially the same for over a decade. Now we had to work out a schedule including 9-month Western Pacific combat deployments with all the attendant alterations to the provisioning, training, and shipyard arrangements we had been used to. At the War College 'Persuasion for Naval Officers' was dropped as a frill inappropriate to the times.

But it was Doug's part of Our Enterprise during this post-convention period that was the most productive.

When they returned from their honeymoon he and Karen went to work full-time on the Goldwater campaign (now doomed even more by Johnson's new militancy in Viet Nam). They were there to see, close up, how campaigns really worked.

Doug entered the fund raising operation and quickly rose to a position of senior coordinator of fund raising activities addressing the truly wealthy.

Large contributions to causes like Goldwater's or ours generally did not come from the first generation to earn a family's wealth. Those folks tended to be more understanding of the problems of people of more modest means and hence less susceptible to our message. Besides, they were still accumulating their wealth and felt they had better uses for their money in that process.

Doug's target subset also did not include the wealthy patrician politicians—the sort of folks like the Rockefellers, the Kennedys, the Cabots, the Lodges, the Harrimans, and the Frelinghuysens—they were personally involved in politics and didn't need other people to mouth their views. They (and many other wealthy families) seemed truly motivated by the 'to whom much is given much is expected' line Doug and I had rejected. Also, the politicians in those families were engaged in political give and take on a wide range of issues and were not so given to Goldwater's absolutes.

No, Doug's target subset of the wealthy was comprised of those who, like us, had been born to wealth, who were interested in the political process only to the extent it affected them, and who wanted to stand apart from the fray but control it. They meant to give orders which were not to be questioned. And they would support only those who would act on those orders. We and they saw politics not as a way to serve others, but as a way to control them.

There was even a sub-set of the to-the-manor-born class that hadn't inherited all their family's wealth themselves. Instead they had inherited the right to direct the distribution of money from their grandpas' charitable trusts. For them the power to distribute the money was an additional claim to fellowship with the other wealthy. Over the years since meeting these types, Doug has been able, through flattery and treating them as the important Allies that they have become, to move a lot of money from grandpas' trusts to our propaganda efforts through Our Enterprise's tax exempt think tanks.

Raising funds among the truly wealthy and the wealth trustees was not simply a matter of making a quick phone call or two and appealing to nation-serving instincts. Those people had to be massaged; their views had to be listened to in detail, and they had to be assured their contributions would honor their views and serve their interests. Doug took his time and gave a lot of his personal attention ministering to those folks at their city dining clubs, on their yachts, at their golf courses, and at private retreats. Having his wife along separated Doug from the usual twenty-something envelope-stuffing eager political neophyte. And it didn't hurt that the wife had Karen's intelligence, energy, attitude, and appearance; that alone marked Doug as worthy of instant respect.

Except for being an RPI engineer instead of an Ivy League liberal arts grad (or dropout), Doug was ideal for the job. His was more than a 'meet, greet, and then hound' assignment.

Even as he traveled the country visiting these people, we still held our discussions-into-dusk—now by phone, usually at 5:30 in the afternoon, Eastern Time (the politics he was involved in is often an evening business). After exchanging our experiences we came to refer to his targets as the 'inherit-a-department-store' set. Of course, the inherited wealth didn't have to come from department stores. It could have come from anywhere—publishing empires, beer, oil, banking, chemicals, even grape jelly.

Schmoozing with these people, Doug learned about earlier activities much like those we had planned. For example, three duPont heirs, working through a couple of the largest companies in the nation, had set up an operation to enlist the people most respected among ordinary Americans—the ones with the highest Character, their clergy—to extol the virtues of capitalism. (Damn, I wondered, had my foc's'l guesses about the core of all the anti-communist rhetoric been right? Well, if so, good for them.)

Most importantly, Doug learned that his targets shared and took their comfort from a common world view. It was one that put them on the pedestal as the world's most important people. That shared world view was Ayn Rand's "Objectivism." Their common bible was her *Atlas Shrugged*. As you know, that's her book in which disaster befalls mankind because the rich masters carrying the burdens of the world (Atlas) weren't being given enough respect so they went on strike (Shrugged) and the rest of mankind fell into chaos.

From Doug I came to see that the reason these folks, Doug's inherit-a-department-store folks, took Rand seriously was because her views held them to be pre-eminently important. In fact, many of them were supporting a foundation she and they established to preach her gospel, give her books free to high school kids, things like that. It was called the Foundation for the New Intellectual, or some such.

So it was that Doug and Karen's work that summer and fall gained us contacts with the right people and insights into their wealth and preferences. By election time we had more than enough of a base from which to draw future allies.

After the election Doug joined a computer company. Both his dad and his father-in-law had counseled him that it would be helpful if he spent a couple of years learning about major corporations from the inside in much the same way he was learning politics from the inside. After that apprenticeship Doug planned to join his family's business.

In January, I left active duty. Now a civilian, I joined my father's businesses in the City, bought and renovated that loft near City Hall, and did my Navy Reserve bit with once-a-month 'Weekend Warrior' duties on an old destroyer home ported in Bayonne.

As for Doug, after a couple of months of corporate indoctrination and product sales training at headquarters, he was also posted to New York. He was part of the team servicing major accounts at the mid-town headquarters of major oil companies.

That spring, together again in New York, we were able to get back in harness working on our plans for an active role in the on-going class warfare. But first, we figured, was to address the three areas that our trip west had shown to be serious gaps in our learning about how America worked.

Reader,

I've never understood how anyone could take Ayn Rand's view of the world seriously. Corporate leaders disappear and there's nobody capable of filling in? Really? Did she never look at children learning and admire the competence of the rising generation?

Kate

How
"Other Religions"
Work

M Y WORK FOR YOUR GRANDFATHER'S investment businesses was demanding; there was so much to learn. Gradually
I mastered enough to make a good living for a lifetime. But
that's not the point of this recitation of Our Enterprise's beginnings. Here
I want to set down what we learned about the three areas bearing on our
war plans that I had resolved to study: religion, prejudice, and the law.

Doug and I started with religion. We wanted to learn two things
about religions: what methods of persuasion religions used to develop and
maintain their following, and how we could use religions to advance our
cause.

We took an adult-education survey course taught by a moonlighting professor from one of the city's universities. The ideas we took away
from those sessions were not the religious views that our instructor intended. Instead, they were based on what he taught viewed in the light of
the reasons we had sought the instruction.

Before I tell you about what we learned I should tell you about a
term I prefer to use. The Navy's rule about not discussing religion in the
wardroom reflects the reality that discussion of a specific religion, among

people professing different religions, is difficult. In the same way, even a critical observation about "religions" risks offending the hearer's emotional commitment to his deeply held beliefs. It still risks offending him because he senses his religion is one of the religions you are talking about.

Nothing's perfect, but "Other Religions" seems to allow a somewhat dispassionate discussion. By "Other Religions" I mean the many social organizations asserting specific knowledge of the Creator and teaching the human conduct required by that Creator.

Our instructor began the course by leading us through an amazing number of ways anthropologists, sociologists, historians, psychologists, economists had viewed Other Religions. For Marx they were an opium-like mechanism for economic oppression (a totally inadequate description, but one not far from our purposes). For Freud they sprang from a neurosis resulting from the need to repress some instincts in order to conform to one's society. Eliade saw them as a struggle to escape meaninglessness.

We wanted to know how Other Religions persuaded their members. Part of that must spring from what function they served for the people in their congregations.

We concluded that Other Religions serve two needs. First, they provide comfort to individuals, especially young individuals, in the face of their awareness of their own mortality. Second, they serve as intergenerational value-transfer mechanisms. They teach members of a society how the society expects them to behave, generally stating the limits society has placed on gratifying instincts that were more useful in humanity's past. For example, the "seven deadly sins" are all rules against excesses in responding to human instincts to do such things as eat, sleep, reproduce, and respect and defend oneself.

Most societies have created religions that teach that conformity to the society's values will give the individual post-mortal significance—an immortal heavenly reward; some advantage in a re-incarnated life; revered memory in the community; and, so on.

Sure, without a religion a person could believe in a creator God and find comfort through compliance with ethical (that is, societally approved) behavior. Such would be a philosophy, a deistic one. But Other Religions are a subset among deistic philosophies that differs from others largely by having a paid staff. Societies have found that paying someone to mind the ethical store, to attend to the comfort/conduct connection, simply works better for society's needs than leaving the matter to individual inquiry.

By teaching ethical behavior and providing opportunities for believers to act ethically toward the less fortunate in the society, Other Religions speak to basic needs of individuals in our highly social species. As a result, people who participate in their religion earn a deep, social, and somewhat righteous satisfaction.

So that's what functions Other Religions served. But of all the things the instructor mentioned it was the work of Emil Durkheim that told us the most about how they work. He drew heavily on studies of South Pacific and Australian aboriginal peoples. It seems that in those regions individual tribes would gather for communal rituals. The tribe would have as its prize possession a stone carving of a symbol associated with the tribe—the Eagle tribe would have an eagle stone, the Koala tribe, a koala, and so forth. At their rituals the rock, this totem, would be elevated in front of those who gathered. Then, often with communal song, an elder would tell the history of the tribe describing God-given values that had brought it safely through to the present. Through such rituals the tribes formed a community in which people identified, and pledged a bond, with those who similarly committed.

Durkheim formulated the statement that Other Religions are a set of symbols through which a society identifies itself to itself. In that sense the cathedrals, whose construction and presence dominated European towns in the Middle Ages, were as much socially-unifying totems as stone koalas. So too was Athens' temple to its protector goddess, Athena. I'm sure you can think of examples from many other cultures.

For our purposes, whether Other Religions are those symbols or merely invoke them was a quibble. The lesson was that symbols have power. Symbols focus power from the community into the hands of the leaders who, in turn, share it with the individual congregants, often in ceremony. Consider the use of the cross in Christian churches and the Torah scrolls in temples. Much the same could be said, in secular ceremonies, about the display of national flags.

Apart from symbols, it seemed likely that a significant number of Other Religions made use of the Big Lie. Consider miracles. Many teach that God worked specific unprovable and improbable acts to show that their religion was His exclusive instrument. If only one religion could be that exclusive instrument, most legends of confirmatory miracles must be Big Lies. In fact, all may be.

What seemed most relevant for us was the strong binding emotional experience the church-goer derives from belonging to the congregation. Being in that group involves some subordination of individuality. But, at the same time, the individual gains a sense of security and comfort, even power, from being part of a community he respects as moral and which respects him in return.

Other Religions often reinforced this binding emotion by leading the members in chorus singing and communal recitation of rote prayers. There is even a theory that the sense of comfort and belonging is heightened further by shared sacrifice. Consider the bonds among male Muslims who unite 5 times a day in bowing prayer; among Mormons who share the 2 year missionary experience; among Catholics who for centuries endured together the obligations of Lent, meatless Fridays, and obligatory Sunday services; and among Evangelicals who tithe.

Other Religions often also convey a sense of self-worth to their members at times of individual significance. At such times—birth, puberty, marriage, and death—members of the paid staff convey the community's respect for the significance of the event through personal attention and ritual. (Doug observed that urban politicians performed a similar function as they appeared at "wakes and weddings, and at every fancy ball." Parallels between religion and politics like that kept popping up. We were on the right track.)

Many people who truly don't believe in Other Religions participate simply because they feel good doing so. The comfort, the security, and the sense of unified righteous purpose serve some of their most important longings.

Our question had been how Other Religions build the foundation from which they persuade people to act. The answer lay in this creation of a moral self-congratulating community of believers. For us, the teaching of the existence and requirements of a God was not at issue. What was central was the use of the emotional power of a group of people unified in the declaration of a common belief; a belief that becomes unchallengeable except at risk of exclusion from the comforting, empowering, group.

That all spoke to the issue of how Other Religions worked. What remained was the question of how we could get religions to work for us. In this country that meant, overwhelmingly, how could we get Christian churches to work for us?

Reader,

I'm a church-goer. Sunday services help keep my ethical compass aligned with humanity. Sure I have my doubts and maybe I'll be as cynical as Dad someday. But right now my religion makes me a better person.

Kate

GETTING
"OTHER RELIGIONS" TO
WORK FOR US

T HOSE WHO FOUNDED AMERICA WERE convinced by their study of history that the union of church and state was a bad idea. The idea that religion and government had separate calls on the lives of their people was as least as old as the "Render unto Caesar..." teaching in three Gospels of Christian scripture.

Obviously, the use of state power to enforce religious thought (by the sword or even simply social rejection) was bad for individuals whose personal spiritual quest brought them to answers that were different than their neighbors' answers.

But it was more than that. The union of church and state seemed bad for the church and bad for the state. It was not that a society cannot harmonize civility and morality. It was that organized Other Religions and governments have organizational concerns. For religions and governments the prime concerns were the same: organizational survival and funding. Alliances between religions and governments addressed those concerns and very often resulted in a government's compromise of its equal treatment of all its citizens and the Other Religion's compromise of its ethical judgment.

If the union of church and state is bad for each, why—throughout history, even unto our time—were there so many state religions?

The answer, of course, was that the arrangement worked. It didn't work from the perspective of fair government or ethical theology, but it worked for the people running the institutions.

Government leaders were advantaged when a favored religion could persuade the schmucks that morality required support of those leaders. The doctrine of the Divine Right of Kings sprang to mind. And then there are the many instances in which clergy have taught that opposition to specific church-endorsed political leaders was sinful.

Government leaders, in turn, could repay the religion's support with the use of government powers to the benefit of the religion's institutions. It was more than Jefferson's idea of mutual protection of abuses; it often included diversion of taxes collected from all the people to the use of the government-supporting denomination.

The union of church and state may be bad, but for the leaders of each institution it worked, at least when their united action was in harmony with the interests of the wealthy of their time and place. We had to map out a strategy to put such united church-state action in service of our interest in wealth in our time.

To understand how we could get Other Religions to serve our ends we had to consider their structure. Some were hierarchical, some of those more so than others. The more hierarchical—that is, the more certainly declarations from a central authority reached the local pulpits—the more readily they could serve our purpose. In terms of organization, the spectrum of Christian denominations across America went from the most highly organized, the Catholic Church, through other episcopal (that is to say, bishop-led) churches to the most independent local church which had no affiliations save those within its congregation.

The range of religions' organizational rigidity was paralleled by the range of conformity they required of the individual congregant. At one end of that spectrum stood the most doctrinal churches—those with a catechism of doctrine which the individual church-goer was told to follow as a condition of membership. At the other end the spectrum were the most "free churches"—those which taught that the scriptures spoke directly to each member, no interpretive presence between the scriptures and the member's soul was appropriate, and the clergyman's input was simply informative guidance.

What all Other Religions had in common was the need for money. Money paid the clergy; money built the churches and staffed the schools; and, money was the key to the performance of charitable works. When we thought through the universal need of religions for money, we came to the crass conclusion that, if we handled the matter with some subtlety, most religions' willingness to help our cause could likely be bought.

That said, we set about to see which religions we should try to work for our cause.

We started with the Census Bureau's annual *Statistical Abstract of the United States*. It reported that the Roman Catholic Church had the most members, about 44 million back then. So, it was the denomination we should consider first. Besides, though I was an Episcopalian, I had attended Catholic schools. The study of Catholics would put me on familiar ground. I already sensed the Catholic Church was pre-disposed to support us as it had supported the wealthy and powerful almost uniformly since it first became a state religion in the 300s.

The average American parishioner of the Catholic Church went to its buildings on Sunday, listened to ethical teaching, sang songs, and experienced a sense of satisfying belonging that was essentially the same as his Protestant counterpart anywhere in the country. He felt comforted attending his Church's services and he did good for his community through its charities and by applying its teachings. Like his counterparts in other religions across the country he knew that he was a better person for his participation. Also like them he would probably say that his congregation's local clergy were among the nicest, most sincere, and most helpful people he knew.

When he heard a sermon calling for some belief or action that didn't make sense, he didn't decide to leave the comfort of his church and seek another. Instead he would turn to his child next to him and say something like my grandmother's maid, Kitty Kelley, told me she had said to her daughter, "Don't listen to what he's saying, Rita. Listen to what he should be saying." Later, Catholics with that outlook of selective obedience would call themselves, "Cafeteria Catholics." Still they learned and respected their church's pronouncements and would defend them even if, personally, they didn't believe or follow them.

And that average Catholic thought himself to be as much a patriotic American as any church-goer anywhere in his nation. His Church taught that he should be so, and his co-religionists had proved their patriotism in many ways. American Catholics proudly served in America's Armed Forces, sworn "to protect and defend the Constitution of the United States."

But at the level of the Papacy, and though a loyal American Catholic parishioner of that time would be offended if you told him so, historically his church had been deeply committed to opposing that Constitution and the founding ideas of his nation. At the Papal level the Catholic Church of those days still longed to restore the Church's golden age, the time when its leaders united with princes and people of wealth to rule the western world.

The typical American Catholic did not see a difference between himself and other religious Americans because he had not read the encyclicals, the teaching letters to all Catholics, of Pope Leo the 13th. And, if he had, he'd work to try to explain away their plain meaning—or simply tell himself, "Listen instead to what he should have said."

In his encyclicals *"Immortale Dei"* and *"Libertas"* Pope Leo raged against just about everything the founding documents of these United States had declared. He taught that the arousal of innovation in the 1500s (the printing press and the Reformation) was "harmful" and "deplorable." It spawned the "terrible" American and French Revolutions "which proclaimed principles at variance with Christian and natural law." Among these offending principles, according to Leo, were the ideas that: governments derived their just power from the consent of the governed; that all men are created equal; that government is not obliged to make a public profession of a specific religion ("the one true religion," confirmed by miracles: Catholicism); that people may publish whatsoever they wished without approval from the Church; that people may hold opinions, act on them, and make them known in public, again without clerical restriction; that people may have such a liberty of conscience as would allow them to worship God or not; and that Church and State should be separate.

In attempting to rationalize these positions the American Catholic parishioner might seek to dismiss them as pronouncements of the 1880s, the distant past. But, our instructor thought, it was not a distant past on the time line of the Church. The Church's effort to restore the pre-Reformation way of the world was certainly alive and well when, a mere 30 years before our session, in the *Reichsconcordat* of 1933, it pledged its local clergy would be loyal and not oppose the policies of the Nazi government in return for protected status for the Church's organization.

Clearly, the Catholic Church was the biggest prize to be pursued in our campaign for religious alliances. It had the most members. It had the doctrine and history most receptive to our stated *mission* of more wealth for the wealthy. It had the most powerful command structure and was thus most able to effectuate any agreement it might make with us. And it was readily disposed to link with governments to advance its institutional needs.

Yet a couple of things our instructor said led us to conclude that there was reason to delay our approach to the Catholics. For one thing, a premature alliance with the Catholics would be off-putting to Protestant denominations which viewed it with a suspicion (though that suspicion was waning in the wake of Kennedy's presidency). Those Protestant denominations were, in their diverse totality, more populous (about 65 million) than the Catholics and could not be ignored. But beyond that, the Catholic Church itself was in the midst of a serious self-examination.

The ongoing Vatican Council, Vatican II, had been convened by Pope John the 23rd to break the 'that's the way we've always done it' mentality of the Church, especially the thinking that had resulted in the institutional Church's conduct before and during the Holocaust. That conduct wasn't just support of state-implemented anti-Semitism; that had an 'always done it' component dating back at least to the Spanish Inquisition and arguably to the time of Constantine. The conduct also included the Church clergy's participation as Croatia conducted its own 1940s holocaust to convert or exterminate Eastern Orthodox Christians of Serbian ancestry.

Pope John had observed all that during WWII as Vatican diplomat. He knew the Church had to change its 'us against the world' mentality if it was to—not only survive—but to square itself with its founding principles.

After he called Vatican II but before it convened in 1962, another issue emerged. The Catholic Church, especially since a 1930 encyclical, had been devoting an unusually large portion of its intergenerational value transfer effort to matters sexual. The FDA's approval of "the pill" in May of 1960 had changed the society-serving basis for those teachings. The result was that the Church's membership was in semi-open revolt against pulpit preachings to a degree that earlier generations would not have contemplated. Cafeteria Catholics were becoming the majority.

Our instructor hoped that the Church after Vatican II would be significantly different than the Church of the previous 500 years. But he knew that rapid change was not the normal way of things in the Catholic Church.

We figured we'd better wait and see.

Naturally, that led us to look toward the next largest Christian denomination. *Stats Abstract* said that was the Baptists with about 20 million members.

Baptists had core values of the independence of individual conscience and the independence of individual congregations. So, it would be a difficult target. But after the American Civil War, one group of Baptist churches in the South had decided to stand strongly independent from the churches of the North (and their carpet bagging moralists who challenged southern attitudes toward freed slaves) and so formed a more interdependent alliance known as the Southern Baptist Convention.

The name of the denomination included "Convention" because it was run in a quite democratic fashion by an annual convention which could be attended by the pastor and a lay representative from each of its congregations, each with a vote.

The *Stats Abstract* reported the Convention had 10 million members, barely more than a fifth of the Catholics. But there were footnotes. It seems that the Census Bureau used numbers reported by the churches and each used its own count. Most relevantly, the Catholics, a church of infant baptisms, counted all baptized members. Protestant denominations usually reported only full—that is, at least teen-aged—members. Clearly, the Southern Baptists were numerically worthy objects of our attention.

The Southern Baptist Convention was a worthy target but presented serious problems. Our first problem was that, true to its Baptist core values, it was a church which taught that the Bible spoke to the soul of each of its readers. It did not seem to be one where we could strike a deal with a central authority, such as a pope, and have the deal be imposed on the souls of church members in short order. The second problem was that, wary of the history of Christendom before the Reformation, it had a strong tradition of support for the separation of church and state.

Still, we needed a way to connect with the force available in this denomination. We didn't develop a complete plan at first. But we did set about to prepare for the day when we would.

Tentatively we figured that one tactic could be having our Allies make contributions to the Convention's seminaries. We figured contributors would be invited to become Board Members, Board Members would select and control faculty, and seminary faculty could establish dogma. Graduates of those seminaries would go forth asserting authority about Biblical meaning that trumped the individual reader's view. In the main, we expected the mass of the denomination's membership would accept such a gradual change rather than abandon the comfort of the fellowship they had known from their youth.

That all seemed a slow process so we'd keep working on the problem and let time present its Music Man Moments. So it was that, later, when chance disclosed that the leadership of the SBC seemed to have gotten too far ahead of its congregations on Civil Rights, we found another way to advance our mission.

At the end of our study of Other Religions we had a deeper understanding of some of the most useful specific weapons of persuasion for our class war. Among them were: the centrality of the social element of persuasion; the power of symbols; and, the functional benefit of the Big Lie. We had a more advanced decision about which *engagements* (gaining control of the Southern Baptist Convention and its doctrines and an eventual political alliance between it and the Roman Church) we should pursue and in what order. And we had a better basis on which to judge the likely success of other religious *engagements* in the years to come.

Reader,

This was really getting troubling. I have come to believe deeply that making the American state an instrument of anybody's church, no matter how noble or 'true,' offends a very fundamental freedom of each of the rest of us.

Kate

THE PSYCHOLOGY AND
SOCIOLOGY OF PREJUDICE

I N GERMANY, IN THE 1930S, a small group of men controlled a nation by inspiring passions of both pride and hatred.

In America, in the early to mid-1960s, the TV screens showed people whose similar passionate hatred was hard to believe. Women, who no doubt could be ever so gracious hosting a tea for other white ladies of gentility, or scurrying among the tables to pour lemonade at their church's "all day sing and supper on the grounds," were screaming hate-filled venom at children walking to school. Policemen and sheriffs' deputies with "Protect and Serve" patches on their shoulders were turning hoses and loosing German shepherds on teenagers peaceably assembled to "petition their government for redress of grievances."

Arousing passion in an audience was one of Aristotle's three ways speech could persuade. Nowhere had we seen passion in a crowd that was half the passion in the eyes of those women and "peace officers." The power of their actions left no doubt that the people under the sway of such emotions were not open to discussion. They would spit in the eye of truth or moderation if it were offered to them. We could see in the faces of those people a passionate blindness to truth and reason that we could use in our plan to get the WESs to vote more wealth for us and less for themselves. We had to learn about the mechanisms, the psychology, of prejudice.

The psychology of prejudice was a hot topic in academia in the middle of the '60s. We didn't have to round up professors to give us private lessons. We simply had to attend one of the many available academic meetings on the subject—and attend prepared to ask, in private conversations, the questions aimed at getting the answers we sought.

We went to one at Columbia University and while we were up at the campus we bought a basic Psychology 101 textbook.

Underlying it all is the idea that humans are societally cohesive, tribal. People are naturally drawn conform to their social surroundings. We learned that almost any idea that gains general respect can produce conforming conduct as if by a societal contagion. Once a critical mass of publicly expressed opinion arises in a society, particularly if it has no respected opposition, the conduct of the average human in that society conforms. Fashion is a simple example; but the phenomenon is not limited to skirt lengths and lapel widths. The conduct of people differs from society to society and from time to time in all manner of things from tobacco usage, tattoo adornment, obesity levels, even to family size—not because the people involved are biologically different—but because they are in different societies. They may be in different parts of the world. Or they may be in the same place but in different social settings of race, religion, or ancestry.

With regard to prejudice, from the meeting and the text we fashioned take-aways resting on three basic concepts: first, humans navigate through their day relying on a series of perceptions and generalizations; second, the basic tribal social behavior naturally creates "in groups" and "out groups;" and, lastly, prejudice requires leadership establish "in the mind" of the "in group" that the members of the "out group" are all the same and threaten the "in group." People, such as Doug and I, who wanted to fan and profit from prejudice had to play on the human tendency to generalize, had to divide the world into "us and them," and then had to create the belief that the "them" are "all the same and they are a threat"

Fine. But what turns that into action? Part of the answer is conformity but a large part is fear. To a psychologist fear is an emotion aroused by the perception of danger—whether that danger is current or in the distant future, and whether the danger is real or imagined. Fear triggers an instinct, the fight or flight response, and the production of hormones such as adrenaline, that improve the body's performance in doing either.

Fear also increases the inclination to communal behavior. I can't help comparing it to the herd behavior I see on TV in all kinds of species faced with threats. Zebras form herds in lion country; wildebeests mass to cross a crocodile-infested river; and herring form into large shimmering balls to escape attacks by sharks or seals.

A professor in a break-out group at our seminar stated the obvious, "prejudice" means **pre**maturely **judg**ing something. But he asked how that was different from what the discussion of perception and generalization had shown: namely, that judgment before all the facts are in is the usual process of human decision-making. Generalization from a limited number of facts is normal. He teased from us an answer that prejudice, as we use the term, is generalization about a category of other people taken to the extreme. Prejudice is generalization-with-blinders-on about the "other's" individuality couple with a level of fear and, sometimes, disgust.

A strident declaration of a threat of great magnitude calls upon members of the "in group" to act for the declared good of the group. At that point the "in group" has perceived, generalized, and allowed its leaders to play on its societal instincts. Group behavior leaves no room for individual empathy. The "in group" is able to turn away from its normal social ethic, for instance "Thou shalt not kill." Instead its members act out of a conviction that loyalty to the "in group" is a higher value.

Remember, those things which we consider ethical rules are often not inborn; they are usually limitations on instincts and passions, limitations passed on as rules of a particular society. How else explain guilt-less headhunting, for example? It follows that a leader of a society—particularly a society in which contrary voices are suppressed—can foment prejudice and then inspire prejudice-based objectively unethical behavior by the same methods by which ethical rules were originally instilled.

Then our professor turned to me and asked what I thought I knew about prejudice. I mentioned characterizing members of the "out group" as not only different but as something subhuman particularly involving the use of visual imagery to disparage the "out group." I was aware that 1930s German cartoonists had portrayed Jews as rats; 19th-century

American cartoonists had portrayed Irish immigrants as monkeys; and, as we were speaking, some American cartoonists were portraying their countrymen of African ancestry as brutish apes. And I mentioned a song from *South Pacific*:

> You've got to be taught before it's too late,
> Before you were six or seven or eight
> To hate all the people your relatives hate.
> You've got to be carefully taught.

The professor said cartoon dehumanization was a common device meant to suggest that aspects of the in group's morality regarding the treatment of human beings did not apply to the treatment of the members of the "animalized" out group.

As for the Oscar Hammerstein lyric, he said that was closer to the truth; you do have to be taught. That is to say, prejudice takes leadership. Somebody has to tell the "in group" that the "others" are a group, its members are all the same, and they are a threat. And often that teaching does come through the mechanisms of the inter-generational transmission of values—the mechanisms of parent to child, teacher to student, and clergy to believer.

But, said, that teaching need not be directed only to youth. He pointed out that history is filled with examples in which political leaders have rallied adults to hateful and warlike behavior by tapping into some unease 'in the mind' of their society and simply, and stridently, declaring that prejudicial action was a requirement for continued acceptance within the "in group." Thus commanded, the adults of many nations have done reprehensible things in their maturity which they in their youth, and the generations before them, would have considered immoral.

(In your time, Kate, Milosevic's leadership of the Serbian nation to violence against domestic Muslims, even in spite of generations of inter-marriages, is a prime example. But of course, you were there and know a lot more about that than I ever will.)

The lessons we took out of the session and the text were that mindless passionate action, prejudice-based action, requires that someone lead a society to a conclusion of "out group homogeneity" ("they are all the same") and that members of the "out group" are a threat. That message is most effective when given to a society isolated from discussion and dissent. That society must be isolated from, or conditioned to disbelieve, any voice which might establish a contrary view. (Naturally, that thought brought to mind Professor Zeman's description of the suppression of the free press in Germany.)

Doug and I wanted to find a way to harness the passions of prejudice in a way as far removed from racism as possible. Attacking people for characteristics they were born with was not only offensive it was, we felt, eventually counter-productive. It would guarantee us permanent enemies. At the same time it could deprive us of possible supporters.

Yet, if the racial passions could help us win our war, we wouldn't oppose their use on mere principle.

At some point it occurred to us that not all prejudice-based hatreds were aimed at things people could not change. Some, particularly those directed against religions, were directed against things people could change—their opinions. Most people, facing the withering hatred for the opinions they held, chose conformity rather than martyrdom. And if prejudice-based hatred could be directed at an "other's" religious beliefs, it could be directed at his political beliefs too.

That realization suggested our best tactical use of the weapon of passionate prejudice in our war. It should be used, consistent with our *strategy*, to inspire hatred for any people or institutions advancing political opinions which would cost us money. "Liberals" must be made the schmucks' hated "others." People receiving government support costing us money must be made objects of the schmuck's disgust—even when the schmucks themselves are one coal mine (or factory) closure away from needing that same support.

In the same way, the schmucks had to be conditioned to see a threat in people or entities that reported facts or opinions supporting an idea could cost us money. Television images of southern repression of blacks may have convinced the wage earning schmucks of the 1960s that change was morally necessary. But would those television images have done so if the same schmucks had been conditioned to believe that television (and press) reports were part of a "Main Stream Media" conspiracy to destroy their beloved nation?

CHANGE THROUGH THE LAW

B Y THE END OF 1965 the only thing left on our check list of subjects we wanted to understand was how the law can be used as an instrument of social change.

As a conversation starter on one of my evening excursions at the '64 convention I mentioned to a recent law school graduate I might want to go to law school. He said a rule of thumb was, "If you want to know what the law was, go to Harvard; if you want to know what it will be, go to Yale; and if you want to know what it is, go to Michigan."

Well I didn't go to law school, but the law's progression from "was" to "is" to "will be" was what I wanted to understand.

In early 1966 I was working on an acquisition with several young lawyers from the firm serving your grandfather's company. I noticed that among them were graduates of the three schools mentioned over drinks in San Francisco. After the deal closed, I convinced your grandfather to ask their law firm to send them to our offices to conduct a two-day session to give me an understanding of legal change so that I could understand how it might be useful in our business over my career. Of course, our business paid for their time as a deductible business expense.

Doug was able to join me for the session. It started with a review of the basics, stuff most people know. Effective law, after all, has to be rooted in its society's common sense.

Law is a body of rules of conduct prescribed by a controlling authority and having binding force.

The rules create rights. In the law a "right" is a legally defensible interest, nothing more.

No right is absolute. Even the constitutional right to the free exercise of religion would not prevent the prosecution of devout fundamentalists who, acting on the authority of Leviticus, c 20, v. 13, murdered a pair of male homosexuals.

Lawyers would say you have a "liberty interest" in swinging your arm in total freedom and, in a wilderness, it would not be restrained. But, despite your interest, your right to swing your arm stops at my chin. That's because society has to establish a balance between your interest in swinging your arm and my interest in being free from violence (and also society's interest in being free of the costs of unrestrained violence between us). My right creates your obligation not to hit me. But my right to be free from violence is trumped when society exercises one of its rights and sends me a draft notice. Its exercise of that right creates an obligation I must honor. And so on. A well-governed society strives for the right balance of liberty and limits.

Every time society decides to respect one person's interest it limits another's. If it respects your interest in your kids' safety, society, through its government, restricts my freedom to drive 90 miles an hour down your street. If it respects your interest in clean well water, through law its government restricts my freedom to put my septic tank anywhere I want. If it respects all Americans' interest in equal job opportunity, its laws limit the freedom some would demand to keep others "in their place." If it respects your interest in prices set by a free market, it denies sellers' the freedom to agree on prices. It's that way across the whole system of legal rights and obligations, from murder to expiration-date-labeling of food, laws restrict unbridled freedom in order to honor other interests. Only with laws limiting demands for unbridled freedom can a society be just and function peacefully.

Reader,

Please permit this marginal interruption. In my classes I make the point that all societies have to deal with freedom-limiting concerns about safety, public health, economic structure, etc. What makes democracies different from kingdoms, dictatorships, and the like is that the choices are made by people chosen by, and answerable to, the citizenry, not by people installed to serve princes, prelates and people of wealth.

But back to Dad's text.

Kate

The next thing the young lawyers taught is that laws established by our society to respect various interests have a pecking order based on their source: first the Constitution; then statutes (and regulations); and, then common law. Their binding effect is generally decided by the courts and enforced (or in the rare case, not) by the executive branch. (And they said we should note that each rank on the pecking order involves people—specifically: legislators; regulators; and, judges.)

They started with the common law. That lowest rank on the pecking order was the place where the earliest forms of law developed.

Ours is a largely English system. In the earliest times in England (and even in earlier societies), when people first decided that maintenance of order required that they resolve disputes by means other than violence, they took their disputes to the leader—a tribal chief, the local king, or such. As societies trended larger and the breadth of the king's jurisdiction expanded, some delegation of authority became necessary.

In the early days of the English tradition people who wished to resolve a dispute peacefully applied to the King. He would issue a writ to the locals such as:

King to the Sheriff: Health.
Take unto your assizes the case of Smith versus Jones and therein do right.

If the facts were in dispute, a jury would resolve them. The Sheriff or a judge would figure out what was a "right," the rule for those facts.

So, for example, if Jones' cattle trampled Smith's crops, Smith might have claimed Jones should pay for the crop loss because Jones should have fenced his cattle. Jones might have defended by arguing to the sheriff or judge that Smith should have fenced his crops. For reasons that seemed right at the time, most judges decided the right rule was "fence your cattle."

After several such decisions, either at the trial or appellate level, precedent kicked in. Judges realized that, at least in such property rights cases, consistency was important to good order. And it also made for a more efficient use of judicial resources. Thus the common law rule—that to protect your neighbor's crops you ought to fence your cattle or pay for any harmful consequences—was established. Today, if a precedential decision comes from an appellate court, like a federal circuit or Supreme Court, it is controlling on all courts subordinate to the deciding court.

Within this common-law system of precedents there can be changes. Judges can recognize that an existing rule of law doesn't fit new circumstances.

For example, when people of the English tradition came to North America, cases of whether you should fence your cattle or fence your crops came up again. Judges in New England saw no reason to change the rule and applied the "Fence your cattle" rule from the old country. But when the same question first arose well beyond the Appalachians there were different considerations. Population densities were much lower. Average annual rainfall was much lower so it took many more acres to support an equal number of cattle. And there was grazing acreage in abundance and minimal economically viable cropland. So the courts announced a "fence your crops" rule and thus created the open range rule that you see involved in many old western movies. Everybody from Bing Crosby to Willie Nelson has sung about this in Cole Porter's "Don't Fence Me In."

To be sure, judges have looked at precedent and then disregarded it for more reasons than the change of the underlying demographic and climatological facts.

For example, there may be a change in the general thinking about a problem. Up until a couple of years before our sessions, when a person purchased an item and a defect in the item caused some harm, the law only allowed that person to sue the one who sold it to him. Then, from the late 1920s to the early '60s, courts of different states recognized that the fault that caused the harm was often that of the possibly distant, and likely more able to pay, manufacturer. So judges gradually changed the common law of liability and the jurisdictional law of whether a distant manufacturer could be called to answer in a local court.

If the common law were rooted in formal (syllogistic) reasoning, once a precedent was established it would remain forever. But the common law recognizes the greater social usefulness of informal logic. As Justice Oliver Wendell Holmes, Jr. put it, "The life of the law has not been logic; it has been experience." In other words, the common law is not rooted in blind principles and syllogisms; it is based on changing facts, their effects, and informal logic.

But enough about the common law.

The next step up in the pecking order is statutory law, the laws passed by legislatures. When the legislature adopts a law, that law supersedes any common-law rule to the contrary within the jurisdiction of that legislature. So, for example, the westward expansion of the American

population changed the population density. Courts were poorly positioned to abandon precedent and use a single case to abolish open range. Legislatures stepped in—starting, I think the young lawyers said, in Indiana—and, in a generally westward series of legislative enactments, abolished open range or relegated it to a county option.

If this business about open range sounds familiar, Kate, you may remember that on our first trip to the West, when you were about seven, I took you to look for this bit of American history before it was all gone. I cherish the day we found it.

But back to law's pecking order. Next are regulations. Particularly since the 1930s there has been a growing practice of legislatures to establish broad rules and create other entities charged with creating and enforcing regulations to give those broad rules detail. For example, under the tax law regulations define which payments are for a repairs that can be deducted as an expense and which are for improvements that must be depreciated over time? The processes by which those regulations are proposed, considered, and adopted present opportunities for achieving change—particularly for people with the wherewithal to monitor what's going on in the agencies in a way that the average citizen cannot.

The legislature can override regulations for any reason it wants. And judges can overturn them if they are improperly adopted or, more often, are obviously inconsistent with the statute they are interpreting.

And judges can overturn regulations, and even statutes, if they find them to be inconsistent with the Constitution—by directly violating it or by being an exercise of power not granted by it.

In short, the places to *achieve* change are in the legislature, in the regulatory agencies, and in the courts. But the place to *control* change is in the courts. The judges are the key.

Often the changes judges make only come about gradually. Our young teachers illustrated this by describing the way Thurgood Marshall and his colleagues set about to change the judge-determined Constitutional rule that "separate but equal" schooling was all that equal protection required of tax-supported school systems. Marshall's main argument was that "separate" wasn't "equal."

He started in the 1930s with a case involving a state's law school for blacks only. If there was one thing judges knew it was that small, low-budget, blacks-only law schools were not the equal of ones conducted by states' major land grant universities. Over the next decade and a half, Marshall's team brought and won a series of cases conditioning the high court to the idea that the "equal" part of "separate but equal" idea was little more than a pretext, a principle used as a screen behind which the unacceptable effect of inequality flourished. It took until 1954 (and a change in the high court's membership) to win their point in *Brown v. Board.*

That was the form by which change happened. The form itself may not have been enough, had not society beyond the courts seen African-American contributions in WWII and Korea and the evil effect of hate-based discrimination in Nazi Germany. From most of its pulpits and in a good deal of its literature American society was reaching a growing awareness that laws discriminating against American citizens of African ancestry were wrong. An important axiom is, "Judges read the papers."

Of course, if you have judges already conditioned to your message, change need not take two decades.

So our question became how do you get judges, particularly on the Supreme Court, willing to do your bidding? The young lawyers thought that was next to impossible. They said that, by and large, the people who had been appointed to the Supreme Court respected it as an institution designed for them to act as wise men—and they tried to do so. Their long-term judicial outlooks were notoriously unpredictable at the time of their appointment. Most famously, Hugo Black, who ultimately joined the unanimous *Brown v. Board* decision, had been a member of the Ku Klux Klan. Once appointed, federal judges were virtually immune from pressure, and intended (by Constitution for reasons explained in the federalist papers and implied in the Declaration of Independence) to be so, since they were given their jobs for life.

Still, the appointment process is the key (and pressure was possible).

The young men also made a point about the role of academics in achieving change through the law. At that time, in the 1960s, legal academia was a heady place where professors were building their careers on identifying things that needed change and arguing for that change. Criminal procedure (where the requirement of *Miranda* warnings is the most well-known change) was one such area to be sure, but there were more. There were also changes in such areas as the legality of inter-racial marriages, free press/slander law, no-fault auto insurance, campaign finance, safety responsibilities of automotive and other manufacturers, corporate governance; and on and on.

Law professors not only sought change through their publication function, they inspired students to consider whether the rules of their time served the people of their time given the facts of their time.

To win our war Doug and I could see we'd need to develop a cadre of professors who would give cover to our movement (and judges who were implementing it). We needed law professors who would provide an air of academic validity to our efforts to disrespect any change that advanced the economic interests of the schmucks.

(Incidentally, we needed economics professors to do the same thing but, as that guy said in the movie *Irma la Duce*, that's another story.)

There seemed to be two ways to get law schools to be weapons in our war. The first was by pushing tax-deductible money at the problem. We could endow "chairs" for professors espousing our cause and have our companies hire those professors, part-time, as consultants. (Later we even funded law schools at the new "universities" of the religious right and had our office holders hire their graduates out of all proportion to the academic merit of those schools and their graduates). The second way—and an important one if ours was to be a successful long term war—would be to establish groups within all law schools where students inclined toward the *status quo* could be identified, inoculated against the allure of change, and started on a path toward taking their place on future appellate benches.

It was clear that these very bright young lawyers were enjoying our session. One of them said that his time in law school was almost thrilling in the way it changed his way of seeing things and thinking about them. The others said it wasn't all that great; still, it was stimulating. But they all agreed that, when they got to their law firm, they faced the mind-numbing work of document reviews for trial preparation or SEC filings. Ugh. They really enjoyed our two-day session because it was giving them a chance to get back to the law's big picture.

At one point I asked them about injunctions and how that judge in Selma could have ordered people not to peaceably assemble.

The Harvard grad went darn near giddy about the history of the English Chancery Courts, King James, somebody called Lord Coke, and the difference between judgments awarding damages and judgments that ordered or prohibited specific behavior.

But the other two guys got closer to my question and talked about balancing the prospective voters' rights to assemble with the community's right to avoid violence. They all agreed that the Selma Judge's ruling seemed ironic, since it was the community's assertion of a right to use violence that was actually in play. But decisions about injunctions are also influenced by the judge's sense of whether the injunction can be enforced. Unenforceable orders could debase the authority of the judiciary. And in a voting rights case in Selma, Alabama, two weeks after three voting right activists disappeared less than 150 miles away, that judge must have had an enforceability concern.

Kate, there's one more thing we discussed in the session that I want to tell you about.

I mentioned to those young lawyers that I wanted to insure that my children and many more generations yet to come could be well provided for. Yet, I had heard there were limits to what I could do. Why? And what could I do about it?

They said the "Why" was that some societies viewed wealth not as a right, but as a tool. According to that view, wealth in any generation should serve as an incentive for contribution to that generation. Anglo-American societies respected the interest of grandparents' or great-grandparents' affections and knew those interests could be part of someone's motivation to make a wealth-generating contribution to society in his lifetime. But those societies saw any interest to favor more remote generations, not as affection worthy of respect, but as current vanity degrading the dignity of the less blessed youth of distant generations.

Our society embodied that judgment in its laws in two ways—legislation and an old, court-made, rule.

First, through legislation, it has taxed the transfer of wealth from one generation to the next. Societies had been doing that at least as far back as ancient Greece. Societies which have not done it, or have done it only lightly, have generally seen cycles of increasing wealth concentration accompanied by increasing civil repression followed by upheaval, often in the form of land reform rebellions.

At the time of our discussions in 1966 America did not tax transfers from one generation to the next which did not pose wealth concentration risks. Dollar amount exemptions did that. But transfers larger than required for the undisrupted operation of a middle class family's finances were taxed at 77%. At that rate, after three transfers, less than two percent of the original wealth would remain. (Doug and I couldn't serve our mission of more wealth for ourselves and our descendants in that tax environment.)

Then there's the court-made rule I mentioned, the Rule against Perpetuities. You might think that a person could end-run societies' grab by directly designating part of the wealth covered by a person's will to go directly to third-, fourth-, and fifth- generation descendants, or by setting up a family trust and only have one transfer. But as early as the 1680s, when wills were new, common law had come up with the Rule as a barrier to such multi-generational wealth-control plans.

Simply put, our young lawyers said, it prohibited a dead hand of the past from controlling wealth in the present. Apparently England even had a similar problem in the days before wills, back in the 1200s. Then the wealthy, particularly the childless wealthy, would often give their land to the Church—which told them the gift would curry God's favor on their judgment day. By those gifts the land was permanently removed from the reach of a major source of government revenue, a system something like estate taxes. Kings who would rule long after those gifts found their ability to tax the wealth of the realm was stymied by the dead hands (*mort main*) of the past which had made those gifts.

Our young instructors went off on a riff on how bizarre it was to speak of the Rule against Perpetuities and "putting something simply" into the same sentence. I sensed that was an in-joke, one open only to former law students who had to master the Rule's complexity, things like the doctrine of the fertile octogenarian, in order to graduate. They seemed to hate it. I put that fact in my memory figuring it would later prove useful.

There were probably 20 more insights that I gained from those two days, Kate. But these have proved to be the most useful ones. When I've gone so far down the list to start talking about something that happened in the late 1200s, I know I've gone on too long.

****

So, Kate, that's all I have for this 'Roots of Our Enterprise,' how we formulated our plan to protect and expand the wealth our families can enjoy. When you and I get together I'll tell you how Our Enterprise has developed since we started and where it stands now. Perhaps I can even get your insights on where Our Enterprise goes from here. See you then.

Dear Reader,

Thank you for reading Dad's history. I'm sure you can see why I asked for your promise of confidentiality. And I'm sure you now know why I need your counsel. I hope this has been helpful.

But there's more to the story.

You will recall that Dad invited me down to the farm for an all-day Saturday meeting at which he and Doug planned to outline how they have implemented the things described in the history—all to the end that they could convince me to join the Enterprise. What follows is the write-up I've prepared for you about that meeting.

Very respectfully,
Kate

The Saturday Conversation: Doug's Role in the Formative Years

I DROVE DOWN TO NEW VERNON from West Point Friday evening. The next morning I showered and dressed in a sort of formal/casual way—slacks, not jeans; loafers, not sneakers; open collar dress shirt, not my usual Saturday work-in-the-garden sweatshirt. I found Dad in the kitchen cooking the pancakes and sausage breakfast that had been a Sunday joy in my youth. Full court press, I figured.

We were finishing breakfast when "Uncle Doug," arrived. He had brought a Box of Joe from Dunkin' Donuts and a warm full bag from Jersey Boy Bagels. We thanked him; grabbed some cups, plates, and napkins; and went into the den. When we got past the pleasantries Doug said, "Perhaps it would be best if I started.

"First I want to answer a question I suspect has been on your mind. 'Why hadn't we invited you to join us before this?' Believe me, it wasn't personal. Long ago, back in Newport, we met with an experienced local lawyer to get his counsel about the problems of long-term partnerships. Among the things he told us was that good two-man partnerships faced their greatest stress when one or both of the partners tried to bring kids into the business. Maybe one of the children might not be competent (at least in the eyes of the other partner), or the children might not be compatible with each other or their elders, or one partner may try to bring in more children than the other. Whatever. But generational transfer was the biggest long-term threat to small partnerships.

"You know that Our Enterprise's goal had included 'more wealth for our descendants.' We always envisioned a day when children would be brought in. But from the outset we agreed that participation would be limited to one child from each family. So it is that our first-borns, my son Paul and your brother Tom, were chosen and you and my other kids were not. Neither your undoubted competence nor your gender ever entered in."

(I hadn't known Paul was involved, but I did know him. Our families had vacationed together for at least a week, and often four, every year throughout my youth. One of our dads' purposes for those vacations was to have all members of the families know and respect each other from their earliest years. As I think of it, for quite a while I had a crush on Paul. One year we even had a bit of a summer romance.)

I thanked Doug for addressing the issue and said that, of course, I had thought about it but it never bothered me. Then I asked him to tell me something about his involvement in all this between the time the Enterprise started and the time I came to know him, roughly the late '70s.

"Sure. Well, as your Dad has told you, in late 1964 I went to work for a computer company for a couple of years. That taught me a lot about modern mega-business. Perhaps even more important have been the friends I made among my customers in Big Oil. Still, holding to plan, after a couple of years I left it to join my father's companies in New York.

"Also, in my free time in those years between Goldwater's 1964 defeat and the 1968 election of Nixon, I did a lot of work for the Republican Party. The Goldwater defeat had been crushing. It was clear to me, but more importantly to the people in the Party, that the Party needed to unite if it was ever going to win again. The Goldwater folks abandoned their leader but nevertheless let the others in the Party know they were in charge. People in the eastern wing of the Party gave in because they knew that without the Goldwater faction they and the remnants of their Republican Party would cease to be a force.

"During the Goldwater campaign I had seen the power of the Democratic machines in the large cities. Some of that power was based on the jobs that winners could give to their supporters. But at a more basic level the Democrats had perfected the tactic of 'identify and pull.' By that I mean they had a well-oiled system of identifying their supporters within each voting district. They kept good records of their names, addresses, and phone numbers, what favors the Party had done for them, and whether they could be counted on to vote for the Party. On Election Day the ward or district leaders would remind the 'identified' supporters of the need to vote. They would provide the voters assistance, if necessary, to 'pull' them to the polls.

"The power of those machines was dwindling, in no small part because Roosevelt's programs had taken the social support needs of the low-income folks from the shoulders of the mayors onto those of the federal government and because, after the war, the urban ethnic neighborhoods were dissolving into the suburbs where political favors were more subtle and the Democrats were not in control.

"Nevertheless, I made it my business to encourage friends on the Republican National Committee, looking as they were for something to offer candidates as a reason to run under its banner, to develop a personal voter identification system nationwide. I urged the Committee to computerize its system with some attention to having the various systems compatible with each other. Computerizing voter records had become easier since, across the nation, more and more Boards of Election were computerizing their records. Particularly in counties controlled by Republicans, we could avoid the data entry expense that the Democrats had borne simply by obtaining a copy of the Election Board's tape of registrants, their party, and their voting frequency.

"That project was by no means complete by the time of the 1968 election, but it had come a long way. As a fully up-to-date computer-industry person I had not only urged it but I had aided its implementation in most states. At that time, 1964—1968, computers were becoming much smaller and more reliable with the introduction of IBM's Sys/360.

"In my efforts I dealt with a great many people in the Party and I had earned a good deal of gratitude and respect. At the same time many of those people had earned my respect; I worked with enough of them to be able to judge who had the means and the energy to get things done and who was 'All hat and no cattle.'

"After Nixon's election in 1968 I was offered a mid-level political position in his administration, in the Department of Transportation. Since I knew something about the shipping industry, that position made a lot of sense for the government, the Party, and me.

"As is the case with most such political appointed posts, my job not only involved daily work with the career government employees who dealt with transportation matters, but it involved significant contact with other junior party operatives in Departments all across Washington. In the Nixon Administration people at my level were generally young and were drawn from both the Goldwater and traditional wings of the Party. A significant part of our jobs was preparing for the next election.

"And we looked beyond that, sharing ideas and preparing for more distant future elections where we could continue to advance the party's business-oriented agenda. We discussed most of the current writings that stated the case for a Goldwater view of America. There were, of course, the Ayn Rand economic pieces. But most of the writings we studied were reactionary, reacting against the largely flower-child, morality-driven popular movements of the 60s. Those movements generally argued that collective human endeavor conducted in corporate and government form was every bit as obliged to act morally as was individual human endeavor. The youth in the streets and the academics in the universities were urging that corporations must concern themselves with racial equality, environmental protection, product safety, occupational health and safety, and on and on. What they viewed as morally and societally necessary, we saw as adding expenses to companies and lowering profits.

"I remember one session discussing a Milton Friedman Sunday *New York Times* Magazine article. In it he declared that it was immoral for a corporation to act morally if it wasn't required to do so by law. For example, by his lights, spending more for socially responsible waste disposal than the law required was, essentially, theft from investors. It was obviously circular reasoning, but it was on our side. He started with the assertion that shareholders (no matter how moral they might be in their personal lives) must have invested to conduct their common enterprise solely for profit, ignoring morality if it were not mandated by law. He concluded, therefore, it was immoral for corporations to act for moral reasons. From our Newport persuasion training I could see this was bootstrapping poppycock, but I could also see it had enough charm that, if repeated often enough, it could persuade—particularly people already inclined, or with a motive, to be persuaded.

"Another discussion focused on an August '71 memo now referred to as the Powell Manifesto. It had been written by a former American Bar Association president whose private practice represented many large companies (notably including Philip Morris during a time it was fighting government efforts to "out" the homicidal nature of its products). He addressed the memo to the head of the Education Committee of the U. S. Chamber of Commerce (a guy who actually had inherited a department store). He also sent copies to others; some reached the White House, he sent one to the General Counsel of General Motors, and Lord knows who else. The memo outlined what Powell thought the Chamber should teach; it was a primer on persuasion for the class war we were entering.

"The memo started by asserting that the American economic system was under a broad attack. Its title said as much: 'Assault on the American Free Enterprise System.'

"For 'evidence' of the 'assault' he gave two examples likely to touch things 'in the minds' of his corporate audience. First, he asserted that Ralph Nader believed that corporate executives who defrauded consumers, poisoned food with chemical additives, and willfully manufactured unsafe products belonged in prison. Second, he raised an alarm about a book suggesting corporations should bear the cost of the environmental effects of their waste disposal practices.

"Having given that evidence, he recommended that the Chamber urge a plan he broadly outlined. Specifically, corporations should pool their wealth (anonymously through a collective enterprise like the Chamber) and undertake a long-term well-financed political effort: to control what was being taught at universities and below; to control the content of TV, scholarly publications, and other media; and, to control the courts."

Doug went on, "I expect to come back to the Nixon reelection efforts and the Manifesto later, but for now, and to keep to your question about the early days, Kate, suffice to say that I left the Administration at the start of the second term in early 1973.

"By that time there were evident changes in my industry. The Port of New York had lost its leading position in the American shipping industry for many reasons, and not one of them was going away soon. For one thing, container shipping had become the norm; it requires more land for staging operations than could be found at a reasonable price around New York harbor, with a limited exception in Newark. There was also the matter of the geology of the harbor entrance. It limited the Port to relatively shallow draft ships which are inherently less economical. And finally, oil was becoming a much greater dollar share of international cargo; and the capacity to handle supertankers, to refine the product they contained, and to access transcontinental pipelines for product distribution was centered on the Gulf Coast.

"So, when Karen and I left Washington, we moved to Texas. That move served the political interests of Our Enterprise as well my shipping business. On the political side, my observations during campaigns, my Nixon years, and the booing of Rockefeller in San Francisco had convinced me that the influence of the East Coast establishment in the Republican Party was vanishing and oil money was taking over."

When Doug had finished his biographical description of those early years he turned to my Dad and said, "You know, Bill, Kate didn't know you in those years either. She wasn't even born. She knows you worked for your father but she certainly didn't know anything about what you were doing in Our Enterprise. Why don't you tell her what you were he doing while I was becoming a Texan?"

Dad's Role in the Formative Years

D AD SHIFTED IN HIS ARMCHAIR. "Sure. Kate, back then, mostly I was building a persuasion organization for the long haul. The people working for me and I reviewed hundreds of newspapers—from rural areas as well as cities. We tracked on-air radio personalities, both religious and political, and reviewed tapes of their shows.

"Meanwhile, like Doug I built alliances with people in the recovering Goldwater wing of the party. We joined (and persuaded our chosen Allies to join) the efforts of that wing to eliminate from office any members of the party who were middle-of-the-road, or had potentially costly compassion for the wage earning schmucks, or, God forbid, were liberal. For starters our hit list was the list of Republican senators who had voted for the Civil Rights Act of 1964. With the help of our Allies we picked them off one by one, as often as not in the Republican primaries.

"If I recall, Kate, your first exposure to a political campaign as a kid was in the Senate primary in which Jeff Bell ousted Clifford Case. New Jersey wound up with a Democrat, Bill Bradley, as a Senator, but the Party was rid of another moderate. Those who wanted to be the Party's candidates of the future had been sent a message. When moderates survived the Party's primaries we simply persuaded our Allies among regular contributors to withhold funds from their general election campaigns. Another message sent."

"I remember." I said. "How old was I, five? Tom and I gave out pamphlets to commuters on the train platforms. But I didn't know we were sending a message to anybody."

"Well, you were and they got it.

"In a related effort we rallied our Allies to use their funding to persuade Democrats who had voted against the '64 Act to swing over to our side. It wasn't that we liked bigots, but we did want people who showed the kind of passion, conformity, and resistance to change that flourished among those people. And, after Johnson, there was no place for them in their traditional party.

"It helped that this could be done with a near-term objective in mind—electing Reagan. He had built a personal political organization that had won him the California governorship. From his organization and the remains of the Goldwater wing he mounted a strong Presidential primary campaign in '76. His campaign almost denied the nomination to Ford, an incumbent first-term President; that hadn't happened since Rutherford Hayes. But that campaign is more memorable as marking the end for the patrician leadership of the Republican Party. That primary season and the general election that followed marked the death of the hopes of Washington and Hamilton for government by civic-minded aristocratic gentry. Reagan, the Goldwater wing, and we were out-flanking the Democrats and ousting them as the party of the little guy. The Dems were speaking to the schmucks' heads for the schmucks' interests; we were learning to speak to their hearts for our interests. We were touching the emotions of the little guy to advance the interests of our new gentry, the inherited-wealth investing class.

"We'll come back to Reagan later. But first I'm sure you remember those vacations we had with Doug and his family over the years."

I couldn't help but smile, "Of course. Bermuda, Aspen, Banff, Sonoita, Seattle, all sorts of great places. You're not going to surprise me. All of us kids knew that, for you and Doug, they were business trips."

"We didn't hide it; they were. Well, at the one we didn't go away for, the one in 1976 when Doug brought his boat to New York for the Tall Ships and the bicentennial fireworks, we did some particularly important noodling. Our organizations were coming together. Rather than support Ford we were sitting out the '76 Presidential elections. We could feel that, longer term, the tide was with us. It was also clear that Reagan was our man, though whether he could beat an incumbent in 1980 was a bit uncertain.

"What got us to thinking was that we had been at our venture for 13 years, the same length of time it had taken the German Movement to put its man in power. The fact that the Thousand Year Reich only lasted 12 more years, together with Reagan's age, reminded us that we had to seriously address how to put our revolution, Our Enterprise, on a permanent footing. That meant younger people. We resolved to figure out how to bring them into our movement.

"We spent the year after the Tall Ships studying the problem and discussing it with our Allies, our permanent staffs, and our professional consultants—particularly college and law school faculty members. We talked on the phone on a lot of evenings; sort of discussions-into-dusk redux. We compared notes at our Christmas vacation that year in Telluride. By that point we had concluded that the best models for recruiting people to a life-long belief system were seminaries. Military academies were a not-so-close second. We studied both of those types of institutions further and finalized our plans that next summer. That was our vacation at Jenny Lake.

"Essentially we decided we wanted to secure the service and allegiance of educated people and do so before or while they were being educated. We wanted to attract many and select the most effective from them. We wanted to indoctrinate them then provide them reasonable early financial rewards for their service. At the same time we'd make a sincere promise of greater status and income for continued productive loyal service.

"We decided on three areas for development. First, we would support and screen the college Republican organizations. Second, we would institute a training school at which we would confirm the doctrines of

Our Enterprise and teach the techniques for achieving its ends. And, third, we would pay particular attention to developing some form of program at law schools.

"By the mid-term elections in 1978 we had developed our means of tracking the college Republicans and were identifying good soldiers for our war there.

"We had established our training school. Doug, ever alert to use Other People's Money and particularly money otherwise going to the government, had even gotten a 501(c)(3) approval for it. That way we and our Allies could fund it with tax deductible contributions. Marginal tax rates had come down, but still over 70 cents of every dollar our training school received would otherwise have gone to the federal government for the WESs' purposes, not ours.

"We were talking up a law school effort with our consultants among the faculties of some of the better known ones, but we hadn't hit on the right vehicle for those efforts yet.

"From that point on I took particular interest in our school, sometimes called our boot camp. The school was primarily for alumni of the college Republican organizations and the alumni of the law schools' organization when we found one. We also invited incumbent politicians and selected members of the broadcast and print media to attend.

"Many of the young folk came in as idealistic as you were when you chose to go to West Point—wanting to serve the country, that sort of thing. We let them know that, like it or not, serving in public office meant politics. We showed them that we had a plan for getting them in office. But they had to learn that success in politics was not about uniting people, it was about dividing them. It meant always attacking, never defending, and never admitting the merit of anything coming from the other side.

"We taught them what message they had to preach to earn our support, and how that message should be delivered. We taught everything from wearing American flag lapel pins (symbols asserting we were the patriots) to the need for adherence to centrally determined themes (message discipline). We let them know that our 'beliefs' were more than suggestions; we were out to establish a strong organization based on absolute message discipline.

"A positive side effect of the school was that it let those who attended know that they were not in it alone; it convinced them that they were part of a 'strong resolute community.' It also taught them that we had standards. They and their peers would be judged by conformity to those standards, and their success within that conformity would determine our financial support of their income and their ambitions.

"Later, in the late '80s Paul, who by then was studying politics in college, pointed out that our tactics were aimed at winning voters. Our precise tactical target should be winning elections. He showed us how we could win elections even if we got fewer votes if we controlled the shape of election districts.

"For example, in multi-district areas, like states, we could shape districts so that most of those who opposed us—say blacks—were crammed into a couple of districts. Housing patterns made that easy. Then we could shape the other districts so that we had comfortable majorities in them. Of course, on a map the districts might look silly. As you know, that practice had been around at least since 1812 when Massachusetts Governor Gerry created a district lampooned as a 'gerrymander.' Importantly, gerrymandering had survived the "one man, one vote" rule the Supreme Court had adopted in 1964.

"Paul also convinced us that there were ways of making it difficult for blocs opposing us to vote (disenfranchising). Of course, one of the more popular disenfranchisement devices, poll taxes, had been outlawed by the 24th Amendment. Others were made more difficult by Johnson's 1965 Voting Rights Act, but judges could change that.

"Our Enterprise built on all that by supporting the election of people generally committed to our views. It was fairly haphazard way until the '90s. But Bush the First's reneging on his 'Read my lips; no new taxes!' pledge made us realize we needed something more binding. The idea of using the Party to elect good people, generally supporting its platform, wasn't good enough. We needed to elect people unmistakably sworn to serve our interests.

"By 1992 we were going public with a stated goal of building a 'Permanent Republican Majority.'

"The next step in our increasing militancy came in 1994. We

started by introducing a requirement that our indebted politicians swear obedience to a written statement of our requirements. In its first iteration the new stronger party discipline was known as 'The Contract with America.' Later, Grover Norquist, a graduate of our boot camp, created a formal written pledge against increasing marginal tax rates (don't hurt the wealthy) and against increasing deductions (don't help the little guys, at least without, dollar for dollar, helping the wealthy). The last time I looked he had something like 238 Representatives and 41 Senators who had actually signed it.

"I'm not saying everything we tried to do in the mid-'90s was a total success. There was one semi-failed attempt that year to publish our creed—a list of articles of faith our politicians had to endorse. But we'll get to that when we discuss religions a bit later."

It seemed Dad had finished so I said, "As I read the 'Roots' I found all the techniques you studied in those early years interesting. And I presume that's the core of what you teach in that school. But has any of it actually been useful?"

APPLICATION OF THE
LESSONS OF NEWPORT

D AD STARTED WHAT BECAME A rapid fire history the early days of the Enterprise. "If anything, it's been more help than we imagined."

"Oh. Okay. But really, have you used any of it?

Doug jumped in, "All of it."

And Dad added, "And we still do, all the time."

"Such as?"

Doug took that one, "Well, let's take an example from those early years, black propaganda and Sun Tzu's teaching about the moral necessity of spying.

"In my days as a backbencher in the Nixon Administration, as we got ready for the 1972 election, I was pushing those lessons in the inter-Departmental political brainstorming sessions we'd been holding since before the '70 mid-term elections. The reception to my ideas varied from tolerance to enthusiastic support. But none were discarded; they became part of the Recommendations for Consideration passed out of the sessions up the chain. By 'up the chain' I mean up to the people who made the decisions—a small group of Nixon loyalists assembled from both major wings of the Republican Party but separate from it. They took ideas from the various brainstorming groups, chose among them, and then implemented the ones they chose. So it was that in May of 1971 the Committee to Re-elect the President, CREEP, voted to allocate a quarter of a million dollars to spying on its opposition in aid of the 1972 campaign.

"The black propaganda idea also worked well; it got Ed Muskie out of the 1972 race (though one of our operatives, Don Segretti, was found out later and convicted). The spying operation was worse. It was ineffective and they were caught.

"When that crew was arrested in the Watergate and its leader told the judge that his occupation was "American patriot," I figured it was time for me to get out of Dodge. I made plans to leave the Administration amidst the turn-over after the 1972 election before things unraveled and finger pointers traced at least some of the idea back to me.

"But those failures were problems of execution of the principles we wanted to deploy. A couple of bungled operations did not disprove the 2400-year-old wisdom of those principles.

"So we have kept at it. I suppose our biggest single success implementing Sun Tzu's morality-of-spying principle came in 1980 when we infiltrated Carter's campaign. We got a copy of the briefing book Carter was using to prepare for the debates with Reagan. The book armed Reagan so that, when Carter pointed out that Reagan had opposed Medicare, Reagan was able to get off his famous "There you go again" line. He said he had supported a better bill. Carter was not prepared to know what bill, if any, Reagan was talking about or why it might not have been better. Until then Carter was seen as the more knowledgeable candidate, the one who had studied and understood the problems of those times. With that line Reagan made himself look like the Professor and made Carter look like someone who should go sit in the back of the class."

"Okay," I said, "so that's a spying success. But has black propaganda ever helped since Muskie?"

Dad answered, "Sure. Think of our 2000 campaign to nominate the guy we controlled, 'W,' instead of this guy nobody controlled, McCain. Early in the year McCain was gaining momentum as a result of winning the New Hampshire primary. Unfortunately for him the next stop on the primary trail was South Carolina.

"As you can understand, we had been able to build a strong organization in South Carolina. It was a state with a long history as fertile ground for our ideas. In the 1780s it had been the state that saved slavery in the Constitutional Convention. In the 1860s it had fired the first shots that turned the secession movement into the Civil War. And in 1960 it was a place Goldwater had singled out, along with Mississippi, as one whose racial attitudes he would not seek to change.

"With our strength there we chose South Carolina as the ideal place to mount a racially-based black propaganda telephone campaign. (You don't put a funding-source tag-line on a phone call.) Our campaign told South Carolina primary voters that McCain had adopted a dark-skinned kid and we suggested he may be the biological father. The result, of course, was that McCain, for all his military service and noble refusal of special treatment while he was a POW, had no chance to win even in the highly military-oriented state of South Carolina. Of course, McCain's honesty about his dislike of the state's use of the Confederate flag helped us too."

Mention of the military brought to mind a related question I had wondered about back in 2004. So I asked, "Weren't you telling your followers in '92 and '96 not to vote for Clinton against Bush the First or Bob Dole because he was a draft dodger and they had served? How could you turn around and convince tell them to vote against Kerry who had been combat wounded three times and for 'W,' the stoned absentee?"

Doug took that one. "First remember that the masses are 'malleable.' Our followers are conditioned to buy what we sell. And remember in that year we were running 'W' for reelection. He had made himself a wartime president and they don't get voted out of office. But to your point, we and our Allies had very good reason to support 'W' because he had delivered during his first term. Mostly by that I mean he passed what are called the 'Bush tax cuts.' Those cuts paid us back, big time, for the help we had given him four years earlier. So money was available.

"With it we mounted what was probably our most effective black propaganda campaign. Students of politics refer to it as 'Swift Boating' and define it as a dishonest attack on an opponent's courage and patriotism. You often hear Democrats telling voters that Swift Boating was dirty pool. But when a WES hears them mention Swift Boating he either has only the vaguest idea what they're talking about or, more likely, no idea at all. Yet, make no mistake. When we used it, the WESs bought it.

"The opponent was John Kerry. In the opposition's eyes he was the ideal candidate. In the war of his generation he commanded a small, fast, lightly armored boat in combat just as Kennedy had done a generation before. Kerry had earned a Silver Star 'for conspicuous gallantry,' and a Bronze Star, and had been combat-wounded three times. (When we mocked him for saying 'thrice' our followers loved it.) And this war hero was also decidedly not someone who thought all wars were good things. After his two tours in 'Nam, he joined the people opposing the War. He didn't sneak around about it; he even testified before Congress that the Viet Nam War was neither in the nation's interest nor consistent with its traditions. For the liberals that testimony was an honest citizen openly contributing to the nation's decision making.

"As you suggested, our guy, 'W,' had spent those years as a civilian (probably often drunk or stoned and certainly not giving the nation a first-hand view of the War and its merits). He was staying the hell away from combat through a part-time gig in the Air National Guard with weekend warrior obligations that he may or may not have fulfilled (the records were 'missing').

"More recently in his first term he had used the 9/11 attack by 20 religious zealots, 19 of whom were Saudis, to start a war against the most non-religious nation in the region, Iraq. It was a war at least as dumb as Viet Nam. I don't think we'll ever know why he did it. I'm pretty sure even he never knew because, let's face it, he was an empty suit fronting for the people actually running his Administration.

"We had to blunt those aspects of Kerry's biography which made him particularly appealing for the time—a war hero with distaste for wars of aggression. So once again we decided to use black propaganda, again in the form of a well-funded Big Lie. We undertook to make him out to be a coward and traitor.

"Our Allies put together a tax-exempt political advocacy group, what they call a 527. It's public information that the 527 received donations from one guy of over $4 million, from another $3 million, another $2 million, and so on down the line. (Mind you, this was only possible through a 527 advocacy group—officially not related to candidate 'W's' campaign. Ha! If some WES had wanted to contribute to Kerry's campaign he could have only given $2,000.) I'm not saying each of those guys was a certified Ally. But that kind of money doesn't spontaneously arrive in the account of a 527 unbidden or by the whimsy of the Tooth Fairy.

"With that money the 527—we called it "Veterans for Truth" or some such—our attack was off and running. It rounded up some "patriots" who felt Kerry's testifying to Congress about what he believed and his other public anti-Viet Nam War efforts were traitorous. Many hated his antiwar position so much they thought that anything that they could say to defeat his candidacy—whether true, exaggerated, or false—was a good thing. They said, or signed quotes our guys had prepared for them, alleging all kinds of stuff.

"We started with TV spots featuring these 'patriots' and including some creative videotape dubbing—like taking a question Kerry was asked and dubbing part of an answer he gave to another question to make him look either dishonest or stupid.

"One of my favorite parts of the caper was that we put the best of it in a 'tell all' book. We paid for enough pre-publication purchases of the book that it hit the bookstores and the top of the bestseller list in the same week. Most schmucks didn't buy or read the book. But they believed that with so much smoke there must be fire.

"The Democrats faulted themselves for being a little bit slow to respond. They weren't slow at all. What they didn't understand was that any response was irrelevant because, as the Modern Experience teaches, demonstrating the falsehood of a Big Lie is too complicated for 'the masses' to follow. And even when the falsehood of a Big Lie is explained, they persist in their belief that at least some of it must be true."

At about that point Dad said, "Those are only examples of some of the techniques. Our day-to-day efforts use them on a more persistent basis. We'll get to more of that, probably this afternoon.

"For now, let's take a break. I need to make a couple of phone calls. I'm sure we all could use some fresh coffee and maybe use the facilities. Then let's meet back on the patio in about 15 minutes and take up the development of the religion aspect of Our Enterprise."

SOUTHERN
"OTHER RELIGIONS"

A
S DAD PROBABLY EXPECTED, I cleaned up the remains of the bagels, put a new filter-full in the coffee maker, and busied myself until we reconvened outside.

Doug began the discussion of what Dad had called the "religion aspect of Our Enterprise."

"I suppose I should start by saying that the shape of what we did is easier to identify now, looking back, than it was as we went through it.

"Remember, our *mission* was gaining more wealth for ourselves and our descendants; we were entering and seeking to win the on-going class warfare. Our *strategy* was to win through the political process. Our main weapons were to be devices of persuasion. We knew a major device of persuasion would be the cooperation of religious leaders, if for no other reason than they had high marks on Aristotle's criterion of 'character of the speaker.' They also had followers who did not expect their declarations to be supported by rational proof; their words were to be taken on faith.

"As soon as Karen and I moved to Texas I sought out some of the politically active and oil-wealthy Texans I knew who were prominent in a local Southern Baptist congregation. I said I was coming from a conservative Dutch Reform upbringing looking for a Southern church that would serve the same spiritual and social needs there in Texas. They welcomed me to join them in their large SBC church where I set about to learn what was happening, on the ground, in the SBC.

"The first thing I learned was that the SBC, with its well-educated clergy, was much more a mainstream Christian religion than I had anticipated. I should have known that the tenet that encouraged members to seek their own meaning from their Bibles would have fostered a tolerant diversity of thought. And it had. For example, I was surprised to learn that at the 1954 convention the Southern Baptists had passed a resolution approving the decision of the Supreme Court directing school desegregation in *Brown v. Board of Education*. Equally surprising, at the 1968 convention they passed a resolution siding with the civil rights movement and apologizing for any activity in the SBC's past that had fostered racial repression.

"But there was resistance in the pews. As one pastor put it to me, 'When people come to a Sunday service they do not want admonition; they want comfort and their beliefs to be confirmed.'

"Back then, in the early seventies, the SBC was as ready for a reactionary change as that sleepy Iowa town in *The Music Man*. The same constituency that was pulling adamant segregationist politicians away from the Democratic Party to our side was pulling a large part of the SBC away from its theological leaders who saw support for civil rights to be a matter of ethics. The path of scripture and reason may point in one direction, but in the pews people's souls sang, 'Give me that old time religion. It's good enough for me.'

"Make no mistake; it was my friends and other long-time SBC members who wanted to act. But by their determination to cause change they were providing us with a Music Man Moment. Let me put that another way: they were the wave; we only had to figure out how to ride it. Their plan was to change the path of the SBC; we decided to help with enough resources to organize and staff their effort in exchange for an unstated and unopposed assumption of post-revolt inclusion of wealth-favoring teachings.

"With the help of wealthy Allies—largely Ayn Randians from the oil patch and members of the inherit-a-department-store crowd—we provided everything they needed to organize their successful revolution. Our idea of change may have differed from their ideas but did not directly conflict with them. We simply suggested soft peddling some of their traditional positions to achieve their goal of reversing their denomination's drift away from segregation and other core aspects of their regional culture.

"We convinced them their change would be easier to achieve if they abandoned their advocacy of the separation of church and state. And it would help if they used their pulpits more as sources of declaration than of guidance. Then we intended to build political support in the pews for our wealth-favoring candidates on the basis of moral issues the Convention would run up the pole while our candidates saluted.

"Tactically, we and they decided to gain control of the SBC by packing the seats at an annual convention. If successful in that effort, they could pass their own resolutions and, more importantly, elect a full slate of their people to lead the SBC.

"Yet in 1975 we saw no reason to hurry. In fact, given the context of the looming 1976 national election campaign there was considerable reason to delay rather than risk a political loss. We were facing the aftermath of the Watergate cover-up and the Democrats' likely nomination of a Southerner governor with serious Southern Baptist credentials.

"Besides, when Nixon fell we were left with a Republican Party led by an open-minded moderate, Gerald Ford. Ford was from the Party's old wing. For example, after the '64 Convention, while he was minority's leader, he tried to make Frelinghuysen its Whip; the Goldwater forces beat that back. And, as President he didn't continue Nixon's fence-straddling encouragement of both wings of the Party. Hell, Ford even made the Eastern Establishment icon, Nelson Rockefeller, his Vice President. About the only thing I can remember he did to appease our side was to allow an Ayn Rand acolyte, Alan Greenspan, to join the Council of Economic Advisors.

"So I was able to use the late-seventies to focus on the work of building our network among the other Southern Protestant churches.

"Looking at Southern religions day in and day out as a resident of the Bible Belt was vastly different than hearing about them briefly described by a moonlighting Professor in New York City. Particularly, I was struck by the power of the successors to the radio preachers we had listened to on our drive west. Radio preachers had become televangelists. Some of them were frocked by ordination within the SBC, some by credentialing by the Assemblies of God, and others by diverse but similar procedures.

"I could see we had to use these preachers in Our Enterprise but my personal involvement with the takeover of the SBC meant that I could not be visible in the efforts to organize them. Still, it was clear that recruiting them was even more important than my efforts to enroll the SBC in our war. If nothing else they offered a more immediate path to the hearts and minds of the WESs in the south. We need only forge strong mutually beneficial alliances with a few of the more emotional and successful televangelists. Through them and their multiple electronic outlets broadcasting the same recorded shows we could reach many more people with a simple, consistent, and controllable message. We could never do anything like that by trying to influence local pastoral preaching through remote pronouncements of the governing body of the SBC.

"I set my staff to look for and evaluate pastors who were preaching a 'God and His purpose for America' line. Some believed it was true; some believed it was financially effective. It didn't matter to us which. That message was ideal for obliterating the separation of church and state. We also decided to favor those with an 'end of times' message. Thoughts of imminent extinction inspired the zealous to a sense of urgency. That urgency could trump, within the hearts of the followers, any instinct to consider a reasoned moderate response to our calls for action. It also lessened the relevance of the traditional moderating political consideration of 'generations yet unborn.'

"With our funding we were able to stoke the ministries of the independent preachers we had selected and help build their churches, mega-churches, and television and radio syndications. We were able to use the power of our purse to insure that their messages continued to be to our liking. As you would expect, since their ministries were advancing religion, they were qualified as 501(c)(3)s. So, the majority of the money we spent on this effort would have otherwise gone for a governmental purpose, not ours.

"Having a separate member of our team work with each one of those avowedly independent ministers, as I was doing with the SBC and your dad was doing among the Catholics as he'll tell you about in a minute, would have been dangerously unmanageable. So we needed to find or create one or more entities through which we could deal with a whole basket of these other churches. The National Association of Evangelicals had been around for 30 years and we hoped to gain influence there. But we could have more direct control if we started our own 501(c)(3). And we had to find a leader for that new entity other than me.

"On one of our family vacations your dad and I discussed what kind of entity would best serve. We decided to pattern it along the lines of Nixon's 'Silent Majority.'

"Just a few years before the Nixon forces had, by simple assertion, proclaimed that there was a 'Silent Majority' (the antithesis of the noisy mob outside the 1968 Chicago Democratic Convention) and it was on his side. The name implied something above and apart from a political party. It was a political force nonetheless. From the perspective of the voter, the neutrality of the title allowed and enabled the allegiance of politically concerned people who were not committed to a specific political party. From the inside, however, it was a purposefully partisan device to gather votes for Nixon Republicans. Nixon and his people put themselves forward as the leaders of this majority by the simple act of saying so. The leaders called upon people to identify with this undefined but high-sounding group. Then they announced the details of that group's 'beliefs' and thereby defined it. The 'beliefs' were, of course, ideas which aligned with the advance of Nixon's power.

"We also discussed the kind of a person who should lead our new entity. We wanted a young male who could appear respectful of his elders (the leaders of individual electronic congregations) yet at the same time project a youthful zealotry and energy which those leaders would embrace and, if necessary, defer to. He had to have shown, in competitive politics, that he was capable of unquestioning obedience. Yet he had to be intellectually agile enough to be Our Enterprise's field general selecting and executing tactics appropriate to the circumstances he encountered in this clergy control engagement. He also had to be someone who was neither troubled by our goals nor interested in shaping them. The way we put it at the time, we wanted someone of intelligence who was able to give us the sort of obedience our ROTC drill instructors called for when they said, 'Mister, when I say "Jump!" the first thing I want to hear out of you is, "Request permission to come down, sir."' For that kind of obedient service we would reward him handsomely.

"After Carter's election, and with the significant help of some of the same people who had funded cause-serving 501(c)(3) think tanks, we were ready to 'go live. Our righteous army was up and running with televangelists leading the way.

"In 1979 my friends implemented their plan to take over the SBC. At the annual convention they ousted the desegregationist leadership by winning the presidency and virtually every seat on the board that would manage the denomination until the next convention. From that vantage they had the ability to install compliant supporters to just about every seat on all the relevant committees including the important Christian Life Commission and the Home Mission Board. They gained control of the funding and of staffing the seminaries. By the mid-1980s they were in complete and virtually unchallengeable control of the public pronouncements of the SBC (though we were having less success in the individual churches). At headquarters, at least, the doctrine that had held the Bible to be unerringly true as it spoke to the soul of each of its readers became a doctrine holding the Bible was literally unerringly true as our clergy interpreted it. The idea of literal truth no longer tolerated Bible-questioning observations by the biologists studying Darwin or geologists doing radio-carbon dating. For some biblical literalists, recent creationists, God's creation happened only so long ago as the biblical "begats" allowed.

"Of course, anyone who resisted was free to leave the SBC. As we had foreseen, most didn't leave because the SBC was a connection to the beliefs of their parents and the spiritual comfort of their youth. We called that the 'Faith of Our Fathers' syndrome. Some of the thinking devout did leave, to be sure; Jimmy Carter and Bill Moyers were the noisiest about it. Even our success with the seminary take-over wasn't complete. Some seminaries, particularly the independently funded ones, did not go along. Still, most individual and corporate members of the SBC family simply went along, as they say, to get along.

"With the SBC and the televangelists in harness we were ready to put the banner of moral issues in front of the WESs and identify as 'moral' our more-wealth-for-the-wealthy candidates. It only remained to announce to the WESs and our candidates a unified 'moral' platform. Your dad, in his work with Catholics, had found the first 'moral' issue for us. We merely had to join our efforts with his.

"So, at this point I think it's time for him to tell you about his efforts in the '70s up here in the North."

"Great," I said. "I'm looking forward to that. Grade-schoolers never really know what their fathers do when they go off to work. But first I need a break."

A Northern
"Other Religion"

WHEN WE RECONVENED I STARTED by teasing my father that as a pre-teen I thought that maybe his office was just a front and he was really a bank robber, or a hit man, or maybe a super-hero. Now I wanted to hear what he had really been doing—at least how he ran "the Catholic part of this operation."

Dad looked down for a moment and went through a little facial ritual he used while he was collecting thoughts: tensing his lips and making a soft tssst-ing sound by pulling in the dampness from the front of his teeth. Then he began, "You have to remember, Kate, I had been a New York City kid. Even in those days affluent City parents were not sending their kids to the public schools. For me that meant nuns in the neighborhood parochial grammar school and Jesuits in high school. In fact, given my lackluster high school grades, it was the Jebbie connection that got me into Boston College. Without that, God knows where... Oh well. Anyhow, that schooling gave me a good base for running the 'Catholic part of this operation' as you put it.

"Being Episcopalian was actually an advantage. The Catholic hierarchy could deal with me on different terms than they could have dealt

176

with a Catholic. They didn't expect me to assume a childlike subservient posture treating them like my "father" or to be disillusioned with them when they made compromises. Still, from school and social acquaintances, I knew a goodly number of affluent Catholics sympathetic to our cause, particularly on Wall Street. They (and judicious contributions) made my introductions and gave me credibility with the hierarchy.

"Besides, in those years right after Vatican II, the Catholics were turning to ecumenism, a much greater level of involvement and encounters with other Churches. So there were many more opportunities to meet, greet, and work with the national Catholic leadership in social situations around the City.

"I should explain a bit more about Vatican II. That Council ended about the time we finished our preparation. Its original goal, to make peace with the Jewish community, had evolved into better relations with other religions generally. In the centuries before Vatican II, including in my parochial school years, the Catholic Church had preached that if a person knew about the Catholic Church and didn't join it, that person was doomed to eternal perdition. After the Council the official Church position was now that 'many elements of sanctification and truth are found outside the visible confines of Catholicism.'

"The Council summed up its work in a series of documents including two I thought remarkable: a *Decree on Ecumenism*; and, a *Declaration on Religious Freedom*. The degree to which those pronouncements repudiated the ideas of Leo the 13th (while throwing Leo a couple of footnotes to suggest that his words provided supporting authority) was, by previous Catholic standards, absolutely astounding.

"My guess is the ecumenism effort to make peace with other Christian denominations, as well as the Jews, was driven by the old political maxim 'The enemy of my enemy is my friend.' After all, all religions were facing the challenges to their traditional explanations as a consequence of Darwin, DNA, and deep space telescopes. Darwin inferred humanity was a relatively recent variation from other species. DNA suggested it was a very small variation at that. Telescopes taught that humanity was barely an impossibly small blip in the vastness of time and space of all creation.

"As a result of the widespread exposure to those scientific ideas, largely through TV, many more people doubted the religious explanations of human uniqueness, direct human creation by a caring God, and the likelihood that even a caring Creator would promise a unique post-mortal reward for human kind. As a result, among religions the main battle was no longer Catholics versus Methodists, etc. It was religion versus non-religion. Through ecumenism Vatican II invited the Abrahamic religions to put aside their differences to face a common foe—disbelief.

"But it was even a bit more than that. In the *Declaration of Religious Freedom* Vatican II had adopted a distinctly Jeffersonian approach—freedom of conscience—that left room for a non-hostile relationship between religious Catholics and nonreligious people to the end that the ethical behavior of all might be fostered.

"From some things our moonlighting professor had said, we figured we'd have to wait and see how Vatican II worked in the real world before acting in reliance on its pronouncements. Consistent with the goal of John the 23rd to 'open the windows of the Church', Vatican II had been held in the presence of Protestant and Jewish clergy. Some modern Catholic scholars who had not previously had any influence at the Vatican were there as well. When the Council closed they all went home but the old guard was still in residence. Among the older hierarchy, ecumenism had its place, but the longing for the comfort of controlling society through the combination of wealth, religion, and central governments was alive and well.

"How the American Church would change was important to us because it had grown more successfully political in the post-war era. In the parishes Senator Joe McCarthy had almost been a saint. The Knights of Columbus had run the campaign to get Congress to pass the 1954 law inserting 'under God' in the 'Pledge of Allegiance' notwithstanding the First Amendment's, 'Congress shall make no law...' (The nation had to steel its children against 'Godless communism,' don't you know.) And Catholic pulpits had been routinely "guiding" voters on the Sunday before Election Day. For example, Prescott Bush, the father of the first President Bush, figured he lost his first Congressional race in Connecticut (by about 1000 votes) because of sermons all across his district on the Sunday before Election Day denouncing his involvement in Planned Parenthood.

"In state legislatures the Church was gaining laws to have all tax-payers pay for the parental costs for parochial schools. A testament to the growing power of the Church (and an example of the maxim that 'judges read the papers') was that one of those laws was upheld in the Supreme Court, 5-4. Not that the case, *Everson*, was a total victory on the march to re-unify church and state. In it the Court unanimously said that, under the Fourteenth Amendment governing post-Civil War America, the states were as bound by the First Amendment's establishment clause as was the federal government.

"But by the mid-'60s, the tide seemed to be turning more secular even in the waning immigrant Catholic neighborhoods. Over Church opposition (based on principle damn it!) states were relaxing divorce laws (based on the effect of inescapable bad marriages on people's lives). And in an increasing number of states—as well as in other nations of the world—the Church's demand for criminal laws against abortion (based on a principle, damn it!) was losing to stronger arguments (based on the effect of the diverse and compelling real life circumstances for which women sought abortions).

"The older Church leaders who were looking for some issue to show and enhance their power were coming up empty. The teaching of the Church's celibate clergy on the immorality of contraception couldn't persuade the post-pill people sitting in its own pews on Sunday; any attempt at national legislation would get nowhere. There was a possibility in 'abortion,' but even there the state-by-state tide was running against. Local churches were barely the equal of local forces—women's groups and libertarians—on the other side.

"Then in 1973 the U. S. Supreme Court gave us the gift that keeps on giving. It decided *Roe v. Wade*.

"That opinion held that, while a state may have an interest in the personhood of a late stage fetus, a woman carrying a fetus had interests as well. Against them the state had no interest sufficient to justify criminalizing any decision she may make about continuing or ending a first trimester pregnancy. The result was really nothing new; it was consistent with historic law throughout Christendom—and certainly the English law this nation inherited in 1776. Under that law terminations before "quickening' (the first kick, about at the end of the 4ᵗʰ month) were not banned even in Church-controlled legal systems.

"The Catholic Church had teachings about abortion before *Roe v. Wade*. They were not central to its message. Abortion was not mentioned in the Baltimore Catechism long taught in parochial schools. (Nor, I might add, was it mentioned in the Bible.) But I will say that the nuns in the schools I had attended taught that it was a sin *except* in cases of rape or incest.

"No one from the secular community denied that abortion could be a moral issue. But, most agreed the government was not in the moral issue business; it was in the keep-order-with-minimal-restriction business. You know, the 'blessings of liberty' and the 'domestic tranquility' business. Sure murder, robbery, arson, rape, and the like were contrary to most moral teachings. But those offences invited government attention and criminal law restraint, not because of their immorality, but because order required that restraint. In the absence of a governmental response those offences they led to reprisals, reprisals led to retribution, and "domestic tranquility" was lost. Property crimes like theft may also be immoral but they were restrained because they threatened the economic wealth-as-a-reward system. Abortion was different; it might be immoral but it did not lead to reprisals or threaten the collapse of civil or economic order.

"Yet Catholic leaders found in *Roe v. Wade* a newly-minted government issue they could rail against on a simple, consistent, nation-wide basis—an issue that could gain the attention of the national media. When the Church leaders made their first responses to *Roe* we sensed that the abortion issue could be the wedge to break the 'urban Catholic' component away from the Roosevelt coalition. If we could stoke the issue and develop a block of voters to office seekers of our choosing, there'd be practically no limit to the ways we could gain more wealth for ourselves and our descendants.

"Through contacts and contributions we encouraged the Church leaders to devote resources to the issue. We urged them that their task was not to persuade Catholic doctors and women that abortion was immoral. Their task was to persuade all Catholics, men and women, that government should use the criminal law to impose that Catholic view of morality on all American women. The nation's women and doctors must be made to fear jail if they did not obey the Church's view of God's law—even if they did not belong to the Church or even if they did not believe there was a God. Women facing all manner of complicated individual situations must be commanded by the state to follow the Catholic clergy's one-size-fits-all moral judgment of what their God would say in every circumstance. And we emphasized that the more they made the issue emotional the easier that would be.

"We strongly suggested to Church leaders that if they could unify their membership on this issue as a voting bloc, we could identify candidates who would not only be supportive on the abortion issue but could return other favors to the Church once in office.

"Members of my rhetoric team worked with Church leaders. Those leaders were already skilled in the techniques of rhetoric.. They were, after all, heirs to 2000 years of persuasion about the unprovable. Together my team and they simplified the message. 'Abortion' became the universally negative word. 'Life' became the universally positive word. Distinctions for rape and incest had to be dropped. The adoption of 'life' as the positive word required a change in the Church's view of capital punishment— ironic considering the Church's historical conduct toward heretics, witches, etc. But the abandonment of past teachings for current advantage was no more of an obstacle for the 1970s Church than it had been for German politicians in the early 1930s welcoming formerly scorned farmers.

"Together we made government criminal law intervention in every abortion decision a simple, 'always and everywhere' morality issue—if the Church's formal, single premise, other-considerations-be-damned reasoning could be merged with a stoked, believing electorate, then the Church and Our Enterprise would have a path to the power we both sought.

"At the time of *Roe v. Wade* there were laws permitting abortion in 20 states—in 16 of them permission depended on considerations that differed from state to state including rape, incest, survival of the mother, deformity of the fetus, and so forth. Those variations were adopted in varying degrees on a state-by-state basis. The variety of laws suggested that society could respect various views of abortion as a moral issue. Whether it was ever an appropriate subject for criminal law was another matter. But Catholic leaders were no more looking for a reasoned discussion or a sound, limited government position, than they had been looking to control the behavior of only those who chose to follow their moral guidance. They were looking for an issue to unify their congregations so that the Church could command the obedience of office holders. They still felt a pull to the good old days, the days before what Pope Leo had called the 'horrible' and 'deplorable' Protestant Reformation and the 'terrible' American Revolution.

"For them the abortion issue held the possibility of advancing the return of the western world to the days when a pope's simple phrase, 'God wills it,' had mustered God-fearing men from across an entire continent and sent them to war.

"To achieve our ends, the abortion issue had to have unifying power. It could not have that if the Church or we were going to acknowledge that the morality of each abortion choice was unique. Therefore, morning-after pills, deformed fetus abortions, mother's life-protecting abortions, and post-rape abortions, and—for some—even birth control pills which inpaired the functions of a first-day fertilized ovum all had to be equated to infanticide. It was the principle, damn it! Ovum fertilization even by the violent incestuous rape of a chained victim was an act of God! It was the principle, damn it! The individual woman's misfortune was God's will; it was her cross to bear. It was society's obligation to use its criminal laws to prevent all women from acting contrary to the Church's morality.

"The Church needed a simple message that every follower could understand, maybe not believe at first, but at least understand; repetition would do the rest. The Modern Experience had taught that in dealing with 'the masses,' issues had to be few, simple, and avoid reasoning in favor of emotion and repetition. 'Abortion' had to become a unitary concept always to be forbidden—not merely morally forbidden—but forbidden by action of government.

"*Roe v. Wade* had transformed the issue into a national one, not a local one. That transformation made it easier for the Church to concentrate its force (Clausewitz), use emotional persuasion by the respected spokesmen in the pulpit (Aristotle), and address 'the masses' with a simple, oft-repeated message (the Modern Experience). The issue was ideal for gathering impassioned followers to fight our class war.

"Also, the abortion issue gave the Catholic Church the chance to assert its leadership within the now-ecumenizing community of Judeo-Christian religions. Soon the Fundamentalist Protestant churches saw the success of the Catholic effort. At that point Doug was able to guide them to join those efforts to seek their own advantage, even though most of the States that had nuanced laws permitting abortion were in the fundamentalist South.

"Before I leave the abortion story I should mention a couple other valuable lessons we learned from the effort and our collaboration with the Church's experienced persuaders.

"We gained an appreciation for the power of reducing a complex issue to a single emotion-laden word. 'Abortion' taught us that our purposes were best served, not by knowing that one picture is worth a thousand words, but by knowing that one emotion-laden word can be worth a hundred thousand rational thoughts. This led to a formation within our rhetoric operation, our 'persuasion directorate,' of a 'packaging department.' Its job is to simplify, down to a single word if possible, any issue worthy of our attention. As the Modern Experience had shown before us, the 'masses,' the schmucks, understand so little of issues that we should turn a complex issue into one headline word. Then we could require our followers to support our view of the now-simplified issue to remain within the comfort of the strong resolute community of belief we had created. 'Obamacare' is a good example of how we apply this lesson.

"Involvement in the abortion battle also taught us anew the value of laying claim to being the party of morality. Issues of morality were issues where reasoned discussion and compromise, the essence of the political processes in a democracy, had no place. For us, as long as we could convince our followers among the WESs that ours was the party of morality, we could more easily persuade them that it was wrong to listen to people who opposed us. The guys behind Goldwater had been ahead of us on this with their emphasis on conscience and their assertions about God's purpose for the nation.

"That same self-proclamation of morality to our comforted believing followers debased the character, the *ethos*, of those who expressed as much as a doubt about our conclusion.

"That's a topic unto itself. But the nub is this: we took the fact of *Roe v. Wade*, united it with the Catholic Church's historic interest in civil control, and massaged it all into a claim that morality rather than the preservation of order was a proper basis for criminal law. Then we had our more-wealth-for-the-wealthy office holders and office seekers commit to carry that banner in return for the support of those whom we and the churches had persuaded."

HARNESSING DIVERSE RELIGIONS TO OUR CAUSE

"**B**Y THE TIME DOUG HAD organized his Southern denominations operations we had an issue-based movement up and running. And the movement was less off-putting to Doug's Southern Protestants than it might otherwise have been before the Catholics' new-found doctrines of ecumenism.

"Later, AIDS and unremitting police brutality brought homosexuals out of the closet and into a world where they could no longer be shamed for what seemed right to them but was repugnant to others. That enabled Doug's contingent in the ecumenical dialogue to add another politically hot 'moral' issue to our arsenal—opposition to homosexual marriage. It didn't trouble the Catholic Church to sign on to that opposition despite its professed understanding that some people are born gay. They just had a God-given higher calling to celibacy. It wasn't about *logos;* it was about an alliance to gain control.

"In fact, ultimately we formalized the alliance between the Catholics and the Evangelicals. That was the 1994 effort I mentioned that didn't entirely work, at least at first.

"Yup, the same year we published the contract with America we announced a written treaty among these diverse religions. You may recall we had envisioned some form of alliance back at the end of our religions course in New York. Now, in our 1994 treaty these formerly warring religions agreed to support a specific litany of issues. We let aspiring politicians know that if they would commit to support those issues they would receive pulpit support and our money.

"The treaty was mainly drafted by a man who had long been on our side and had a well-deserved reputation for nasty suppression of disagreement with it. That was the drafter of Nixon's enemies list, Chuck Colson. After his release from prison he garnered religious 'creds' with a 'reformed and repented' tack and soon had a well-funded, recent-creationist, fundamentalist 501(c)(3) church up and running. Colson's ministry's unifying community outreach was prison reform advocacy. Along with him, among the drafting 'participants,' were representatives of some Catholic Archdioceses, both the Christian Life Commission and the Home Mission Board of the SBC, and leaders of the Assemblies of God.

"The treaty, entitled *Evangelicals & Catholics Together: A Christian Mission in the Third Millennium*, committed the denominations to stop recruiting each other's members (a practice that it called "sheep stealing") and instead turn their efforts against the forces of secularization. The treaty, generally called ECT, went on to verbally genuflect toward the concept of the separation of church and state (it was especially fond of the 'free exercise' provision of the First Amendment—on the 'no establishment' clause, not so much). It asserted the Dominionist idea that the denominations and their members have a responsibility to use government for the 'right ordering of civil society.' It invented and proclaimed a major premise that the American 'constitutional order is not just of rules and procedures but is most essentially a moral experiment.' (You can imagine the range of arguments we can craft with that as a major premise.)

"Then it turned to the issues. It started in a declaratory mode by asserting that 'abortion on demand…must be recognized as a massive attack on the dignity, rights, and needs of women.' It went on to list opposition to birth control, equality for gays, and 'statist' decisions which made the poor wards of the state government—i.e., welfare. Then, not to be all negative it endorsed government support for parochial schools, 'legitimate' censorship, and honoring Christian culture and the work of 501(c)(3)s. Most importantly for us, to insure that the treaty advanced our *mission*, we made sure that it contained a strong endorsement of free markets (despite what it recognized as their potential for 'grave abuse').

"The Treaty received an initial favorable response—including the endorsement of the Catholic Cardinal in New York as well as political televangelist/presidential candidate Pat Robertson, Ralph Reed from the Moral Majority, a representative of the 501(c)(3) American Enterprise Institute, and the others. But for the general membership of the SBC it smelled of too much political power for Rome. So it wasn't as powerful as we hoped, but it remains a good catalogue of religion-related issues we require our aspiring politicians to espouse.

"By the way, the ECT movement still has legs. In the summer of 2013 it published a 9 page paper on its view of religion and law which nets to an anti-abortion message surrounded by a lot of legalistic mumbo-jumbo.

"We haven't yet won the anti-gay marriage issue and we may not. But we haven't won the abortion issue either. However, with repetition we've been gaining enough polarized single-issue voters to help elect our more-wealth-for-wealthy politicos. Ya' gotta love it.

"But it's time for lunch. We could rustle something up in the kitchen. But it's a beautiful day and you've got that convertible, Kate, so let's go out. We could grab a sandwich at the Hickory Tree Deli, go to my Club, or go to a restaurant. Your pick. What do you say?"

I didn't feel like just picking up a deli sandwich (no matter how good) and, for now, the Club held a fresh, sad memory of the family gathering the night before Tom's funeral. So I said, "Let's get a booth at the Black Horse Pub. I'll be glad to put the top down so you young guys can get the breeze through your thinning hair."

With that we broke, washed up, got our jackets, and joined up again at my car.

A Short Drive
Through the Forest

AS I GOT IN THE car I asked Dad and Doug to wait while I started the engine and put the top down. Then Doug got in the back seat and my father joined me in front.

After a bit of meandering over a few narrow but paved country roads typical of Dad's tax-averse township, we picked up the two-lane Tempe Wick. There we drove under the not-yet-fully-leafed canopy of hardwoods, past the entrance to the National Historical Park, and on toward Mendham. The day was precisely the kind you picture when you buy a convertible. It had a pleasant feel of awakening life all the more welcome after the tough winter lowlighted by Tom's death.

The abortion discussion had bothered me. For a time I worried about seriously changing the tone of the day. I drove slowly enough to allow conversation over the breeze, yet I kept silent about my thoughts for an uncomfortably long time. But finally I asked, "Do you really want these people to win? I mean, more than one Catholic I've served with has told me, 'Abortion is immoral and it should be illegal. But if my daughter needed one, I don't know what I'd do.' Really, do you want to make all abortions illegal?"

Dad got mildly huffy and said, "First of all, that's not our intention. As I keep saying, our intention is 'more wealth for ourselves and our descendants.' Abortion, win or lose, is only a means to that end—a battle, an engagement, in our war. And, frankly, the longer the issue is unresolved the longer religious voters will be putting our politicians in office. So, no, we don't want them to win; we want them to work toward winning. But really what if they won, so what? If they do, it doesn't matter to our goals in this war."

That did it. "What? You're men, well over 70, not likely to get pregnant, so it doesn't matter? You say you're concerned for your descendants? Some of us are—and more will be—females. Suppose one of your granddaughters, Terri or Joy, were raped; or suppose she were impregnated in some other family-unwelcome way when she had a couple too many, or even while she was simply careless; would you still say it doesn't matter? Or suppose she were happily pregnant with two youngsters at home to care for but there were complications and she were advised she would not survive the next delivery? Or suppose she were advised that the fetus was profoundly mentally impaired. I've known parents who discovered that burden after delivery and bore it for decades with love. They're saints. But do you really want your government ordering your Terri or Joy to bear that burden if they could avoid it?"

For the first time that day I had shown something more than a 'take it all in' response. Dad met my slightly aggressive tone with a stern, defensively belligerent tone of his own. "Come on, Kate, don't give me that 'You're a sexist pig' shit. Laws against abortion won't affect you, Terri, Joy, or any of our descendants. Our family has money. An easy three-day round trip to any of a hundred other cities around the world could and would solve the problem."

"Oh yeah. Like where?"

"Well, for example, Rome. You or Joy could receive a perfectly legal, safe, procedure in a fine hospital within 2 miles of the Vatican."

Doug had also been disturbed by my outburst and chimed in with a sarcastic, "You know, Bill, if she wanted to extend her stay an extra week we could probably get her a private papal audience while she was in town. At least we could have under the last guy."

"AAARGH!"

"No, really. Even simpler than that, we could get one of our business contacts in Rome to FedEx her one of those RU-whatever-it-is pills, the 'up-to-40-mornings-after' pills—they're legal there—and she wouldn't even have to leave Atlanta."

I wanted to scream but thought better of it. I had turned off Tempe Wick and was about to pass a barn that, from earlier trips, I associated with static on my radio. I used to think, "Maybe a ham radio." Then, "Grow lights for an indoor pot growing operation? I wonder..." This time I decided that, in this affluent gentleman's-farm country, it's probably just an alarm system to protect a barn full of vintage cars or some such. In any event, that thought process bought my mind the time to turn off the heat under my boiling psyche.

I decided to de-escalate the tone and bring up another question that I had considered back on the patio. It had been made more relevant by Dad's concept of keeping the abortion issue alive indefinitely So, I asked, "Okay. So you're gaining the benefits from having your selected politicians in office. But what are the churches really getting? I mean especially if you keep the abortion battle going but unresolved? Won't the churches see that they're being used or even just lose interest for lack of results?"

During the brief heated exchange Doug had unbuckled his seatbelt and leaned toward the space between my shoulder and Dad's. Now, sensing and then mirroring my de-escalation maneuver he said, "Don't worry, Kate, we've thought of that. We know, and the office-holders of our Party know, that they have to deliver something to the churches. We have pay them back. And I mean pay them. Remember, money is as important to religious clergy as it is to executives in any other business. It pays their salaries.

"That's why that 'faith-based initiatives' business was such a wonderful idea. You couldn't expect the damn liberals to block programs helping the poor, afflicted, or addicted. And the religions were running programs for those people already. Financially speaking, those programs were already on the expense side of their ledgers. Federal government payment for those 'initiatives' increased the revenue side, did not increase the churches' expenses, and left the other parts of the churches' revenues, money collected from church members and such, freed up for the clergy to use in other ways: larger churches, more land, higher salaries, even settling lawsuits. Beyond that and as icing on the cake, a church with an active charity operation gave greater social satisfaction to its members. Often that means more contributions from them—even more revenue for their clergy to use.

"Of course, while Congress wouldn't block faith-based initiatives, it wouldn't vote for them either, so 'W' and his aggressive Evangelical Attorney General pulled it off by executive actions. They distributed church-destined money into diverse department budgets in untraceable amounts. They knew the *mission* and the *strategy*; they knew the place of the pay-back-the-churches *engagement*. Their *tactics* were well chosen and opaquely executed. They even subbed out a goodly part of the job of choosing recipients to a politically loyal televangelist."

Dad then added, "And don't forget ours is the party of school vouchers. We'll talk about that another time. But for now, just look at every school voucher dollar as ninety-some cents going to the gross revenue of a Catholic parish or another religious congregation with a school.

"In short, 'abortion' in particular and religious denominations in general, produce a voting bloc. That voting bloc installs our people in office. Our people are able to deliver 'more wealth for the wealthy' and to repay the churches for their support. Churches realize their efforts have been rewarded, so they continue the efforts into the next election. Beautiful."

For a moment Dad seemed to be reflecting on a memory. Then he said, "You know, we've often wondered whether we would have known enough to select this religion *engagement* in our war if we hadn't taken that drive across country—or, if when we did, we had one of today's multi-station satellite radios."

We crested the last hill right where Mendham's tall wooden Presbyterian Church stood alone, sunlit white above the trees that sheltered the village's other buildings. There we turned right, down toward the village traffic light. Then we took a quick left onto Main Street and an even quicker right into the driveway of the Pub.

35
LUNCH AND THE LAW

T HE BLACK HORSE PUB, ON the left of the drive, was once a stable for the 1740's Inn on the right. Its entrance is on the broad side of the stable facing the valet parking stop between the Pub and the Inn. In keeping with the fact that the Pub asks patrons to eat in a stable, it offers casual dining. But from the heavy, wood-framed, clear glass doors inward, it does so with class.

The large room immediately through the doors is undeniably all barn. No low ceilings here. The room is tall-to-the-rafters post-and-beam construction open all the way up to the visible underside of the roof's wooden shingles.

But it's at eye level that the room says "class." From the stone fireplace at one end of the room to the floor-to-roof-peak windowpanes at the street end, the style is bright oak accented with impeccably shined and lacquered brass. The most welcoming features are the booths along the walls. Each is raised two steps up from the floor and is comprised of a thick oak table framed by high-back benches made of the same solid, well-varnished oak. In keeping with the stable motif the tall seat backs that separate the booths have the look of the finest stalls at Churchill

Downs. They provide a privacy that no booth at a diner could approach.

We were shown to a booth near the far right corner of the room. I knew our waitress, Kathleen, from as far back as the dinner with my Mom and Dad the night before I left to become a Cadet. As soon as she came to our table and her Brooklyn-accented 'I heard about your brother, I'm so sorry' 'How's your Mom doing,' and the 'How have you beens?' had run their welcome course, we each ordered diet sodas and Dad ordered a pound of steamed shrimp as a shared appetizer.

While we waited, Dad and I went directly into a restaurant-waiting-time, people-watching game we had played since I was about 12. We took the roles of Sherlock and Mycroft Holmes one-upping each other "reading" people, as those characters had while evaluating a man standing on the sidewalk across the street from Mycroft's office. We invited Doug to join us.

Around the room there were mixed groupings: husbands and wives back from Saturday morning "togetherness shopping"—for furniture, or maybe selecting hardware for the new kitchen cabinets, we gauged; a grandpa was presiding over a table of 8 including a small birthday granddaughter, the little girl's father was ethnically different so there probably was a story there but true to the best of contemporary America it was not on display; and, in each of two different booths a 50-something couple was treating an aged mother to a lunch "out" and, we deduced, reporting such as they thought they knew of her grandchildren's college careers.

There was one booth away from the walls, sort of behind the hostesses' desk and thus in the center of the room. There a 20-ish woman was talking up a storm, gushing actually, apparently trying to impress the bewildered young man across from her. He had the body language of a crawfish trying to back away from my grasp in a cold creek of my youth. Doug had picked up on the game and said, "Let me take this one. Let's see. Bright, sun-lit space. Public, neutral territory. I think we are witnessing the first meeting of two people who, before today, have only 'met' on the Internet." Both Dad and I nodded and gave Doug a "Spot on."

Then six large men in black leather jackets entered. We couldn't help but notice because, while they waited for the hostess to select their table, they blocked a good deal of the light coming through the glass doors. They were led past us to the corner round-tabled booth behind me. As they passed, their smiles, open jackets, and the shirts under them declared that they were no threat; just buddies from a police force 'down'a shaw.' They were using the spring day for an outing of the Monmouth County Harley Owners' Club (according to the backs of their jackets) before the summer at the shore took weekends away from them. There was no need to play Sherlock on them.

Kathleen returned with the drinks and shrimp and we gave her our main course orders.

It seemed that neither Dad nor Doug had planned a topic for this break in our day, so I took the lead. I said, "Tell me how you addressed the legal end of your Enterprise."

Dad seemed surprised to be brought back to our day's agenda. He paused, pondered, and then started, "OK. Back in the 70s, our plans for the legal operation had two major *engagements* in mind. The first was continual effort to install federal appellate judges who had rock solid loyalty to the cause and to block the nominations of those who did not. The second was the systematic suppression of efforts by practicing trial lawyers to accomplish change.

"But to understand where we are now I think I should start the story in the early '80s, with The Federalist Society.

"I've mentioned that law schools in the '60s were hotbeds for the incubation of change. Students arrived with about as naïve a view of reality as we had at the end of our college and service years. They might have even liked *The Conscience of a Conservative* if they had read it, and they probably had. They found themselves in law school for several reasons. Some were there because they heard they could make good livings as lawyers. Others were there because they had political ambitions and figured the law had been the usual path for earlier generations. Many others were there simply because they graduated from college unprepared for anything specific and needed a graduate school that would postpone the draft until they were over-age or ineligible due to parenthood—a grad school that didn't require completion of the kinds of prerequisite courses that medical, business, and, let's say, oceanography schools did.

"But soon after they arrived on campus they learned that law school was not about money, politics, or avoiding Viet Nam. It was about a profession dealing justice, a system for improving the lot of the American people of their generation by adjusting the rules of society to fit the facts of their time. In short, the law schools were giving a rising generation of future politicians and judges a message that was directly opposed to our cause.

"Around 1981 or '82 a few guys imbued with our view that such change was unwelcome came up with a way to grab the students, particularly the politically inclined, before they were exposed to the intellectual allure of the law's tradition of evolution.

"Their solution to the problem was to form a society of mutual support, something like Yale's Skull & Bones, but without the secrecy or admission restrictions. By membership in the society young lawyers would commit to oppose change, to resist the attempts by professors to educate them toward the law's possibilities, and to view their law schools as trade schools teaching about what the rules are, not about the law's search for new rules for their times.

"From its outset The Federalist Society has called upon the neophyte law students to see their chosen profession as 'strongly dominated by a form of orthodox liberal ideology which advocates a centralized and uniform order.' (OK, so it's a Big Lie, we are the ones who want uniform order—we tolerate nothing that detracts from profit maximization and wealth enhancement values. But, hey.)

"Anyway, the 'centralized' part is right. Liberals do tend to see the United States. as a nation, not as a collection of states. They see the original Constitution as rejection of the weak central government model the Federalist Papers argued against. They see the Civil War and the 14th Amendment it produced as a complete rejection of the State sovereignty model that the Confederates had announced in their Constitution.

"The Federalist Society dogma also posits that "it is emphatically the province and duty of the judiciary to say what the law is, not what it should be." Sounds bizarre, but that's what the Society says; at least it did the last time I looked at its website. And, as I've said, it seeks to catch the young students as early as their entry into school. You know, 'you've got to be taught before it's too late…'"

Doug interrupted, "Kate, it's even better than that. They now publish a pre-law-school reading list. It doesn't have anything on it to teach their prospects how to succeed in law school. Instead it seeks to fill them with works preaching our message. When last I looked it did contain two listings actually about law schools but they're just how to identify (and presumably avoid) professors who might make them less conservative. Can you imagine? Going to a university primed on how to avoid learning to look at things differently? You can't make this stuff up. I love it. "

Dad resumed, "For such a society to have an attention-holding appeal for aspiring politicians it had to be able to present itself as a pathway to wealth-funded participation in the electoral process. Membership had to be more than a résumé item to get them in the door of our political party. It had to be an introduction to people who were willing to give substantial money in support of aspiring office seekers who, in turn, could be counted on to advance our policy. That's where we and our Allies fit in."

I interrupted. "Do you mean to tell me your Allies would throw money at every law grad just because he joined some club?"

"That's my Kate," Dad said to Doug, "Right to the nub.

"Of course not," he went on, "the local Societies' faculty advisors give us feedback on the members who have shown both loyalty and talent.

"I'm not saying who first came up with the idea for the Society. But I will say that people with authoritarian reactionary loyalist credentials were involved from its earliest days. Among them were Robert Bork, Antonin Scalia, and Ed Meese.

"Bork and Scalia were men of considerable academic achievement, but they were difficult people. They would more naturally ridicule a person who disagreed than respectfully reason with him.

"And they had proven loyalty to our cause. Bork, you may recall, did Nixon's dirty work during the "Saturday Night Massacre" (after two old school Republicans, Richardson and Ruckelshaus, refused) by firing the Watergate Independent Prosecutor because that prosecutor was being independent. Shortly thereafter Scalia proved his loyalty when, from the Office of Legal Counsel, he gave Gerald Ford the party-desired opinion that the Watergate tapes belonged to Nixon, not to the United States. Of course, the courts quickly decided otherwise.

"At the time the Society was formed, Meese was a loyal authoritarian advisor to President Reagan. He had been so from at least the time he advised California Governor Reagan on how to suppress the student uprising at Cal Berkeley. He continued during the Reagan presidency as

Attorney General advising on the air traffic controller's strike, Granada, Panama, and who knows what all else.

"Well, that Society got up and running. Not surprisingly it was well-funded quickly. Now it is functioning as a very successful launching pad for adhering politicians and judges. Let me give you some examples…"

With a small raise of his hand Doug interrupted and took over the lesson. "Before we get to the judges, I want to mention some of our efforts to stop the evolution of the law that trial lawyers achieve when they ask courts to reach new common law statements of what ought to be; new ideas of what is 'right.'

"It started when Nixon's first appointment to the high court, Warren Burger, speaking at an American Bar convention, kicked off an initiative to increase the use of arbitration instead of trials. Arbitration decisions are private, virtually unreviewable, don't involve juries, and often don't even give their reasoning. They just state the result. Remember, it is through the appellate and academic review of an opinion's reasoning that the law's view of what is right evolves. No review, no evolution.

"Another program to stop the WESs from putting their hands in our pockets has been a considerable effort to limit the ability of lawyers to bring cases on their behalf. Individual WESs, feeling themselves wronged by one of our companies (you know, exploding gas tanks, misrepresented drugs, chemically polluted wells, that sort of thing), were bringing too many cases asking juries filled with other WESs to make our companies pay enough to get the injured back to near even in their lives. On a state-by-state basis, our indebted office-holders have passed a gang of laws called 'tort reform,' or 'product liability reform.' (I'm sure you guessed the idea to call them 'reforms' came from our packaging department.) These laws have improved the profit margins of companies, lessened courts' review of their conduct, and limited contingent fees, the cash flow supporting yet further suits.

"The last of these lesser programs I want to mention is still on-going. We're continuing legislative and judicial efforts to limit class actions and punitive damages for the same reasons as the other reforms. Without punitive damages an injured WES can only recover the value of his injuries, less the probably 40% goes his lawyer, experts, and other trial expenses."

"OK," I said. "But let's get back to judges. For now just tell me about the High Court."

Doug continued, "Sure. We've learned a lot about judicial appointments over the years. We were never going to allow one of our presidents to appoint a Democrat. Eisenhower did that when he appointed William Brennan. His term lasted 34 years and he fought against us every day of it.

"But let's start with Nixon. He led the party like the guy in the circus or the Wild West show who rides by standing on two horses. The two horses he rode to office were the business-oriented Eastern Establishment and the fully authoritarian reactionary right, the Goldwater faction.

"Before the 1968 election, when Chief Justice Warren, a Republican, saw that fellow-California-Republican Nixon was likely to win, he tendered his resignation so President Johnson, a Democrat, could fill the seat. Damn traitor. But the Republicans in the Senate filibustered Johnson's appointment and held the seat open until Nixon was sworn in.

"For his first couple of appointments Nixon picked experienced Republican jurists with a fair likelihood of serving as wise men, acting as society at large would act when confronted with the cases before them. He first picked Warren Burger for Chief and, the next year, Harry Blackmun for an Associate Justice seat. Sure, Burger came with 'roll-back the Warren Court' speeches on his résumé. And Blackmun was Burger's buddy with ten years of middle-of-the-road service as an Eisenhower appointee on a Circuit Court.

"But, by 1971 when Nixon had a chance to appoint two at the same time, Burger and Blackmun had started to drift to the center. That's when our forces insisted that at least one of the new appointees must be a clear apostle of our cause, preferably a young one.

"In the 64-year-old Lewis Powell the Eastern Establishment thought it got one of its own, a respected business-favoring former President of the ABA. In fact Powell was far more a class warrior than that. He was the foremost spokesman for using the political power of corporate wealth to raise the interests of corporations above those of the little guys. Two months before his appointment he had written that Manifesto I mentioned earlier. In essence he preached that corporations had to aggressively enter the political fray if they were to hold off the forces advancing the WESs' profit-limiting interests. Fortunately, his Manifesto was not yet public when his confirmation hearings were held.

But Nixon gave our side an appointee with no hint of establishment respectability—a 39 year-old Goldwater speech writer, a firebrand that Haldeman once described as 'far to the right of Pat Buchanan.' That was William Rehnquist. He had a states' rights view that he based on the 10th Amendment; it essentially ignored the 14th Amendment, the Civil War, and the 19th and 20th centuries.

"President Ford made the next appointment, Paul Stevens, who started out middle of the road but, with Burger and Blackmun, drifted toward to the other side, the risk our young lawyers had warned us about.

"With Reagan we finally had control. His first appointment fulfilled a campaign promise to appoint a woman. The one he appointed, Sandra O'Connor, started and stayed loyal to our cause, voting with her friend from law school, Rehnquist, about as consistently as possible.

"Antonin Scalia was next. Perfect. I had seen him around in the Nixon administration, but really didn't know him. As I have mentioned, he had loyalty credentials dating from at least the time of his advice about the ownership of the White House tape recordings during the Watergate cover-up. He was also in the Federalist Society from its earliest days."

As I recall, Dad spoke up at that point to make some personal comments on Scalia. He said, "I find him particularly fascinating because, like me, he was a graduate of a New York City Jesuit high school and continued with the Jebbies in college—he at Georgetown. He grew up in the Catholic Church pre-Vatican II and my sense is that he was the kind of kid who hung with nuns and priests more than with the kids on his block. I figure he was a lot more comfortable with the certainty of syllogistic thoughts during the drone of the Latin mass than he was sitting on the running board of a parked car waiting for his turn at bat in his street's stickball game.

"He grew into manhood about as opposed to change as anybody on the planet. We couldn't have found a person more opposed to the 'harmful' and 'deplorable' 'arousal of innovation' since the 1500s without exhuming Pope Leo. He coupled that with an aggressive but fundamentally defensive and visceral disrespect for the discretion, the judgment, of his contemporaries.

"He knows the common law system of decisions, academic analysis, criticism, and the resulting evolution of society's rules. He just rejects that system with the argument that predictability is more important than case-by-case just justice. He said as much. Ironically he did so in his Oliver Wendell Holmes, Jr. lecture at Harvard. (I say 'ironically' because probably no man in American history despised exalting principle over effect more than Justice Holmes.) Even the title of Justice Scalia's lecture, 'The Rule of Law as a Law of Rules,' let you know he was a man given to the comfort of syllogistic reasoning from established principles and not given to the discretion, empathy, or compassion that informal logic with its consideration of effects would impel. If forced to deal with the concept that a purpose of the Constitution is to establish justice, he'd probably say that predictability is justice. But that's just assertion of a principle—the effect is to turn over the rules of contemporary society to the long-dead judges who made rules in the context of earlier times. It's a sure way to ignore the changes in society that bring new ideas. But, hey, it works for us."

With that Doug resumed his description of Our Enterprise's appointments to the Court.

"Next came Reagan's appointment of Bork. We had our friends in the leadership the Southern Baptist Convention endorse him quickly. But Bork's arrogant disrespect for just about everybody but himself, particularly including the Democratic senators who had to consent to his appointment, together with his Watergate involvement, made his confirmation impossible. His academic writings didn't help either—arrogant and antediluvian. We wound up with Anthony Kennedy. Kennedy's still there and he has been fairly true to his reactionary credentials as they existed at the time of his appointment. But the swing of the Court to our side has been so dramatic that he now looks almost like a neutral.

"Incidentally, every time we block a Democratic judicial nominee we tell our faithful 'they started that sort of thing with Bork.' That gives our followers more reason to hate the liberals. We don't mention our side's 1968 filibuster to block Johnson's appointment of Warren's replacement.

"Then Thurgood Marshall retired. We knew for the Thurgood Marshall seat we had to find a black. What with our political alliances with racist elements we hadn't cultivated a whole lot of blacks to draw from. But we did have Clarence Thomas.

"Thomas had been the black face of the Reagan administration as the chairman of the Equal Employment Opportunity Commission. There his greatest success was doing nothing of note to help people of color in almost 8 years. He thereby proved his loyalty to the *tactics* we had chosen in our class war. We also had controls on him. First, he showed evident delight at being treated as a buddy by our well-connected and deep-pocketed Allies. And, second, we have had a significant effect on his family income by employing his wife. She's a bright lady who has been a lobbyist and an aide to Congressman Dick Armey (a House Majority leader after being one of our 'supply-side' economics professors). She has also been a long time well-paid consultant to the Heritage Foundation. More recently she has made a pretty penny associated with the Tea Party movement in a couple of different ways.

"One of the most comical instances in Thomas's tenure was when he was caught having failed to disclose how our Allies' payments to her had supported his family. I don't know how much it was, the financial disclosure forms only require the source of a spouses' income, not the amount. I've seen it said to be as high as $1.6 million in total with over $600,000 from the Heritage Foundation alone. Anyhow, it was some significant number. What was this Supreme Court Justice's reason for not reporting it? He said he didn't understand the ethical disclosure forms he was required to fill out. (He's a Supreme Court Justice and the forms have about as many spaces to fill in as your driver's license renewal form.) You can't make this stuff up.

"Incidentally, his record on the Court on Civil Rights issues has been just as we would have wanted—against affirmative action, gay rights, criminal procedure rights, and so forth. About the only rights he has defended are gun rights. Ideal.

"By the time of the 2000 election we had a pliable 7-2 Republican majority on the Court. You remember, that was the election that came down to the recount of the ballots in Florida. We won the election 5-4."

I interrupted. "I have often wondered about that. Here you had a majority of justices committed since Goldwater to states' rights, literal strict constructionists all. And until that case the states had a right to determine how the electors in their state were chosen. Yet your court trumped Florida's right, specifically the right to run a recount, for what they somehow found to be an unwritten Constitutional national interest. Weren't they..."

Doug cut me off. "You're back to that principle thing again, Kate. Remember, consistency is the hobgoblin of small minds. The principles we invoke from time to time are for the WESs' consumption. Our Allies know to judge us by what we do, by effect; and they were pleased.

"'W' could only appoint two justices in his eight years. The first was John Roberts. O'Connor wanted to retire during Clinton's later years but she loyally held off until a Republican administration came into power. Once 'W' was in, she tendered her resignation pending confirmation of her successor and 'W' nominated Roberts to her Associate Justice seat. Roberts had been a clerk to Rehnquist who recommended him highly. While the confirmation process was going forward Rehnquist's health failed and he died before the confirmation. So 'W' changed the nomination and put Roberts up for the job as Chief. O'Connor held off her resignation until Samuel Alito was nominated and confirmed.

"The Alito appointment is a study in just how good we have become at this process. He was an ambitious young man who made no bones about wanting to be on the Supreme Court; it was even mentioned in his law school yearbook. He knew how to play the game. Though he was already out of school when it was formed, he joined the Federalist Society. (Hell, I don't know, he may have even invented it.) When he applied for a job as Deputy Assistant to Reagan's Attorney General Meese he had touted his conservative philosophy and went out of his way to be critical of the Warren Court decisions on criminal procedure (again, *Miranda* and such), on the separation of church and state, and on 'one man one vote.' He got the job and worked for Meese in that position for two years. Then he spent three years as U. S. Attorney for New Jersey before Bush the First nominated him to a circuit court. There he played the game even better, going out of his way to file anti-abortion dissents in every case he could.

"Most people in, or following, the judiciary took note. As I followed his career he reminded me of the kid in parochial school who keeps raising his hand buzzing, 'S'tr, S'tr, S'tr' to get the nun to call on him. But it worked.

"It worked because we also know how to play the game. Remember Sun Tzu's bit about bestowing rewards without respect to customary practice? Well, Supreme Court appointments are a great example of appointments that used to be given according to a customary practice—the custom of balance. Typically they were one from New York, one from Virginia, one from Massachusetts, and so on; or one Episcopalian, one Methodist, one Jew. Later they became one Catholic, one black, one female, and so forth. In those days presidents were looking for a Court that would reflect and be sensitive to the nation's diversity and changing values. We stopped that. For us the determining criterion is rock solid loyalty to our side of the class war.

"We have a lot of lawyers in our following, but demonstrated unfaltering loyalty to our cause is not that common among them. Our cause requires that we stoke the Catholics and our southern denomination supporters on the *Roe v. Wade* issue. So we were looking for a judge who is known to go out of his way to write unnecessary anti-abortion opinions. Do you think if we ignored Sun Tzu and bestowed Supreme Court seats by custom we would have two Italian-American Catholic justices born in the Trenton Diocese? No way. But the appointment of two justices, Scalia and Alito (or 'Scalito' as the press calls them), with total disregard for the custom of geographic, religious, or even ethnic diversity, sent a message to every ambitious young judge or judge wannabe in the Republican Party.

"Don't get me wrong—Alito, Scalia, Roberts, Rehnquist, Kennedy, and Thomas—they're all bright people. But there are a lot of bright people in this country who aspire to such jobs. By awarding appointments on the basis of unwavering loyalty to our issues we do more than control the kind of drift we saw with Justices Black, Blackmun, and Stevens. We set up a system which allows us to 'employ the entire army [here, the judiciary] as you would one man'".

Our waitress came back and asked if we wanted to order coffee or dessert. Dad looked at his watch and said, "No thanks, Kathleen. We'd better be getting back." With that he gave her a credit card.

THE RIDE BACK

WHILE DAD PAID I WENT outside, gave the parking attendant my stub, and described my car. After he jogged down the drive to the back lot Doug and Dad came out and joined me. While we waited, Dad pointed to the Catholic Church down a bit on the opposite side of the street. He told of how, according to one local version of the story, a recent pastor's 'truth and reconciliation' efforts to heal the parish after his predecessor's altar boy scandal had made some important contributors uncomfortable in their pews. That cost him his job. Dad's palms-up, head-tilting, eyebrow-lifting shrug was a silent commentary on "Other Religions'" recurring tension between ideals and funding.

The attendant brought my car up quickly. I tipped him; we got in and set out to retrace our route back to the farm.

After I made the tight turn by the Presbyterian Church and returned to country driving I asked, "Did you ever come up with anything like the Nuremberg rallies?"

Doug said the closest thing they found at first were Evangelical "Crusades." "Take Jimmy Swaggart's, for instance. At his Crusades in the spring of 1981 in Kansas City and Dallas he followed his always entertaining gospel music with a simple clergyman's proclamation of the blessings of grace in his life and the lives of others. Then he ended with a call for the congregants to accept Jesus and receive personal salvation. Even in Charlotte in November of '82 the message was still traditional 'Come to Jesus' and personal, though with a bit more warning of hell's fire.

"But that changed over the next half year. In that half year Reagan gave his rousing government-against-abortion speech at the March convention of the National Association of Evangelicals (better known for its last minute add-on as the 'evil empire' speech). And it also included Swaggart's personal visit with Reagan. So, the message of his Crusade in Atlanta in May of '83 was no longer about personal morality. It was a call for support for a national governmental role in advancing Christian morality. Pure Dominionism. He started his central sermon with his own seriously misinformed version of the collapse of the Roman Empire, transitioned to the collapse's supposed parallels with contemporary America, ranted about abortion, praised Reagan, and damned liberals. The people who filled the seats in that basketball arena took it all in without objection because, as usual, they were there prepared to take the preacher's words on faith. The people seated there were as unquestioning and transfixed as the people standing in the Nuremburg Sportplatz 50 years earlier.

"But, Bill, persuasion is your part of Our Enterprise. You should take it from there."

Dad said, sure, "For a while, beside mass religious gatherings we couldn't find anything that enabled us to have the followers succumb *to the magic influence of …mass suggestion*. After all, except for Evangelical Crusades, when TV came in, mass gatherings had gone the way of the buggy-whip. But there were other key things about the Nuremberg rallies. One was that they used the spoken word, not the written, to persuade. Another was that their format did not permit dispute or contradiction. And attendance at the rallies was free. So we looked for a forum that had at least those features.

"Our first success was with talk radio. It doesn't have the immediacy of stirring up emotions in a crowd, then having those emotions persuade individuals within in the crowd. But it came close.

"Each show takes an event of the day (often obscure, sometimes invented) as the base for launching the discussion. (That follows directly from the teaching by the leader in his book that member of the masses will more readily consider an idea conveyed by the *spoken word...especially if he gets it for nothing, and all the more if the headlines plastically treat a topic which at the moment is in everyone's mouth.)* The event serves as a seed crystal dropped into a super-saturated solution of anger, hate, and fear born of the listener's sense of powerlessness in the face of his diminishing income and advancing science's impact on the certainties of his youth.

"The shows start with the event-based rant directing hate and scorn at government, the media, and anyone who is currently speaking for a value that might cost us money. The hate and scorn, the insults, are in a style that aggressively rejects language that might show respect for those with different ideas or race. Such respect itself is coded and then scorned as 'political correctness.'

"Next carefully screened calls come into the show from 'the common man' usually praising and reinforcing the rant; giving it what amounts to an 'Amen!' Men listening while driving cars home from work, or while driving trucks on the ranch or the road, identify with the callers. They sense that, in vehicles all across the country, there are others just like themselves. In their isolated and moving passenger compartments they feel the 'immediate, sociologically fulfilling power of belonging to a strong and resolute community' of the kind Dr. Zeman had described back in that session in Newport.

"For some of these radio efforts we screened different personalities and built syndicates of stations for them. Then we funded their broadcasts—largely with our Allies' deductible corporate advertising dollars. Sometime radio personalities were funded with money originally contributed on a tax-deductible basis to a 501(c)(3) think tank—Limbaugh had The Heritage Foundation; Hannity and Beck had their equivalents.

"These guys know the lessons of the Modern Experience. They use *more radical and inflammatory* speech as an attention-getting, entertaining way to attract an audience. Their messages are addressed *exclusively to the masses* at a *low intellectual level* and *particularly tak[e] into consideration the emotions of the masses.* Following the pattern of the WWI propaganda the leader described, *at first the claims of propaganda were so impudent that people thought it insane; later, it got on people's nerves; and in the end it was believed.* Actually, Limbaugh spelled this out quite well in an interview which has made its rounds on the web. And remember a lesson of the Modern Experience was that movements are driven by agitators who knew the psychology of the WESs' emotions. Our showmen fill that bill in ways Doug and I could not.

"We were able to give the shows free to local radio stations all across the country, pre-packaged with 4 commercials per hour from our Allies, and allow the stations to fill their coffers with whatever they could get for selling the other spots in the hour. The broadcasts' messages *'plastically treat'* the real or invented events of the day by wrapping them around our core messages: government is bad; the nonconforming press (a/k/a 'Main Stream Media' or 'MSM'), is bad; and, unregulated industry is good. Nowadays, given our sources of funding, the oil industry is particularly singled out for praise. The showmen target its critics for scorn—they mock Al Gore and global warming at every turn and especially during every cold snap.

"These talk radio personalities sneer at any people who speak for any interest that could cost us money. They particularly single out women who speak for those interests and suggest that strong women are a threat to males neutered by their economic slide. Limbaugh calls such women 'Femin-nazis.' His rant against Sandra Fluke, for testifying in defense of health insurance coverage for contraceptive pharmaceuticals before an all-white-male, all-Republican, House Committee hearing is a classic. The showmen's favorite female target remains Hillary, though Nancy Pelosi is worth at least one shot a week."

I came back at that one, "That one always got me. Sometimes I listen to those shows and I wonder what an American grandmother who has been serving her country for decades could have done to be so worthy of the level of hate aimed at her."

Dad explained, "What she has done doesn't matter. There are at least a hundred of our followers who hate her for every one who could tell you anything she has done. Our showmen have convinced them that hatred of her is required of listeners if they are to be loyal members of the pack. Once convinced to hate her, they wouldn't believe a thing she had to say, even when she was urging something that would help them. Believe me, this stuff works.

"The radio personalities also attack generalized movements that disagree with us like Moveon.org, Acorn, and so forth. They ridicule those groups constantly so, for the listeners, the groups become the hated 'others.' With every hate-inspiring identification and dismissal of someone or something as an 'other,' a follower becomes bonded as one of our 'us' and more determined not to be, and not to listen to, a hated one of 'them.'

"Our advisors have said that such hatred comes naturally in part because it is a way for an economically unsuccessful "follower" to avoid hating himself for being a victim of events as we ship his job offshore. We simply give him a target for his anger other than us.

"At the same time the showman hails our Allies and their programs, our think tanks and their position papers.

"People and movements aren't the only object of ridicule. Any government policy which could cost us money is ripe for attack. And, equally or more importantly, we ridicule each as another example of how government policies are always bad. It is standard operating procedure to mock—not analyze the pros and cons of—a policy to establish it as bad and then assert, as to government policies generally, 'they are all the same' and 'they are a threat' to your liberty. Result—one more brick in the wall that we were building to block government implementation of any program that might lessen our profits.

"On the whole, the power of talk radio is amazing. Here's a Wage Earning Schmuck driving on a safe, government-funded highway, looking at less smog-filled skies, perhaps driving along a river cleaner than it was 50 years ago. Even within 5 feet of him, his car has seat belts and air bags. His steering column is collapsible, no longer a rigid spear aimed at his chest waiting for a front-end accident to pierce his heart. His ignition key is no longer a cleaver aimed at his knee cap, and there is no steering wheel horn ring poised to rip his face or gouge out his eye on impact. He's far safer; from 1968 to 2008 American highway fatalities dropped from 55,000 to 34,000 while vehicle miles traveled almost tripled. He's getting at least twice as many miles per gallon as he used to and his catalytic converter is removing over 90% of the pollutants leaving his exhaust. Those gallons no longer contain brain-damaging lead; and as a result, his granddaughter's blood lead levels are less than one-fifth of what his were at her age. All this because his countrymen, informed by Main Stream Media and acting through their government, have raised their values of safety, health, the environment, and mileage efficiency above our profit maximization value.

"Each of those improvements is a result of what Powell's 1971 Manifesto decried as an 'Assault on the American Free Enterprise System'. Wage Earning Schmucks are better off. And most of the old companies—and some new ones—are meeting the new requirements—requirements that the 'free-enterprise' marketplace would never have imposed.

Yet here we are floating the mocking voice of talk radio into WES's passenger compartment and convincing him to vote for our 'free market' candidates by using Reagan's mellifluous mantra, 'Government is not the solution to the problem. Government is the problem' or by using the old quote Goldwater revived in his book, 'That government governs best which governs least.' No facts support these assertions. But they are simple, and they have been repeated over and over until our conditionsedWage Earning Schmucks believe them. *[T]he most brilliant propagandist technique must confine itself to a few points and repeat them over and over.* I love it.

"Our success with talk radio led one of our Senior Operatives into the TV 'news' business. He's gathered a whole stable of on-air types and writers trained in the techniques of the Modern Experience. Following the Powell Manifesto dictum that our spokesmen be attractive, he has filled his on-air news staff with lots of pretty girls. His on-air types have become skilled at taking the daily talking points sheets developed at our persuasion ministry and distributed through our chosen outlets (including the RNC and, when our guys held it, the White House). They take the talking points and develop them into on-air scripts, using such of the techniques as they have found work, considering their individual personalities and their individual audiences. Their feedback and our market research review of the effect of their presentations are very helpful in developing follow-on material."

Doug broke in, "Kate, I'd like to get back to your question about our Nuremberg rally substitutes. Eventually, your Dad found another gloriously effective one—e-mail."

That surprised me and I said so. I said, "How can an email work like a Nuremburg rally? For one thing, emails are writings, not speech. For another, an email reaches a reader when he is alone, far removed from the emotions of a crowd. And emails allow dissent; they are a forum for discussion, not a pathway for one-way unchallengeable declarations."

Dad cut me off. "They only seem so, Kate. Let me explain."

37
THE EMAILS

"WE ACTUALLY STARTED TO USE emails to serve another function of our 'propaganda ministry.' That was market research. Sending an email is like dropping a stone into a pond; if the message is well received it spreads outward far beyond the original recipients. We can send several such messages and, every so often, include pictures or other attachments or links. A recipient who wants to see the attachment has to click in a way that enables us to record how many people we are reaching.

"Gradually we came to learn how the natural conduct of a follower receiving a message advanced our cause. In the first place, particularly if it is humorous, he forwards it to a group of friends thereby expanding its reach. But more than that, his forwarding is an act of adding his personal endorsement to our message; it subtly suggests to his friends that agreement with the message is a term of their friendship.

"It is important our emails take a strong and *basically subjective and one-sided attitude to every question* they deal with. They must not present ideas tentatively implying a respectful, 'what do you think?' If one of a sender's friends fires back a disagreeing reply, possibly in a 'Reply to

211

All' format, the sender (or another guy receiving the original forwarded message) will, almost certainly, snap back with an abusive, personal
attack on the dissenting responder. Even if not, the original sender will
most likely delete the dissenter from his mailing list. Remember, the cornerstone axioms of our persuasion operation include 'do not tolerate dissent' and 'dissenters must be scorned or worse.' The dissenter need not
immediately feel himself ousted from the 'strong resolute community' or
from friendship. But in the long run he'd be isolated, particularly if the
original email was sent to his friends, old teammates, or even co-workers,
one of whom may soon be his boss.

"Whether with disclosed or undisclosed addressees, it doesn't take
long for a WES receiving emails, particularly humorous ones, to decide
to forward some to his friends. Pretty soon this process becomes a major
part of his expression, his thought-content communication. The people
in his email chains become a strong 'in group' identifying for him who
'us' is. For the person who did not oppose the original email but wasn't
sure he agreed with it, the Nuremberg mass rally psychology soon sets in,
*when the visible success and agreement of thousands confirm the rightness
of the new doctrine and for the first time arouse doubt in the truth of his
previous conviction—then he himself has succumbed to the magic influence
of what we designate as 'mass suggestion'.*"

"But what are the themes?" I asked.

"There are several. First, we have to attract followers. For that we
hold out our community as a welcoming one comprised of the hard-work-
ing core of our nation, the 'real Americans' who have a sense of humor.
Then our followers are encouraged to believe that we and they are better
than the 'others' who are unrighteous and beneath us. Each of those
others—be they blacks, gays, Hispanics, Muslims, eggheads, atheists, un-
skilled laborers, unemployed, and most of all liberals—are, to our followers, all the same and they are a threat. We promote distain for those
'others' as so ignorant, evil, or unworthy that they should not be listened
to or even spoken to in a respectful conversation. As one of our craftsmen
put it, 'our main job is to instill an atrophy of empathy.' Empathy for the
less fortunate can cost us money."

I said, "Thanks. This is all new, or maybe it's just because it's after a heavy lunch. Forget for a minute the themes and the mechanics of how it works. Can you give me an example of the kind of emails you're talking about?"

"Sure. We plan to give you plenty of examples back at the farm. But first let me say that a sample or two won't give you the full picture of the effect of our email campaign. That campaign includes some ordinary political commentary criticizing something the other side did. And, for about a year, it has included a daily summary of Fox News 'on air' points. But those emails only serve as background for the mass of others aimed at gathering followers and getting them to hate and disrespect other Americans, those who oppose our 'more wealth for the wealthy' goals. These emails come in both text and visual form. Those in text form are not constrained by *ethical values such as truth.* Any individual visual email, standing alone, could be dismissed as childish, unlikely to persuade anyone. But in their context within the couple-of-dozen-emails-per-week campaign they are important tools for binding together the mutually reinforcing, self-righteous community of our followers."

Dear Reader,

Before I continue reporting on the Saturday conversation let me say I have scanned a couple thousand of these emails while I have been writing and editing these notes. Perhaps out of a sense of whimsy, but mostly to let you know I'm not exaggerating, I have decided to insert some of the visuals into this report where they seem appropriate. For example, regarding the idea that the emails should only be forwarded to believers, not to elicit dissent or discussion, consider this one:

⚡ IMPORTANT ⚡
This is not sent for discussion.
If you agree, forward it. If you don't, fine, delete it.
I don't want to know one way or the other.
By me forwarding it, you know how I feel.

Or on convincing the followers that they should not speak to, or listen to any liberal:

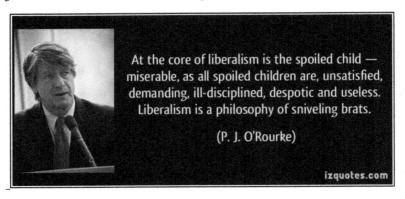

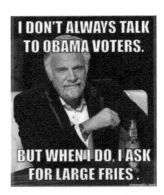

Kate

But let me get back to my notes on Saturday's conversation; Doug was about to describe some examples of emails sent to gather and stoke committed, comforted followers.

He said, "Consider one where we first praised Lee Iacocca as a wise man and great American who should be listened to. Then we took his scathing indictment of 'W' from his 2007 book, and by simply substituting "Obama" for "Bush," we made it into an Iacocca rant against Obama.

"Then there was the one where we recycled a stoke-the-believers piece we did in 1999 when Barbara Walters was going to name Jane Fonda as one of the 100 most influential women of the 20th Century. We edited it and republished it saying Obama was about to give a traitor (Fonda) an award. He wasn't."

Politicians, Wars, and Scandals come and go, but hating Jane Fonda is forever.

Jane Fonda Memorial Wall

"OK, I get it—the Big Lie in visual form. But what happens when you get caught?"

"Nothing, Kate. These emails are untraceable so _we_ never get caught."

"All right. Let me put it this way: what happens when the lie is exposed?"

"Again, Kate, nothing.

"First, remember—telling WESs, 'the masses,' that it's all a Big Lie at best only leaves them believing some of it must be true.

"Second, the revelation of the Big Lie will not reach as many people as the lie itself. Very few of our believers, people who have hatred for liberals 'in the mind,' are going to go to *Snopes.com* or *Factcheck.org* to find out if the piece that they find so satisfying is actually dishonest. Like the people in 1970s pews we mentioned, they don't want to be challenged; they want to be comforted in their pre-conceptions. Maybe among a million who received the e-mail less than a thousand will check. That's about the same ratio the Modern Experience gave when it taught that *only 1 in 10,000 read the press or pamphlets of their opposition to obtain a balanced view.*

"And, just to be sure, we have sent emails attacking *Snopes.com*, so that our followers have it 'in the mind' to distrust that reference. Some of the attack-*Snopes* emails are guilt-by-association attacks alleging a George Soros connection (which *Snopes* expressly denies)—and asserting Soros is an 'evil man.'

I HOPE GEORGE SOROS WILL GO TO HELL FOR WHAT HE DID TO THE JEWS DURING THE SECOND WORLD WAR IN BUDAPEST

"The World War II reference is to the fact that when the Nazis took over his native Hungary, Soros' Jewish father hid him in a convent school. Like any parent he wanted his child to survive, so told him to act as if he were a Christian—and he did. OK, the email is a bit over the top since Soros was only 14 when the war ended in Europe. But, if the email helps us get our followers to hate a liberal, tarring him as a Jew sharing the guilt of the Holocaust, it works for us.

"Sometimes our emails attack a *Snopes* report as a Big Lie even though it wasn't. One example was a *Snopes* piece debunking one of our emails about Obama nominating Kagan to the Supreme Court because Kagan defended Obama against claims he's not a citizen. (Our 'grain of truth' was that, as Solicitor General, Kagan had defended cases where the President was a defendant due to his office. But she did not defend him against 'birther' charges.) Our email was false, so it was better to attack *Snopes* for saying so (emphasizing the 'grain of truth' of her representation but without refuting the details of the *Snopes* analysis of the nature of the representation). How many schmucks would know the difference anyhow? Lord knows, though caught, we weren't going to apologize.

"Back to your question about what happens when our Big Lie is totally exposed: remember, a believer will want to rationalize. For example, if he has our world-view 'in the mind,' if it is one of his enthymemes, he might well say to himself, 'Well, Obama may not be going to give Fonda an award this time. But it's only because he hasn't gotten around to it, damn liberals!'

"Lastly, if by some means the believer is cornered and must admit that some unknown person of his persuasion lied to him in the email, he'll say, 'Well, the other side does it too. Damn all the politicians. I'll still vote for our side.' Of course, it isn't true that the other 'side' does it too, at least not yet—someday they may catch on and decide to 'fight fire with fire.' That will only make it easier for us.

"But the fact that a WES is seeing things as 'our side' versus 'their side' means we have already won him. At that point he is no longer listening to the reasons for or against a new idea that might cost us money; he is opposed to it without giving it a hearing as a matter of his committed membership in the community of our followers, 'our side.' The disjointed issue-by-issue approach of our adversaries, those who speak for all manner of WESs' interests which might affect our profits, is nothing like the monolithic power of the single-minded rhetoric of Our Enterprise, promulgated, as it is, across multi-media: talk radio, television news, print, and email."

One of the things he said caught my ear, so I asked, "You said something like 'the other side doesn't do it too.' Does the other side use emails?"

Doug said, "They do and we monitor that. They're pathetic. The average involved Democrat gets 4 or 5 emails a day, more in an election year, about what our followers get. The Dems' emails presume the recipient is already a believer and is thoroughly up to date on the issues. Their emails look the same day after day. They say something like: 'Are you as concerned about issue X as I am? Send money.' Or, 'Take my word for it; Thus and So has given $4.1 million to run slanderous ads against one of our candidates. Give $3.'

"In short, their emails seek money from the already persuaded. They do nothing to persuade the masses. They address an imminent election but none of them has a Sun Tzu-inspired aim of winning the battle before it is fought. Nobody who gets one is going to forward it to any friends. Their emails do nothing to arouse the recipients' emotions; there's no attempt to foment hatred; no offer of membership in *a strong resolute community.* Our emails seek voters to become our followers; theirs seek dollars for their coffers so they can fund some unidentified argument in the future. Our messages, though constant at the core, differ from day to day playing off *'what is on everyone's lips.'* Theirs? Well nothing gets old faster than repeated requests for money. To add to the ineptitude, remember the Modern Experience taught that a not-yet-committed person will consider an idea *especially if he gets it for nothing*? These guys are putting suggestions of future messages packaged with a request for money. And, as their recipients tire of the repeated begging, these geniuses are getting shrill.

"To put it bluntly, their email efforts are a joke. In the last presidential campaign cycle I only saw one that approached the core of what's going on. It argued that Sheldon Adelson could give $100 million to Romney's political campaign and, if Romney won and delivered on his tax promises, Adelson could be ahead by $2.3 billion."

I was nearing the farm and driving fairly slowly. Even so, while trying to get my head around a $2.3 billion tax break I banged into one of the unrepaired January potholes left by the under-funded Road Department of Dad's always tax-averse township. I thought of the cost of the wheel alignment I'd need when I got back home.

THE EMAIL COLLECTION

T HE DAY HAD CONTINUED TO warm up. I made the season's first pitcher of our family's standard summer beverage, double strength Crystal Light Lemonade, and set out some glasses and a plate of Mint Milanos from Dad's trove in the freezer. Then I waited for Dad and Doug to finish some phone calls and join me back on the patio.

When Dad came out he was carrying four thick ring notebooks. As he plopped them down on the stone wall that bordered the patio he said, "We told you we had a bunch more emails to show you. Well…." He made a two-handed, Vanna White-like gesture in the direction of the books to indicate they were now mine.

He went on, "We want you to take Tom's place. He was in the middle of taking over our persuasion operation. We wondered about the best way for you to see how we use all the theory about rhetoric—the use of prejudice, the formation of a unifying group, the variety of fallacies, the declarative semi-syllogisms, the *ad hominem* attacks, and all that. Finally we figured that this collection of emails was about as good a way as any. Many are short, punchy. But if you read through the mass of them each can work like the single frame in a reel of film. Pretty soon they'll blend together and you'll understand the whole picture.

I said, "Obviously I don't have time to go through them now. But I will take them and look them over. But let me ask something about them. On the drive back you mentioned a couple of the anti-Obama emails: one about Jane Fonda and another—shall we say 'adapted' from Lee Iacocca's book. Are there others as intentionally dishonest as those? Are they all that way?"

Dad answered, "Well, here's 'Lee Iacocca Speaks out on Obama' (by the way, we've just re-issued that saying Iacocca is 94 and has just written a book…as if the book were a new one). And here's 'Never Forget a Traitor.' They were two of our most effective.

"Not all of our emails are false and most that are contain a grain of truth that aids their credibility. Most of them scorn or mock Obama or some other leftie, or dismiss one of their ideas, or denigrate liberals in general and specific liberal leaders in particular.

"But just staying with the ones that you would say were intentionally dishonest, here are some that use the device of false attribution. This one praises the Prime Minister of Australia for an anti-Muslim rant she never gave. Here's one, 'I'm 76 and I'm Tired' that we invented and attributed to Bill Cosby (before his fall from grace) attacking welfare, Islam, tolerance for other cultures, and global warming. Here's another that attacks separation of church and state; at one point we attributed that one to Andy Rooney and, at another time, Paul Harvey. Here's one of the versions of a rant we wrote, 'A Very Important Read.' For that one we recited the credentials of a Professor at the Naval War College, David Kaiser, and then attributed the piece to him. (His web site denies he wrote it, but which of our followers is going to find that?) And while we're on the category of false attribution, we had long circulated a get-mad-at-Congress piece, but at one point we updated it to rope in some lefties by saying that Warren Buffett was asking recipients to send it to at least 20 others.

"One of our totally false ones told our followers that Obama is becoming dictatorial by an overwhelming and unprecedented use of large numbers of Executive Orders. (*Reader, I've attached this one as Appendix C. -Kate*) The email has the appearance of truth because it lists specific Orders by number and asserts what they contain. For example it starts by saying that Obama issued Executive Order 10990 allowing the government to take over all methods of transportation. Actually JFK issued executive Order 10990 in February of 1962 (before Obama was 1 year old) to reestablish something called the Federal Safety Council. The falsehoods run through the email's list until its last. It ends by blaming Obama for issuing Executive Order 11921 reportedly allowing government control of production, energy, wages, credit, and the flow of money. Actually Gerald Ford issued Executive Order 11921 in June 1976 (Obama wasn't out of high school) to adjust existing emergency procedures to align with organizational and functional changes in the federal government.

"The email's declaration that Obama's rate of order issuance far exceeds that of other presidents is just as false. It asserts that Obama has issued more than a thousand in 6 years; the truth, as of 12/23/13, was 166 in 4 years 11 months. The email's table says FDR issued 11 in 16 years; he actually issued over 3,400 in 12 years and 1 month of war and depression. All of that can be checked easily, Order by Order, at the National Archives' website,www.archives.gov. Our email even gains an air of authenticity by daring its readers to check it out, but how many of our target WESs are going to do that? No, the vast bulk of our followers are going to accept our facts and deepen their rage that their beloved democracy is being displaced by, as our email puts it, 'Emperor Obama.'

"Then there are the false-with-a-grain-of-truth emails. One of my favorites is the one where we showed a picture of a sign from a Muslim-owned store in Texas announcing it will be closed on September 11, 2009 in memory of the martyrdom of Imam Ali. (*Appendix D. -Kate*)

"As you'll see our email declares that 'Imam Ali flew one of the planes into the twin towers' referring, of course, to the September 11 event 8 years earlier. The truth is that Imam Ali was Muhammad's son-in-law who was murdered in 661 A.D. as part of the dispute over who had a right to succeed Muhammad as the religion's leader—the dispute that split Islam into Shi'ite and Sunni factions. The event is commemorated by many devout Muslims every year on the 21st day of Ramadan. In 2009 that day, which floats according to a lunar calendar, fell on a September

11. Who among our target audience is going to pick up that we're using a fallacy of verbal trickery we learned in Newport, by shifting the meaning of 'September 11' from an ordinary calendar date [in 2009] to code words for the horrors of 2001. And even among the few of our supporters who check, most will cheer us for scoring points for their side.

"Or take another one. We put out quite a stream of false emails describing what our packaging division named Obamacare. One theme we've used several times, and are still using, has to do with a tax provision in the law. Our emails called it 'sickening' and 'hidden.' Here's one from that campaign,

Subject: HOME SALES TAX
Yet another way **the middle class is getting screwed**!

When did your home become part of your health care? After 2012!   Your vote counts big time in 2012, make sure you and all your friends and family clean the white house. It is critical.
HOME SALES TAX
I thought you might find this interesting, -- maybe even SICKENING!   The National Association of Realtors is all over this and working to get it repealed, -- before it takes effect. But, I am very pleased we aren't the only ones who know about this ploy to steal billions from unsuspecting homeowners. How many realtors do you think will vote Democratic in 2012? Did you know that if you sell your house after 2012 you will pay a 3.8% sales tax on it? That's $3,800 on a $100,000 home, etc. When did this happen? It's in the health care bill, -- and it goes into effect in 2013. Why 2013? Could it be so that it doesn't come to light until after the 2012 elections? So, this is 'change you can believe in'? Under the new health care bill all real estate transactions will be subject to a 3.8% sales tax. **If you sell a $400,000 home, there will be a $15,200 tax. This bill is set to screw the retiring generation, -- who often downsize their homes.** Does this make your November, 2012 vote more important? Oh, you weren't aware that this was in the ObamaCare bill? Guess what; you aren't alone! There are more than a few members of Congress that weren't aware of it either. You can check this out for yourself at:
http://www.gop.gov/blog/10/04/08/obamacare-flatlines-obamacare-taxes-home
I hope you forward this to every single person in your address book.
VOTERS NEED TO KNOW.

"It's false. There is a grain of truth, of course. Obamacare does contain a new 3.8% tax. So, if a Wage Earning Schmuck looked up the law, he'd find the 3.8%, conclude we were correct, and agree that the 'others,' the damn 'liberals,' really were a threat, out to screw him when he retired. We figured that would ratchet up his prejudging hatred of liberals and make him more unwilling to engage with them in any discussion about the nation's future."

Doug took over the explanation. "Fact is the 3.8% tax provision wasn't hidden at all. It was put in the health care law because it makes our people's kind of income, investment income, subject to the same 3.8% tax which WES and his employer have been paying for Medicare. Before Obamacare our kind of people—those whose income came from investments, not wages—had Medicare benefits ever since Medicare started in 1966 but they never had to pay into that program.

"The 3.8% tax, the one our email intended to enrage the WESs about, is a tax on investment income; it is certainly not a tax that only applies to the capital gain on a home sale. It especially doesn't apply at all to the sale of a residence by 99% of wage earners."

I asked, "Why not?"

"Well first, the emails have the 3.8% tax on the sale price. The tax is only on the gain, not the price. And then it's only on the taxable gain."

"OK," I said, "but that can still reach a lot of modest income Wage Earners; they often have a gain when they sell their houses."

Doug went on, "True, but rarely taxable gain. When most WES families sell their homes the first $500,000 of gain is not taxable. Beyond that there is a $200,000 income requirement that kicks in under some formula. For the average WES's family to face the email's asserted $15,200 tax it would have to have a $900,000 gain on the sale. In short, the tax is not a problem many WESs, or as the email puts it 'middle class' or 'retirees,' have to pay.

"But from a grain of truth, a 3.8% tax aimed at making our class of wealthy folks pay for their Medicare just as WES pays for his, and with a little creativity, our emails told our community of ready-to-believe followers that Obama was out to screw WES homeowners like them.

"The damn liberals probably thought they were serving the WESs when they put this level-the-Medicare-playing-field provision in the law. But our emails gave the WESs yet another reason to feel that they were victims of a determined villainous enemy. Even if it didn't add to their hatred of liberals, at least it made them mad about a specific new tax that ran against our mission of getting more wealth for ourselves and our descendants. Thus prepared, our WESs would rejoice at efforts by our politicians to repeal the tax that did not really apply to WESs' homes but did apply to all our gains from the stock market and from our sale of companies, mineral rights, farms, and all manner of other assets.

Dad changed the subject by pointing with pride to another group of emails his persuasion troops had generated. "Here are some other emails that show how our operatives apply our techniques to advance our strategy when there's an event in the news that we can use. Remember, persuasion can be effective *all the more if the headlines plastically treat a topic which at the moment is in everyone's mouth.* We cooked up a 'disrespect Obama' email series regarding the day when a Muslim doctor went on a murderous hate-driven shooting rampage at Fort Hood.

"First, we had one telling a story in which 'W' acted with compassion for a soldier shot in the event and Obama didn't. (We invented everything we said about Obama in that one. But the moment gave an opportunity for an *ad hominem* attack and we took it; it was simply throwing more fuel on the constant fire of hate we roast him on.)

"In another we asserted that the murdering doctor was an Obama advisor—showing his name on a formal-looking list under the letterhead of a long-standing government medical advisory panel. The murderer wasn't an advisor on the panel; the list was of people who had attended one of the panel's seminars during the first year of the Obama presidency. We didn't mention that the murderer had signed in at the same seminar the previous year during the 'W' administration. Which of our followers is going to look that up?

"We fired off another Fort Hood shooting email designed to appeal to our gun rights constituency. It mocked the Obama administration for 'its policy' of not allowing people other than base security officers to carry loaded weapons on most military installations. The 'do not carry guns on base without permission except for base security and training' policy is a debatable one. You could agree with it after a respectful reasoning discussion or not. At least you'd have to admit that reasonable people could differ about it. It seems a reasonable way to lessen the chance that people in the military and their on-post families would have to worry about some distraught, military assault rifle-toting 19-year-olds going nuts. But hey, in our one-way emails we could mock (not analyze the effect of) the regulation to inspire the Wage Earning Schmucks to hate Obama, hate the damn liberals, and hate the stupidity of all government regulations. So we did.

"The truth, of course, is that the policy which our email described as 'Obama's' was adopted—and made immediately effective in a Department of Defense Directive—more than 16 years before Obama took office—during Bush the First's presidency. It remained in effect all during Clinton's and Bush the Second's. But Obama was in office at the time of the Fort Hood shooting, so *Post hoc* it must have been <u>his</u> policy.

"We got to recycle that one a few years later when there was another murderous military base rampage at the Washington Navy Yard, this time by a Buddhist, not a Muslim. That time our emails inferred it was Clinton who took guns away from the troops at the Navy Yard.

"This one started when one a newspaper on our side, *The Washington Times*, blamed the Navy Yard shooting on a 'Clinton-era military base gun ban.' Apparently the paper was referring to an Army Regulation implementing the already-in-effect Bush the First-era Department of Defense Directive. It had taken the Army a year to adopt that implementing Regulation, until 2 months after Clinton got in office. Well, the shooting happened after that, so, *post hoc*, Clinton must have been at fault. We morphed that news story into an email and voila!

In the one-way world of our email chains, what an <u>Army</u> Regulation had to do with the <u>Navy</u> Yard shooting was not something we had to explain.

"Still, the most common email themes feed on the frustration of the lower middle income white worker as his ability to provide for his family diminishes. His status is going to get worse, and our ability to enlist him to our cause will get better, as time goes on. In his lifetime the U.S. has gone from 50% of the world economy to 25%. When fully adjusted to a boundary-less world, it will be 6%. So far he has been able to soften the blow to his household's standard of living by sending his wife to work. But that is a cushion against decline that, once used, is no more. The same factor, the U. S.'s diminishing share of world production, makes it urgent for our class, the guys gaining the profit from domestic production, to make higher profits and pay lower taxes now so we can gather the wealth we need to invest overseas before domestic opportunity ends.

"Usually we try to convince the schmucks that the blame for their declining purchasing power belongs either on them because of bad public schooling (their public schools, good or bad, are a needless cost to us) or, most often, on the presumptively non-working, lazy, blacks. That's a theme we have used forever. Goldwater ranted about it. Reagan used anecdotes and inferred they were typical. And in his campaign Romney dismissed an imaginary 47% a (figure that had to include your friends, military and other government retirees, by the way) for sucking the life out of the system. We've sent out hundreds of emails making the same point."

I nearly laughed. "Come on. Most of the nation's poverty-easing effort is now in tax credits for the working poor. The 'welfare' you complain about, twenty years after reform, has a lot less effect on a Wage Earning white American's purchasing power than a small wobble of the interest rate on the federal debt. How do you get a minimum wage white laborer or store clerk to identify with you and your inherit-a-department-store buddies instead of with minimum wage black laborers or clerks? How do you sell him that an imaginary horde of shiftless blacks are a cause of his problem?"

Because it's 'in his mind,' my dear, 'in his mind.' Everybody doesn't know what you think they do. People 'know'—they have 'in the mind' and act on emotional responses to—what has been repeated to them over and over, especially if the message confirms their belief that they, as members of our community, are worthy and 'others' are not. They're inclined to believe the 'lazy parasite' line because it triggers a comfortable self-justifying 'us vs. them' emotion.

"Anyway, racism still sells. Not for everybody maybe, but for enough. We've generated hundreds of race-based emails selling the 'us vs. them' theme. Some are really good. I gave a bonus to the guy who came up with this one:

Subject: Aspirin Tax???

It appears that Obama is going to impose a 40% tax on aspirin, just because it's white and it works!!!

Thought you would like this one...

"Succinct and funny. The aspirin email is a great example: an *ad hominem* attack on Obama that hit the racist theme, the working white versus the non-working black theme, and our anti-tax theme—all in one sentence. You'll see a lot of racist stuff in the notebooks.

"You'll see that our racist stuff uses stress-release humor as much as possible. Our emails speak to our followers and the non-committed in a way that, psychologically, releases their hostility toward 'others,' a hostility which society has repressed as 'politically incorrect.' The release helps build a bond with others (including the sender) while giving the reader communal protection for his belief of his superiority over the target of the joke.

"We have another related series running, both in the email format and on Fox News. It plays on the "black man in the White House wasting your money' theme. We'd have one of our media outlets, preferably off-shore, invent some numbers and report extremely expensive presidential junkets—$400 million to India, $60—$100 million to Africa, 24 teleprompters and 6 doctors to London—that sort of thing. They make up exaggerated costs of presidential trips (including the wild guesses at the cost of secret service protection, related trade mission's transportation and lodging, and such). None of that can be confirmed or refuted due to the long-standing Secret Service policy of not revealing such costs. Then we'd have our domestic media outlets feign horror at the dollars "reportedly" involved. That way we suggest the invented 'facts' are true. When we put those 'facts' in emails we certainly make no effort to compare the cost of Obama's trips with those during our guys' administrations over 20 of the previous 28 years. That's just another application of the *very basic first axiom of all propagandist activity: to wit, the basically subjective and one-sided attitude it must take to every question it deals with.* Our message is, this is a liberal black man, damn him, and he's been wasting your money.

"And of course what we can do for a presidential official visit we can do to a fare thee well about a presidential vacation."

I instinctively made a slight, shuddering, shake of my head as I drew in a breath. Then I said, "All the while you are telling white wage earners to blame their families' economic decline on imagined shiftless blacks, it is really your 'Enterprise' and its members, not their black countrymen, who are bleeding them. You're the ones blocking minimum wage laws, attacking their unions, and exporting their jobs offshore for lower wages and less regulation."

Dad nodded. "Partly it's us. Can you blame us if our capital can move to other countries and their labor can't? And it's not just us. Don't underestimate the effect of the electronics revolution; with on-line bill paying there's less need for postal clerks; with word processors and copiers there are fewer secretaries per executive; bar codes and scanners have simplified warehousing, distribution, and supermarket checkouts; and, on-line ordering means fewer brick-and-mortar stores and less construction work to build them.

"And that's just the effect of integrated circuits replacing brains. The next wave is the communications revolution facilitated by those integrated circuits. When WES was growing up, the U.S. was the world's only large common market. For all sorts of reasons now gone he could earn relatively high wages in occupations needing little schooling. That'll soon be a thing of the past, and not just for laborers. Lawyers, radiologists, architects, accountants, and all manner of such folk are just beginning to feel the effect of their competitors having access to infinite web-based libraries full of the information they had to learn in school. And communications makes it easy for those competitors—in India, China, or wherever—to reach to American professionals' clients in the professionals' neighborhood. All labor is getting cheaper from increased supply; capital is not.

"We even have friendly religious leaders talking about a moral imperative to send jobs to lower wage ("more needy") parts of the world. What's important is that the more frustrated WES gets, the more he supports us and our 'old time values.' You're forgetting, this is war, Kate."

I wasn't forgetting but I said, "I know the old saying that 'the first casualty in war is truth.' But usually that means that at the beginning of a shooting war the press only reports what helps the national effort."

"Maybe so," my Dad replied, "but just because our war is a class war doesn't mean truth can't be the first casualty.

"But let me get back to your question. I'll give you another group of emails you'd probably call false. These usually involve something true, but out of context, which we use in emails with the message, 'Obama insults your values. Be enraged.'

"Many of these emails are particularly targeted at current and former members of the U.S. military. The aspect of our campaign addressing the military is particularly strategic and particularly intense. Identifying ourselves with the military cloaks us with some of its nobility. It also gives us entry into an already formed brotherhood inclined to unquestioning obedience. And we may need a military which believes we righteously stand for the all it is sworn to protect and defend. They will obey. Remember, it was the military that allowed Reagan to break the air traffic controllers' strike.

"There are hundreds enrage-the-military emails on all sorts of themes. Most imply that Obama disrespects them, *e.g.*:

"Still others imply that opposition to Obama and liberals is nigh-on-to an official Armed Forces imperative.

"Another of our campaigns quotes Obama saying, 'America is not a Christian nation'."

I perked up and said I had seen some of those, "What he said was America was not just a Christian nation but one which defends religious diversity. That's a statement to which Jefferson, Madison, and Thomas Paine, the authors of the *Virginia's Statute for Religious Freedom*, *Memorial and Remonstrance against Religious Assessments*, and *The Age of Reason,* would have shouted 'Amen! You understand!' I'd even put George Washington on the list for his 1790 letter to the Jewish community in Newport. Even the SBC, before 1979, would have given Obama an 'Amen!'"

"That may be. But within the schmucks' reinforcing and comforting community, among those white Christians who already have it 'in the mind' that their religions are under attack, this campaign remains useful; it also plays equally well on broadcast media and from friendly pulpits."

"Come on, Dad, why would any sane American think his religion is under attack?"

"A couple of reasons, Kate. For one thing, by his lights, it is. The Schmucks see our attacks on atheism and secularism as righteous evangelism. But he sees every assertion by one of "them" of an atheistic belief, or a secular scientific view of the cosmos, or sometimes even any tolerance of a non-Christian faith as an unrighteous attack on his religion. Such is the nature of discussion about religion. It's just another example of why such discussions were *verboten* in wardrooms.

"Second, our followers feel attacked because we repeatedly tell them they are. We mock every Christmas card that says 'Happy Holidays' or 'Seasons' Greetings' as 'political correctness' run amok and blame liberals for starting a war on Christmas. If a liberal had a chance to respond to our emails he might say that he was respecting people of a different culture because the parable of the Good Samaritan taught him to do so. But our emails are one-way, so he'll never get to tell that to our followers and, even if he did, they so disrespect him they wouldn't listen.

"There are other reasons the Schmucks sense their religion is under attack. We repeat the theme as often as possible. For example, we had the Catholic bishops denounce the liberals and Obamacare for requiring health insurance to cover birth control pills as an attack on the Catholic Church. Its own parishioners use birth control. But many of these same parishioners will take offense at Obamacare because their Bishops tell them it is an attack on Catholicism.

"Remember, our followers are people more given to accept than question, especially if the statement contains a tinge of threat to them from the "'other.' None of them is going to challenge us just because some health insurance company, seeking to post a better quarterly report, arbitrarily refused coverage to a relative who was seriously ill. He's going to believe what we have repeatedly told him: Obamacare is an attack on his religion.

"But enough about your question about 'dishonest' emails. In judging emails or other media used by Our Enterprise, you have to remember one of our cornerstone axioms from Newport, 'The advancement of the enterprise, not some nicety of factual accuracy, is the test of the value of any utterance.'

"As you read through these emails, Kate, you will find that we routinely exaggerate or even invent the actions of our opponents before inviting our followers to hate and despise those opponents. It's an electronic form of the straw man fallacy we heard about in Newport."

That prompted me to ask, "What about some of those other fallacies that persuade, ones you learned in your Newport sessions? Attacks on opposing speakers, *Ad hominem*? Reducing to the absurd? Guilt by association?"

"Well I've told you about the *ad hominem* (or should I say *ad feminem?*) attacks by our radio showmen aimed at Hillary Clinton and Nancy Pelosi. They have their parallels in our email operation which I'm sure you'll see when you go through the notebooks."

I saw many; here are a couple:

"Our *ad hominem,* ridiculing attacks against Obama are constant.

These attacks need have no connection to any policy or proposal; they need only foment or cement an 'us vs. them' response among our followers. Many attacking him use the age-old dismiss-him-as-subhuman technique often used in fomenting or applying prejudice:

BREAKING NEWS

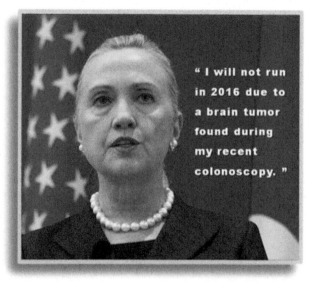

" I will not run in 2016 due to a brain tumor found during my recent colonoscopy. "

This old photo just brings a tear to my eye!

Rare photo of Ronald Reagan babysitting Barack Obama in early 1962

The skunk has replaced the eagle as the new symbol of the American Presidency. It is half black, half white, and everything it does, stinks.

"And, naturally, we link sneers at him with sneers at others:

Obama is thinking: "This proves I am not a Muslim—no Muslim would kiss a pig."
Pelosi, Miss Lube Rack, 1955, is thinking: "I've had so many face lifts, you are actually kissing my ass."

In other news... We all remember when KFC offered the "Hillary" meal, consisting of 2 small breasts and 2 large thighs. Now, KFC is offering the "Obama Cabinet Bucket". It consists of nothing but left wings and chicken shit.

As you review the emails you'll see that we employ guilt by association in attacks on people (for example, we impugn the Clintons by saying their daughter's father-in-law was a crook, and we ridicule Obama by things we say about his grandfather and showing nude photos of his mother). We do the same thing in attacks on ideas (often we spit on ideas by linking them with some damn liberal; our invention of the term 'Obamacare' is just one example). But we use 'guilt by association' imagery as well:

Fonda Speaks To Vietnam Veterans At Anti-War Rally

Actress And Anti-War Activist Jane Fonda Speaks to a crowd of Vietnam Veterans as Activist and former Vietnam Vet John Kerry (LEFT) listens and prepares to speak next concerning the war in Vietnam (AP Photo)

"Society's needs come before the individual's needs."
-Adolph Hitler

"We must stop thinking of the individual and start thinking about what is best for society."
- Hillary Clinton

"You'll also notice, most of our emails don't speak to issues; they simply dismiss liberals as not worth talking to—like Reagan's use of the old comedian's barb that they knew a lot, but what they knew was wrong. That works to unite our followers no matter the issue of the day.

"But you've been putting your question in terms of dishonesty, of lies. I would not call our emails lies. Lying involves a consideration of truth and a decision not to use it. In our operation the truth doesn't matter. What matters, as I keep telling you, is whether the statements advance the *mission* and *strategy*. We publish 'facts' with no regard for whether they are true or false. That's not the same as a lie, big or small. Maybe you saw that Princeton Professor's little book describing our approach to persuasion. He pretty much nailed it."

I winced; I had seen it. He was referring to Professor Harry Frankfurt's short hard cover essay with an attention-getting title: *On Bullshit.*

RANDOM QUESTIONS

I LOOKED FOR SOME WAY TO change the subject, so I started asking random questions that had occurred to me during the discussion.

Many of them had to do with the management of such an avowedly unorganized operation. My training and experience was entirely with hierarchical organizations, those with concerns of rank and file, spans-of-control, and defined measurable responsibilities at every level, and—above all—an identified leader. For the most part, Reader, those questions don't bear on the advice I am asking of you. So I'm leaving most of them out of these notes.

There were some questions you might find relevant though.

The first was that I asked my Dad how he would define this 'Main Stream Media' his people were always talking about. I told him I generally get who they mean—*The New York Times*, CBS, NBC, the *New Yorker*, *Rolling Stone*, and so forth. And I was sure they didn't mean Fox News, *The Washington Times*, or *Investor's Business Daily*. But what made an operation Main Stream Media? Being MSM seemed to me to be something like what Justice Stewart said about pornography, he couldn't define it but he knew it when he saw it.

I said I had tried to define it. At first I thought maybe it's that Main Stream Media start with facts and reach conclusions; the Enterprise's media seemed to start with a conclusion and gather or manufacture facts to fit. But I found that wasn't always fair. Sometimes the stories MSMs select do have a leftist lean to them, even if those stories are reported accurately.

Dad grinned and said, "You're catching on, Kate. Remember we are not a rigid rank-and-file organization. With a couple of exceptions our non-MSM media are Allies, not subordinates. We try to keep the definition of MSM fluid so we can turn our scorn on any of our media that drift toward the center (as the *Chicago Tribune* has in my lifetime). But, if you have to have a definition, the general idea is that MSMs report facts and give diverse opinions which presume that society's agreed objective is the common good. When our media report facts and give opinions they start with the idea that society's agreed and morally imperative (but unstated) objective is more wealth for the wealthy. Of course, that's our objective, not society's—at least not yet.

"Beyond that, MSM believes its purpose is to inform and sometimes persuade the public on issues. Our outlets know their main to purpose is to divide the public into "us" and "them." To that end they select stories, report facts, and, with embellishments invoking patriotism and Christianity, give opinions with much more emphasis on principles, much less emphasis on real world effect, all with a background drumbeat of judgment of persons—good guys versus bad guys."

Next I asked Dad if they ever used the "Right to Work" tactic of giving a "Who-could-be-against-that?" name to a law that misleads about the law's meaning.

He said, "Sure. All the time. Think the 'Patriot Act' (a law virtually repealing Constitutional protections in the name of anti-terrorism), 'No Child Left Behind' (a law designed to allow and fund flight from integrated classrooms thereby leaving a lot of children behind), 'The Class Action Fairness Act' (which a Democratic Congressman accurately called a 'payback to the tobacco industry, to the asbestos industry'), and 'The Defense of Marriage Act' (which doesn't defend any marriage but denies equal treatment to some). And we were able to get the WESs to support the massive reduction in the Estate Tax for the rich (remember, the estate tax didn't apply to WESs' families) simply by linking it with an emotion-laden word. We called it a "death tax" and, for a time, repealed it. A Wage Earning Schmuck rarely knows anything about the content of laws. If he approves of the title, he approves of the law and, if it sounds like a moral issue is involved, in the next election he'll reject any politician who opposed it and look favorably on the character, the *ethos,* of any who voted for it."

He went on, "Oh, and by the way, this 'name of the law' thing works in reverse too. The damn liberals tried to hang a happy title on their health care bill, the Affordable Care Act. It put some of WES's health care costs on us. So, our outlets drenched the law with venom calling it 'Obamacare.' Not only did we pull the teeth out of their happy title, but every Wage Earning Schmuck we had convinced to hate Obama instinctively hated the law for its title, no matter what benefits its text gave him." Unfortunately, for now, we've lost that battle.

Next I asked, "What about guilt by association other than showing a war hero dissenting from the war alongside a person you've styled as a traitor? I got the impression from the 'Roots' that it was a particularly useful device."

Dad responded emphatically. "It is. Absolutely it is. It's actually the core of much of what we do and it's particularly effective against the damn liberals while they are powerless to use it against us.

"Think about it; think about how change comes about. Take civil rights. I don't care if it's rights for blacks, women, gays, Muslims, or left-handed freckled-faced gorillas. Or consider opposition to wars like Viet Nam, or Iraq, or Afghanistan. Or even consider the 'Occupy Wall Street' crowd feebly protesting taxpayer-enabled multi-million dollar bonuses to guys who lost their firms billions and cost the home-owning wage-earning families much of their wealth. Change on issues like those is never immediate because the first awareness of a need for change is not apparent to everyone at the same time. So the first people to believe a change is necessary are on the fringe. Sometimes they're wrong and sometimes they're just early. Either way they can get impatient and make noise to get their view across. The next thing you know they're picketing, or burning draft cards or a flag, actions that offend even most people outside our comforting community.

"At that point we crank up our media to denounce the fringe—paint them with guilt (for their form of expression, we rarely take on the idea directly) and make them an object of hatred. Then we identify them as liberals and—here's where the guilt by association kicks in—associate that form of conduct with <u>all</u> liberals. In short we invoke "They're all the same." We insinuate that every person who favors unions, feels charitably toward the unemployed, or thinks gays should receive equal protection is as evil as Jane Fonda aiming anti-aircraft guns at American fliers. We shame the people away from the liberal end of the spectrum and draw the uncommitted toward our community, toward being followers. Later we associate any new ideas we oppose with those now-more-hated-than-ever liberals.

"Every movement, even those the mass of Americans will later adopt, has early supporters who give us an opportunity to bring more followers into the fold, rolling them up like wet snowflakes into a solid ball about to be an unthinking snowman's body.

"By the time the masses adopt the change, we've faded into the background. What do we care if the masses come to respect blacks, or conclude a war was wrong, or decide that the Constitutional idea of 'equal protection of the laws' mandates the legality of gay marriage? What do we care about the changes as society adjusts to post-pill realities? We're about wealth, remember? By the time the masses have decided the early activists on an issue were right, we're on to the next issue, scorning the next fringe activists, and rolling out the welcome mat for those threatened by change to find comfort within our self-proclaimed righteous community.

"Believe me, this stuff is powerful. When you think about it, a lot of our early success in pulling wage earning schmucks from the Roosevelt coalition was based on the average citizen's revulsion at the law-breaking sit-ins of the early-1960s and the tactics of the anti-war movement culminating outside the Democratic National Convention of 1968. We just had to sell the idea that Democrats, liberals, do that sort of thing; we don't."

"Come on Dad," I objected, "your authoritarian reactionaries have their own lunatic fringe: white supremacists, the KKK, The Aryan Nation, James Earl Ray, David Koresh, Timothy McVeigh, Terry Nichols, and on and on. And they don't burn flags to make their points; their ideas drive them to kill people."

"Sure, but the open-minded main stream media is not going to assert that all authoritarian reactionaries, much less all "conservatives," are like that. They have no reason to associate the guilt of those folks with our followers and then cry, as we do, 'America! Love it or leave it!' While they focus on reporting facts, our outlets focus on dividing people. We make sweeping scornful associations and, as night follows day, the good people who are offended by the other guys' fringe become our followers."

I paused, cleared my throat, and pointedly turned toward Doug to ask a money question. "Back when you were discussing paying law professors who would teach your doctrines, you mentioned something about having to do the same with economics professors. What was that all about?"

"Remember the old axiom holds that politicians are nothing more than the instruments of dead economists? When we started, the prevailing economic view was based on the writings of John Maynard Keynes. Keynes essentially says that when the private sector is not buying enough to keep a decent level of employment, government should step in and create demand. Then jobs will follow; individual purchasing power will return, and things will turn for the better. That's a very wage-earner-favoring view.

"We needed economics professors to preach (that is to figure out, write about, and teach) a wealth-centered economic theory. What they came up with was a defense of the Coolidge/Hoover view of the world which liberals call trickle-down economics. Our professors put a new coat of paint on it and called it 'supply side economics.

"We also needed to disparage any government regulation that could add costs to our companies' production. Even Friedman (who railed against minimum wage laws, redistributive tax policies, public housing, public education, public national parks, and so) acknowledged some government role in limiting some side effects of our activities—stream pollution for example—effects he called 'neighborhood effects.' Nonetheless he disparaged regulation by decrying regulation's own 'neighborhood effect' of loss of freedom and government's inherent ineptitude.

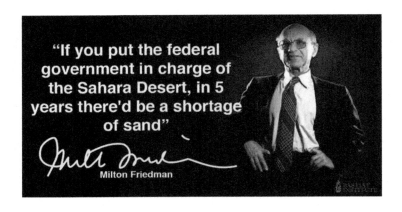

"If you put the federal government in charge of the Sahara Desert, in 5 years there'd be a shortage of sand"

Milton Friedman

"Hogwash, but it charms our followers.

"So, our supply side professors preached that if you let companies produce for lower costs (less regulation, lower wages at home or overseas, whatever) things will be hunky-dory because goods will be cheaper. They could generate lots of data and reams of graphs to support that view.

"Everyone knows that lower costs can mean cheaper goods, by itself an economically good thing. But if cheap goods come from lower wages, higher unemployment, and no values-based regulations (such as those addressing occupational health, pension protection, the environment, etc.), those lower costs may not 'promote the general welfare.' For people who don't need the dignity provided by a job, our kind of people, the 'supply side' idea works. But even economically, it can leave the much larger segment of society with neither a job nor money to spend. For such people ever cheaper goods will not improve their lives when they can no longer afford those goods.

"We showered our professors with prizes and our money. They got academic glory and we gained academic cover for our more-wealth-for-the-wealthy politics. One 501(c)(4) even bought the rights to screen appointments for economics professors at the state university of one of our largest states—and the right to monitor the professors' continuing supply-side orthodoxy."

"Our effort with professors was necessary to create the color of a dispute too complicated for a WES to understand. Then we characterized Keynesian economics as the 'soft cousin of Communism.' The WESs who had our righteousness 'in the mind' needed no more."

Our conversation left those points and we went back and forth on other ideas as they popped into my head. Dad and Doug were also on a roll about things popping into their heads. They swapped war stories ("class war" stories, that is) as my questions reminded them of forgotten battles in their 50-year campaign.

They rambled about the success of gerrymandering in the districts for the House of Representatives. The laughed about how, all the while they were deriding affirmative action, they used it (and blacks' demands for districts which would elect black Congressmen) to their advantage. In large, partially urban states, every time their redistricters drew lines to create two virtually 100% black (Democratic) districts they could draw other lines to create five districts with an insurmountable 60/40 Republican majority. They talked about how they were amazed how precisely they could carve up a state with government-provided tract-by-tract census data on race and an ordinary laptop. In such states no amount of open debate of the issues was going to change the outcome of an election. In 2012 the Democrats won the national popular election for House seats by 1.4 million votes but the Republicans won an overwhelming and well-disciplined 34 seat majority. Gingrich crowed the result was a mandate for their side. By implementing the elections-not-voters tactics Paul had suggested, the Enterprise had lost the vote but won the election!

Doug went on about how that Congressional majority had the power to bring the world economy to its knees. Then both of them winced as they spoke of how that power almost did. That happened when their 'don't think, just obey' politicians in the House threatened to block a rise in the debt ceiling if they didn't get repeal of Obamacare. There would have been default on the American Treasury bonds, the world-wide anchor of financial value if their 501(c)(3)s hadn't stopped the madness.

They spoke of their on-going efforts to carry gerrymandering further by having specific states shift their electoral college rules from a winner-take-all format to a congressional district format (e.g., in 2012, Pennsylvania's 20 votes went to Obama; under a congressional district format he would have lost something like 13-7 even though he would have won the state's popular vote by about a million).

They joked "Voter fraud has to be stopped, don'ja know." They couldn't point to any examples of voter fraud, but the idea that it might exist seemed reason enough to purge voter registration books of all black men whose names match names on the lists of vote-ineligible felons (Florida, 2004). It seems the noble "principle" of preventing election fraud by disenfranchising even made its way into the 2012 National Republican Platform by an amendment pushed through at the Platform Committee—over a very timid expression of an "effects" worry by the only black delegate Dad saw in the committee room.

They lamented that for the longest time the Enterprise' cleverest plans to suppress black voters in the South were blocked by the need for prior federal approval of any changes under the Voting Rights Act of 1965. Damn LBJ. But now, after the 2013 decision by their Supreme Court in Shelby County v. Holder, that obstacle was declared unconstitutional as discriminating against the South. All bets were off unless Congress could re-adopt the restriction and apply it to all states, but no way would the Enterprise going to allow such a bill to get out of Committee.

Doug and Dad could have rambled on about these successes until the cows came home. But there were more important questions I wanted to get to.

RESULTS AND TAXES

S O FAR THE DISCUSSION HAD mainly been about objectives and means—specific plans and devices of persuasion to get votes for their sworn-to-obey politicians. But we hadn't yet discussed how this all played out in their class warfare.

So I asked, "This is all impressive; but I'd like to know, has it been worth it? I mean, has it worked for serving your mission—increasing your wealth and the wealth of your descendants?"

Dad answered, "Wonderfully. The wealth of the guys in our set has increased so dramatically compared to the guy in the middle that even the dolts in Main Stream Media are noticing. There are books like Tim Noah's *The Great Divergence*. But those sources mainly focus on growing <u>income</u> inequality—they talk a lot about the top 1%. Not many of them focus on the growing <u>wealth</u> inequality."

"OK. You're getting the votes and you're getting richer. But are those two facts connected? How does having the votes translate into your personal advantage?"

"Well, mainly through changes in taxes."

I had been wondering about this since I read the Dad's history of the Enterprise when it spoke of taxation items as possible future *engagements*. I knew Doug to be the Enterprise's financial guy so, recalling my study of Federalist #10, I asked him, "It seems to me that every dollar the wealthy class saves is a dollar out of the pockets of the WESs. Am I right? If I recall, Madison said something like, 'no legislative act gives greater opportunity for predominant parties to trample on the rules of justice; every shilling overburdened on another is a shilling saved to their own pockets.'"

Doug seemed surprised that, as he put it, "My boy Madison" had seen through their idea more than 175 years before they thought of it. Nevertheless he rattled off the changes they had won for themselves on tax rates through 2013: they dropped the highest ordinary income rate from 91% to 36%; capital gains from 25% to 15%; dividends from 91% to 15%; interest income from 91% to 36%. (There has been a slight increase in rates for the rich on their upcoming 2014 returns, Doug said. But he viewed those changes as temporary, to be reversed when their guys got back in complete control in 2016.)

I asked whether there were similar changes for the average wage earning guy. Doug cited some changes in marginal rates. I said that it didn't sound like the middle guy had benefitted by the ballyhooed tax cuts their votes had enabled.

Doug agreed and said the bite on the middle guy wasn't just rates. Those folks had lost some of important deductions. "We've eliminated deductions for all interest payments except for his mortgage, for example. Even on mortgage payments the average guy used to be able to deduct interest on a refinancing up to his original purchase price of his home. Now he can only deduct re-fi interest up to the remaining balance of his original mortgage. And he used to be able to deduct all his state taxes; now he generally can't deduct what he paid in sales tax.

"Beyond that, over a certain limit of income even his still-allowable deductions get reduced. Above a family income of about $150,000 or so he loses deductions because 'he's making too much.' That's the Alternative Minimum Tax, the AMT. For you, a single mom, it starts somewhere, if I recall, around $110,000 or $115,000."

I interrupted. "Well, isn't the idea of the AMT to plug loopholes for the wealthy? I mean, the alternative minimum tax—it applies to the wealthy folks too, doesn't it?"

"Do you just read the headlines? The devil is in the details, Kate. The AMT is aimed at the middle class, the upper income Wage Earners. It doesn't affect the truly wealthy in any significant way. Generally we don't have mortgages; we own debt-free inherited property. Our purchases of assets are often through private corporations so any interest payments are still deductible. As to sales tax, our annual personal purchases are a smaller share of our income than are the personal purchases of the WESs. Their trips to the barber and the dentist cost the same as ours and their trips to the supermarket and dry cleaners only cost a little less. With the AMT, the upper end wage earner loses his property tax deduction but the truly wealthy guy doesn't lose his special treatment on dividends, capital gains, or municipal bond interest. Think about it, the AMT taxes the higher income wage earner on money he doesn't have (because he paid it to his mortgage lender or to the local government in real estate taxes), but AMT refuses to tax a truly wealthy man on extra money he does have (because of his special breaks in the federal tax code for capital gains and dividends)."

Enough already! All this—rates, deductions eliminated, the AMT—was becoming just a blur of numbers and concepts in my head.

I decided to ask my question a different way. I said, "Please stop. All these rates for this and rates for that, deductions eliminated, special breaks retained for the wealthy: I'm missing the big picture, sometime you're talking about marginal rates, some fixed rates, some breaks lost apply to the wage income of the average guy and benefits gained apply almost exclusively apply to your passive income set. What about the effective rates? Has the effective rate for the really rich gone down? And has the effective rate for the average guy gone down as well? What's the effect on your class warfare?"

Dad answered, "There's my Kate again, going right to the bottom line. I knew that you'd ask that and wouldn't take an answer of generalities. So I looked it up on the IRS website about Statistics on Income. Remember that in my written history I said that in 1963 the highest group, the taxpayers in the top category (those who reported income over

$1,000,000) actually paid—their effective rate—a little over 46%? Well, in the most recent available Statistics on Income, those for 2011, the richest category (the taxpayers who made over $10,000,000) paid an average of about 24.5%. That's a 47% cut in their effective rate. That's right; our guys' tax rate has been cut almost in half. Figuring the average taxpayer as best I could from the IRS's tables, in 1963 the median taxpayer paid just under 9.3%; in 2011 he paid just over 12.1%, a 30% increase. Simply put, we're winning."

Doug added, "And our victory over the middle guy is not just because of more taxes for him. It's not always that a dollar less tax for us is a dollar more tax for him. It could be a dollar less value to them in some other way. Sometimes, and I mean rarely, the government chooses to spend a dollar less for every dollar less of tax we pay. That's a dollar less for some program to help the WESs or serve one of their values. But usually the government doesn't spend less; it just prints more money. That's wealth out of the WESs' pockets through inflation."

"But isn't it also wealth out of your pockets?"

"No, or at least not so much. Remember, there's a difference between current income and wealth. An increase of inflation, measured by the Consumer Price Index, has a lot more effect on the WESs than on us. That's because they spend a much higher percentage of their income on consumer goods. So a drop in the current buying power of their current wages hits them harder. The guys who really get hurt with inflation are the paycheck-to-paycheck families and the retirees. When the government prints more money, it's the purchasing power of their income and savings that falls.

"Wealth barely feels the hit. With inflation it's the value of money that goes down; but the true value of other forms of capital generally stays the same. For other assets, it's only the price in dollars that changes, and it goes up. If you own a factory producing a valuable product for the world market, with inflation you'd still own a factory producing a valuable product for the world market. Sure there could be some interim adjustments. But ultimately they reach a new balance. Through it all, you'd own a factory that had fairly constant true value.

I scanned my notes from Dad's history and decided that we had covered what I wanted to ask about the kind of taxes paid in April. So I asked Doug, "In Dad's history he also mentioned estate taxes. How have you done with them in terms of your mission?"

"Well remember, our mission is more wealth for ourselves and our descendants. Judged by that measure, estate tax rates are really the biggest game in town.

"When we started in 1963, estates were taxed, but only above an exempted amount. Enough was exempt so as not to disrupt a middle-class family's economics. But, exempted amount aside, our kind of wealth was being taxed at 77%. So offspring of wealthy parents, when they inherited an estate, only received 23% of it after tax. Gradually, over the decades when our guys were in power they cut the tax and thereby raised the percentage of the estates the offspring received: during the Ford Administration we raised their cut to 30%; in Reagan's we raised it to 45%.

"'W' did even more for us. He phased in lower taxes and higher exemptions so that, by 2010, the estate tax was eliminated. By 2010 our guys were no longer in control; Obama was in. There was a heated battle over restoring the estate tax but, since we won the mid-term election in 2010, we came out all right. As it stands now, in 2014, the exemption is $5,340,000 and the tax rate is 40%; that is, the offspring keep 60%. So, even ignoring the jump of the exempt amount from insignificant to over $5,000,000, during our participation in class warfare the share of an estate going to the children of the wealthy has gone up from 23% to 60%, a 261% increase in money received. For WES's kids, over that time, nothing changed.

"Our success of estate taxation will reach more than just the children and the grandchildren. Consider what happened to an estate passing down to succeeding generations under 1963 rates. It would be taxed once going to the children, the second time going to the grandchildren, and a third time going to the great-grandchildren. Those great-grandchildren would only get 1.2% of the original estate.

"But the politicians we put in office changed all that. Under 2014 rates those great-grandchildren, the third inheritors, would get 21.6% of the original estate. And, under 2014 rates the <u>eighth</u> generation would get more than the 1.2% that went to the third generation in 1963. If you figure

25 years between estates it meant that a 2014 grandpa will be remembered fondly by the generation celebrating the New Year in 2200.

Doug continued. "It's even getting far better for us. We started a campaign against the Rule against Perpetuities our young lawyers told us about, and we're winning. It's a state issue, and in some states we have won. On a billion dollar estate (and, according to Forbes, at least 400 Americans are worth over a billion) every generation from the first onward would have the benefit of (that is, be able to have the income from) $650 million. The money goes in a trust, and because in those states there is no Perpetuities Rule, the trust can go on forever, there's no taxable event (like a death) as each new generation comes to the trough."

I asked, "How did you pull that off?"

"Simple." Doug said, "The Rule is a common law creation so legislation can change it. We let our indebted politicians at the state level know we want it repealed. We get our bankers to give our legislators cover. They give committee testimony that repeal will be good for the state as it will allow it to get a bigger percentage of the nation's trust business. That even sounds good to most Main Stream Media statehouse beat reporters. Other legislators either don't care or have a general feeling from their law school days that the rule is a useless pain in the 'butt-tocks.' In short, no one speaks for retaining the old Rule."

"But Doug, that sounds like you're saying that you've pulled that off in state after state. Does that tactic work in all states?"

"It doesn't have to. People from any state can put their money in a trust in a state where it has worked. But, yes, when an idea like that works in one state we export it to other states via the American Legislative Exchange Council, ALEC."

I interrupted to ask, "Who pays for ALEC?"

Doug answered and went on. "To some degree WESs pay for it; ALEC is a 501(c)(3) and in many states our politicians in the legislature vote to have state tax dollars pay a state's ALEC dues.

"Probably none of the WESs has any idea how drastically the Rule's repeal will affect wealth distribution in their grandchildren's generation.

Dad chuckled as he weighed in, "Let some Wage Earning Schmuck turn to his church for promise of post-mortal significance. We've got politicians insuring we'll have a welcome effect on our children's children for frickin' ever."

I didn't rise to the bait, but turned back to Doug and said, "You're telling me that while your politicians keep talking about the need to lower taxes, they've lowered your ordinary income tax bill, your capital gain tax bill, your dividend tax bill, and your estate tax bill—and the WESs have gotten, essentially, nothing."

"Yup."

"How do you get away with it?"

My Dad, Our Enterprise's persuasion director, took over, "That's what we've been telling you, Kate; that's what Our Enterprise does. We do it, essentially, by persuading a large passionate segment of the WESs to hate those who speak for their pocketbook interests. Instead we persuade them to love us for our apparent concern for their religions, their patriotism, and our assertion that we are working toward a more prosperous America. We persuade them to hate (and not listen to) liberals as wrong, stupid, unpatriotic, irreligious, and a lower despicable life form—a "them." Then we get our followers to elect our politicians. In 1963 Americans' idea was that wealth in any generation should be a reward for contribution to that generation or one shortly before it. Since then we've had our radio, TV, and think-tank lackeys convince the American wage earning schmucks that 'It's our money damn it, keep your hands off.'"

I asked, "Don't the wage earners fight the way you're taking money out of their pockets and opportunity out of their kids' future just to make you richer?"

"Not really. They don't understand the magnitude of it. And maybe, at some level, they don't begrudge us lower taxes. Hell, they probably dream that someday they'll be rich; or maybe their kids will be."

I huffed, "That's not likely. With fewer good factory jobs, your attacks on their tax-supported schools, and the growing wealth disparity, this country has fallen way down the ranks of countries where a climb from poverty to wealth is possible. I mean the extraordinary few—guys like Steve Jobs, Warren Buffet, Bill Gates, Sam Zell, some super athletes, and the CEOs you've anointed as long as they have their companies toe your line—can rise. But the common man's ability to work his way up the ladder from the farm, mine, or checkout counter to a lifetime factory job, to foreman, etc., and to educate his children for a better station, that ability is fading away. American companies and capital are closing their factories here and producing goods with cheaper labor in other countries."

Dad came back at me, "Well the schmucks sense that, but they don't really understand the link between the big picture and their votes. They have a patriotic belief in the America of their dreams—'The Land of Opportunity.' As a 2009 Pew research report said, the schmucks believe that America ranks first in opportunity for upward mobility. Of course you're right about the reality, according to Chicago Fed studies, the U. S. ranks behind at least 9 other countries, just in Europe. All the while WES keeps hearing about us as the Party that understands business and is seeking a More Prosperous America. In a way he's like the frog in the pot. As long as you apply the heat under the pot slowly he'll keep thinking it's tolerable until he can't think anymore."

I blinked, gathered myself, and turned to Doug, and changed the subject. "Let's leave that. Doug, what about tariffs? Dad's writings about the start of your enterprise said they were an impediment to your companies moving jobs offshore for cheaper wages and more profit."

Doug, apparently glad to have my attention again, put down his glass and said, "The big picture is that tariffs as a percentage of the value of goods imported has gone from about 7.3% of imported value in 1963 to about 1.3% today. Reagan and Bush the First essentially did away with wage/job protectionism."

"What about Social Security?"

"That's still a bother. It still doesn't apply to our kinds of income. But the Social Security Trust Fund holds federal government obligations that will have to be redeemed out of general tax revenue. And you have to figure that the eventual shortfall of the Trust Fund will have to be paid with general tax revenue as well.

"We've been at this problem for a long time. Reagan used to tell a charming little story about how a WES could buy a voluntary retirement insurance policy for less than he paid Social Security. The story inferred that government inefficiency was the problem and we'd be better off with a voluntary program. It was a simple answer using a simple story but it had logical holes you could drive a truck through. Our boy WES probably didn't see the holes, but he sensed it was a bad idea for him.

"When Reagan got in office one of the first things he tried to do was seriously cut the benefits. He lost 96-0 in the Senate. Unanimously, for God's sake! Of course that was long before 1994, when we went to strong party discipline. We won't lose like that again. To date, we haven't been able to dent social security. But we haven't stopped trying and among the WESs we're getting more and more loyal-follower-induced adherence to our views all the time. When, after some inevitable scandal or just a longing for change for change's sake, they put our guys in complete control, we'll be able to pull it off."

Since we had returned from lunch our discussion had been going on for a little over two hours. I suggested a break and said that, when we reconvened, I intended to ask about whether Our Enterprise had success in areas other than taxes.

41

RESULTS OTHER
THAN TAXES

T HE DAY WAS COOLING AND a breeze was coming up. During the break Dad had put a kettle on. He set out tea bags, mugs, sugar, honey, lemon, and cream on the granite counter that separated the kitchen from the great room. As we gathered again we each made up a mug to our taste and brought it into the den. Then, after Dad turned the TV on just long enough to check some scores, we went back to meeting mode.

Doug asked me if there were any particular engagements of Our Enterprise that I had intended to ask about.

"Sure. Dad's 'Roots' mentioned payment for use of federal lands and payments for extracting assets from federal property. I took it that oil was representative and the biggest item. I figured he was saying that, with your indebted politicians in office, the government would sell you the in-ground oil belonging to 'We the people' cheaper than you could get it elsewhere."

Doug cleared his throat, made a nervous pause, and said, "That's about it. But even though that's exactly what's happening, it's not simple."

"What's not simple? 'We the people' own it. 'We the people' sell it to your oil companies. There's a price."

Doug closed his eyes, then glanced over at Dad as if to ask permission to tell me there was no Santa Claus. When he looked back at me he said, "Hunh! I can tell you've never been in the business of contracting with the government, Kate. Let me walk you through it. To start, the price is a percentage of something and the something is the 'value of production.' I can tell you there are loopholes in that. But let's just stick with the part of the price that is the percentage.

"Yes, that percentage is low and our indebted politicians were the ones who lowered it. For decades the rate was an already low 25%. Then, just before we went looking for funds from the oil patch for the 1988 election, the Reagan administration lowered the rate to a flat 12.5%, It has been 12.5% ever since."

"How does that compare to what other countries sell their oil for?"

"Again, a complete answer is not simple, but the short answer is that it's cheap, real cheap. The Government Accounting Office said that the 'government take' in the Gulf of Mexico ranked 93rd among 104 oil and gas fiscal systems evaluated."

"You said the answer is not simple. That seems simple enough."

"Only seems so, Kate. The concept of 'government take' is a gimmick the guys in the oil patch like to use. They used it to provide the data to the GAO for that report. It includes taxes that every other corporation pays. From the companies' accounting point of view that way of looking at the "price" of the oil is mixing two expense items, 'cost of goods sold' and 'taxes.' If you were to ask a dressmaker what she's paying for her fabric she wouldn't add in her income tax.

"But even if you buy the gimmick word 'take,' compare the U.S.'s 'take' of even 41% to Norway's North Sea oil 'take' of 84%. You don't see Norwegians fretting about impending bankruptcy of their Social Security program. Egypt, Indonesia, Malaysia, and Columbia 'take' more than that. Iran at 93% and Venezuela at 95% topped the list. And make no mistake; oil companies are still able to make money buying their oil from those guys.

"But, Kate, don't get too focused on the sale of oil from federal territory.

"The more important oil-company-favoring arrangement has to do with oil on private lands. The states, not the feds, control that oil. The states don't usually claim to own it the way, say, New Jersey owns the groundwater beneath your dad's farm. So the states don't sell the oil although most do charge a severance tax. Except for Alaska those taxes are even lower, a lot lower, than the cut the feds take—they average about 5%. Even then they have lots of exceptions. For example, Texas' 4.5% rate drops to 2.25% if the operator uses an "enhanced extraction method" and North Dakota's law is nominally 6.5% but it is full of exemptions such as no tax for the first 18 months for this, or none of the first 10 years for that, or a lower rate if it's from the Bakken formation, etc., etc.

"In short, the states' rates start low and have more loopholes than Chantilly lace. Overwhelmingly, the state severance tax laws read like they'd been written in rooms full of people who could profit from lower taxes—with nobody representing John Q. Public present.

I said, "That's always struck me as a 'pump America first' strategy, not very good in the long term."

Dad smiled. "It's good for us. But not as good as it could be. Consistent with the idea that we need a strategic petroleum reserve, the feds do impose a rough limit on pumping by prohibiting export of domestic oil."

"Point taken," I said. "Let's shift again, this time to any ways you have benefitted by your control of the Court."

"You mean besides electing 'W'?"

"Well, you've already mentioned that".

"That's true. Well, the Court has advanced our cause in more ways than we anticipated and more ways than I have time to tell—at least if we're going to finish today. Take some examples.

"In *Matsushita*, the courts took a 'see no evil, hear no evil' hands-off approach to international trade regulation and they gave judges a lot more power to keep cases away from juries.

"The Court also took the right to a jury trial away from the little guy in securities fraud cases in the *Byrd* line of cases which essentially mandated arbitration. That, of course, cut off the development of the law of securities fraud through the common law process.

"In *Massachusetts v. EPA* the Court came close to establishing that an administration's regulatory agencies could render a Congressional law meaningless by exercising 'discretion' not to decide a case brought under the law. We'll win that soon, and with it more power for our side

"Then, when the law putting 'under God' in the Pledge of Allegiance reached the Court in a case (*Newdow*) brought by a father of a schoolchild, our Justices let the law stand; they threw the case out because there had been a divorce and he was not the custodial parent, though he still had parental rights and obligations. He lacked 'standing' don'cha know. Judicial procedure over Constitutional rights to serve our base— certainly not the approach the *Roe v. Wade* court took.

"That was just one of several cases endorsing our follower-unifying 'religious morality' propaganda. We've got two more coming up before the end of the Court's year, *McCullen v. Coakley* and *Burwell v. Hobby Lobby Stores, Inc.* My sources at the Court tell me we'll like the way they come out.

"Let me give a totally different example. As you know, one of our pet projects is school vouchers. Vouchers serve two of our constituencies. They put money into the coffers of religions with parochial schools. They also give parents help with a way to avoid sending their kids to desegregated schools."

I thought he was over-stating the racial effect of vouchers so I asked, "Come on, don't they give black parents the same opportunity to send their kids to parochial schools?"

"That may be true, at least as to skin color, and even then not always. And sure, nowadays even most bigots will tolerate, even patronize, some upper class blacks. But those schools need not accept, and can be quick to expel or flunk out, a black kid who doesn't meet their subjective standards. The result is still segregation; parents who don't want their kids to go to a school where they'd have to socialize with 'them' have the government vouchers paying for their 'white flight.'

"Anyway, in 2002, in the *Zelman* case, the Court approved school vouchers. Then, in 2011, in the *Hibbs* case, it did that one better. It approved a law from Arizona that allowed parents to reduce their state taxes, dollar-for-dollar (up to a limit) for tuition to parochial schools. That's better than vouchers! It decreases money available for other WES-favoring programs, just like vouchers. But it is little help to low income families who have little or no tax bill to apply the credit against. It's not segregation purely by race, but by income. The children of the well-employed are separated from the children of the lowest class. Talk about winning a battle in class warfare! It's economic segregation, a big step toward creating a permanent lowest class. And yet, our followers in that class see us as heroes for helping their church schools. Yet affluent kids don't ever have to sit in a class with 'one of them.' Ya' gotta love it!"

I still had some doubt that Our Enterprise's control of the courts was that secure. So I said, "Well, what about the fact that your side lost the Obamacare case?"

Dad laughed at that. "Jeez, you really do only read the headlines. And if <u>you</u> only read the headlines, just think how much less a Wage Earning Schmuck reads. The decision to uphold the law was 5-4, but only as a tax. Roberts' opinion was a brilliant win for us. He gave us a 5-4 majority on all the non-tax issues. And it left the Obamacare issue open for us to use in the next election.

"His opinion establishes a view of states' rights (state sovereignty, the term he used right out of the Constitution of the Confederate States of America), a view which was supposed to be buried by the Civil War. Roberts' opinion is a pure Rehnquist view that neither the Civil War nor anything else about the present or the last 225 years matters in understanding the Constitution. Remember? 'Original Intent.'

"But the Court gave us our biggest win came when it neutered bi-partisan congressional action (McCain/Feingold) to limit the power of our wealth to influence elections. That was *Citizens United*. The opinion took the idea of free corporate commercial speech (advertising and such) and expanded it to give corporations 'free speech' rights to fund elections and overwhelm the voices of human citizenry. With *Citizens United*, we, the wealthy of our time, had gained at least as much control of the ruling princes of our time as the wealthy of Renaissance Italy had over the princes of theirs. "

"*Citizens United* converted the American idea of democracy from one where each individual has equal political power to one where each discretionary dollar has equal power. The power of each schmuck shrinks to the power of the discretionary side of his purse. It is becoming the

America we designed."

Dad was near beaming he was so proud.

I was flabbergasted; outraged, actually. But I knew from the exchange about abortion on the drive to lunch that I had to keep a lid on my thoughts if there was to be any hope of a future civil relationship. If I hadn't forced myself to silence I'd have probably gone steely-eyed, set-jawed, and commandingly quiet as I said something like, "Your America is certainly not the one I've been sworn to protect and defend for more than half my life."

For most of those years I've been teaching some core ideas of that America: it was formed to serve the public good and to control the main enemy of public good, private interest; the principal task of its government was the regulation of competing interests; its biggest internal threat to its survival has always been that small groups that would seek to advance "unequal distribution of property" or to pursue "their zeal over different opinions about religion."

I taught Madison's idea that such groups were "the source of mortal diseases under which popular governments have everywhere perished." I'd studied the history that had convinced Madison that in the democracies of the past, men "of sinister design," by success with "the vicious arts by which elections are too often carried" had first obtained the vote of the common man and then overcome the common man's interests.

Now, here I was, face to face with two men of such design. What confounded my instinct to aggression was that one of them was my father.

I searched for a way to change the topic or end the discussion. Maybe seeing my stress, Dad raised both hands and said, "But enough of all these details. Kate, we'd like to take you to a good dinner and outline our specific proposal. Bernards Inn or that new steakhouse in Morristown? Your pick."

I said that I knew the Bernards Inn and would be comfortable there, so it was my pick. I also said I'd like some time to make some phone calls—check in with Joy in Georgia and call Tom's widow, Diane, and see how she was getting on, that sort of thing—and freshen up and change. I'd need a bit more than an hour. Dad said that 'sounds like a plan;' he'd make reservations for a time about two hours or so out.

WHERE DO I FIT IN?

W E ARRIVED AT THE INN a bit before our reservation time, ordered a round of drinks from the bar, and settled into the armchairs in front of the fireplace in the hotel's lobby. Dad had his usual bourbon, Doug a single malt scotch, while I had a merlot. We made small talk—my promotion, Doug's new boat, whether Dad could get tickets in the unlikely event the Knicks made the NBA play-offs—you know, things to pass the time until our table was ready.

It was ready just about as we finished that round. As we settled at the table I started, "Today was fascinating. But just exactly what are you proposing for me in Our Enterprise?"

Dad began, "First of all, our proposal is not just about Our Enterprise. After all, Our Enterprise is not a revenue producing entity. So our proposal includes taking Tom's place in our investment businesses in New York. He was managing a staff of cracker-jack MBAs who run portions of the investment portfolios of our clients. I say 'portions' to make the point that we never manage more than 20% of any client's investments. We don't want to make serious political enemies if we have a glitch. It will take some time for you to learn the details of what the MBAs do, but your leadership training and experience should allow you to manage them well right from the start. That job will give you an annual income in the $5-$10 million range."

I acted as if the numbers were unimportant and said, "Well, a central part of my West Point view of leadership involves knowing my people's values, then showing them how they can serve those values by our common enterprise. Why should those people work for me?"

"I'll get to that in a minute.

"As for your role in Our Enterprise, we'd like you to take over Tom's place. He had just about taken control of the rhetoric operation, the 'persuasion directorate' if you will."

"You mean the Ministry of Propaganda."

"Precisely. But remember, we're more careful about the words we use.

"We also want you to be a member of our Management Committee. Right now it's comprised of Doug, his son Paul, and me, sort of like the permanent members of the UN Security Council. We often share our decision-making with other major players; though, since we're not about ego, they are not subordinates nor do they see themselves that way. One way we share some decision-making is through our sponsorship of a roundtable that discusses how we similarly-minded folks should concentrate our 'philanthropy' to best advance our common cause.

"The results of the last election suggest that the Committee needs input from someone of your gender. It looks like the abortion issue may soon be costing us more single-issue voters than it's gaining. And we seem to be having some real problems with the gay marriage issue. We've already started to back off on that one. We'll need your thoughts about whether we should abandon either of those engagements or seriously modify our tactics in them, and, if so, how we can keep the Catholics and the Evangelicals in harness.

"And the Committee needs someone of your comparative youth. For Our Enterprise to succeed it has to make judgments based on a thorough understanding of the times as they change with each new generation. Doug and I are not Facebook or Twitter people. As we age it is harder for us to grasp, as instinctively as we need to, all the factors involved in the choices before us. In the same way, in the future, you will not be part of a new generation with its tools and common understandings. We can't even anticipate what those times will bring."

I said, "That committee, I notice you didn't call it an Executive Committee. What does it do?"

Dad answered, "It does execute, of course. But more importantly it tries to identify opportunities and problems, assess them in light of our *mission*, and craft responses. To use the Clausewitz framework, it serves as our General Staff. It identifies *engagements* that should be fought and recommends *tactics* to be employed in them. Then it designates (or should I say, invites) individual members of the Committee or other Allies to conduct the *engagements* by marshaling and employing such resources and alliances as seem appropriate.

"I must also mention that each member of the management committee also has fairly heavy social responsibilities. In the main these are used to build and serve our alliances. All the while they also generate the contacts among the wealthy, the customers upon which our investment business depends.

"Because we convince the IRS that the nationwide socializing is a sales effort for the investment business, the business pays for it as a tax deductible expense.

"And, realize, top grad schools are cranking out MBAs by the bushel. So, our investment business is delivering services of a type where many people possess the knowledge necessary to provide the service. In that kind of a setting, it is the people who control the customer contact that derive the lion's share of the wealth generated by the service. By controlling the client interface you'll protect our business from client defections should some of our well-paid MBAs get go-it-on-their-own ideas. Your control of the clients is the answer to your question about why the MBAs will work for you. Their skills are worth zilch without clients."

"OK. I get that. But, back to the committee—how do you identify problems?"

"Essentially, just by looking for them. You'll have to be alive to the possibilities lurking in changes in society. People on the committee simply have to be looking and aware, just as Doug and I were in the early days when we were on the lookout for Music Man Moments. That's another reason why your younger eyes and understandings can be important to our success."

He continued, "I'm pretty sure you've already thought of problems facing us as you have been listening to all of this. Am I right? Go ahead, give it a try. What do you see as a problem?"

That question called on me to give insightful opinions about a whole operation I hadn't even known about a few days before. Still, the dynamic of the day required that I say something. I shrugged my eyebrows as a recognition of the question, looked down for a about a half a minute, then took a stab at an answer. "Okay. I figure a 'problem' is something your opponents can use to defeat you. Sun Tzu would say that the biggest problems are likely to be those that can defeat your strategy and those that will attack your alliances.

"Your Enterprise is, essentially, an alliance between, on the one hand, the economic interests of the wealthy people you serve and, on the other hand, the non-economic interests of the people whose votes you need to serve them. But you've known that from the outset.

"What caught my eye is that conflict is so fundamental that it goes all the way to the philosophical level.

"The idea that your alliance patches together Ayn Randians and the American military is obscene. She taught that 'If any civilization is to survive, it is the morality of altruism that men have to reject.' Altruism is the core value of the American military. Every individual in it is living the altruistic belief that there are some values worth defending, even by risking his or her own life. Even if there were no military, those Americans and millions more would put their lives on the line to try to protect or save to save their child—and would probably do the same for their neighbors' children as well.

"And one of your other alliances poses an even deeper conflict, the one between the philosophy of the Ayn Randians and the philosophy of the Christians. Frankly, from the time you made me read *Atlas Shrugged* when I was in high school, I've never understand why anybody treated Rand seriously."

Dad's body language was showing that he was antsy about having given me reign to possibly criticize his life's work. So, at this point he pushed back. "Come on. She was raised in Russia. She knew firsthand the problems with Communism's total power in the hands of corrupt government functionaries."

I broke back in to pursue my point. "But she knew next to nothing of the western tradition that had worked toward an optimal amount of government power somewhere between total and none. She rejected total governmental power on the basis of her experience, then she preached a 'no governmental power' Utopia on the basis of nothing more than her arrogance. Apparently it never occurred to her that the society she preached, one devoid of communal power, was the kind of society that led the whole of mankind to accept the idea that some government, however flawed, is better than none.

"But whether she was talking through her duster or not, the fact is you can't reconcile *Atlas Shrugged* and the Christian Scriptures. I mean, wasn't one of the heroes of *Atlas Shrugged* a guy, Ragnar Something-or-other, who robbed from the poor to give to the rich because the rich deserved it?"

Dad calmed, "True."

"Well, Matthew, Mark, Luke, and John would not have written *Atlas Shrugged*. It seems to me that, in biblical terms, your enlistment of religions in your cause is an example of using people inclined to serve God to serve Mammon. Remember, your Evangelicals have a Bible that teaches if there was one thing that brought the Christ to rage, it was making the temple a den of thieves.

"I also think your basic alliance is particularly vulnerable to a rise in the education level of the citizenry. I mean the whole idea of Our Enterprise is to evade the natural tension between, on the one hand, those wealthy you serve and, on the other hand, the masses of paycheck-to-paycheck Christian wage earners who provide the votes you need. Your strategy to control the politicians is to control the vote. Your strategy to control the vote is to persuade the voters that you speak for their nation's traditions and their personal his religion. That makes your Enterprise vulnerable to the possibility that they may come to really understand Judeo-Christian thought and what their nation's traditions are, particularly the views held by the truly educated people who shaped the Constitution."

Dad nodded and answered. "Right. But we do work to address all that. We have long and constantly criticized public schooling and promoted homeschooling. And we fund the related work of the Christian fundamentalists to provide homeschooling textbooks, curricula, and web-based instruction that distinctly reject secular explanations of, among a lot of other things, American history.

"Now we're having some great successes with expanding that effort to the public school systems. We've gained control of state Boards of Education and used their buying power to demand production of textbooks conveying views that help us and suppress the views that don't. Texas, with its large population and its unified purchasing program, was key. When we added Florida we had a critical mass."

I said something like, "I teach history and I admit history books are written by the winners and have the winners' bias. But how do textbook writers, even ones you are paying, change history to teach what you want taught?"

Doug took up the question as if it were one about the mechanics of the change. "Well, one simple way has been to eliminate the sections on Madison, Jefferson, and the like from their books and then bulk the books back up by adding comparable sections about Reagan."

Dad was more blunt and addressed my question as I had intended it, as one about the morality of tinkering with historical truth. "When you think about it, parochial school textbook publishers have done that sort of thing forever. The nuns that taught me used textbooks that taught the American Revolution by giving more space to Bishop Carroll of Carrollton than to George Washington. For them, a Catholic, Commodore Barry—a worthy, to be sure—was the 'Father of the American Navy.' But for the people at Annapolis (who should know) and just about everybody else in the nation that title belongs to John Paul Jones.

"Oh, and one more thing about our control of education: we've been working to centralize control in the national government. That way we can have our partisan office holders—you know, the likes of Bill Bennett—eventually decide the content of standardized tests and, through them what is taught at the local level."

I tried to interject a zinger. "I thought that Goldwater's book which set out the fundamental principles of 'conservatism' said that the Constitution 'does not permit any interference whatsoever by the federal government in the field of education.'"

Dad looked down, clenched and released his left fist, gave his head a single quick shake, then leaned forward, resumed a soft and continuous head shake, and in a lighter manner than his now-redder face revealed said, "Jesus, Kate, you keep sliding into that old consistency trap. That was a principle he declared to achieve the effect of restoring segregated schools. It has no place where the effect we seek is control of the ideas we need lodged in the minds of American youth in order to win our class war."

I decided not to respond. Instead I went back to my argument that the Randian/Christian interface was a structurally weak point in Our Enterprise's foundation, "It's more than the idea that Christian teaching is at odds with Rand's. The Ayn Randians are at odds with just about everything you have your cooperating Christian denominations teaching."

I told them I knew something about the foundation Rand started, The Foundation for the New Intellectual. I had been following it since some of its representatives had approached me at a conference a few years back about working her books into the West Point curriculum, or at least distributing her books at the Point for free. I mentioned that The Foundation had morphed into the Ayn Rand Institute, the ARI. I knew that the Institute's mission statement is pretty explicit about the battlefield for converting America to unbridled capitalism being the educational institutions 'where students learn the ideas that shape their lives.'

So I said, "From what I've seen from the ARI, Ayn Randians are avid libertarians. They argue for a whole bunch of individual freedom ideas that you may have to reject to keep your religions in harness. On abortion, the ARI favors a woman's right to individual choice. The ARI also favors an individual's right to assisted suicide. It is firm on the need for the separation of church and state. It is against faith-based initiatives and the teaching of intelligent design as a rebuttal of Darwin. And I could go on."

Dad countered, "Yeah, but it's on our side opposing the damn tree-huggers and affirmative action."

The pace of the discussion was quickening. I snapped back, "True. But my point is that generally it is openly hostile to the religious right. Someone looking to attack your real alliances will focus on the tension between the teachings of Rand and Christ as viewed by each side of the divide."

Then Doug weighed in, "To some extent you're right. But remember we're not allied with the teachings of Christ; we're allied with specific Christian denominations and independent evangelists on the basis of their financial and power interests.

"In any event, we have thought about that problem. We have already put a plan in motion to defuse or weaken that kind of attack from the Randians before it comes. It's a simple application of Sun Tzu's idea of winning the battle before it is fought.

"Remember that, when describing the ARI, you said Rand's 501(c)(3) Foundation for the New Intelligence 'morphed' into the ARI? The ARI is technically not the Foundation she started. Well now we have some disgruntled ARI folk who have formed a competing 501(c)(3) organization and assert that it is more truly the heir to her thought. Our idea is that their entity can draw contributions away from the ARI, emphasize the economic side of Rand's thought, and soft-pedal or ignore the rest. Remember it is the economic side of her preaching, the righteous exalted position it gives to the wealthy, that has attracted their money to keep her ideas alive. Which Randian 501(c)(3) do you think the wealthy are going to support going forward?

"Still," he continued, "I'm not sure that's answer enough. As you pointed out, for the Christian churches we still have that Ragnar What's-his-name problem."

I pushed back to carry my ideas further, "You know, it's not just the incompatibility of Randians and Christians; it may also be an incompatibility between your authoritarian reactionary version of conservatism and the libertarians. Maybe the libertarians' natural alliances are with the left."

Doug said, "We've always worried about that. Somehow they don't see the government as their instrument to gain liberty from oppression coming from wealth. We pitch them that the left is for big intrusive government. So far that's been enough to keep them in the fold."

"Intrusive?" I almost gagged. "Intrusive? Suppose I were pregnant and seeking an abortion in Texas? What's more governmentally intrusive than the government requiring a doctor (under threat of criminal fines and loss of license for performing an operation without 'informed consent') to shove a 10-inch ultrasound wand up my lady parts, to make sure the volume is up while he looks for heartbeat sounds, while he displays the images, and while he describes what the images show—then sending me home for a day to think about it? Why? It's because your government of that state commands doctors to deliver the dominant religions' view of the morality of a woman's choice. And why does your state government do that? To convince your voters that your party is righteous so they'll give your party the votes it needs to win your class war against them. That's why. The political right's not intrusive? My foot!

"For me the real 'why' is: why do the libertarians tolerate intrusions like that?"

"Well, like the man said, 'politics makes strange bedfellows.'" That was dad's first reply. Then he added, "But more fundamentally, libertarians are more emotional, more given to absolutes. The left is too fuzzy for them. Emotionally, the libertarians fit with us better. We declare firm beliefs; the left explores doubts

"Oh, and by the way, remember your question about laws with misleading titles? That Texas law you've been describing about mandatory intrusive ultrasound, we gave it gave the title 'The Women's Right to Know Act.'

"But since you've identified a key *engagement* (let's call it 'continued inclusion of libertarians among our followers') I'd reckon you should be able to devise *tactics* to win it. More to the point, you clearly have a good feel for what we do on the Management Committee. Have you thought of any other problems we may face?"

I drew a breath while trying to calm myself and return to at least one of the many thoughts Our Enterprise had triggered in my mind during the day. After a long pause I said, "Well, your attempt to hide the strings and the string pullers is wearing thin. Talking heads on Fox News have been shown with your daily talking point sheets in their hands. Even if they hadn't been, the uniform language all their commentators use in their daily rants makes the strings and the command to be repetitive pretty obvious. And every now and then one of your former hired hands "outs" the process. One of "W's" White House Press Secretaries did that in his book, *What Really Happened.* And the whole nasty side of your strings to your puppets in the conforming media came out in the Scooter Libby trial for his criminally 'outing' a CIA spy to get back at her husband for writing about the intentional dishonesty used to justify starting the second Iraq war.

"Another thing that's wearing thin that may pose a serious problem is your cash-driven hold on the Christian churches. The Catholics are absolutely key to your plan, but they now have a pope who seems to be on to the incompatibility of Randian and Christian thought. In his 'exhortation' about the Joy of the Gospel, *Evangelii Gaudium,* he tagged your supply side trickle-down economics as unproved bunkum, a sales device to justify making the rich richer and the poor poorer. He said it rests on a rejection of ethics and of morality; and he spoke of it a form of enslavement.

"In the same exhortation, while he did hold to the idea that abortion is immoral, he didn't say anything about any need for criminal laws to stop it. Now he's calling asking church leaders to take a fresh look at government's obligations to same sex couples, at contraception, and who knows what all else. Suppose, at the end of some such conference, he gets up in that window and says something like, 'The conference has concluded that the Church should and will continue to teach the immorality of masturbation, divorce, homosexual practices, adultery, premarital sex, and abortion. However, while giving guidance to its faithful, the Church must respect the individual moral judgments of those believers in their personal circumstances, and respect as well the consciences, the individual judgments, of the contemporaries of the faithful outside the visible confines of Catholicism. Accordingly, and in keeping with Christ's teaching that the spheres of God and government are separate, the Church will not henceforth urge or support governmental action to criminalize personal choices on these matters.'"

Dad said, "He'd only do that if he doesn't understand the link between American abortion laws, its delivery of our political office holders who serve his church's income. We'll make sure he does. We've already started. Right after *Evangelii Gaudium* Limbaugh jumped on him to remind him he needs money to run the Vatican so he ought to shut up and look where that money is coming from."

I left the Catholic side of that risk and said, "Your hold on the Evangelists is weakening too. A few months ago even the Jimmy Swaggart Ministries' magazine, *The Evangelist*, took a featured a swipe at Dominionism.

"I've also thought of another problem, though it only deals with a detail, not the core, of your plan. If 'problem' means a threat to your objective of more wealth for yourselves and your descendants, I think you'll have a problem with your efforts to eliminate the Rule against Perpetuities. It's not that I think your adoring followers will ever catch on to what you're doing and its effect on their grandkids. But I do think the federal tax policy wonks will see echoes of the old English *mort main* problem, the effect of charitable gifts from long-dead hands. They'll pick up on that as their revenues decrease."

"But what can they do? It's a state issue."

"They could urge a tax on what are, essentially, generation-skipping trusts. For example, Congress could say that such a trust must pay, as a tax, a percentage of the fair value of its assets every 20 years. I'd expect that kind of a tax would likely be at the then-current estate tax rates so you'd be back where you started."

Dad looked mildly startled. "Well done. I hadn't thought of that. But we do have a couple of hundred indebted Congressmen who have signed Grover Norquist's 'no new taxes' pledge. And every one of them knows damn well that if he breaks his pledge he'll have a well-financed opponent in the next primary. And he'll have a lot less support if he wins the primary; just ask Bush the First about 1992 after he welshed on his 'read my lips' pledge. Remember, we only need 40 senators to filibuster and block any attempt to pass that tax. So we probably already have mechanisms available to meet that challenge if it ever arises.

"Actually, our lawyers tell us that the main problem with our tactic of killing the Rule against Perpetuities is that more and more descendants are suing to set aside the trusts in order to 'get <u>their</u> money.' The damn ingrates.

"Anything else?"

"Sure," I said, "several things strike me from the 2012 election.

"For one thing, your free-form organizational ideas allowed something no well-run business would tolerate. In businesses and in the military, people controlling the money supervise, evaluate, and reward other people doing the work; the clerks who issue the purchase orders don't double as clerks on the receiving docks. In the last election you let the people doing your propaganda work raise their own money and even evaluate themselves by running their own polls. People running that kind of operation have incentives to keep the money for themselves instead of applying it to the *mission* at hand."

Doug nodded agreement, "I take it you mean Karl Rove running his own Political Action Committee."

"His apparent structure at least. I don't know how any specific one of your apparent operatives allocated the funds contributed by your Allies between the tasks to be done and their own income for doing them. But I am saying that, as a matter of structure, you have to be on the lookout for the effect of structural weakness in your non-traditional organization."

I went on, "And another thing, your movement seems to be getting old—not enough fresh input. I mean, for example, in 2012 Ralph Reed came back out of his consulting practice to try to lead the Christian right through something called the Faith and Freedom Coalition. It seemed like he was trying to run his own, new, Moral Majority. But it lacked the youth, the 'virginity' if you will, of the original.

"Also, your visual emails seem aimed at the juvenile inmates at some 1950s all-white-male college Animal House."

Dad flashed back by saying I was reacting to the emails on too high, too elitist a plane. He told me to remember that they were running a campaign addressed to the Wage Earning Schmucks, or as the leader would have said, "the masses." "Remember," Dad said, the leader taught "*[T]he greater the mass it [the message] is intended to reach, the lower its purely intellectual level will have to be. The more modest its intellectual ballast, the more exclusively it takes into consideration the emotions of the masses, the more effective it will be."*

I nodded and went back to listing problems I foresaw for the Enterprise. "Even more fundamentally, your success with your 'more wealth conservatism' has been so complete that 'more wealth conservatism' and 'Republican' have become synonyms. There's no room left for an Eisenhower—someone in the Party who can say he's a conservative on economic issues but liberal on social issues. There's not even room for a Nixon, someone who can see the reason for, and sign, a stronger Clean Air Act or a new Clean Water Act. Your emails mock as 'Republicans in Name Only', RINOs, the likes of Bush the First, John McCain, and Chris Christie. Sarah Palin is even saying Reagan wasn't conservative enough. That can't be good—you may see it as important for your goals, perhaps, but it can't be good. Where are the heirs to the middle of the Party?"

Dad fought against that one. "It may not be good as you see it, but it is essential to our goal because 'liberal on social issues' would cost us money. You're forgetting that movements like ours must not tolerate dissent. And Palin's point is that Reagan did backtrack a bit when experience with his first tax cut disproved our hirelings' economic theory that lower tax rates would mean more tax revenue—you probably remember that, "the Laffer curve." (Arthur Laffer, by the way, is still making a living espousing efforts to cut taxes on the wealthy.)

"As for the heirs to that wing of the party, they are politicians—people more interested in the ego rewards of holding office than any noble cause. Look at 'W.' Look at Mitt Romney. Even look at our local congressman, Peter Frelinghuysen's boy Rodney. All are children of men who opposed us—the elder Romney and Frelinghuysen back in '64. 'W's' father did it in the 1980 primary against Reagan, when he pegged our tax plan as 'voodoo economics.' All three 'heirs' and hundreds, maybe millions, like them across the country stay loyal to the Party they were born to and spout the party line we give them.

"We do give some effort to the care and feeding of the heirs to the Eisenhower wing of the Party to prevent their total flight. Take for example our almost-neighbor, Christie Todd Whitman. She had little to commend her to public office except her dad was highly regarded as a leader of the state Party in the Eisenhower days. She got the nomination for governor, won against a weak opponent, and then totally botched the state's pension funding problem. But when some poli-sci grads told us we needed some appearance of balance in W's administration (she was a pro-choice woman) he gave her the Environmental Protection Agency (a post as far away from abortion issues as possible). Of course, she wasn't allowed to do anything about the environment that would cost us money. She wasn't even allowed to mention global warming. At her leaving-of-fice press conference the only accomplishment she could point to was an emission standard for bulldozers that wouldn't go into effect for about 6 years. No harm to us, but she was a mild message to the children of the leaders of the Party's Eisenhower era that they have a place as known entities on our side of the political line compared to anonymity on the other side.

"And even among the rank and file there are fourth- and fifth-generation Republicans whose families joined it because it was the Party of Lincoln who freed the slaves. Many of them inherited such emotional revulsion for the other side that they couldn't leave the Party even while it became the party of Strom Thurmond and white supremacists. Doug's parents went to their graves as perfect examples of this political version of the 'Faith of our Fathers' syndrome— 'Republicans' forever even though the meaning of the word had entirely changed."

"Maybe," I said trying to get back to my list of problems from the 2012 election, "but the next observation I'd make, and maybe this is a result of your total success I just mentioned, is that to win the Party's primary a person—say a Romney—has to say stuff way off the mainstream, your stuff. Then when he tries to come to the center for the general election, people notice the shift and don't know which version of him they'd be voting for—so they don't vote for him. And they're probably right; he'd likely immediately focus on being reelected and obey the commands of the moneyed end of the Party that he needed to win the last election. Put another way, he'd likely work harder to check off the items on the 'Mandate for Leadership' checklist the Heritage Foundation will give him after the election than to fulfill anything written in the Republican Party Platform or anything he promised in a campaign speech.

"Lastly, and related to all that, you've let the money run the Party with total disregard for neutral public policy types. Your campaign organizations don't do anything more than spout off on polarizing issues like outlawing abortions and gay marriage, making all government (except the military) smaller, and lowering your taxes."

Dad was starting to look a little agitated, the way he had looked on the ride to lunch. He almost barked saying, "We're running a war, Kate. You don't win wars by moderation."

"Maybe. But maybe not. Was Goldwater right when he suggested moderation wouldn't win the Cold War? It seems to me that you're thinking too much Clauswitz and not enough Sun Tzu. I guess I'm not given to absolutes. Sometimes I even incline to a Clausewitz-ian 'it depends.'"

Through all this the dinner had been ordered, served, eaten, and cleared.

Finally, Dad's agitation faded into a smile, perhaps a bit forced, but a smile nonetheless. He said, "You know, what I like best about your comments is that they make it clear you understand what we've been saying, you look at it all a bit differently than we do, and you're not shy about saying so. You're more than capable of making some very valuable contributions to our Management Committee.

"Let's leave the details of the Committee and tactical issues of the moment. You have our offer. What do you think about all this and when can you join us?"

"Dad, you know I have to think this over. Let's break for now and go back to the farm so I can get some sleep. I'll need time and a clear head to deal with all this."

THE LAST SATURDAY CONVERSATION

W HEN WE GOT TO THE farm Doug took his leave. Dad and I each gave him a hug and thanked him for the day. His car crunched down the pebbled drive, turned left, and became just a pair of red lights moving off into the dark.

With a gesture, Dad silently suggested we talk a bit further by walking into the den, pouring some B&B into a couple snifters, and setting them down while gesturing for me to sit on the sofa. Then he relaxed himself into his recliner facing me diagonally across the coffee table.

He started, "I'd have to be blind not to know you've been a bit restrained all day. Now that Doug's gone, tell me what you really think."

I begged off. "I really have to think about it all, sort it all out, there's so much to digest."

"Come on, you must have some impressions."

"Impressions? Sure. But they're still on the details, not the big picture. They're more along the lines of your question to me at dinner about what problems I see with the Enterprise."

Dad took a breath, a sip, then kissed in some liquid from the front of his teeth and said, "Well, OK. That's a start."

I began. "First, when I was a kid, young people were very aware of the environment. We knew government had to do something or we'd all be in trouble, large regions of America might even become uninhabitable, aquifers would dry up or become so polluted there'd be no drinking water. The Republican Party I was born into had a good claim to be the party of the environment because of Nixon's Clean Air Act amendments, the Clean Water Act, and his formation of the EPA.

"Nowadays, young people know there's an even bigger problem. If global warming is not stopped this whole planet may well become uninhabitable. So what's the platform of the current Republican Party? That Congress should:

> prohibit EPA from moving forward with new greenhouse gas regulations that will harm the nation's economy and threaten millions of jobs over the next quarter-century. The most powerful environmental policy is liberty, the central organizing principle of the American Republic and its people. Liberty alone fosters scientific inquiry, technological innovation, entrepreneurship, and information exchange. Liberty must remain the core energy behind America's environmental improvement.

"That's high sounding bullshit, pure and simple. Let your allies in the oil patch make money without regulation and the world will be a better place? And you've got as one of your leaders, Jim Inhofe, the Senator from the American Petroleum Institute and author of *The Greatest Hoax: How the Global Warming Conspiracy Threatens Your Future*. What kid is going to grow up in a Republican family, as I did, proud that his is the party of the environment?"

"Kate, the only thing left of that Republican Party is the name. We're not trying to convince those kids that we are the party of the environment. Hell, we've got parents convincing them that seeing Al Gore's movie, *An Inconvenient Truth*, is nigh on to a mortal sin. We've got a stronger message for those kids: we are the party of certainty in uncertain times, a fortress against change. We are the party of Liberty! Of Freedom! Of white America! Of the American flag! We are the party of righteousness, the party of Jesus!

After a long-ish pause he said, "Anything else bother you?"

"Well, for one thing I think the racial side of your Enterprise has gotten out of hand. I know racism enabled you to pull the Solid South out of the Roosevelt coalition.

"And I watched Reagan rant about welfare cheats, always illustrating his point with an anecdote (real or imagined) about a black welfare family. His apparent point was that welfare cheats were a reason to eliminate welfare. But he never argued that bank robbers were a reason to eliminate banks. His real point was that the cheat he portrayed was always was one of 'them,' a black.

"And I saw Bush the First's Willie Horton campaign ad. The pretext for using the ad was as a commentary of his opponent's continuation of a prison furlough program while he was Massachusetts governor. But that wasn't the message and everybody knew it. It wasn't about a white inmate that went AWOL from a prison furlough. It was about a black who went AWOL and raped a woman in another state.

"Your enterprise has consciously played on separating white 'us' from black 'them.' And now, all your maneuvers to prevent 'voter fraud' have been totally transparent devices trying to keep the blacks you have alienated from voting.

"You know I've seen a lot of your Enterprise's emails before. You have a lot of followers in the military; I get these emails every day from all over the world. Hardly a day goes by when I don't get an email inviting me to laugh at, and think of myself as separate from and superior to, my countrymen of color, many of whom wear the same uniform I do.

"Anyhow, there was an email I'd seen earlier this spring. While I was getting ready this evening I pulled it out of the binders you gave me because I wanted to talk about it. Then I couldn't bring myself to pull it out at the restaurant. It seems to be from the 'hate Obama' campaign suggesting unprecedented extravagance by the <u>black</u> family in the <u>White</u> House. It's not even arguably clever like the aspirin one." I handed it to him:

CAN YOU GUESS WHAT THIS IS?

It's the next thing the US taxpayers will have to pay for!

MICHELLE OBAMA'S

HIGH SCHOOL REUNION !!!!!!!

"That's revolting. Though I'm sure your followers think it's funny.
"And how about this one?

Subject: Obama's replacement
He is laid back, looks equally intelligent, and appears to have what Obama lacks.

"But whether you like it or not, times change. For example, even if racism gave you a lever into governance of the Southern Baptists, the good people in its management and in its pews have moved on. Sometime in the mid-'90s the SBC reaffirmed its approval of the civil rights movement. More than that, its members seem to have decided that they have a lot in common with people of faith who were also people of color. Your racist emails are going to do you more harm than good with that church.

"And the racial breakdown of the votes in the last Presidential election should have shown you that your problem of losing touch with the times is even bigger. The Hispanics are here."

"Look Kate, one of the benefits of the free-form structure of our alliances is that the racist email folks have no apparent connection to our own-the-pulpits folks. And we know the lessons of the last election. That's why we've got the Party talking up its 'Party of Lincoln' heritage."

"Come on, Dad. That's not going to sell after almost 50 years of the 'Southern Strategy.' Do you really think African-Americans are going to forget all that? That they're going to remember Lincoln and forget stuff like Goldwater's votes, Reagan's stories of black welfare cheats, and Bush's Willie Horton ad? Do you think they're going to forget any of the last 50 years while emails like that "Reunion" one are still going out?"

"Actually, Kate, I do. A Wage Earning Schmuck, black or white, knows a lot less than you think he does. He will know what we have our "respectable" people, our talk radio hosts, and our pretty girls on Fox News repeat and repeat to him. And if you think back to what we told you about how the email chains work, the black WES won't be getting that email. Some day we will abandon racist themes, but we'll do so on the basis of effect not principle. When they hurt our cause of more wealth for ourselves and our descendants we'll stop. For now they help so we'll keep using them.

"But I agree that email crossed the line. It's a prime example of why we need to pay attention; we have to lead, manage, and coordinate, the messages in our campaign. We just can't give general guidelines and have some schmuck, somebody who's probably working for us because he's a believer, go off and do what he thinks best, unsupervised. By the way, the guy that produced that one has been reined in. He recently produced the 'race traitor' email that essentially said that liberals are so fixated on race that they're the racists."

"Come on, dad. By that logic Martin Luther King's call to judge children by their character, not their color, was racist.

"But OK." I said, "Let me give you another thought I've had about your Enterprise. You started this effort to exploit the vulnerability of democracy to the passions of the voters. You did so because you were worried that the wage earner and the unemployed guys would vote their interests, not yours. The worry about that possibility in a democracy has been around at least since the Greeks first studied government. When Aristotle wrote about it in *Politics* he thought a constitution was best if all the citizens held power, had a common education, and they sought the good for all citizens, not just a few. Second best, and more realistic, would be a constitution controlled by a numerous middle class. Your Enterprise is out for unequal good and to minimize the middle class—and it is succeeding. When it does, what then?"

"Hopefully, by that time, we'll have enough and it'll be invested all over the world."

"Dad. Do you really think there is such a thing as enough? I've watched you talk about this all day. You seem to be treating this as a game."

"Well, Kate, I'll admit it is fun. But I sense you mean something more than you're saying."

"Of course. You know I've read most of your emails. I've watched a lot of Fox News. Even on summer deployments, with Rush Limbaugh on Armed Forces Radio and The Patriot Channel on Sirius/XM radio, I've been awash in your Enterprise's messages. Frankly, I don't buy any of it."

"Of course you don't, Kate. Neither do I. The last person Our Enterprise would want leading it is somebody who believed that stuff. That kind of person would be the kind who authored what he called that 'jungle bunny' reunion email; one who couldn't *tactically* abandon an *engagement* when abandonment best served the *strategy*.

"But you're back to judging the message by its truth. I've been trying to make the point over and over that this is war and the merit of the message has to be judged by whether it serves our mission. You've got to judge it that way."

"Maybe. But I do need time to digest it all, Dad.

"But so far, each time each time I try to think about the big picture I get a feeling that it's not good for the country. Through scorn, hate, and religion you're building a tribe of followers and pitting them against other Americans as if they were in a separate nation. You are training your tribe, your followers, that loyalty to tribal values requires them to hate, before they listen to, other Americans who incline to urge government to honor values other than your profit."

As I said that I was looking directly into Dad's eyes and I could see that he was pained that I put my reservations on that basis. He wanted me to view it from his so he said, "Well, Kate, you may be right. But it's good for us. It's good for our family…" He paused. I could almost see clouds of thoughts about Tom's death pass behind his eyes. He went on more quietly, "or at least what's left of it."

He slowly came back from those thoughts and went on, "But our family is not just me, or you and me. It's also the grandchildren—Tom's kids, Bob and Terri, and your daughter, Joy—and generations that we'll never know. Our Enterprise is a worthy effort because it will make their lives better. And Doug, Karen, and their family for generations will be served as well. All of us will be far better off than Doug and I could have dreamt back on the foc's'l of the Oldendorf."

"True," I said as I shrugged, put down my drink, and stood up. "Like I said, Dad, I've got to a lot of thinking to do to sort this all out." He rose when he saw me getting up. I went over, gave him a hug, then stepped back, gave him a nod and a "Love you a bunch, Dad," and went upstairs to me old childhood bedroom.

I shut my mind to escape everything we had talked about through that day, consigning those thoughts to some future time. I tried to lose myself in the reality of the familiar room. Back in that childhood, during nights in that room I had thought a lot about the darkness, infinity, and the place of my short life in it. This Saturday night I couldn't face those thoughts either. Instead, I resorted to a skill I developed with the Army in the field: I just put my head on the pillow, forced my mind to profoundly dull topics, and fell asleep.

44
END NOTE

R EADER, THE NEXT MORNING I told Dad he had given me a lot to think about, but I'd get back to him as soon as I could. If I accepted I'd have to notify the Point quickly so it could find a historian replacement for the fall semester.

I'm in my forties and reasonably accomplished. You'd think I'd be a model of a self-confident adult human being. But we all doubt. And we all meet decisions in the context of the society we live in; mine is the military, a society apart. You have lived a life in a broader world. I need the kind of wisdom born in that world.

Dad's offer is a challenge to my values so profound that I feel I'm lost. It's as if my mind's boat was cut loose from its moorings and drifting in a fog.

Obviously I am a believer in the America of my mind. But does it exist? Can it?

Naively or not, I believe in an America that, as Reagan said, is a hope for mankind. It is a light to a way for ordinary people to live lives of choice, as more than servants of princes, popes, and people of wealth. I have given half a lifetime to learning and preaching that hope; teaching that America allows people to decide things for themselves and the rules needed to govern them in proportion to the numbers of those people, not their wealth. I've never thought America was perfect. But I believed it had the mechanism—the process reborn in the 1500s of honest and mutually respectful, if uncertain, discussion—to cure and redress its imperfections.

Before all this I was already worried that modern communications and current wealth concentrations were a threat to idea-diversity and open discussion. That was the idea behind the Johns Hopkins article I'd been writing. Now I don't have the neutralizing distance that an academic needs to write about such an issue. I'm not the one to do a disinterested academic's analysis of Madison's theories and today's realities, about whether wealth concentration and its focused use of media are allowing private interest to defeat public good. Nor am I the person to suggest that wealth's use of the rhetoric of deceit and division has created a well-nigh religious conviction of the righteousness of one faction, exactly what Madison feared as "the source of mortal diseases under which popular governments have everywhere perished."

Besides, it's not my place to publish (and have my Dad read) what is likely to be a public indictment of his life's work.

Are my beliefs false? Is Dad's world view reality? Is social control by wealth the inevitable ordained way of things?

Even if it is, can I participate in fomenting in the Enterprise's followers enough disrespect, absolute certainty of moral righteousness, and hatred that they will not respectfully listen to and discuss new and different ideas? Can I ever come to think it's right to imbue followers with so much hate toward anyone, even liberals and the MSM, that just a few of the inner circle can use that hatred to control the nation?

Already the lockstep discipline of Congress shows that a small cadre of decision makers, puppeteers outside Congress, can pull the strings of the supposed national leaders. The Enterprise has momentum; the puppeteers are steadily gaining power; today Congress, tomorrow the nation, and then? That scares me. Yet, on a personal level, Dad's offer is for me to be one of those puppeteers.

Should I accept? From what you know of me, can I? And if I don't, will it matter—not just to me and my descendants, but to the Republic? If not, is there any other way to deal with Dad's offer that I'm missing?

Reader, from the real world, and not from the ideal-filled, military, fairy tale life Dad says I've been leading, what do you think I should do?

Please, I need your wisdom and your common sense. Call me. Or, better yet, set your ideas down and send them to me at:

http://www.aParticularWoman.com.

Thank you,
Kate

EPILOGUE

THE TALE TOLD IN THIS book ended in late spring 2014. I finished the book in September 2014 and set about to find a way to get it to market. Letters asking agents to look at it were met with silence or uniform responses that netted to "I've never heard of you; don't bother me." Expected. Understandable. But discouraging.

As I dallied, daunted, a year passed. As it did, events moved on.

There has been a touted-to-be-remarkable compromise by which Congress approved a budget. The compromise involved the right's apparent concession to allow continued funding of Planned Parenthood in exchange for the lifting of a decades-old ban on exportation of domestic oil, a 10% draw down of the strategic petroleum reserve, and a couple of 'hands off' directions to regulators regarding campaign finance. So, faced with a choice between serving the religion-based demands of their constituents or serving big oil, the Enterprise's obedient congressmen opted to serve big oil. They expanded its markets at the expense of the nation's long term interest in having petroleum reserves. At the same time they appeared to preserve the anti-Planned Parenthood issue for the future (it proved to be a very short time to the future). As "Dad" said on the "ride to lunch," "the longer the issue is unresolved, the longer religious voters will be putting our politicians in office."

In *Obergefell v. Hodges* a majority of the Supreme Court declared that, given the many diverse secular consequences of marriage in our society, state bans on gay marriage deprived people of liberty without due process or equal protection of the laws The dissenters, in their various opinions, generally lamented that Justices, including themselves, could declare, in light of new understandings and circumstances, that the way people had always done things violated the Constitution. (By such reasoning, we would still have segregated schools, forbid interracial marriages, and permit coerced confessions as evidence.)

Also, in Supreme Court matters, 79 year-old Antonin ("Mere factual innocence is no reason not to carry out a death sentence") Scalia died of natural causes during a free stay in the *El Presidente* suite at a luxury hunting ranch in Texas. From the right, conspiracy theorists quickly crowed that he was done in by a Democratic administration intent on defending Obamacare, or the EPA, or whatever. From the left people futilely sought to know who else was on the junket, what influence they sought, and how many similar junkets there had been.

Pope Francis also weighed in with a second revolutionary message, *Laudato Si*. In it he forcefully echoed and expanded upon the message of Al Gore's movie, *An Inconvenient Truth*: global warming is real, manmade, and presents a serious moral problem for all the lives, human and otherwise, that will be lost as a result. Further, he urged people to realize that "economic interests easily end up . . . manipulating information so that their plans will not be affected." This put some politicians in an awkward place. They had won the blessing of the Enterprise by proclaiming their religiosity while, with equal voice, mocking climate scientists who warned of a need for ending dependence on carbon fuels. Forced to choose, mostly, they said something like they'd listen to the Pope on other issues of morality but they'd take their climate science from scientists. Which ones, they didn't say; but see the book or the documentary, *Merchants of Doubt*.

The hideous racist slaughter of a pastor-legislator's entire family led a state government to remove a Confederate flag, the prime emblem of white supremacists, from the state house grounds—in South Carolina, of all places. Mississippi still flies its flag defiantly.

The Affordable Care Act (ACA, i.e., Obamacare) was upheld in the Supreme Court for the second time. Sixteen million more Americans now have health insurance. And national health care costs are rising more slowly than they have in years. At my last count, the Republican majority in the House of Representatives has passed destined-to-be-vetoed bills to repeal all or a substantial part of ACA 61 times. Evidently, meaningless demonstrations of loyalty to their financial backers are more important than attention to the nation's other problems.

Through it all, those with the money to do so continuously worked to divide the country by arousing passion-based, profit-serving disrespect in the hearts of their tribe of low-wage-earning followers. In keeping with the idea of plastically treating the issues that are on everyone's tongue, very few days passed between a European aviator's suicidal/mass-homicidal plunge into the Alps before the email circuit was ringing with a call for a German copilot to fly Air Force One. The visual messages of the unworthiness of Democrats and the presumed-to-be-lazy unemployed continued:

In mid-December, I received the 7th annual (and false) alarm that, with that black non-Christian Democrat in the White House, the government's National Christmas Tree had become the National Holiday Tree. This year's alarm went on, in a falsely-attributed diatribe, to decry the never-happened tree-name-change as symptomatic of a threat to our children who, denied government-sponsored prayer and bible reading in public schools, will not learn that murder and stealing are wrong.

Best of all, in the presidential primaries, a self-funded entrant put himself before the hate-united but previously intentionally leaderless army of followers. He proclaimed their victim-hood and scorned the evil threat of all manner of outgroups. Thus—with the force of a bully/blowhard (known to all of us from our schoolyards)—he became the army's leader. With each arrogant declaration of his own "greatness" and every dose of scorn hurled at "others" he pulled the non-scorned followers closer. The list of scorned grew by the day and included each of his individual adversaries, whole categories of people (e.g., Muslims, Mexicans, women), and nations (China and Russia)—it even included American servicemen captured in battle who had honorably endured years as prisoners of war. The Enterprise and its Allies were blind-sided. They had created the army intending to offer it, along with their funding, to the candidate who most agreed to do their bidding. The bully/blowhard is now marching toward the general election at the head of that army of followers pre-conditioned to confront the fears of their real world with hate rather than with understanding.

As for the Republic? Well, The Federalist who spoke of "the vicious arts by which elections are too often carried," must be in dread.

Very respectfully,
Jack Lynch

ACKNOWLEDGMENTS

D ECENCY DEMANDS A SHOUTING GRATITUDE to many who have brought this book far above what it would have been if it had come from my keyboard alone.

Of course, my principal debt is to my wife, Doreen, for her moral support of the effort and her technical support of its production.

Likewise the book's production would not have been possible without the energy and efforts of Tom Coultas and Graham Schreiner at One Source Press; their help through the drafting years sustained me.

I am indebted more than I can say to my excellent and experienced editor, Kathleen Daley. If there is anywhere in the text which seems to belie her prodigious attention to detail it is likely because I snuck in a note or two after her last review.

Along the way I have been encouraged, taught, and saved from errors by people with far more substantive knowledge than I. Principal among them have been Charlie Courtney, Jay Hellstrom, Beth Knorr, Blair MacInnes, and Doug Simon. Their tolerance of my barely rudimentary knowledge of their fields can only have been based on their friendship, which itself is an honor I cherish.

The courtesies extended me by Colonel Pilar Ryan, USA (Ret.) grounded my mind's-eye construct of my central character. My time with her deepened my awe of those who teach the young folk who will make it their life's work to protect and defend the right of the rest of us to speak, believe, and behave as they might not.

Finally, I must thank the research librarians from Morristown, Boston, Newport, and the University of Pennsylvania who willingly and professionally responded to questions that must have seemed to them to have been born out of the blue.

But it took much more for this book to reach you. It would not have reached you but for the experience and sound guidance of Matt Balson of Berwick Court Publishing Co. It was Matt who led me through the maze of the self-publishing universe. Matt also arranged for the excellent services of Mitch McNeil, who produced an artistic, coherent, and compelling cover out of the jumble of my far less artistic thoughts.

AFTERWORD

Beware of false prophets, which come to you in sheep's clothing, but inwardly they are ravenous wolves. Ye shall know them by their fruits.
Matthew, c. 7, v. 15-16.

Sheep's clothing, a comforting thing, can come in the form of patriotism and religion—themselves good things. Today that clothing conceals spirits that are ready to ravage the common man for their own advantage. Their efforts bear fruits in the form of massive tax and other political advantages for those with the wealth and stealth to wrap themselves in those forms. But they harbor an even deeper threat—to the intended functioning of our Republic.

APPENDIX A

DOUG'S EXCERPTS FROM *MEIN KAMPF* ON ORGANIZATION
(CITATIONS ARE TO FIRST MARINER BOOKS EDITION, 1999)

[The first period of activity in a movement is designed] to fill a small nucleus of men with the new doctrine. **581**

Every movement will first have to sift the human material it wins into two large groups: supporters and members.

The function of propaganda is to attract supporters, the function of organization to win members.

A supporter of a movement is one who declares himself to be in agreement with its aims, a member is one who fights for them.

The supporter is made amenable to the movement by propaganda. The member is induced by the organization to participate personally in the recruiting of new supporters, from whom in turn members can be developed. **581**

Propaganda tries to force a doctrine on the whole of a people; the organization embraces within its scope only those who do not threaten on psychological grounds to become a brake on the further dissemination of the idea. **582**

[I]t is the highest task of the organization to make sure that no inner disunities within the membership of the movement lead to a split and hence a weakening of the movement's work. **584**

[The organization] must see to it that ... [the] core alone shall lead the movement. **585**

[T]he more radical and inflammatory my propaganda was, the more this frightened weaklings and hesitant characters, and prevented them from penetrating the primary core of our organization. **586**

[And he was certain that a movement run on dictatorial principles will, in a state with majority rule] someday with mathematical certainly overcome the existing state of affairs and emerge victorious. **589**

APPENDIX B

DAD'S EXCERPTS FROM *MEIN KAMPF* ON PROPAGANDA

[Human and ethical values such as truth] are inapplicable to propaganda. **178**

Propaganda... must be addressed always and exclusively to the masses. **179**

[T]he greater the mass it is intended to reach, the lower its purely intellectual level will have to be.
The more modest its intellectual ballast, the more exclusively it takes into consideration the emotions of the masses, the more effective it will be. **180**

[A]ll effective propaganda must be limited to a very few points and must harp on these in slogans until the last member of the public understands what you want him to understand by your slogan. **180-81**

[T]he very basic first axiom of all propagandist activity: to wit, the basically subjective and one-sided attitude it must take to every question it deals with. **182**

The people in their overwhelming majority are so feminine by nature and attitude that sober reasoning determines their thoughts and actions far less than emotion and feeling. **183**

[T]he most brilliant propagandist technique must confine itself to a few points and repeat them over and over. **184**

[O]nly after the simplest ideas are repeated thousands of times will the masses finally remember them. **185**

At first the claims of propaganda [here he was describing English propaganda in WWI directed at Germany] were so impudent that people thought it insane; later, it got on people's nerves; and in the end it was believed.
[T]he spiritual weapon can succeed only if it is applied on a tremendous scale, but that success amply justifies the cost. **186**

[On related matters I should note that the leader had little regard for persuasion through written media. He felt only 1 in 10,000 read the press or pamphlets of those they don't already agree with to obtain a balanced view. But it was otherwise with the spoken word. The man in the street will] consider it especially if he gets it for nothing, and all the more if the headlines plastically treat a topic which at the moment is in everyone's mouth. **478**

APPENDIX C
EMAIL ON EXECUTIVE ORDERS

Subject: As I Said—It Is Here Now!!

For the SHOCK of your life, take 1 minute to comprehend what you read below. During our lifetimes, all Presidents have issued Executive Orders.

For various reasons, some have issued more than others. These things will directly affect us all, in years to come. Question is: Do YOU care enough to send this, 'shocking info,' to people you love and others?

NUMBER OF EXECUTIVE ORDERS ISSUED by U.S. Presidents in the last 100 years:

Teddy Roosevelt—3
All Others until FDR—0
FDR—11 in 16 years
Truman—5 in 7 years
Ike—2 in 8 years
Kennedy—4 in 3 years

LBJ—4 in 5 years

Nixon—1 in 6 years

Ford—3 in 2 years

Carter—3 in 4 years

Reagan—5 in 8 years

Bush—3 in 4 years

Clinton—15 in 8 years

George W. Bush—62 in 8 years

Obama—923 in 3 1/2 years! More than 1000+ and counting Executive Orders in 6 years...

Read some of them below—unbelievable!

Next step -dictatorship. (Looks like we are there already!) If you don't get the implications, you're not paying attention. How come all the other presidents in the past 100 years have not felt it necessary to INCREASE GOVERNMENT'S POWER OVER THE PEOPLE with more than 1,000 Executive Orders? This is really very scary. And most Americans have absolutely no idea what is happening.

YES, THERE IS A REASON THAT THIS PRESIDENT IS DETERMINED TO TAKE CONTROL AWAY FROM THE HOUSE AND THE SENATE.

Even some Democrats in the House have turned on him, plus a very small number of Democrat Senators have questioned him. Rightfully so. - WHAT IS OBAMA REALLY TRYING TO ACCOMPLISH????

Remember what he told Russia's Putin: "I'll be more flexible after I'm re-elected".

Now look at these:

EXECUTIVE ORDER 10990 -- allows the government to take over all modes of transportation and control of highways and seaports.

EXECUTIVE ORDER 10995 -- allows the government to seize and control the communication media.

EXECUTIVE ORDER 10997 -- allows the government to take over all electrical power, gas, petroleum, fuels and minerals.

EXECUTIVE ORDER 10998 -- allows the government to

take over all food resources and farms.

EXECUTIVE ORDER 11000 -- allows the government to mobilize civilians into work brigades under government supervision.

EXECUTIVE ORDER 11001 -- allows the government to take over all health, education and welfare functions.

EXECUTIVE ORDER 11002 -- designates the registration of all persons. Postmaster General to operate a national registration.

EXECUTIVE ORDER 11003 -- allows the government to take over all airports and aircraft, including commercial aircraft.

EXECUTIVE ORDER 11004 -- allows the Housing and Finance Authority to relocate communities, build new housing with public funds, designate areas to be abandoned, and establish new locations for populations.

EXECUTIVE ORDER 11005 -- allows the government to take over railroads, inland waterways and public storage facilities.

EXECUTIVE ORDER 11049 -- assigns emergency preparedness function to federal departments and agencies, consolidating 21 operative Executive Orders issued over a fifteen year period.

EXECUTIVE ORDER 11051 -- specifies the responsibility of the Office of Emergency Planning and gives authorization to put all Executive Orders into effect in times of increased international tensions and economic or financial crisis.

EXECUTIVE ORDER 11310 -- grants authority to the Department of Justice to enforce the plans set out in Executive Orders, to institute industrial support, to establish judicial and legislative liaison, to control all aliens, to operate penal and correctional institutions, and to advise and assist the President.

EXECUTIVE ORDER 11921 -- allows the Federal Emergency Preparedness Agency to develop plans to establish control over the mechanisms of production and distribution, of energy sources, wages, salaries, credit and the flow of money in U.S. Financial institution in any undefined national emergency. It also provides that when a state of emergency is declared by the President, Congress cannot review the action for six months.

Feel free to verify the "executive orders" at will.....and these are just the major ones. I'm sure you've all heard the tale of the "Frog in the Pot"... Watch Obama's actions, not his words! By his actions he will show you where America is headed.

If THIS IS DIFFICULT TO BELIEVE, THEN PROVE TO YOURSELF IT'S WRONG - Google it!

APPENDIX D
EMAIL ABOUT IMAM ALI

Subject: Fw: Sign in Mall in Texas UNBELIEVABLE
This is scary

READ CAREFULLY........... This is so "Unbelievable"..... In Houston, Texas, Harwin Central Mall: The very first store that you come to when you walk from the lobby of the building into the shopping area had this sign posted on their door. The shop is run by Muslims. Feel free to share this with others.

In case you are not able to read the sign below, it says, **"We will be closed on Friday, September 11, 2009 to commemorate the martyrdom of Imam Ali."**

Imam Ali flew one of the planes into the twin towers. Nice huh?

Try telling me we're not in a Religious war!
THIS HAS NOT BEEN AROUND....**SO MAKE SURE IT
DOES!
PLEASE PASS THIS ON TO EVERYONE YOU KNOW
AND HAVE THEM DO THE SAME**

BIBLIOGRAPHY

American Academy of Pediatrics, Committee on Environmental Health. Lead Exposure in Children: Prevention, Detection, and Management; subsection: Decline of Lead Poisoning in the United States. 116 Pediatrics 1036 (2005).

American Legislative Exchange Council. ALEC: History. http://www.alec.org/about-alec/history/ (accessed 12/28/2012)

Angloinfo. Termination of Pregnancy and Abortion in Italy. http://rome.angloinfo.com/countries/italu/abortion.asp (accessed February 13, 2012).

Aristotle. *Politics.* Translated by Benjamin Jowett. http://www.mit.edu/aristotle/politics.html (accessed April 25, 2014).

Aristotle. *On Rhetoric: A Theory of Civic Discourse.* Translated by George Kennedy. New York: Oxford University Press, 1991.

Bell, Jeffrey. *The Case for Polarized Politics: Why America Needs Social Conservatism.* New York: Encounter Books, 2012.

Bernays, Edward. *Propaganda.* 1928; repr. Brooklyn: IG Publishing, 2005.

Brock, David and Rabin-Havt, Ari. *The Fox Effect: How Roger Ailes Turned a Network into a Propaganda Machine.* New York: Anchor Books, 2012.

Bunch, Will. *The Backlash: Right-Wing Radicals, High-Def Hucksters, and Paranoid Politics in the Age of Obama*. New York: HarperCollins Publishers, 2010.

Carroll, James. *Constantine's Sword: The Church and the Jews, a History*. New York: Houghton Mifflin Co., 2001.

Catholic Church, Paul VI (promulgator, not author). Declaration of Religious Freedom, *Dignitatis Humanae*: On the Right of Persons and Communities to Social and Civil Freedom in Matters Religious. http://www.vatican.va/archive/hist_councils/ ii_vatican_council/documents/vat-ii_decl_19651207_dignitatis-humanae_en.html (accessed April 27, 2104). 1965.

Catholic Church, Second Vatican Council. Decree on Ecumenism, *Unitatis Redintegratio*. http://www.vatican.va/archive/hist_council/ii_vatican_council/ documents/vat-ii_decree_19641121_unitatis-redintegratio_en.html (accessed April 27, 2104). 1964.

Clausewitz, Carl von. *On War*. Translated by J. J. Graham, Edited by Anatol Rapoport. Pelican Edition, London: Penguin Group, 1982.

Colson, Charles, et al., Evangelicals & Catholics Together: The Christian Mission in the Third Millennium. reproduced at: http://www.firstthings.com/article/2007/01/ evangelicals--catholics-together-the-christian-mission-in-the-third-millenium-2 (accessed April 25, 2014). 1994.

Danforth, John. *Faith and Politics: How the "Moral Values" Debate Divides America and How to Move Forward Together*. New York: Viking Penguin, 2006.

Department of Defense Directive, Number 5210.56: Use of Deadly Force and Carrying Firearms by DoD Personnel, February 25, 1992.

Federalist Society. Home Page, Our Purpose. http://s3.amazonaws.com/atrfiles/files/ files/112012-113thCongress.pdf (accessed May 14, 2014).

Francis. *Evangelii Gaudium:* Apostolic Exhortation of Pope Francis on the Proclamation of the Gospel in Today's World. http://w2.vatican.va/content/francesco/ en/apost_exhortations/documents/papa-francesco_esortazione-ap_20131124_ evangelii-gaudium.html (accessed April 25, 2014). 2013.

Francis, *Laudato Si*, Encyclical of the Holy Father Francis On Care for Our Common Home. http://w2.vatican.va/content/francesco/en/encyclicals/documents/papa-francesco_20150524_enciclica-laudato-si.html (Accessed December 15, 2015) May 24, 2105.

Frankfurt, Harry. *On Bullshit*. Princeton: Princeton University Press, 2005.

Friedman, Milton. *Capitalism and Freedom*. Chicago: University of Chicago Press, 1962.

Friedman, Milton. "The Social Responsibility of Business is to Increase Profits." *The New York Times Magazine*, September 13, 1970.

Freud, Sigmund. *Jokes and Their Relation to the Unconscious*. 1905. Standard edition Translated by James Strachey. New York: W. W. Norton, 1960.

General Accountability Office. Report to Congress. Subject: Oil and Gas Royalties: A Comparison of the Share of Revenue Received from Oil and Gas Production by the Federal Government and other Resource Owners. GAO-07-676R Oil And Gas Royalties. May 1, 2007.

Goldberg, Michelle. *Kingdom Coming: the Rise of Christian Nationalism*. New York: W. W. Norton, 2006.

Goldwater, Barry. Acceptance Speech, Republican National Convention, 1964. http://www.washingtonpost.com/wp-srv/politics/daily/may98/goldwaterspeech.htm (accessed May 16, 2014).

Goldwater, Barry. *The Conscience of a Conservative*. Shepherdsville, KY: Victor Publishing, 1960.

Gordon, Colin. *Growing Apart: A Political History of American Inequality*. http://scalar.usc.edu/works/growing-apart-a-political-history-of-american-inequality/index (accessed May 14, 2014).

Hacker, Jacob S. and Pierson, Paul. *Winner-Take-All Politics: How Washington Made the Rich Richer – And Turned Its Back on the Middle Class*. New York: Simon & Schuster Paperbacks, 2011.

Haight, Jonathan. "What Makes People Vote Republican." *The Edge*, September 8, 2008. http://edge.org/conversation/what-makes-people-vote-republican (accessed May 12, 2014).

Hitler, Adolph. *Mein Kampf*. Translated by Ralph Manheim. First Mariner Books Edition, New York: Mariner Books, 1999.

Holocaust Education & Archive Record Team. The Jasenovac Extermination Camp. http://holocaustresearchproject.org/othercamps/jasenovac.html (accessed July 17, 2013).

Jefferson, Thomas. A Bill for Establishing Religious Freedom, Printed for the Consideration of all the People. 1779. Accessed through the Library of Congress: http://www.loc.gov/exhibits/jefferson/jeffrep.html (accessed May14, 2014).

Kearney, Ryan. "Rightwingers Are Blaming Bill Clinton for the Navy Yard Shooting". *New Republic.* September 17, 2013.

Krebs, Christopher. *A Most Dangerous Book: Tacitus's "Germania" from the Roman Empire to the Third Reich.* New York: W. W. Norton & Co., 2011.

Krugman, Paul. *The Great Unraveling: Losing Our Way in the New Century.* New York: W. W. Norton, 2005.

Leo XIII. *Immortale Dei:* Encyclical of Pope Leo XIII on the Christian Constitution of States. http://www.vatican.va/holy_father/leo_xiii/encyclicals/documents/hf_l-xiii_enc_01111885_immortale-dei_en.html (accessed April 25, 2014), 1885.

Leo XIII. *Libertas:* Encyclical of Pope Leo XIII on the Nature of Human Liberty. http://www.vatican.va/holy_father/leo_xiii/encyclicals/documents/hf_l-xiii_enc_20061888_libertas_en.html (accessed April 25, 2014), 1888.

Limbaugh, Rush. (Methodology video) Accessed through an article by Leslie Salzillo, Rush Limbaugh Reveals How He Dupes the Dittoheads. November 28, 2013. http://www.dailykos.com/story/2013/11/28/1241236/-Rush-Limbaugh-Reveals-How-He-Sucks-People-In-Video# (accessed May 14, 2014).

Limbaugh, Rush. Accessed through ABC News Report: Rush Limbaugh Calls a Female Georgetown Student a Slut. March 2, 2012. http://www.youtube.com/watch?v=Jfb9f7yFYgw (accessed May 14, 2014).

Limbaugh, Rush. It's Sad How Wrong Pope Francis Is (Unless It's a Deliberate Mistranslation by Leftists). November 27, 2013. http://www.rushlimbaugh.com/daily/2013/11/27/it_s_sad_how_wrong_pope_francis_is_unless_it_s_a_deliberate_mistranslation_by_leftists (accessed May 14, 2014).

Luther, Martin. *On the Jews and Their Lies.* Translator not stated. Los Angeles: Christian Nationalist Crusade, 1948. http://www.remnantresources.org/Archives/Books/TheJewsAndTheirLies-Luther.pdf (accessed May 12, 2014).

Madison, James. Memorial and Remonstrance Against Religious Assessments. (1785). http://religiousfreedom.lib.virginia.edu/sacred/madison_m&r_1785.html (accessed May 14, 2014).

Madison, James. *The Federalist Papers, Federalist No. 10: The Union as a Safeguard Against Domestic Faction and Insurrection.* http://thomas.loc.gov/home/histdox/fed_10.html (accessed April 25, 2014), first published November 23, 1787.

Menand, Louis. *The Metaphysical Club: A Story of Ideas in America.* New York: Farrar, Straus and Giroux, 2001.

Mooney, Chris. *The Republican War on Science.* New York: Basic Books, 2005.

Noah, Timothy. *The Great Divergence: America's Growing Inequality Crisis and What We Can Do about It*. New York: Bloomsbury Press, 2012.

Norcross, George. "Americans for Tax Reform: Federal Pledge." http://s3.amazonaws.com/atrfiles/files/files/112012-113thCongress.pdf (accessed May 14, 2014).

Novick, Sheldon. *Honorable Justice: The Life of Oliver Wendell Holmes*. Boston: Little, Brown and Co., 1989.

Ody, Elizabeth. "Dynasty Trusts Let Wealthy Duck Estate, Gift Taxes Forever." http://www.bloomberg.com/news/2011-07-28/dynasty-trust-let-u-s-wealthy-duck-estate-gift-taxes-forever.html (accessed April 6, 2012).

Oreskes, Naomi and Conway, Erik M., *Merchants of Doubt: How a Handful of Scientists Obscured the Truth of Issues from Tobacco Smoke to Global Warming*. New York: Bloomsbury, 2010.

Phillips, Kevin. *American Theocracy: The Peril and Politics of Radical Religion, Oil, and Borrowed Money in the 21st Century*. New York: Viking, 2006.

Pius XI. *Casti Connubii:* Encyclical of Pope Pius XI on Christian Marriage. http://vatican.va/holy_father/pius_xi/encyclicals/documents/hf_p_xi_enc_31121930_casti-connubii_en.html (accessed April 25, 2014). 1930.

Powell, Lewis. "Confidential Memorandum: Attack on the American Free Enterprise System;" (to Eugene B. Syndor, Jr., U. S. Chamber of Commerce). August 23, 1971. http://law.wlu.edu/deptimages/Powell%20Archives/PowellMemorandumTypescript.pdf (accessed May 15, 2014).

Press, Bill. *The Obama Hate Machine: The Lies, Distortions, and Personal Attacks on the President – And Who is Behind Them*. New York: Thomas Dunne Books, 2012.

Rand, Ayn. *Atlas Shrugged*. 50th Anniversary Edition. New York: Signet, New American Library, 2007.

Rand, Ayn. Lecture — Faith and Force: Destroyers of the Modern World, Yale University, February 17, 1960, Excerpts. http://freedomkeys.com/faithandforce.htm (accessed 11/15/2014).

Reagan, Ronald. Labor Day Speech at Liberty State Park, Jersey City, New Jersey. September 1, 1980. http://www.reagan.utexas.edu/archives/reference/9.1.80.html (accessed May 16, 2014).

Reagan, Ronald. Remarks at the Annual Convention of the National Association of Evangelicals in Orlando, Florida. March 8, 1983. http://www.reagan.utexas.edu/

archives/speeches/1983/30883b.htm (accessed May 16, 2014).

Reagan, Ronald. Speech – 1964 Republican National Convention. (The speech was not given there, see http://blog.constitutioncenter.org/2012/08/the-myth-of-reagan%E2%80%99s-gop-convention-speech-in-1964/), http://lybio.net/ronald-reagan-speech-1964-republican-national-convention/speeches/ (accessed January 16, 2012). Also available on Youtube described as "given at the convention:" http://www.youtube.com/watch?v=yt1fYSAChxs (accessed May 16 2014).

Reagan, Ronald. Ronald Reagan/Jimmy Carter Presidential Debate. October 23, 1980. *http://www.reagan.utexas.edu/archives/reference/10.28.80debate.html (accessed May 16, 2014)*
.

Republican Party. *Platform 2012: We Believe in America*. http://www.com/2012-republican-platform_home/ (accessed May 14, 2014).

Scalia, Antonin. "The Rule of Law as a Law of Rules." 56 U. Chi. L. Rev. 1175 (1989).

Smith, Hedrick. *Who Stole the American Dream?* New York: Random House, 2012.

Stern, Seth and Wermeil, Stephen. *Justice Brennan: A Liberal Champion*. Boston: Houghton Mifflin Harcourt, 2010.

Stiglitz, Joseph. *The Price of Inequality: How Today's Divided Society Endangers Our Future*. New York: W. W. Norton, 2012.

Sun Tzu. *The Art of War*. Translated by Samuel B Griffith. London: Oxford University Press, 1963.

Texas Women's Right to Know Act. Tex. Health & Safety Code §171. http://www.statutes.legis.state.tx.us/Docs/HS/htm/HS.171.htm (accessed May 14, 2014).

United States Treasury Department, Internal Revenue Service. *Statistics of Income…1963, Individual Income Tax Returns, Table 1*. Washington, U. S. Government Printing Office, 1966. http://www.irs.gov/pub/irs-soi/63inar.pdf. (accessed June 30, 2014).

United States Treasury Department, Internal Revenue Service. *Statistics of Income…2011, Individual Income Tax Returns, Table 2*. http://www.irs.gov/uac/SOI-Tax-Stats-Individual-Income-Tax-Rates-and-Tax-Shares#_tables. (accessed June 30, 2014).

Vogel, Kenneth and McCalmont, Lucy. "Rush Limbaugh, Sean Hannity, Glenn Beck Sell Endorsements to Conservative Groups." Politico, June 15, 2011. http://www.politico.com/news/stories/0611/56997.html (accessed January 22, 2012).

Washington, George. Letter to the Hebrew Congregation of Newport. August 18, 1790. http://www.tuorosynagogue.org/index.php/history-learning/gw-letter (accessed May 10, 2014).

Weiss, Gary. *Ayn Rand Nation: The Hidden Struggle for America's Soul*. New York: St. Martin's Press, 2012.

Woodham-Smith, Cecil. *The Great Hunger: Ireland 1845-1849*. New York: Harper & Row, 1962.

Zarefsky, David. *Argumentation: The Study of Effective Reasoning*. 2nd Edition. Chantilly, VA: The Teaching Company, 2005.

Zeman, Zybnek. *Nazi Propaganda*. London: Oxford University Press, 1964.

CASES

Everson v. Board of Education, 330 U.S. 1 (1947).

Brown v. Board of Education, 347 U.S. 483 (1954).

Roe v. Wade, 410 U.S. 113 (1973).

Dean Witter Reynolds, Inc. v. Byrd, 470 U.S. 213 (1985).

Matsushita Electrical Industrial Co., Ltd. v. Zenith Radio Corp., 475 U.S. 574 (1986).

Bush v. Gore, 531 U.S. 98 (2000).

Zelman v. Simmons-Harris, 536 U.S. 639 (2002).

Elk Grove Unified School District v. Newdow, 542 U.S. 1 (2004).

Hibbs v. Winn, 542 U.S. 88 (2004).

Massachusetts v. Environmental Protection Agency, 549 U.S. 497 (2007).

Federal Election Commission v. Wisconsin Right to Life, 551 U.S. 449 (2007).

Citizens United v. Federal Election Commission, 558 U.S. 310 (2010).

National Federation of Independent Business v. Sebelius, 567 U.S. 1 (2012).

Shelby County v. Holder, 570 U.S.   , 133 S. Ct. 2612 (2013).

McCutcheon v. Federal Election Commission, 572 U.S.   , 134 S. Ct. 1434 (2014).

McCullen v. Coakley, 573 U.S.   , 134 S. Ct. 2518 (2014).

Burwell v. Hobby Lobby Stores, Inc., 573 U.S.   , 134 S. Ct. 2751 (2014).

Obergefell v. Hodges, 578 U.S.   , 135 S. Ct. 2584 (2015).

CPSIA information can be obtained
at www.ICGtesting.com
Printed in the USA
BVOW07s2027150716
455505BV00005B/3/P